"AREN'T YOU GOING TO TIE ME UP?"

Jake turned back and stopped in front of her. "If you leave the cabin, you'll have to deal with Bobby or Luis. You ought to know by now what will happen if they get their hands on you."

Allie shivered. "I won't leave."

"Good, now get in bed. If I wanted to rape you, I'd have done it long before this."

"Why haven't you?" The words were out of her mouth before she could stop them. Allie cringed at the astonished look on his face.

"You want me to rape you?"

"No! Of—of course not. I just wondered . . . you know, why you hadn't. I'm sure if my roommate had been the one hiding in your cabin, you would at least have considered the idea. It seems kind of insulting in some way."

His mouth edged up at the corners. Then the faint smile slowly slid away.

She stood frozen as he reached up and touched her cheek. "Well, now, I wouldn't want to insult a lady."

Also by Kat Martin

HOT RAIN

KAT MARTIN

ZEBRA BOOKS
KENSINGTON PUBLISHING CORP.
www.kensingtonbooks.com

Chapter One

"Are you sure about this, Chrissy?" Mary Alice Parker glanced worriedly from her friend to the gleaming white yacht bobbing at the end of the wooden dock. "You've always hated boats. Forgodsake, you get seasick on the way to the mall!"

Chrissy just grinned. "I don't hate boats—especially not boats like that one." Flipping her long dark brown hair back out of her face, she tipped her head toward the sleek, fifty-three-foot Bertram that her latest boyfriend, Donnie Markham, planned to take her out on for the day. "Getting seasick is the part I hate and today I'm wearing 'the patch.' If I weren't, I'd be in trouble the minute we got out of the bay."

With her dark eyes and full-busted figure, Christine Chambers was the exact opposite of Allie, who had wavy short blond hair, blue eyes, and a slender, almost boyish physique. But the pair had met at San Diego State, and though Allie had dropped out at the end of her junior year, their friendship had endured, becoming even stronger through the years.

"Look—here comes Donnie." Chrissy waved and called out to the attractive, darkly tanned man in the flowered short-sleeved shirt, white pants, and navy deck shoes stepping out of a long white Cadillac limo. The car wasn't his, Allie knew. Like the yacht, it belonged to Dynasty Corporation, the import-export company Donnie worked for, one of several expensive autos the company kept to wine and dine its wealthy clientele.

Donnie stopped beside them on the dock, gave a cursory nod of greeting to Allie, but his attention was fixed on Chrissy, his eyes drifting over the tank top and shorts she was wearing, leaving no doubt of the way he intended to spend his afternoon aboard the yacht. "You ready to go, babe?"

Chrissy took his arm and gave him a sexy hug. "I'm ready whenever you are." She was used to the way men looked at her, and there were plenty of them. Chrissy used her body the way Allie used her head, both of them in a constant search for what would make them happy. Chrissy jumped from bed to bed, Allie from job to job, but so far neither of them had found the answer.

"Have fun," Allie called after them as the couple walked away. Chrissy turned and waved, then snuggled closer to Donnie and they continued toward the yacht.

Allie watched them climb aboard and disappear into the cabin, thinking of Donnie Markham and wondering why her best friend always picked losers. Markham might have money—an endless supply it seemed, which he tossed around as if he'd won the lottery—but he also had an attitude. He was shorter than average, and though he was extremely well built, he had a little-man complex that sat like a rock on his shoulder.

In the beginning, Chrissy had liked the expensive gifts and the attention Donnie lavished on her, but lately she'd begun to have her doubts. It was only a matter of time, Allie knew, before Chrissy realized Donnie Markham was just another in a very long line of men who weren't the least bit right for her.

Allie reached the iron gate leading up from the dock and shoved it open. Walking toward the parking lot where her brand-new chartreuse Volkswagen bug was parked, she took a last look at the yacht, *Dynasty I,* shading her eyes against the brilliant San Diego sun glinting on the bright blue water. The boat had already left the slip and was heading toward Point Loma, looking smaller and smaller as it grew more distant.

Allie started to turn away, to continue on to her car, when a bright light flashed at the corner of her eye and her gaze swung back to the yacht. A fierce explosion rocked the bay. Allie stood rooted to the earth, her chest knotted so hard she couldn't breathe as the beautiful boat splintered into a million pieces and burst into a glowing ball of flame.

Chapter Two

Wearing a pair of tortoise sunglasses and the short black skirt and white blouse that were the uniform of a waitress at the Raucous Raven Bar and Grill, Allie Parker shoved through the doors of the San Diego Police Department.

Nearly two weeks had passed since Donnie and Chrissy had been killed, and she still couldn't think of it without crying. The apartment just wasn't the same without her best friend's constant chatter. The rooms were less bright without her gaudy clothes strewn over the ends of the sofa, her endless stream of novels sitting in piles on the floor.

Chrissy's things were still there: slacks, shorts, blouses, costume jewelry, endless boxes of shoes. Her family lived in Boston and they hadn't yet come to get them. Two days ago, her mother had called to ask if Allie could possibly find time to box them up and ship them home.

"I'll be happy to do that, Mrs. Chambers," Allie had said, though packing Chrissy's things hadn't made her the least bit happy. Every time she pulled out one of Chrissy's sweaters, painful memories arose. Chrissy and Allie at San Diego State, trying out for the women's swim team. The two of them double-dating, snickering about how the guys they were with were such a pair of geeks. Hiking together up in the dry inland hills.

Even worse, when she began to pack the gifts Chrissy had received from Donnie Markham, more recent memories crept in.

"I'm worried, Allie," Chrissy had said one morning before Allie had left for work. "Donnie's been acting kind of weird lately."

"Weird how?" Allie asked, setting her coffee mug down on the kitchen table.

"He keeps talking about his boss. He says he's tired of taking orders, tired of being Baranoff's lackey. He says in another couple of weeks things are going to change." Chrissy shook her head. "The way he looks when he says that stuff—it scares me, Allie."

When Allie packed the expensive heart-shaped diamond pendant Donnie had given Chrissy the week before the accident, Allie recalled the reason for the gift.

"Donnie and I had a fight last night," Chrissy had said.

"A fight? What were you fighting about?"

"I asked him about his job. I wanted to know what he did for Dynasty Corporation that paid him so much money."

"What'd he say?"

"He went crazy, Allie—I mean ballistic. He said the way he got his money was none of my business. I swear, for a minute I thought he was going to hit me."

"You told me he had a terrible temper. You'd better be careful, Chrissy."

Chrissy bit her lip. "I hate to say this, but you don't think he might be involved in something illegal?"

"Illegal? You mean like drugs or something?"

"Yeah."

Actually, the thought had occurred to Allie more than once. In fact, the troublesome notion was the reason Allie was standing in front of the sergeant's desk at the police department, asking for Lieutenant Hollis, the detective who had come to her apartment after the accident to discuss the case.

"You'll find him through the doors on your left," the sergeant said. "I'll let him know you're here." A black officer, at least twenty pounds overweight, directed her through a set of swinging doors into another section of the building.

"My name's Allie Parker," she told one of the uniformed women behind a row of desks. "I'm here to see Detective Hollis."

The woman pointed with the end of a pencil toward the skinny, red-haired man standing just a few feet away. He turned toward her as she approached.

"I'm sorry to bother you, Detective Hollis. You probably don't remember me, I'm—"

"Mary Alice Parker. Your roommate was killed in that boating accident last week. What can I do for you, Ms. Parker?"

Allie removed her sunglasses, though she knew her eyes looked red and swollen after packing more of Chrissy's clothes that morning. "I came to talk to you about the case. I was wondering . . . you know . . . if anything new has turned up."

The detective frowned. "I'm sorry for your loss, Miss Parker, but—"

"Allie," she corrected.

"I'm sorry for your loss, Allie. From what you told us, Miss Chambers was a very nice person. But there really is no case. Accidents happen. More than seventy gasoline-powered boats blow up in this country every year. I know, because I looked it up. The damn things are a hazard."

"But what if it wasn't an accident? What if Donnie Markham was involved in something illegal?"

"Drugs, you mean?"

"I—I don't know. I just . . . Chrissy was worried he might be into something like that and now . . . now both of them are dead."

Hollis exhaled a breath. "I'm sorry, Ms. Parker, there hasn't been a whisper of illegal drugs or anything else connected with Markam or the company he works for. Unless you've got some sort of proof, I'm afraid you'll have to accept the fact your friend's death was an accident."

Allie shoved her sunglasses back over her eyes. "Well, thanks for your time, Lieutenant."

"Let me know if there's anything else you need."

The only thing she needed was a way to end the nagging doubts that were driving her crazy. It was stupid. There was no real reason to believe the explosion was anything other than a very unfortunate mishap. Chrissy had always had bad luck with men. Markam probably just capped the list. Still, Chrissy's words continued to plague her.

You don't think he might be involved in something illegal? It scares me, Allie.

The words rattled around in her head all the way back to her chartruese Beetle. What if he was? What if he had had enemies, men powerful enough to have him killed? What if Chrissy was simply an innocent bystander who had happened to get in the way?

If that was the case, then the explosion on the boat was actually murder.

Allie shivered behind the wheel though the late March day was San Diego-warm. When she reached her apartment on Juniper Street, she went straight to the computer in her bedroom. At night, after she got off her day shift at the Raucous Raven, she and a friend she worked with were taking computer courses over the Internet. Allie was learning how to design and administer websites. So far she liked the challenge, and the pay was great for jobs in the field.

Even before she'd enrolled in college, Allie had been trying to discover what she wanted to do with her life. Since the day she dropped out of school in her junior year, still uncertain which direction to take, she'd tried everything from dental assistant to cruise ship social director, looking for a job that would be interesting and fulfilling.

Maybe computer science would be it.

Seating herself at the keyboard, Allie brought up a search engine and typed in DYNASTY CORPORATION. Their website appeared and she skimmed through it, then began a search for other information. An hour later, she knew a lot more about the company than she had before. The owner, Felix Baranoff, was CEO and Chairman of the Board. Markham's name wasn't listed among any of the top executives. Allie wondered, as Chrissy had, what he had done for Dynasty that paid him so much money.

She typed his name into a couple of different search engines. His name didn't show up anywhere on the Net, but Baranoff's did. She found a number of newspaper articles about him and quickly printed them out. Felix Baranoff, it turned out, was a Russian immigrant. In the Cold War days, at the age of seventeen, Baranoff had jumped ship in South Africa, made his way to South America as a crewman on various boats, and eventually arrived in the United States.

He'd earned his fortune through "grit and hard work," according to *Business Magazine*, to become one of the most successful import-export dealers in the country. He had a fabulous art collection and a twelve-thousand-square-foot house on a cliff overlooking the beach in San Diego.

And he didn't sound the least like a man involved in anything illegal.

Allie searched for another half-hour, but still came up with nothing of any importance, only the name of the insurance company that Dynasty Corporation used. Albright Insurance proudly listed Dynasty as one of their clients in a magazine ad. There was a local branch, she saw.

What could a quick visit hurt? Chrissy had been her dearest friend. She owed it to their friendship to be certain her death was the accident it seemed.

And if it wasn't—well, then the police should do something about it.

At two o'clock on Monday, after her lunch shift was over, Allie walked behind the bar to retrieve her purse. The Raucous Raven, in the Gaslight District of downtown San Diego, was a hot spot. Decorated in the style of the eighteen-nineties, with a long oak bar and etched glass windows, the place served great food and didn't scrimp on the drinks. And the people who worked there were friendly.

"Hey, Allie—where you off to in such a hurry?" Barbara Wallace, a daytime bartender and the friend she was taking computer courses with, was thirty years old, two years older than Allie. She was petite and black-haired, an attractive divorcee with two darling little boys, Ricky and Pete.

"I'm going over to Albright Insurance. They're the company that insured the boat Chrissy was on. I want to ask them a couple of questions about it." Barb had known Chrissy Chambers, of course, and how hard Allie had taken her friend's unexpected death.

"You still don't believe it was an accident?"

"Actually, I haven't got a clue one way or the other. I'm just nosing around a little. I want to be sure everything is what it seems."

"You don't think the cops have already done all this?"

"I don't know. Somehow I doubt it. Felix Baranoff is a big political contributor here in town. He's got friends in high places, so to speak. I don't think the police would want to make an enemy of him, and I'm certain the mayor wouldn't."

"Has it ever occurred to you, if there is something shady going on and you keep asking questions, you might end up in trouble yourself?"

Allie shrugged. "To tell you the truth, I hadn't thought about it. Besides, I don't think the questions I'm asking are going to make anybody angry."

"I hope you're right." Barb mopped at a spill on the bar. "I don't think Chrissy would want something happening to you because of her."

True enough. Chrissy had been the sort of person who liked everyone she met, and she would never have wanted anyone hurt because of her. But Allie was hardly in danger. She was just going to ask the insurance agent a couple of questions. If nothing seemed out of the ordinary, she would be satisfied and let the matter drop.

"Did you pass your systems and network support series?" Allie asked Barb.

"As a matter of fact, I did. I start the Windows Advanced Series next." Both of them were enrolled in classes through a company called Total Training Solutions, Barb hoping for a better job and more income to take care of her boys, Allie searching, as always, for a career that would truly interest her.

"I'm almost done with Website Administration," she said. "I'm really enjoying it so far." Allie grabbed her purse, a big khaki canvas bag fashioned like a backpack that carried everything from her makeup kit to a palm-sized screwdriver set and everything in between. Allie believed in being prepared. She rounded the bar, heading for the door and Albright Insurance.

"Hey, wait a minute," Barb called after her as she pulled the heavy door open. "What makes you think that insurance company is going to answer your questions?"

Allie frowned. "Good point." She glanced down at her short black skirt and crisp white blouse. "Maybe I'd better go by my apartment and change."

"Into what, for instance?"

"Into a nice, conservative suit, something a secretary from Dynasty Corp might wear."

Barb frowned. "I thought you said you weren't gonna make anyone mad. I doubt Felix Baranoff or anyone else will appreciate your masquerading as one of their employees.''

Allie grinned. ''Then I better make sure they don't find out.'' With that, she whisked herself out the door.

Forty-five minutes later, she was parked at the curb in front of the office, a three-story glass building on Seventh Street. Inside the second-floor office, half a dozen agents worked behind their desks, a computer station set up at each one.

Dressed in a plum-colored suit and heels, a plum and yellow print scarf tied at her throat, clothes she had worn when she'd worked as a temp for Kelly Girl, Allie walked over to the receptionist.

''Could you tell me which agent handles the Dynasty Corporation account?''

The gray-haired woman stared at her over the top of a pair of half-glasses. ''Any of our agents can help. We're all computerized now.''

''Thank you.'' Allie scanned the room for a likely suspect, then chose a young man in a conservative gray suit and red-striped tie who looked to be four or five years younger than she was.

She stopped beside his desk and gave him a sunny smile. ''Hi.''

The young agent smiled back. ''Hi.'' He shoved to his feet and extended a hand. ''I'm Bill Burns. What can I do for you?''

Allie shook it. ''My name's Dorie Rankin. I work for Dynasty Corporation. Mr. Baranoff's secretary asked me to stop by and pick up a copy of your file on the *Dynasty I*—that's the boat that blew up in the harbor last week. Apparently after the accident the file got misplaced. Do you think you could do that for me?'' She smiled again. She didn't have Chrissy's voluptuous, man-killing figure, but she'd always had a knockout smile.

"Sure. I can do that. No problem."

No problem? No way. It couldn't possibly be that easy. But then who would imagine someone besides the insured wanting a copy of the file?

The young man, Bill, she remembered, began to type words into his computer. A few minutes later his printer started humming, spitting out half a dozen pages.

He handed them over, along with a pristine white, letter-sized envelope to put them in. A very efficient young man.

Allie looked down at the pages.

"Anything else I can do for you?" Bill asked almost hopefully.

Allie read the information and worriedly bit her lip. "I hope Marge will be able to decipher all this. She's got to explain it to Mr. Baranoff, you know. He'll expect her to know the details."

"Here," Bill said, reaching for the papers, "let's see what it says." He scanned the first page, reading through the abbreviations that looked like Greek to Allie.

"Apparently Dynasty Corp had three boats insured with us. *Dynasty I* was the oldest and smallest." He glanced up. "Still a fabulous boat, don't get me wrong. God, I'd love to own one of those babies."

Allie just kept smiling. "What else does it say?"

"It says Mr. Baranoff got lucky. He had just upped the amount of the policy three weeks earlier. We did a reappraisal at the time, to ensure the value was there, but with inflating boat prices, there wasn't a problem. The yacht was professionally surveyed, found to be seaworthy and mechanically sound, and the coverage adjustment was made.''

Allie frowned. "If the boat was sound, why did it blow up?"

Bill skimmed down the page. "Apparently a gasoline leak developed. Fuel spilled into the bilge below the engine room. Terrible thing, but stuff like that happens sometimes."

"Anything else Marge ought to be able to tell him?"

"Well, he doesn't have to worry about lawsuits. Even if the families of the victims should sue, the company has a gigantic liability umbrella. We'll reach some sort of settlement and that'll be the end of it."

A lawsuit. It had never occurred to her that Chrissy's family might want to sue the owner of the boat that killed her. The Chambers family wasn't rich. Chrissy's sister was away at college and the tuition wasn't cheap. Mr. and Mrs. Chambers could probably use the money. Allie would drop them a note when she got back to her apartment.

"Well, that's about it," Bill said. "Let me know if there's anything else you need to know."

"I'll do that, Bill. You've been a real prince. Thanks so much for your help."

Allie clutched the file as she slid behind the wheel of the Volkswagen. So Dynasty had raised the insurance on the boat just before it blew up. A very timely move. Very timely.

Still, as Helpful Bill had said, it might just be a stroke of good luck.

What a shame Chrissy's luck had been so bad.

Chapter Three

Allie told herself not to go. She had covered every avenue she could think of, and except for the fact that Dynasty Corp had raised the amount of insurance on the yacht, she had come up empty-handed. It was time to resign herself to her friend's death and put the matter to rest.

And she would, Allie vowed. Just one quick stop at the marina where *Dynasty I* had been docked and she would end her so-far-futile search. Besides, it was Monday, her day off. What better place to spend it than down at the harbor?

Except that the moment she reached the parking lot, she was assaulted by terrible, heart-breaking memories: orange and red flames clawing their way into the sky, greasy black smoke roiling over the surface of the water, the chilling wail of sirens in the warm morning air.

Allie steeled herself, locking the painful memories away.

As it had been that fateful morning, the late March day was glorious, not a single cloud to mar the blue dome of a sky. Mission Bay glittered like a perfect gem in front of her, dotted with distant sailboats, expensive powerboats, and even an occasional Windsurfer.

Dressed in a bright orange tank top, a pair of khaki shorts, and new white Reeboks, her canvas purse slung over her shoulder, Allie made her way toward the slip where the *Dynasty I* had been tied.

The iron gate was locked, Allie knew. Donnie had given Chrissy the number code to unlock it, but the day Allie had given her friend a ride to the harbor to meet him, she hadn't been paying attention.

Pulling on her light blue windbreaker, she busied herself with the zipper as a man with three unruly children approached the gate. He punched in the proper numbers, the gate swung open, and he followed his kids down the gangway. Allie caught the gate before it closed.

She headed down the gangway to the floating wooden dock, checking to see who might be around, hoping she might find someone who had seen something that day, someone who might know something about the *Dynasty I* or the explosion that had blown the boat and her friend to bits.

Scanning the row of yachts on each side, she wandered toward the impressive yacht tied up at the end. She spotted the *Dynasty II* in its slip and remembered it from before, a plush, sixty-five-foot Voyager, but the magnificent *Imperial Dynasty*, taking up the entire end of the dock, hadn't been there that day. It was at least seventy-five feet long, low and sleek, reeking of money and class. Several crewmen worked aboard her, scrubbing the decks and setting her in order.

She wandered closer, waved, and called out to them, "Beautiful boat," she said.

An older, wizened man with skin so darkly tanned it looked black, grinned and waved back. "That she is, miss."

"Her owner must be very proud of her." Inwardly she smiled, thinking it sounded more like they were discussing a dog than a ship.

"Mr. Baranoff, the owner, he just got her . . . maybe three, four weeks back. Up till lately, he spent most of his time on that boat there."

He pointed to the *Dynasty II,* also an impressive yacht though not quite in the league with *Imperial Dynasty.*

"I heard he lost one of his boats in an accident last week."

The old man lifted his wide-brimmed straw hat and scratched his head. "Terrible thing it was, too. Two people got killed, you know."

"Yes . . . I read that in the paper. Did you know them?"

"Not really. I was workin' on this boat, getting it ready to bring down from San Pedro. We just got in a couple of days ago."

A couple of days ago. Convenient. Even before the boat blew up, Baranoff had a replacement for *Dynasty I.* Allie waved goodbye and the old man went back to work. She glanced toward the *Dynasty II,* bobbing at the end of a rope not far away. It looked to be deserted.

Allie wandered in that direction. *Dynasty II* was the boat that Baranoff had used until a couple of days ago, the old man had said. Fleetingly, she wondered what she might find aboard. Nothing of any consequence, she was sure. It was time she faced reality. Even if Donnie had inadvertently been the cause of Chrissy's death, there was no way to prove it. There never would be.

She started past *Dynasty II,* but her feet seemed to slow of their own volition. The old man was hard at work, tossing orders to a younger crewman who disappeared on some errand below. The man with the three kids had boarded a boat called the *Mary-ann* and headed out into the bay.

There was no one around. It would be so easy just to step over the side of the boat and duck out of sight below. It would only take a minute to glance around the captain's cabin. She had no idea what she was looking for but maybe that was good. It just meant she could keep an open mind.

She didn't realize she was moving till her feet hit the deck and she shoved through the door leading into the main salon. It was gorgeous, done in navy and mauve. She glanced past the mirrored, built-in bar to a modern galley that boasted double stainless sinks and even a microwave.

A door at the far end of the room stood ajar. She made her way in that direction and descended to a pair of cabins, each with its own separate bath. Instead of going in, she went back to the salon and crossed to the aft end of the boat. A door at the end opened into a set of spiral stairs curving down to the captain's quarters.

It was as beautiful as the rest of the boat, done in mauve and pale green. A queen-sized bed stretched beneath a row of portholes. The spread and curtains all matched, the bathroom—*head,* she silently corrected, remembering her days aboard the cruise ship—was mirrored, the lighting state-of-the-art, the shower, glass-enclosed.

Baranoff sure knew how to live.

A built-in teakwood desk sat against one wall. She hurried in that direction, pulled open the top drawer, found a compass, a brass protractor, pencils, pens, and a small hand-held computer. The second drawer down held papers. She had just started to riffle through them when the sound of voices coming from above made her blood turn ice-cold.

Ohmygod!

Easing the drawer closed, she crept across the deep pile carpet to the stairs. She had closed the door at the top, thank God. Soundlessly, she climbed up to hear what was going on, her heart hammering away. It sounded like three different men, all of them Hispanic.

"You sure this is good stuff, man?"

"The best, man. This shit's pure Peruvian flake. You can't get any better."

Allie gripped the stair rail. *Ohmygod!* Baranoff *was* involved with drugs!

"How much?" the first man asked.

"Thousand a ball."

"Okay—give me two balls. Two ounces is enough to start."

One of them chuckled. "You got it, man. Let me see the color of your money."

Allie swallowed hard. She had come aboard to find some kind of evidence—and just like Barb had warned, now that she had, she was in major trouble.

She glanced around the cabin, looking for a way to escape but the sound of another voice, this one deeper, harder, jerked her attention back to the door.

"What the hell's going on?"

She caught the sound of scuffling feet as the men moved away from each other. "Nothing, man, just a little business deal, that's all."

"You dumb sonofabitch." A body slammed hard against the door and Allie bit back a scream, praying it would hold. "Get out!" the latest arrival said to the guy who was buying the drugs.

He didn't falter. She heard his footsteps as he bolted for the door, raced across the deck, and scrambled off the yacht. On the other side of the door, the man with the deep voice still railed at the other two men.

"Have you two lost your minds? Or maybe you just have some sort of death wish."

"I told you, man, we were only tryin' to make a few bucks."

"Get that shit out of here, Lopez," he said. "I don't care what you do with it, just get it gone."

"What a minute, Dawson," the first guy said, and his body slammed a second time hard against the door.

"You wanta argue about this, Bobby? You're lucky I don't beat the crap out of you." He released his hold and the man slid down the door. "Use your head, Roberto. Valisimo will kill you if you botch this operation trying to line your pockets with a lousy few thousand dollars."

Roberto said nothing, then she heard him sigh. "Okay, so maybe you're right."

"No question I'm right. Now why don't you take a walk, cool off a little, and take a look around, make sure you got everything you need."

Roberto left the cabin, but the man with the hard-edged voice remained.

Lord, don't let him come down here.

There was no way she could leave until the men were off the yacht. In the meantime, she would simply have to wait. She glanced around the cabin, looking for a place to hide. Deciding on the head, figuring the odds were in her favor since there were probably at least three bathrooms aboard, she went in and quietly closed the door.

They won't stay long, she told herself. Why would they? They didn't sound like the type of guys to be heading off on a pleasure cruise. The minute they were gone, she would escape—and head straight for the SDPD and good ol' Lieutenant Hollis.

Instead a few minutes later, she felt a vibration beneath her feet. Allie's stomach collapsed into a terrified knot as the powerful engines of the *Dynasty II* roared to life and the boat began to head into the bay.

From the inside steering station just above the main salon, Jacob Michael Dawson worked the controls, easing the yacht out into the water. Everything was in order, ready for the eight-day journey that would end a little south of Matzatlan, and ultimately in Belize.

Jake thought of the man who waited for them there. If the rest of Valisimo's men were as dumb as the two on his payroll in L.A., the general might as well forget winning his so-called People's Revolution. Christ, if the cops had gotten wind those idiots were selling drugs . . .

He didn't even want to think about it.

Jake dragged his wraparound sunglasses off the top of his head and shoved them over his eyes. He'd been working on this deal for more than a year. He wasn't about to let some meathead like Bobby Santos blow it for him.

Careful to keep the boat below the five-mile-an-hour speed limit in the harbor, Jake watched the shoreline slip past, long stretches of white sand beaches, fabulous waterfront homes. Though he lived in an apartment in L.A., he'd always loved the ocean. And boats. He loved the feel of the throttle vibrating beneath his hands, loved the way the water stretched out endlessly in front of him. And a boat like this . . . This was living—big-time.

They made it through the bay and into the open sea in less than twenty minutes. The oversized fuel tanks were filled to capacity. Jake pressed the throttles forward till the boat was moving at around twelve knots, a good speed to conserve fuel and still make their scheduled appointment.

Three hours passed. Roberto spelled him at the wheel. Roberto "Bobby" Santos was maybe twenty-five, a small, wiry man with slicked-back hair cut short and a scar that bisected his left eyebrow. While he settled himself behind the wheel, Jake went below to the galley to make himself a sandwich.

Time slipped past. Luis took his turn at the helm. He was an inch or two taller than Bobby, his straight dark hair long, pulled back in a queue, the sides shaved a couple of inches above his ears. He wasn't as much of a smart-ass as Bobby, but somehow that worried Jake more.

Three more hours passed. During the night they would take two-hour shifts, so no one would fall asleep, but for now the sun was still up and it was his turn again. He was heading toward the helm when he heard Roberto's voice coming from the aft ladder that led to the captain's cabin. What the hell was he doing down there?

He started in that direction then heard a second voice, this one higher, distinctly feminine.

Sonofabitch!

"Let me go, you jerk! You're hurting me!"

Bobby dragged a woman, fighting and screaming, up the stairs and hauled her into the middle of the salon.

"Look what I found." An excited smile cracked across his dark Hispanic features. "I heard a noise. It sounded like it came from your cabin." Another smile, this one leering, glued to the woman's small breasts. She was maybe twenty-seven or twenty-eight, with big blue eyes and a cap of short blond hair that curled around her face. She was pretty. And she was terrified.

At the moment, so was Jake.

"Real nice of your boss to provide us a little entertainment," Bobby said. Holding her around the waist, her back pressed into his chest, Bobby ran a hand over her breast. The woman drove an elbow into his ribs and he grunted. The smile slid off his face. "Do that again, bitch, you're gonna be very sorry." The blonde paled, and Bobby's leering smile returned. "You know what I'm gonna do to you, *chica?*" His fingers tightened around her breast but this time she didn't move, just turned those big baby blues, round as saucers, in Jake's direction.

He steeled himself against their silent plea for help, hating what he was about to do, knowing he didn't have any other choice. Not if she wanted to live.

"Who the hell are you? And what are you doing on this boat?"

She swallowed. He watched the lump go up and down the arch of her throat. She had a tiny waist and legs that went forever.

"I—I just . . . I've, um, always wanted to go out on a yacht, you know? I thought you'd just be cruising around for a couple of hours. I thought it would be fun, that's all. I—I didn't think you'd even know I was here."

Bullshit. Jake didn't know what the hell she was doing aboard, but he didn't think she was there for a pleasure outing. "Who else knows you came aboard?"

She blinked once too often and Jake knew whatever she said was going to be a lie. "I told a couple of my friends. They'll be worried when I don't show up for work. They'll call the police. They'll—"

"Let me get this straight. You told your friends at work that you were going to sneak aboard the *Dynasty II* and go for a pleasure ride when you didn't even know it was going to leave the slip. I don't think so. I don't think anyone has the vaguest idea where you are."

"I—I mentioned this boat—the *Dynasty II.*"

"Yeah, well, you sure picked the wrong boat, lady."

"I think she picked the right boat," Bobby said. She was nearly as tall as he was, maybe five foot five or six. Bobby ground his pelvis suggestively against her bottom.

Just then Luis came into the room. "Hey, Jake, it's your turn to—" He broke off when he saw the girl. "Fucking-eh! Where'd you find that little piece of heaven?"

Jake looked at the lust on Roberto Santos's face,

spotted the instant hard-on Luis Lopez sported, and knew his options had just gone to zero.

He reached out and grabbed hold of the girl, jerked her away from Roberto and hard against his chest. "You're right, Bobby. I guess this is the right boat. You found her in my cabin. That's where she stays until I get tired of her. When I do, you two can have her."

"No way," Bobby whined. "I found her. The pussy belongs to me."

Valisimo's men were tough, but he was tougher and they knew it. The eight years he'd spent in Army Special Forces was the reason Baranoff had hired him, the reason he was running this operation.

"I said the girl is mine. Luis, you get back to the wheel. I'll be there as soon as I've had a taste of her." He felt her stiffen and tightened his hold, crushing her breasts against his chest. Big blue terrified eyes stared into his face. "You hear that, Blondie? You do what I tell you and maybe you won't get hurt."

"This ain't right, Dawson." Bobby took a threatening step forward.

Jake straightened to his full height and stared at Roberto over her head. Standing nearly a foot taller than either of the two Latino men, his size alone was intimidating. He was in charge of this operation and they'd been told to follow his orders, but Bobby was a hothead and Luis a wild card he hadn't quite figured out. If he backed down now, the girl was in serious trouble.

He gripped her arm and turned her toward the ladder leading down to his cabin. "You heard what I said. Now get your sweet ass down those stairs."

* * *

Allie stumbled down the ladder into the cabin, the big black-haired man with the hard-edged voice right behind her. He was at least six-foot-four, two hundred pounds of solid muscle and bone. He was tanned and lean, a set of iron-hard biceps bulging from the sleeve of a worn khaki T-shirt. Faded, soft blue denim jeans clung to narrow hips and the long bones and sinews in his thighs.

The insane thought occurred: *If you have to be raped, what better man for the job?* Hysterical laughter warred with hysterical tears. Oh, God, Chrissy would have loved him. Unfortunately, Allie wasn't interested in the least.

In fact, she had never been more frightened in her life.

"What—what are you going to do?" She edged away from him to the far side of the queen-sized bed.

His mouth barely curved. "What do you think I'm going to do?"

"Please . . . I just wanted to go for a ride. You seem like a nice enough man." That was a laugh. He seemed like the devil incarnate. "Couldn't you just take me back?"

"Sure. And the minute you got off the boat, you'd go singing to the cops about Bobby and Luis and their little business deal."

"I wouldn't do that. I promise I won't tell anyone."

"So you did hear what went on. I figured you did."

Dammit, how had she let him trap her that way? "I didn't hear anything, and even if I did, I won't tell anyone."

"No, you won't, honey, because you aren't going back. Not for a while, at least." He started toward her, a panther on the prowl. His eyes were the most intense shade of blue she'd ever seen.

Allie backed away. "Stay away from me."

"Not on your life, sweetheart."

Her heart thundered. She feinted right, then darted left, planning to go up and across the bed, but instead of ducking around to block her as she had figured he would, he simply caught her ankle, jerked her down, and lunged on top of her, crushing her into the mattress.

Allie bit back a shriek of pure terror. *Oh, God, oh, God.* Her heart thumped like a drum against her ribs. Her breath came in short, erratic little puffs. Jake Dawson pinned her down with his big hard body. She looked up, into fierce blue eyes that had tan lines in the corners.

"Scream," he said softly, the sound so deep and rough it vibrated across his chest.

"Wh-what?"

"I said scream."

She just stared, trying to make her fuzzy mind work, which it completely refused to do.

"Dammit, lady, do you want those guys to rape you? I said scream." When she still didn't comply, he swore a word she would rather not have heard, jerked her tank top down, used both hands to rip her lacy bra in two, and his lips crashed down over hers. He kissed her hard, plunging his tongue inside her mouth, rubbing a thumb roughly over her nipple. A little whimper of fear bubbled up but every other sound was locked tight in her throat.

Lifting his head, he stared down at her. There was hunger in those penetrating eyes and pure, raw lust etched into his face. Her whole body clenched in terror—and Allie let out a bone-chilling scream.

She screamed again, even louder, and couldn't believe her good fortune when he rolled away from her and got up from the bed.

Lounging in a chair across the room, Jake checked his watch. Fifteen minutes. Kind of a quickie by his standards. His reputation would suffer, but he guessed he'd have to live with it.

A few feet away, the girl huddled in the middle of the bed, her knees pulled up to her chest, her arms wrapped protectively around them. She'd retrieved her windbreaker and pulled it on over her tank top. He felt bad about the bra, but he had a role to play and there was nothing he could do about it. If she wanted to stay alive, she would have to do what he told her. Exactly what he told her.

Fear was the best way to accomplish that.

Jake uncrossed the legs he'd stretched out in front of him and slowly came to his feet. "What's your name?"

She looked up, eyed him warily. "Allie."

"Alley? Like a dirty little street behind a bar? That's not much of a name for a woman."

She made no reply but her mouth flattened out.

"I'd advise you to stay down here, Allie. You'll be safer that way." He reached into the closet and dragged out a faded blue chambray shirt, pulled it on over his T-shirt against the faint chill in the early evening air. "Apparently you don't get seasick."

She shook her head. She had the shiniest blond

hair he'd ever seen. "I worked for a while on a cruise ship."

He nodded, started toward the stairs. Damn, he hated blondes. Well, that is to say, he loved them—always had, but he hated that he loved them. He especially liked the ones with long hair and big tits. He'd married two of them. Both times had been a disaster.

Jake took a last glance at Allie. Thank God, this one's breasts were small, not big and round, the way he liked them, though the sweet little points had felt damned good in his hands. Better yet she was slim, her hair cut short, almost boyish, not much of a temptation at all.

He noticed the sexy way it curled around her face. He thought of those long, tanned legs, remembered lips as soft as any he'd ever tasted. His body tightened, began to go hard.

Damn, he wished he'd never kissed her.

"One more thing," he said.

Those big eyes followed his every move. She looked smart enough, but she was probably as dingy as every other blonde he'd ever known. Inwardly, he smiled.

What are the worst three years in a blonde's life?
Third grade.

"You'd be wise to keep your mouth shut about what goes on in this room. As far as Bobby and Luis are concerned, from now on you belong to me. You'd better make sure they believe it."

She swallowed hard and nodded.

Jake didn't say more. He'd done his job. She was scared spitless of him; she'd do what he told her. He wished he could just let her go, put in someplace in Baja and send her on her way. It was impossible. She'd go to the authorities the minute her feet hit the pavement. He couldn't afford for that to happen. Too much was at risk, too many lives at stake.

Closing the door at the top of the stairs, he pretended to fasten the zipper on his jeans, then the buttons on his shirt as he crossed the salon on his way to relieve Luis. *Just take it easy*, he told himself. *A week from now, you'll be in Belize.*

But his sixth sense told him it wouldn't be that easy.

Jake just prayed nothing else would go wrong.

Chapter Four

Allie paced back and forth in the cabin. Night had settled in and the wind had kicked up. Through the row of portholes above the bed, stars glittered like diamonds in black velvet, and a quartering moon formed a path across the sea. Frothy white foam skimmed along the hull as the yacht plowed ahead, its big engines easily propelling the boat through the water.

Allie glanced at the brass ship's clock on the wall. Ten P.M. They'd been away from the harbor for twelve hours. Twelve hours! It felt like twelve days. How much longer did the men plan to be gone? What was their destination?

What would they do with her once they arrived?

Allie shivered. What a mess she'd made of things. The knowledge that she had probably been right and Chrissy's death was somehow involved with illegal drugs was little consolation. From where she sat now, there wasn't a darned thing she could do about it.

Allie sighed as she peered, for the twentieth time, out of the nearest porthole. At least so far they hadn't hurt her. She thought of the man, Jake Dawson, big and tough, dangerous-looking, exactly the sort of man you would picture doing something illegal. Why had he only pretended to rape her?

A shiver of fear ran through her as she remembered his savage attack, ripping open her bra, brutally kissing her, roughly palming her breast. He had wanted to frighten her and he had done a good job. Why had he stopped when he did? Or perhaps he merely planned to wait until his companions weren't lurking outside the door.

Like right now, she thought, her heart kicking up as the door to the salon swung open and Big Jake Dawson walked in. Unconsciously, she backed away as he started down the spiral stairs, but he barely tossed her a glance, just crossed the cabin and disappeared inside the head.

She had to admit he was impressive, tall and lean, long-waisted, with an incredible set of shoulders. His hair was black and wavy, long enough to curl at the base of his neck, and he was flat-out handsome.

Not pretty. Not hardly. His face was too angular for that, his cheekbones too high, his mouth too hard.

She heard the commode being flushed and a few minutes later he reappeared, making the cabin feel even smaller than it did already. He cast her a look she couldn't read, then calmly began to unbutton his shirt. The fear she had been fighting returned with bruising force.

"Wh-what are you doing?"

A smooth black eyebrow went up. "Getting ready for bed."

Ohmygod! "I'll fight you. You'll probably win but I'll do some damage before you do. I've had self-defense classes and I've gotten pretty good at protecting myself."

He grinned. He actually did. "Now that sounds mighty tempting. I was planning to get some sleep—I've only got four hours until my next turn at the wheel—but I suppose if you promise to make it that much fun—"

Allie bristled. The big jerk was laughing, making a joke at her expense. "You're saying you're not planning to rape me?"

"I thought you figured that out before."

"I thought maybe you were just . . . you know, waiting."

His eyes ran over the windbreaker she wore though it was warm in the cabin, continued down her hips and legs. "Maybe I am."

Allie glanced away, hoping he wouldn't see how frightened those words made her. "Why don't you just let me leave? There are lots of places you could stop, small harbors where—"

"I told you why. I don't want you running to the cops and that's exactly what you'd do."

It was useless to argue. She could tell by the implacable look on his face. "Then what are you going to do with me?"

He paused in the middle of shrugging out of his shirt. "I'd say that's up to you. Behave yourself and once we get where we're going, I'll let you leave."

She wondered if he meant it. She told herself he did.

Her stomach growled and she realized how long

it had been since she'd eaten. "I don't suppose you'd happen to have anything to eat."

He took off the shirt, leaving him in the khaki T-shirt he wore underneath, and cast her a considering glance. "There's sandwich stuff in the galley. Luis has gone to bed. Roberto's at the wheel. Just don't go anywhere else, and get back here as soon as you're finished."

He was letting her go up to the galley by herself? Her pulse took a leap. They were too far away from land for her to swim to shore, but there was all sorts of stuff in the galley that she could use for weapons. She had a little pocketknife, one of those fold-up scissor–nail file sets, and some other miscellaneous stuff in her canvas purse, which she'd stashed beneath the sink in the head; but nothing that would really do any damage.

She kept her expression carefully blank. "Thanks. I'll be right back."

Allie raced up the ladder and headed straight to the galley. She hadn't eaten since breakfast and she was starving, but protecting herself was more important. She rummaged through the drawers, found a four-inch paring knife that looked good and sturdy and shoved it into the back pocket of her khaki shorts. A heavy, long-shanked screwdriver went into a pocket of her windbreaker. She shoved a steak knife with a serrated edge along the side of her leg beneath her sock, and a can of Pam cooking spray into the other pocket of her jacket.

Afraid to take too much stuff for fear the men would notice, she settled down to making herself a ham and Swiss sandwich.

God, it tasted like mana from heaven. She finished the sandwich, along with a glass of milk, and headed back downstairs.

Unfortunately, Jake Dawson was waiting.

He caught her the minute she reached the bottom of the stairs and shoved her up against the wall.

"What are you doing!"

"Just a precaution. I like to be sure I'm going to wake up in one piece." With that he began to search her, patting her down, finding the can of Pam and the long-shanked screwdriver in the pockets of her windbreaker, jerking them out and setting them down on the dresser.

"Well, well. I guess you were planning to do a little cooking down here in the cabin. Or maybe make a few repairs?"

Allie clamped hard on her tongue, though silently she cursed him. Jake unzipped the windbreaker and jerked it off her shoulders, saw that she wore the orange tank top without a bra, which he, of course, had ruined.

He whirled her around to face the wall, lifted her hands up and placed them palms down against it, then proceeded to pat down her bottom. Allie tried not to blush, but heat roared into her face. He found the paring knife, of course. He also found the steak knife she had shoved into her sock.

He turned her to face him, caught the angry flush in her cheeks. "You're quite resourceful, Allie." He was smiling, but there wasn't a trace of humor in his face. His T-shirt and shoes were gone. He wore just his jeans and they rode low on his hips. She found herself staring at the six-pack muscles across his stomach, the curly black hair that fanned out over his chest.

He toyed with the paring knife, the sharp edge glinting in the lamplight. "I wonder . . . would you have tried to use this on me?"

She didn't answer. Just lifted her chin and gave him a mutinous glare. She was scared of him. Maybe she could make him a little bit scared of her.

"Get over on the bed."

Her stomach dropped to her toes. "Why?"

"Because I need to get some sleep and now I know I can't trust you to stay here while I do. Now, get on the bed."

She only shook her head.

Jake walked over to the built-in dresser and jerked open the top drawer. There was a coil of line inside. He dragged out a length, cut it off with his pocketknife, and started toward her. Gripping her arm, he tied one end of the rope around her wrist and the other around his own.

"What are you doing?"

"Just what I said—going to bed." Jake hauled her across the room, tossed her down on the bed, and stretched his long body out beside her.

Allie prepared herself, certain this time he would force himself on her. Instead he clicked the light off on the bedside table and plumped the pillow behind his head.

"Get some sleep," he said gruffly, turning a little away from her onto his side.

Allie lay next to him, stiff and wary, staring into the darkness, waiting for his next move. Instead, just seconds later, she heard his even breathing and realized that he was asleep.

Dammit to hell! She was wide awake and shackled like a prisoner—exactly what she was—and the big jerk was already sleeping! So much for making him afraid of her.

She stared up at the ceiling, waiting for her heart to slow, fighting the exhaustion sweeping over her.

She didn't dare fall asleep—did she? But as the boat plunged through the waves in its hypnotic, rocking rhythm and the engines purred deep in the hull, her eyelids grew heavy. She tried to forget there was a man lying next to her, that any moment he could awaken and do God only knew what.

Instead she thought of Chrissy and how much she missed her. She thought of her parents living in San Marcos, a little town north of San Diego, and wondered when they would begin to worry about her.

She wondered if she would ever see them again, if she'd ever see Barb or any of her other friends, and if anyone would think of feeding Whiskers, her little orange calico cat.

She tried not to cry, but the tears she'd been fighting finally came. She wept silently until she fell asleep, wishing she hadn't been such an idiot, wishing she had listened to Barb, wishing she were back home in San Diego.

She awakened hours later, her wrist tied to the headboard, the rope just looped, not even a serious knot. Jake was gone, returned to his duty at the helm, and it wasn't yet dawn. An icy calm settled over her. She was still alive, still unharmed, and she wasn't the sort to give up without a fight.

Sooner or later, she vowed, she would find a way to escape.

When Jake had finished his shift and returned to the cabin, he found Allie asleep in the chair, her feet tucked up beneath her, her head nodding forward. She was a pretty little thing, with softly feminine features and big blue eyes. He smiled as he thought of the knives, screwdriver, and cooking spray. Not a bad try. She might even have fooled Bobby and Luis.

What do you do when a blonde throws a pin at you? Run like hell—she's got a grenade in her hand!

He chuckled to himself and wondered again how she'd been unfortunate enough to wind up on the boat. There was a chance she worked for Baranoff, of course, another set of eyes and ears for his employer, but he didn't think so. Baranoff would have expected the men to use her and she didn't look all that used to being used.

Jake kicked off his deck shoes, stripped down to his jeans, and lay down on the bed. He thought about tying her up again, but he was a very light sleeper and it was almost morning. He slept for a couple more hours, awakened at six forty-five, and got out of bed. Allie jerked awake when she heard him moving around and inched back even farther in the chair.

Jake ignored her. Instead, he went into the head, stripped off the rest of his clothes, and stepped into the shower. She was still sitting in the chair when he emerged, freshly shaved, to pull on a clean T-shirt.

He studied her a moment, trying to decide what to do with her, trying to ignore those long, tanned legs. "You've got fifteen minutes to shower, then I want you upstairs."

A muscle tightened in her cheek. She came to her feet and surprised him with a sharp salute. "Yes, sir, Captain Jake."

"I'm not the captain. I'm the guy who's screwing you, remember? And if you don't, I imagine those other two can handle the job for real, if that's what you want."

The color drained from her face. "No . . . that's not what I want. I'll do whatever you say."

"Good. I'm tired of eating sandwiches. From now on, you're going to cook. Nobody gets a free ride around here."

"But I don't know how to—"

His hard look cut her off. She moved cautiously past him into the head, and he heard the shower go on. Fifteen minutes later, she appeared at the top of the staircase in the main salon, her hair still wet but already beginning to curl. She wasn't wearing makeup, but she had great bone structure, nicely shaped eyebrows, and pretty pink lips, the kind of face that didn't really need any. He pointed her toward the galley.

"Roberto and Luis could use a decent meal, too. You'll find eggs and bacon in the refrigerator. There's plenty of bread for toast."

Ignoring whatever it was she started to say, he walked out of the salon and made his way out on deck. The wind whipped through his hair, and a warm sun beat down on his back. They were making good time, and the oversized fuel tanks gave them good range. They wouldn't make their first fuel stop, in the little Baja village of Tortugas, until tomorrow morning.

He glanced toward the galley, but couldn't hear anything except the roar of the engines and the wind sailing past his ears. He'd have to lock her in the cabin when they got there. He didn't know how far she would go in an effort to escape, but he didn't want to take any chances.

He saw Luis walking toward her across the salon. Maybe he shouldn't have let her come up, but he couldn't imagine her being locked up down there for a week and they really could use a cook. He just wished she wasn't such a tempting little piece.

And he hoped she played her role as his reluctant bedmate well enough for those two jackals to leave her alone.

Allie shoved the bacon around in the skillet, trying to dodge the blistering pops of grease that kept stinging her hands and legs. She grabbed a hot pad, carefully lifted the skillet, and dumped some of the grease into a second pan, sending a spray of hot grease and smoke into the air. Gingerly hopping out of the way, she reached for the eggs.

She had intended to cook them over easy, but the first yolk broke in the pan and so did the second. Scrambled eggs it would be. She dumped in eight eggs, two apiece, and stirred them around in the skillet.

In the past few years, she'd had a jillion different jobs trying to find out what she really wanted to do, but cooking wasn't among them. None of the domestic arts appealed to her, though she really loved kids and had always looked forward to someday being a wife and mother.

Allie stirred the eggs, which were beginning to stick to the bottom of the skillet. Using a spatula, she scraped at them madly, saw that the rubber spatula was melting among the eggs, swore, and tossed it into the sink. The bacon was turning black and a column of smoke rose up from the pan. She was about to snatch it away when the smoke alarm went off with an angry buzz, and Jake stormed into the galley.

"What in the hell . . ."

"I told you I didn't know how to cook!" she

shouted above the roar of the alarm. Jake just kept walking, a murderous scowl on his face. Turning away from the fury in his eyes, Allie reached for the bacon pan, but Jake's big hand grabbed her wrist.

"Use a hot pad, dammit!" He plucked one up, wrapped it around the smoking skillet, and set it off to the side of the stove, then did the same with the eggs. "I don't believe this. You can't even fry an egg?"

She started to tell him there were a dozen other things she *could* do, but the minute she opened her mouth, his dark look cut her off.

"Never mind. I'll fix breakfast. And I better not find out you did this on purpose."

Allie said nothing, just backed a safe distance away to watch him work. He moved with a brisk economy of movement and an odd sort of grace for such a big man. In minutes, he had more bacon cooking and the rest of the eggs scrambled with onions and tomatoes, simmering in just the right amount of grease.

"I'll get the plates," Allie heard herself say, probably because her mouth had begun to water from the delicious cooking smells. Ten minutes later, Jake was filling the dishes with perfectly crisp bacon, golden scrambled eggs, and crisp slices of buttered wheat toast.

"Take this up to Roberto." He handed her a plate and she took it up the ladder to the helm. Luis was filling his plate when she returned.

His eyes ran over her windbreaker and shorts, down the length of her legs. "Hey, man, how was she?" he said to Jake.

Jake gave her a leering smile, but his eyes were

filled with warning. "Better than I thought she'd be. I think I'll keep her for a while."

Luis looked disappointed. Knowing how important it was to play her part, Allie stiffened. "What kind of man forces himself on a helpless woman?"

Jake smiled wolfishly. "It's okay, baby. I won't tell 'em how much you liked it." As an actor, he wasn't half bad, but then, neither was she. She'd been in a half-dozen little theater productions during the years she had considered becoming an actress.

Allie bristled even more, playing her role as best she could. Even knowing the rape was a lie, feeling those intense blue eyes on her, it was suddenly hard to swallow her bite of eggs.

They finished the meal in silence and Jake ordered her to clean up the dishes. Afterward, no one tried to stop her when she went outside and made her way up to the bow. The hours slid past and she finally returned to the cabin.

After the breakfast fiasco, she wasn't asked to cook supper, but the men expected her to clean up the galley. When she'd finished, she returned to the cabin. The routine that night was much the same. Jake tied her wrist to his and went to sleep.

In the morning, he cooked breakfast, she cleaned and afterward she returned to the bow. The early-morning sun sliced down from overhead when she realized the yacht was moving closer to shore. Jake was once more at the helm, guiding the boat toward a speck of land in the distance. They were stopping to refuel, she realized, her pulse jumping up, beginning to thrum with hope.

Just stay calm, she told herself. *This is your chance to escape.*

She'd had enough of Jake Dawson and his lowlife friends. She was getting off this damnable boat—come hell or high water.

Jake shoved his wraparound shades over his eyes and settled himself comfortably in front of the wheel. In the distance, Bahia de Tortugas nestled like a welcome mirage in a dry stretch of cactus-covered sand. There wasn't much there, only a cluster of thatched-roof houses, a cantina, and a small marina. About the only good refueling spot since they'd passed Ensenada and the sort of place they could slide in and out of with the least amount of hassle.

Jake caught a glimpse of orange tank top and blue windbreaker, saw Allie standing near the bow. He would let her get a little fresh air, then take her back down to his cabin.

Damn, he wished he could just get rid of her. Not only was she likely to get herself killed— For chrissake, the woman couldn't even cook!

Why do blondes hate making chocolate chip cookies? Too hard to peel the M&M's!

Remembering the joke did nothing to lighten his mood. He waited another thirty minutes, changed course a little to intercept the village, called for Luis to spell him at the wheel, and went after the girl.

He found her near the bow, the wind tossing her shiny blond hair. The windbreaker blew open and he caught the outline of small, upturned breasts and the sharp little points of her nipples. His loins began to fill and he forced his eyes away. Damn, he hated blondes.

"Enjoy your walk?" he asked, once more under control.

She gave him a vapid smile. "Actually, I did."

"That's good, because you're going back down below for a while." He caught her arm though she tried to elude him and steered her back inside. He gave her a nudge toward the stairs and followed her below.

"I'm barring the door," he said, "so you might as well forget trying to get out."

Allie just smiled. "I don't know what you're so worried about. We're in the middle of nowhere. I can hardly get off the boat way out here."

"Really? What if I said that if you promised to keep your mouth shut, I'd let you stay here?"

Her whole face lit up. "Would you? Oh, God, that would be terrific. I won't say a word to anyone. I won't do anything but find a way to get back to—"

"That's what I thought." Jake crossed over to the built-in dresser, jerked open the top drawer, and pulled out a couple of handkerchiefs. He hadn't meant to tie her up, but one glance at the line of portholes over the bed and he could already hear her yelling for help.

"Sit down on the end of the bed."

She eyed him with suspicion. "Why?"

"Just do it, dammit." He grabbed her arm and jerked her down, picked up the length of line he had used during the night, and tied her arms behind her.

When she started to protest, he stuffed one of the handkerchiefs into her mouth and tied the other around her head to hold it in place. Allie cursed him behind the gag, or at least he figured she was calling him something he'd just as soon not hear. He left the cabin and closed the door, leaving her fuming at the foot of the bed.

Wedging a chair beneath the doorknob, he returned to his duties at the helm.

Chapter Five

Damn him! Allie wiggled her wrists, trying to untie the line, but it was no use. She looked up at the little portholes above the bed, wishing they were bigger or she were a whole lot smaller, determined to at least get rid of the gag so that she could shout for help.

As the boat drew closer to shore, Allie rushed into the bathroom, turned so she could use her bound hands, and dragged her big canvas purse out from under the sink. Carrying it over to the bed, she dumped the contents in the center, then grabbed up the little fold-up scissors. They were pretty small, not really meant for something as strong as the line. The pocketknife might work better. Allie fumbled, finally got the little knife open, and began to saw madly at her bonds.

They were nearing the dock. She could hear the

change in the pitch of the engines. She sawed and sawed and finally sliced through the rope. With a little cry of triumph, she untied the handkerchief around her head, spit out the gag, and ran over to the portholes above the bed. The boat eased up to the dock, and whoever manned the helm cut the engines.

The group of men on the dock began speaking in Spanish and she heard Roberto answer. Living in San Diego, she had taken Spanish in high school and also in college. She wasn't all that great, but she could get by. She listened now, understanding a surprising amount, biding her time, her heart thudding away. If she yelled too soon, one of the men would come down and silence her.

Allie shivered at the thought.

She glanced toward the stairs. She considered shoving the chair beneath the doorknob, but couldn't figure a way to make it work on the spiral stairs. Wondering if there might be a small lock on the inside of the door, she quietly climbed up, and there it was. It wasn't much of a lock, but it was better than nothing. She punched the little button, prayed the men hadn't heard the click, and crept back downstairs.

Long minutes passed. She bit down on the end of a finger and started to chew, then realized what she was doing and jerked her hand away.

She hadn't chewed her fingernails since she was a kid. She wasn't about to start the ugly habit again. She wouldn't let them have the satisfaction.

Allie stared out of the porthole. They were in Bahia de Tortugas—Turtle Bay—or so the sign read over the fuel pump. At least four Mexican men swarmed over the dock, filling the yacht's big fuel tanks, filling the water tanks, and hosing off the decks. Mexican women in colorful long skirts and white cotton blouses began to gather, hawking eggs and produce and unleavened Mexican bread.

The yacht's arrival was an exciting event. More and more townspeople continued to gather around.

Allie glanced toward the door, hoped the lock would hold at least for a few precious moments, and started to yell for help.

Conversing with one of the women, a pretty little black-haired girl with an armload of brown and white eggs, Jake halted midway through his purchase.

Sonofabitch! Allie was yelling, making enough noise to wake every dead Mexican within a hundred miles, telling the world in English and surprisingly passable Spanish that she'd been kidnapped, and beseeching someone to help her.

Luis and Roberto were farther down the dock, haggling with a fishmonger for a fresh catch for supper. Their heads snapped up at the ruckus aboard the yacht and Jake started running. He vaulted the side of the boat, hit the deck like an Olympic sprinter, slammed through the glass door into the main salon, tossed the chair aside, turned the knob on the door, and nearly knocked himself out when the door didn't open.

Sonofabitch! Gritting his teeth, he slammed his shoulder against the wood and sent it crashing against the wall, damn near knocking it off its hinges. He took the stairs in three bounds, took three more strides, and hauled Allie off the bed.

"Shut the hell up!" he warned, gripping both her arms and jerking her hard against him.

Allie just kept yelling. He clamped a hand over her mouth, wrenched one of her arms up behind her, which at least put an end to the noise, retied her hands with the piece of line that hadn't been sawed in two, and stuffed the gag back into her mouth.

"Christ, are you trying to get yourself killed?" *Why don't blondes call 9-1-1 when they need help? They always forget the 1-1.*

Cursing softly, he hauled her over to the chair, slammed her bottom down hard on the seat, and used the other half of the rope to tie her feet. He had plenty of line. He jerked another four feet out of the coil in his drawer, cut it off with his pocket-knife, and tied her to the chair. He could hear her yelling behind the gag, but it wasn't doing a lick of good, and at least this would keep her out of his hair while he figured out what to do.

Spotting her canvas tote and wondering where she'd had it hidden, he strode over and began to rummage through the pile of junk in the middle of the bed—everything from breath mints to lipstick; a pocketknife, which she'd obviously used; tiny folding scissors; and a plastic case that held miniature screwdrivers. He'd never seen anything like it.

Roberto appeared at the top of the stairs. He cast a furious glance around the room, seemed pleased when he saw her bound and gagged and tied to the chair.

"Hey, man, there's some guys up here. They want to talk to you about the woman who was screaming."

Christ. Raking his hair back out of his face, Jake took a calming breath and climbed the stairs.

Two of the local *policia* and an older, gray-haired

man who appeared to be the village spokesman stood on deck.

"There was a woman, señor," the leader said in broken English. "She was yelling very loudly, asking us for help. Everyone heard her."

Jake scratched his head and tried to look embarrassed. "I'm really sorry, Señor . . . ?"

"Delgado. I am the mayor of Bahia de Tortugas."

"Yeah, well, I'm really sorry, Mayor. The woman you heard was my wife. I'm afraid she's got a little drinking problem. *Boracho,* you know?" He mimed upturning a bottle and pouring liquor into his mouth. "This morning . . . well, she was feeling a little under the weather so I let her put some whiskey in her coffee. Apparently, she had a little too much."

Jake reached into the pocket of his jeans and pulled out his wallet. "I didn't want her to embarrass herself, so I locked her in our cabin. I can see now, that was a mistake."

While he talked, he thumbed through the wad of greenbacks in the bill compartment. "I know your time and trouble are worth a lot. Perhaps I can repay you all for the trouble my wife has caused." He dragged out a stack of hundreds, began counting them into the mayor's palm.

"I don't know, señor. We would all feel better if we could speak to the woman."

Christ. He counted out another two hundred. "I assure you she's unharmed. She's already sleeping it off."

Roberto smiled and chimed in. "*Sí,* Señor Dawson's wife, she goes a little loco sometimes, but she is all right now. The liquor—it's no good for her, *comprende?*"

Jake counted out two hundred more. He was at six hundred and counting. He wanted to strangle the little hellion below.

"You are certain the señora, she is all right?" one of the policemen asked, which prompted Jake to add a couple of hundred more.

"Like I said, she's sleeping it off."

The men seemed satisfied at last. The mayor smiled. "If there's anything else you need, señor—food? Supplies? Anything at all, just let us know."

Jake gave him a toothy smile. "Everything's fine. As soon as the tanks are full, we'll be out of here."

The mayor nodded. "Have a good journey, Señor Dawson." He counted the money as he climbed off the boat, the policemen eyeing their share.

Mordida was the way in Mexico, bribery paid to officials for any infraction of the law—or just about anything else. Aside from that, they were good people who rarely interfered in other people's business.

Right now, Jake was damned glad.

"Maybe you should teach her a lesson," Roberto said, once the men were gone. He glanced toward the door leading down to the master's cabin. "Or if you want, I could do it for you."

The look in Roberto's eyes gave Jake a chill. "I'll take care of it. Just pay for the fuel and let's get the hell out of here."

Roberto's mouth edged up, but the hard look remained in his eyes. Damn, where had the general found these two?

Almost wishing Allie's ploy had worked and she had actually escaped, Jake headed down the stairs.

* * *

Allie heard the broken door being shoved open and looked up to see Jake at the top of the stairs. Fury etched his features into hard, unbending lines, and the muscles across his shoulders strained beneath his T-shirt. A tremor of fear ran through her. She had known the risk she was taking when she tried to escape. God, what would he do?

His footsteps pounding down the stairs sounded like gunshots. Allie steeled herself as he jerked the gag out of her mouth and untied her hands and feet.

"You little fool." Gripping her arms, Jake hauled her out of the chair and slammed her against the wall. "What do I have to do to make you understand? If you don't do what I say—exactly what I say—these guys are going to kill you!"

Allie stared into his face, just inches away from her own. "What about you? Are you going to kill me?"

He swore a vulgar word. "Right now, I'm tempted." He let go of her arms and stepped away, raked a hand through his wavy black hair. "Look, Allie, I can hardly blame you for trying to escape. Maybe I even admire you for it, but it isn't going to work, and all you'll manage to do is get the hell beat out of you—or worse."

Allie didn't reply, but a shiver ran through her. He was fighting to control his temper. A beating was the least she expected.

"You'd better stay down here for a while. Bobby's looking for blood and Luis is dying for an excuse to screw you."

Allie bit down on her trembling lip. She wanted

to go home. She wanted to see Whiskers. She wanted to be with her friends and family again.

"Christ, don't cry," Jake said.

"I'm not crying." Allie blinked and a tear ran down her cheek.

Jake swore an oath she couldn't hear, turned, and started for the stairs. Allie watched him go, remembering the hard look on his face, remembering the threat he had made, telling herself it didn't change things.

No matter what Jake Dawson did, she wasn't giving up until she got off the boat.

"I'm sorry to worry you, Mrs. Parker, but Allie hasn't shown up for work for the last three days and I'm really getting concerned." Barb's fingers tightened around the phone. She hated phoning Allie's mom, but she didn't know what else to do. "This morning, I went over to her apartment to see if maybe she was sick or something. When she didn't answer the door, I used the key she keeps under the flower pot on the porch, but there wasn't any trace of her, and Whiskers hadn't been fed."

"Oh, dear Lord. Allie would never go off without getting someone to take care of Whiskers."

"I know, Mrs. Parker, that's why I called. I took Whiskers home with me, so you don't have to worry about that, but—"

"Allie wouldn't go away without telling someone. Something's happened. We have to call the police."

"That's what I thought, too." Barb looked over at Detective Reynolds, the tall policeman standing on the opposite side of the bar. He was a regular at the Raucous Raven, though she hadn't really ever talked to him until now. Today, when he came in for lunch, she had cornered him and asked for his help.

"There's a policeman here now," she said, "a detective named Reynolds. He wanted me to call you first, and anyone else I could think of who might know where Allie is. After that, if we still haven't found her, we'll need to file a missing persons report."

Mrs. Parker started crying, and Barb's worry shot into the stratosphere. She worked to keep her voice from betraying her concern. "It's going to be okay, Mrs. Parker. Allie's smart and you know how resourceful she is. She'll be fine. This is probably just a mistake."

But she didn't really think so. Barb hung up the phone feeling slightly sick to her stomach. She hadn't mentioned Allie's belief that Chrissy's death might not have been an accident. She hadn't told Mrs. Parker that her daughter had gone on a one-woman crusade to uncover information that might prove Chrissy and her boyfriend were murdered.

But Barb had said exactly that to Detective Reynolds.

"I take it her mother also believes something may have happened to her," he said. He was dark-complexioned, with thick brown hair and a pleasant smile, a handsome guy, Barb had always thought. Right now she just hoped he was good at his job.

"She's really worried. She and Allie have always been close. I don't think Allie would purposely frighten her for any reason."

"We'll have to talk to her, and to Allie's father, of course."

"He's retired. He's probably out on the golf course."

"You said she went to see Detective Hollis about Chrissy Chambers's death."

"That's right. She thought maybe Felix Baranoff or someone in Dynasty Corporation was involved with illegal drugs."

"Why would she think that?"

"Something Chrissy said, I guess. She was afraid that Donnie Markham was in some kind of trouble."

"Interesting."

"Very interesting, considering now something's happened to Allie, too."

"We don't know that yet." The guy next to him at the bar waved an empty highball glass. Barb went to refill the drink then returned.

"I've called everyone I can think of," she said. "I don't know what else to do."

"If you can find someone to cover you long enough to file that report, I'll drive you down to the station."

Barb started untying the red and black Raucous Raven apron she wore over her short black skirt. "Give me five minutes. I'll find someone." She hurried toward the back, worry making her hands shake. Dan Reynolds knew Allie Parker. She had waited on him a dozen times. He had known Chrissy Chambers even better—since he had undoubtedly slept with her.

Reynolds knew both of the women. If he was in a hurry to get the search for Allie underway, Barb was even more worried than she was before.

* * *

Two more long days passed. Except for an occasional walk on deck, Allie stayed below. At night, Jake tied their wrists together, dragged her down on the bed beside him, and promptly fell asleep. In the daytime, he left her alone.

They were due for another fuel stop. Based on how long they'd been able to travel the first time, they would have to find a harbor pretty soon. After her escape attempt, Jake had rummaged through the contents of her purse and removed anything she might be able to use against him.

Allie felt a shot of satisfaction as she thought of the little Bic lighter in the inside zipper compartment that Jake had missed and she had stashed beneath the mattress.

She had been on deck for the better part of an hour when she felt the subtle shift of the wind and knew it meant the boat was changing course. The yacht arched in a slow turn and the shoreline moved into position ahead of them, a long thin finger of sand interspersed with green.

"Where are we?" she asked as Jake walked up beside her, though she figured he probably wouldn't tell her.

"Puerto Magdalena." He cast her a hard, dark glance. "I don't suppose I could trust you to stay below and keep quiet."

"Oh, but you could. I promised I wouldn't—"

"That's what I thought." Gripping her arm, he tugged her toward the door leading down to his cabin. Knowing she had no choice, Allie preceded him down the stairs.

"I promised you I'd be quiet," she said. "Isn't that good enough?"

"No." Reaching into his dresser drawer, he dragged out the pieces of line he had used before.

"I really hate doing this, but I don't have any choice."

"Surely you could—" The gag went in, cutting off her words. He bound her wrists, then her feet, sat her down in the chair and tied another rope around her, and left her there. "I'll untie you as soon as we leave."

Allie sat there cursing him, waiting impatiently for the ship to dock. Once the engines were shut down, she could hear the men up on deck, all three of them departing the yacht. As soon as the boat was empty, Allie set to work, scooting the chair to the side to the bed, groping beneath the mattress to pull out her little emergency Bic.

It wasn't easy tied the way she was. She fumbled with the lighter, trying to burn the line, but it seemed impervious to the little flame. Knowing time was of the essence, she resigned herself to being tied, and started scooting around in the chair, hopping and dragging it from one place to another, retrieving some discarded paper from the waste can, bunching the comforter, sheets, and blankets into a pile in the middle of the bed.

It took forever to get the portholes open, but somehow she managed to get the end ones undone. Exhausted, she leaned back in her chair to study the soon-to-be bonfire she had made in the bed.

The plan seemed a good one, considering her limited options. Once she got a blaze started, smoke would billow out the open windows. Jake and the other two men might see it and rush back to put it out, but there was every chance that other men would come as well. Finding her bound and gagged, they would realize she was in trouble.

Someone would help her—they had to.

This time she was determined to succeed.

Taking a breath for courage, praying she wasn't about to go up in flames along with the mattress, Allie lit the papers she had laced through the pile and waited for the little blaze to smolder to life.

As soon as she was sure she had it going, she scooted as far away as she could get, said a quick prayer that the smoke wouldn't get too thick before rescue came, and waited for the excitement to begin.

A prickle of unease teased the back of Jake's neck. It was a feeling he rarely ignored and he wasn't about to ignore it now. From the start, he'd had a bad feeling about leaving Allie alone for so long; now his sixth sense was shouting out a warning. Ducking beneath the low door of what passed for the local grocery store, his arms full of supplies, Jake headed for the boat.

Down the block, he passed Luis and Roberto, who sat at the bar in Pedro's Cantina—an open-air shed with a thatched roof and six stools—drinking straight shots of tequila. He told them to be ready to leave in twenty minutes and continued toward the boat.

He had almost reached the marina where the *Dynasty II* was docked when he saw the first wispy tendrils of smoke rolling out of the portholes.

Sonofabitch! Tightening his hold on the bags of supplies, furious at being duped again, he raced down the gangway, leapt onto the deck, tossed the groceries aside, and slammed through the door leading below. At least she hadn't been able to lock it this time.

Jake blinked against the smoke beginning to fill

the cabin. A stack of bedding smoldered in the center of the bed, refusing—to his great relief—to burst into a decent flame. Still strapped to the chair, eyes two round blue pools, Allie tried to scoot away from him. Her already pale face turned sheet-white as he pulled a knife from the pocket of his jeans and flipped open the blade—not a dinky little affair like hers, but a long-shanked, serviceable piece of steel that could gut a man if the need arose.

Allie's big eyes slid closed and she trembled.

Good, he thought. *I hope to goddamn hell she's scared.* Jerking open the closet door, he reached down and cut the rope that bound her to the chair, hauled her to her feet, and shoved her in.

Cursing her and every blonde he had ever had the misfortune to meet, he slammed the door, whirled the chair around backward, and crammed it under the knob.

He could hear her calling his name behind the gag but he ignored her. Wrestling the smoldering comforter off the bed—all she had managed to ruin—he carried it into the shower and turned the water on.

A few minutes later, satisfied he'd finally found a way to keep her out of trouble, he left the cabin to finish refueling and making ready to leave.

He cast a final glance at the door to his cabin and an uneasy tremor ran down his spine. Thank God he was the one who had seen the smoke—not Bobby or Luis.

Allie's chest hurt as she thought of her failure and fought her growing fear. She slammed her shoulder against the closet door one last time, but the chair refused to budge and she knew it was useless to continue. Her shoulder aching, she leaned against the wall of the tiny, airless space that was maybe three feet across and the width of a clothes hanger deep. Only a thin crack of light seeped in from under the door, and the smell of burnt cotton tinged the heavy air.

Allie fumbled around inside the closet, telling herself to relax, trying to get comfortable. A sport coat, a couple of pairs of slacks, and a pair of leather shoes were the only clothes inside, yet the confining space had her nerves frayed raw and her mind on the edge of panic.

Since she was eight years old, she'd had a phobia of closed-in spaces. Ever since the Friday afternoon she had been playing in an open trench in her backyard. The construction company had dug it to repair a broken pipeline, but they had already finished and left for the day.

As soon as the workmen were gone, she'd headed straight for the trench, thinking how much fun it would be to play war with the twin boys who lived next door, using the trench as a fort.

She was digging madly away, trying to build up her fortifications, when the dirt caved in and instantly she was buried, everything but her nose and the top half of her head covered by the fallen earth.

Fear unlike anything she had ever known descended on her that day. Her parents hadn't found her for nearly three hours, and she had been hysterical when they did—and terrified of anyplace too confining ever since.

Allie dragged in a calming breath, but it was hard to do with the gag in her mouth. She was breathing way too fast, her palms sweating, the walls of the closet beginning to close in. She closed her eyes and tried to imagine herself in a place of serenity, as the doctor at the phobia clinic had told her to do, though it had never actually worked.

Another few minutes passed and the panic increased. She tried to move her arms, but Jake had bound them securely. She tried to spit out the gag, but it was tied too tight.

Her chest muscles contracted. It was getting harder and harder to breathe. She felt as if she were buried, trapped as she had been before. She started jerking her hands, trying to free her wrists, no longer feeling the pain of the rope cutting into her skin. The panic continued to build. She banged her shoulder against the closet door again, then slowly sank down to her knees.

Her breath wheezed in and out. Dear God, she was going to suffocate, going to die right there on the closet floor! Tears filled her eyes and slid down her cheeks, wetting the gag, which felt swollen twice its size inside her mouth.

Allie stared at the door, but no longer saw it, just the darkness that sucked her in and wouldn't let her escape.

Swearing, determined to make the girl understand once and for all the danger she was in, as soon as the yacht was underway, Jake returned to his cabin. What the hell was the matter with her? Was the little idiot actually dumb enough to believe she could best three hardened men?

He cursed as he reached the bottom of the stairs and started toward the closet. Hearing a series of thumps, he realized Allie was banging against the door. Dammit, didn't she know when to give up?

Determined to scare her badly enough she wouldn't give him any more trouble, Jake jerked open the door. Slumped in the bottom of the closet, Allie made a pathetic little whimpering sound and not the least attempt to come out.

Jake's chest squeezed. His hand shook as he hauled her up, limp as a rag and barely able to stand on her feet. Her eyes looked glassy, the pupils abnormally dilated.

"Easy, baby." Sliding an arm around her waist, he held her while he untied her wrists. They were bleeding, he saw, rubbed raw in her effort to get away.

Dammit to hell. Certain he knew what was wrong, he untied the gag and pulled the handkerchief out of her mouth.

Allie looked up at him and burst into tears.

Damn, he hated a crying woman, especially when he was the cause. "It's all right," he soothed, tightening his hold, wrapping his body around her, cocooning her in his warmth. "You're all right now."

He could feel her trembling. He sat down on the edge of the bed, eased her down on his lap, and just held her. He'd known hardened men who were claustrophobic, guys who washed out of Special Forces because they couldn't crawl through tunnels or stand the feeling of being trapped underwater in scuba gear.

He smoothed back her wavy blond hair, sifting his fingers through it, tucking a strand behind her ear. It felt soft as silk, different from the hair-sprayed, overbleached blond hair on the women he had dated, including the two he had married. He could feel her breasts pressing into his chest, remembered the way they had felt beneath his hands, and his loins tightened. Jake forced himself to ignore it.

Reaching down, he tipped her chin with his fingers. "You all right?"

Allie straightened a little, nodded.

"You're claustrophobic?"

She worried the edge of her lip. "Since . . . since I was a kid. I was digging a fort in our backyard when it caved in and I was buried. I guess I never got over it." For the first time she realized she was sitting in his lap. Her face flushed and she slid away, coming unsteadily to her feet. She must have felt the vibration of the engines because she glanced toward the disappearing shoreline.

"We're underway again. You're going with us, Allie. You might as well get used to it."

Allie said nothing. He didn't miss the despair in her eyes.

"There's some ointment in the head. Let me take care of those wrists." He went after it, returned a few minutes later. Allie still stared forlornly out the porthole. He led her back to the chair and started smoothing salve over her wrists.

"You're going to kill me, aren't you?" she said softly.

Jake paused. For the first time since Roberto had found her, he considered telling her the truth. As fast as the idea surfaced, it died.

"I told you before, if you behave yourself, I'll let you go when we get where we're going."

"And that would be . . . ?"

"South of where we are now."

"If you're going to let me go then, why won't you let me go now?"

"You know why. Because we can't afford to take

the risk. You've caused enough trouble already. We don't need any more."

"But—"

"You're going, Allie, and that's the end of it."

She didn't argue. As soon as he'd finished bandaging her wrists, she returned to staring out the porthole.

"What's your name?" he asked, more curious about her than he should have been.

Allie eyed him warily. "You know my name."

"I mean your last name."

"Parker."

"Allison Parker?"

"No."

She didn't offer more and he didn't press her. The less he knew about her, the better. When he came down to check on her a little before supper, he found her sleeping, exhausted from her ordeal.

Jake thought about what he'd told her, that they would let her go once they reached their destination. The truth was, he couldn't let her go—not until this whole mess was over. She knew the name of the boat—which would implicate Felix Baranoff. As soon as she got back to San Diego, she'd go directly to the cops and the whole deal would be blown. Worse than that, if she went to the Mexican police, they might set the *Federales* after them.

Jake couldn't let that happen. Not at any cost.

He wished like hell he knew what to do.

Chapter Six

Seated behind his gleaming rosewood Louis XIV desk, Felix Baranoff checked his gold Patik Philippe wristwatch. Two minutes to ten.

To his right, he heard a single sharp ring, pulled open the drawer, and took out his private cell phone, a number listed under a fictitious name that even his secretary knew nothing about. Eve Holloway was efficient and trustworthy. Once he'd even enjoyed her in bed. But there were a few things better off kept private, and his relationship with General Alejandro Valisimo was one of them.

"*Buenos dias*, Alejandro." Felix spoke five languages fluently and a couple of others passably well, but he preferred to converse in English, since it always kept his clients, mostly foreign, a little off-guard. His tone was relaxed, carefully light. He had been waiting for this call. There was no need to worry . . . not yet.

"I am calling to confirm our meeting. The boat is underway?"

"That's correct." Felix was a big man, stout through the shoulders and chest. His dark brown hair had a few streaks of gray at the temples, but those, women said, only made him look more dignified.

"And your man . . . Dawson, is it? He has the items requested?"

"Jake Dawson will be bringing the first shipment, just as we planned."

"Good. My men will be waiting at the rendezvous point. If the boat does not arrive within twenty-four hours of its scheduled time, I will be in touch."

"It'll be there, General. Dawson's a dependable man."

"He had better be," Valisimo said, and the phone went dead.

Baranoff's mouth thinned. He didn't like Alejandro Valisimo. The general saw himself as a patriot dedicated to "The People." He treated anyone who profited from his efforts with disdain. Felix saw him as a zealot, bent on self-destruction, and was happy to help him along his chosen path . . . for a price.

Returning the cell phone to the drawer of his desk, he rose and walked over to the window. His office faced San Diego Bay, not a cheap location, but he could afford it.

He carefully reached down and picked up the exquisite Tang Dynasty horse sitting on a Hepplewhite table. The horse, though nearly priceless, was just one small piece from a collection that was world renowned.

Felix loved to collect. Seventeenth-century Flemish paintings and Italian sculpture, rare Chinese jade and exotic Japanese silk screens. And his personal favorite, exquisite golden artifacts from ancient civilizations.

He set the Tang Dynasty horse back down on the table and turned toward the lighted case that held a golden necklace worn by the Egyptian Queen Hatshepsut in 1500 B.C.

It took money to buy such valuable art. Felix had worked hard all his life to own the treasures he wanted.

He thought of Alejandro Valisimo and his silly little revolution. He thought of what lay beneath the deck of the *Dynasty II*, and he smiled.

Evening set in. Allie awakened to find the cabin bathed in shadows. Through the porthole, she watched the sun sink low on the horizon, turning the sky an orangey gold. It was warmer tonight. The farther south they traveled, the hotter it got. She was glad it was only the end of March—correction—today was the first of the month, April Fools' Day, and the joke was definitely on her.

Her stomach rumbled. She thought of going up to the galley for something to eat then wondered if Jake had barred the way. She doubted it. There was no place for her to go, and whenever she was on deck, one of them always kept an eye on her. She started up the stairs, got as far as the door, but the sound of men's voices kept her from going any farther.

"The woman's trouble," Bobby Santos was saying to Jake. "You can't control her, give her to me. I'll make sure she keeps her mouth shut."

"Hey, man, I'll take care of her," Luis offered. "I'll fuck her so hard she won't be able to get out of bed."

Both men thought that was hilariously funny. Jake didn't join in the laughter. "I told you, the woman belongs to me for as long as I say."

"Yeah, well, that sucks, man," Bobby grumbled.

"You don't like it?" She heard the sound of Jake's chair sliding back. "Maybe you'd like to do something about it."

Bobby didn't answer. Jake Dawson was big and tough, sure of himself in a way neither of the other men were. She didn't blame Bobby for not wanting to fight him.

"I didn't think so," Jake said.

He was defending her again and she couldn't help wondering why. Was there really such a thing as a bad guy with a good heart? Or was it something more sinister, something he wanted from her that he could get only by biding his time?

She thought of what had happened in Tortugas, remembered the way he had cared for her after he had found her in the closet. She could still feel the imprint of his big, hard body wrapped around her, infusing her with its warmth.

Outside the door, she heard Bobby leave the salon and return to the helm. Gathering her courage, she joined the other two men. Jake had fixed some sort of fish stew and it smelled delicious. A man who could cook—and looked as good as he did—under different circumstances, he would have been a treasure. She ate the bowl of stew he set in front of her, then cleaned up the galley after she was finished.

When he came into the cabin that night and began to strip off his clothes, she looked at him in a way she hadn't before, the way Chrissy might have looked at him. What she saw made her breath catch. Shoulders so wide they barely fit through the door to the head, and a flat, rock-hard stomach. Sculpted muscles in a smooth, tanned back, eyes a beautiful deep blue, and a face that, if it hadn't been so hard-edged, would have made a woman dizzy.

Allie mentally shook herself. Maybe she was succumbing to the Hostage Syndrome, beginning to see her captors as saviors instead of the ruthless, drug-dealing kidnappers they were. The truth was, she had no idea what Jake Dawson's intentions might be. There was more than a good chance he meant to kill her.

He cast a glance in her direction as he stripped off his T-shirt and tossed it over a chair.

"Get in bed. I need to get some sleep and I can't do it with you prowling around the cabin."

She watched him warily, surprised when he ignored the drawer where he kept the rope and started instead for the opposite side of the bed.

"Aren't you going to tie me up?"

He turned back, stopped in front of her. "If you leave the cabin, you'll have to deal with Bobby or Luis. You ought to know by now what will happen if they get their hands on you."

Allie shivered. "I won't leave."

"Good, now get in bed. If I wanted to rape you, I'd have done it long before this."

"Why haven't you?" The words were out of her mouth before she could stop them. Allie cringed at the astonished look on his face.

"You want me to rape you?"

"No! Of—of course not. I just wondered . . . you know, why you hadn't. I'm sure if my roommate had been the one hiding in your cabin, you would at least have considered the idea. It seems kind of insulting in some way."

His mouth edged up at the corners. Then the faint smile slowly slid away. Inside his faded jeans, he went hard. It didn't take an expert to recognize the thick ridge pressing against his fly or know exactly what it meant.

She stood frozen as he reached up and touched her cheek. "Well, now, I wouldn't want to insult a lady."

Allie opened her mouth to say something—anything—but before she could formulate the words, one of his big hands slid into her hair and he dragged her mouth up to his for a kiss. His lips were softer than they looked and his hands were stronger.

He held her immobile, taking what he wanted, turning her head one way and then another, claiming hot, wet kisses, taking her deeply with his tongue.

Allie felt plundered, savaged. On fire.

His chest was bare. Hard muscle and curly black chest hair pressed into her breasts, and every time he moved, her nipples rubbed against her cotton tank top. His thigh found a place between her legs and an ache throbbed there. His mouth felt hot and wet and wonderful.

Jake deepened the kiss and her knees turned to jelly. Her lungs refused to drag in a sufficient amount of air. Somewhere in the distance, she heard a little moan and realized it came from her.

Ohmygod! Allie jerked away at the same instant Jake released her and took a step backward. For a moment, both of them just stood there, breathing too fast, staring at each other as if they couldn't believe what had happened.

"Sonofabitch," Jake said, raking a hand through his too-long black hair.

Allie said nothing, but she couldn't have agreed with him more. What in God's name was the matter with her? The man was a kidnapper, a criminal, maybe even a murderer. And she had kissed him!

Allie backed away. "I—I'm sorry."

Intense blue eyes fixed on her face. *"You're* sorry?"

"Yes, I . . . That was a stupid thing to do. I'm your prisoner. You're a . . . a . . . well, you're some kind of desperado. I shouldn't have said what I did."

An eyebrow arched up, along with a corner of his mouth. "Asking if I'd thought about raping you, you mean."

She swallowed—hard. "Well, yes. I mean, it was really dumb to—"

"Just so you know—I like my women willing, Allie. But I've thought plenty about having you." The amusement slowly faded. "Thanks to what just happened, now I'll think about it a whole lot more."

Allie said nothing, but a little tremor ran through her. She told herself it was fear. She watched him round the bed to the opposite side.

"By now you know I'm not going to force you. I'm tired of sleeping in these damnable jeans so I'm taking them off. You don't like it—don't look."

With that he unbuttoned the waistband and unzipped his fly, slid them down, and pulled them off. She told herself not to look, but her eyes refused to go anywhere else. He wore small white briefs, and when he climbed beneath the sheet, she saw his legs were as long and muscular as the rest of him. And if the bulge in front was any measure, he was very well endowed.

"Get some sleep," he said gruffly.

A nearly naked man lay under that sheet. It was bad enough when she had been forced to sleep beside him and that was before he had kissed her—and he'd been wearing a lot more clothes.

"I'll sleep in the chair tonight."

One blue eye cracked open. "You'll sleep in the bed so I can keep track of you."

Allie shook her head.

"You want me to tie you up again?"

With a sigh of defeat, she sat down on the edge of the bed and took off her sox and Reeboks. Refusing to crawl under the sheet, she lay down on top and drew the blanket up over her, ignoring the smell of burnt wool.

"Those clothes can't be any more comfortable than my jeans," Jake said without opening his eyes. "If you want, I'll dig out one of my T-shirts for you to wear."

"No! I—I mean, no, thank you. I'm fine just the way I am."

Jake snorted in disbelief, but he didn't press her. In fact, he seemed relieved. Rolling onto his side, he punched the pillow a couple of times and stuffed it beneath his head. Allie tried not to think of all that dark skin and hard muscle lying just inches away.

But it was a very long time before she fell asleep.

Detective Dan Reynolds stepped into the glass-enclosed office and closed the door. Thin, red-haired Archie Hollis was already there. Both Dan and Archie had been assigned to the Parker case, since Archie had spoken to Allie in regard to her roommate's death and Dan knew a little about both of the women.

Sitting across from them in a chair behind his desk, Captain Tom Caruthers took his glasses off and rubbed the bridge of his nose. "So what have you got so far?" Caruthers was black, about five-ten, and built like a fireplug. He was street savvy, bulldog stubborn, and the best captain Dan had ever worked for.

Hollis answered, "No all that much, sir. We checked her apartment. The place was in order, nothing disturbed. If somebody snatched her, they didn't do it there. We interviewed the neighbors. None of them saw anything out of the ordinary. According to a couple of them, the Parker girl was well liked and friendly. No enemies they could think of. No serious boyfriends. She didn't date much. Her roommate did, though." He flicked a glance at Dan. "I guess she got around pretty good."

Dan ignored the jibe. He'd dated Chrissy Chambers for maybe a couple of weeks, but the only thing they'd had in common was sex. She liked it hot and so did he, but when they woke up together in the morning, there never seemed to be anything to say.

Oddly enough, even after the affair had ended, they'd stayed friends. Chrissy liked everyone. She never made an enemy, not even the men she slept with. She was just that kind of person.

"How about the all-points on the car?" Caruthers asked.

"Nothing yet," Dan said, "but it's one of those metallic lime green Volkswagen bugs—not hard

to spot. Sooner or later it's bound to turn up somewhere."

"It's been at least five days. Check the towing
companies. See if maybe it's sitting in a lot somewhere."

"I'm already on it," Dan said.

"Anything else?"

"According to her friend, Barbara Wallace,"
Dan added, "Allie paid a visit to Albright Insurance, the company that covered the boat Christine
Chambers was killed on. Archie and I spoke to
a guy named"—he flipped open his little spiral
notebook—"Bill Burns. Burns didn't know her by
name, but he recognized the photo. Said she called
herself Dorie Rankin. She told him she worked for
Dynasty Corp and asked for his help." Dan fought
a smile. "Burns gave her everything she wanted."

"Which was?"

"Information on the *Dynasty I.* Apparently she
learned that the insurance on the yacht been raised
just before it blew up."

"Lucky for Baranoff," the captain said dryly.

"I guess that's what Allie thought."

"Sounds like she was trying to turn up that proof
Hollis told her she needed."

"Maybe," Archie said. "But I doubt she uncovered anything useful."

"Why not?" Dan asked.

"Because Felix Baranoff isn't the kinda guy to
worry about some dingbat blonde, that's why. He's
got more money than God and he's a regular philantro—philantro—"

"Philanthropist," Dan finished.

"Yeah. Last year he even gave a big chunk of
change to the Police Department Widows and
Orphans Fund."

Dan reached up and loosened his tie. Wearing the damned thing was the worst part of being a detective. "I'll admit it isn't likely, but there is a chance Allie Parker stumbled across something she wasn't supposed to know and somebody did something to keep her quiet."

"Well, it's too soon to speculate." The captain stood up from his chair. "You two keep after it. And keep me informed. With Baranoff's name being bandied about, this could turn into a very high-profile investigation."

Dan made no reply, but he didn't like the direction this was taking. And just like Barb Wallace, Dan was worried about Allie Parker.

Another day passed, along with another restless night. Jake had been awake the better part of an hour when a thin gray tendril of light seeped in through the portholes above the bed. He stretched a little, trying to ease the kink in his neck. Though it smelled faintly of smoke, the cabin was roomy, and luxurious by any standards, yet with the slender woman asleep at his side, it felt cramped and airless, not nearly big enough for the two of them.

Jake cast a glance at Allie, who lay curled up just inches away. His turn at the wheel didn't start for more than an hour and his eyes felt gritty from lack of sleep, but there was no way in hell he was going to get any rest.

Damn, he wished he hadn't kissed her.

He noticed the soft curve of her lips, the smooth, peaches-and-cream color of her skin, and his groin began to throb. He was hard as a stone and achingly uncomfortable. He had been that way, off and on, since the day Roberto had found her.

Damn, he hated blondes. They had a way of getting under his skin at the worst possible times. He thought he'd be immune to this one, but he had rapidly discovered he wasn't. He wanted her. Wanted to be inside her.

Damn.

Why don't blondes talk while they're having sex?

Their mothers told them not to speak to strangers.

Jake ground his jaw. He and Allie were strangers, and blonde or not, he didn't think she was the type for casual sex—to say nothing of the fact he was on the job and doing his best to keep her safe.

Grumbling a swear word, he climbed out of bed and padded into the head. He turned on the shower and set the temperature lower than he liked. It woke him up the rest of the way and got rid of his morning hard-on. Which made it easier to think.

Mentally, he went over the events so far. Until Allie Parker had been found aboard, everything had been going exactly as planned. The yacht, the perfect cover, was loaded and heading south right on schedule. The authorities kept watch for boats smuggling drugs into the States. A big, expensive sport-fishing yacht like this one would hardly be smuggling goods in the opposite direction.

And the Baranoff name provided a cover of its own. The *Dynasty II* had been traveling these waters for years, taking Baranoff's wealthy clients on luxury cruises. On the surface, this was just another trip.

Jake thought about the satellite phone in the pilot house. He knew exactly what Baranoff would tell him if he discovered there was a woman aboard.

"There's no room for failure," the man had said. "Bear that in mind and do whatever is necessary."

When Baranoff said, "Do whatever is necessary," he meant exactly that, and there was no doubt the other two men had been given the same instructions.

Dressing in cutoff jeans in concession to the growing heat, Jake thought of Allie and a chill worked its way down his spine. There was no way in hell Baranoff could find out she was on the boat. No way. Was there? Christ, he really hoped not, but the man was smart and he had nearly limitless connections.

As soon as his shift came up, Jake decided, the satellite phone was going to go temporarily out of order.

Chapter Seven

She was going stir-crazy. If she hadn't known it was impossible in a sunny, luxurious cabin, she would think she was getting claustrophobic again. Allie paced back and forth across the thick mauve carpet. The truth was she just wasn't the type to spend so much time doing absolutely nothing.

Jake had warned her to stay below as much as possible, and so far she had. But she'd hoped by now the yacht would have reached its destination. Unfortunately, they were still at sea, still underway, and she couldn't take a whole lot more.

The sun beat down through the portholes, making the cabin unbearably warm. It was too hot for her windbreaker, but she didn't dare go on deck without it. She dragged it over her orange tank top, which, along with her khaki shorts, badly needed washing, and started up the stairs.

Luis stood in the salon when she opened the door. "Hey, baby. You come up to get your itch scratched?" He gave her a lecherous grin. "You tell Jake, he ain't got what it takes to keep you happy, Luis will be glad to take care of you."

Allie ignored him. Luis was always saying something like that. "Where is he?"

"It's his shift. He's up on the bridge."

And where is Roberto? she wanted to ask but didn't. It was important neither of the two Hispanic men know how frightened she was of them. And she really did need some air. She was desperate to stretch her legs, and she wasn't letting Bobby Santos or anyone else keep her from it.

She shoved open the glass door and went out on deck, sucked in a deep breath of warm, salty sea air. So far the weather had been mild and sunny, just a few fluffy clouds in the sky. Today was the hottest day yet, the temperatures in the high eighties.

She wandered toward the front of the boat, enjoying the rush of wind and the clear blue sea that stretched out in front of her. Then the engines ceased their roar and silence fell over the boat. It came to a rolling stop and settled deeper into the swells.

She started to go inside and find out what had happened, but whatever it was, it wasn't going to change her circumstances and she was enjoying the rare moment of freedom. Shading her eyes from the sun, she studied the horizon, straightened, then looked harder.

Whales! She was so excited that for one sweet moment she forgot she was a prisoner. Forgot she was stuck on a boat headed for God-knew-where, an uncertain future ahead of her. She wanted to share her excitement, and for that single sweet moment, Jake's name rose on her lips.

Reality surfaced. Jake was her captor, not her friend, no matter that he had protected her.

No matter that he had kissed her.

A huge gray body surfaced in the water, followed by a monstrous tail, and a rush of pure joy ran through her. Perhaps it was a message, a sign. Life could be so good, so sweet, even when things looked bleak. She watched another beautifully curved, massive gray tail flip high in the air then sink gracefully out of sight beneath the surface of the water, and a feeling of awe settled over her.

She was grinning, thinking that perhaps the message she'd received in watching the whales was one of hope. Life was precious, and very much worth fighting for. She was going to survive this adventure and she would be a better, stronger person for it, once she got back home.

The conviction grew so strong she almost didn't hear the faint squeak of rubber-soled shoes on the deck behind her. Turning, she found Bobby Santos standing just inches away.

"You saw the whales?"

She tensed. "Yes. They were beautiful."

"*Sí*, beautiful . . . like you, *chica*." Reaching out he touched her cheek, let his hand run slowly along her jaw. Allie fought a shiver of revulsion. She cast a frantic look over his shoulder, wondering where Jake was, wishing he would miraculously appear.

"He is working down in the engine room, checking on a problem with the pump." Roberto closed the distance between them, forcing her back against the stainless steel railing that enclosed the bow. "I think it's time we got to know each other better—don't you?"

Her chin went up. "I know you as well as I intend to." Allie tried to brush past him, but he blocked her way, forcing her back to the rail. "Get out of my way."

Bobby moved closer, pinning her with his body, pressing his pelvis into hers. "You don't want to mess with me, *chica.*" One of his hands slid inside the windbreaker and he cupped a breast. "I could hurt you so easy." His fingers tightened around the soft flesh and he gave it a painful squeeze. "It would be smarter just to give me what I want."

Her heart pounded. She wanted to scream, wanted to turn and run. Instead, she held her ground. "I'm not giving you anything, Roberto." Twisting away from him, she started walking away. Instead of fighting her, Bobby moved with her, using her own momentum to help him spin her around, catching her behind the knee, bringing her down on the deck and coming down hard on top of her.

She landed with a painful thud, knocking the air out of her lungs. Bobby's heavy weight made it difficult to breathe. She felt his hands, one of them rubbing her breast, the other groping between her legs. His eyes were dark and flat and filled with determination.

Allie swallowed against the bile rising in her throat. Fear warred with fury. She had taken self-defense classes for nearly six months. She knew what to do—and dammit she would do it—no matter the consequences.

She forced her body to relax, and smiled up at him. "Maybe you're right," she said, sliding a hand behind his neck as if she meant to kiss him. "I give it to Jake. Why shouldn't I give it to you?"

Bobby's eyes gleamed with triumph. He fumbled

with his zipper, bent his head to kiss her, and Allie
slammed a knee into his groin.

"Aiyeee!" Roberto howled, rolling away from
her, clutching his crotch as Allie sprang to her feet.
"You bitch!"

Whirling away from him, she started to run, but
Bobby's hand lashed out and caught her ankle. He
twisted and brought her crashing back down on
the deck.

"You wanna play games?" He was on her in an
instant, grabbing her wrists, pinning them beside
her head, holding her down with his body. She
thought she heard something and prayed it wasn't
Luis. She could feel his erection pressing into her
stomach and fear sparked another jolt of fury. With
a sudden jerk, she freed one of her hands and
raked her nails down his face.

"Puta!" Roberto hissed in pain and grabbed her
wrist. Allie fought like a wild thing and shoved
him with all of her strength, but Roberto held
her immobile. She struggled against the hand he
wrapped around her throat and began to squeeze,
turning the world fuzzy and dim. Then Jake
appeared out of nowhere, grabbed Bobby by the
back of the neck, and dragged him off her. Jake
whirled him around as if he were made of balsa
wood and slammed him against the sloping Plexi-
glas windows of the pilot house.

"I told you I don't share." Jake's face was con-
torted in rage, his blue eyes almost black. Long,
tanned fingers curled into the front of Roberto's
pristine white short-sleeved shirt. "The girl is mine
until I'm finished with her. Since I'm running this
operation, that's the way it's gonna be. You got
it?"

Roberto wiped at the thin lines of blood trailing

down his cheek. "I got it." Cruel black eyes bored into Allie. "When this is over, *chica,* I'm gonna kill you."

Jake dragged him up and slammed him again. "You aren't killing anyone. You're not fucking them, either. You're here to do a job. That's exactly what you'll do."

Roberto said nothing for the longest time. Finally, he nodded, but his surly expression never changed and his dark gaze remained on Allie. He was warning her, telling her he would do what Jake said—for now. But the time would come when he would make her pay.

An icy shiver ran over her skin, though the day was already warm.

Jake let go of Roberto's shirt. "Get below," he said to her. When she didn't move fast enough, he wrapped a big hand around her arm and practically jerked her off her feet as he towed her along the deck and into the salon. He slammed the cabin door and followed her descent down the stairs, which was more than a little unsteady with her legs shaking as badly as they were.

Forcing herself to face him, Allie blanched at the dark look on his face and steeled herself to face his wrath. In a remote corner of her mind, she wondered why she wasn't more frightened.

"What the hell's the matter with you? I told you not to go on deck alone."

"I—I thought you were up on the bridge."

"Since you didn't bother letting me know you'd left the cabin, I went down to the engine room. Your little stroll gave Bobby exactly the chance he's been waiting for."

A surge of anger straightened her spine. Allie clamped a hand on her hips. "Oh, so it's my fault.

Your friends are pigs who can't control themselves, and I'm the one who's to blame?"

"They aren't my friends. I figured you knew that by now." There was something in his face, something that looked remarkably like concern. Reaching out, he caught her chin, tipped it up to examine the bruises that were forming around her throat. "I'm sorry he hurt you. You gonna be all right?"

His voice had an odd note of softness. She was shocked to realize that he had been afraid for her. "I'm okay. Thank you for what you did."

"When I came out of the engine room, I saw you through the pilot house window. That's how I knew you were in trouble." The corners of his mouth inched up. "I guess you really do know self-defense."

She couldn't resist a grin. "I got an A in the class." It was ridiculous to stand there smiling at a man who held her prisoner. The lack of oxygen must have affected her brain. "I didn't make it easy for him. Still, if you hadn't come along when you did . . ."

His amusement slowly faded.

"Bobby's stronger than he looks. And he's flat-out mean. I don't know how long I can keep him under control. From now on, stay out of his way."

Allie looked up at him. "Why do you keep protecting me, Jake?"

"Maybe I've got a thing for nosy blondes."

"And maybe you're just not the same kind of man they are. Why don't you tell me what's going on? What has Felix Baranoff got you and those two lowlifes doing that you can't let me off this damned boat?"

His eyes turned as hard as Roberto's. For the first time she was actually afraid.

"What do you know about Felix Baranoff?"

She took a step backward. "Not . . . not much. I know he probably killed my roommate, Chrissy Chambers."

He drilled her with a look. "Christine Chambers was your roommate?"

"She was also my best friend."

"That's it, isn't it? That's what you were doing on the boat? Snooping around, trying to dig up information about what happened to the Chambers girl."

"Yes—and I did, didn't I? I found out Felix Baranoff is involved in illegal drugs."

"Did you tell anyone you were suspicious of your roommate's death?"

She chewed her lip, trying to decide how much to say. Maybe if he knew she had talked to the police, it would help protect her. "As a matter of fact, I told several people—including a detective named Hollis on the San Diego Police Force."

"Yeah?"

"That's right. In fact, I mentioned the possibility that Baranoff was involved in drugs. They're probably looking for the boat right now."

"Yeah? So you told this detective you were going to sneak aboard Felix Baranoff's yacht and see if you could find evidence he was smuggling drugs— and Hollis thought that was a brilliant idea."

Her face flushed. "Well, not exactly like that."

Jake stared at her for several long moments, then the tension eased from his shoulders. "I hate to disappoint you, Allie, but Baranoff's reputation is impeccable. The police aren't going to give your story the least amount of credence."

Impeccable? Credence? Big words for a criminal. Allie wondered exactly who Jake Dawson was. "In time, they'll figure it out. You're just lucky they haven't caught up with you yet." Jake said nothing. Allie had the strangest urge to reach out and touch him. "You could stop this. It isn't too late, Jake. Instead of going through with whatever Baranoff has planned, you could be one of the good guys."

The edges of his mouth inched up. "A good guy, huh?" He had the nicest mouth. She remembered the heat of it moving over hers, remembered the taste and the unexpected softness, and a curl of warmth slid into her stomach.

"I'll give it some thought, Allie." Turning away, he started toward the stairs. "I'll bring you some ice. You can wrap it in a towel and use it on your throat."

Allie watched him disappear up the stairs. She wondered what had happened to Jake Dawson to make him turn bad.

Morning drifted into afternoon. The sun beat down, hotter than a stolen hubcap, but Bobby thought it felt kinda good. Standing on the aft deck outside the main salon, he took a drag on his cigarette, tilted his head back to absorb the rays, and let the smoke drift out through his nostrils.

He reached up and touched the scabs forming on his face, long thin rows going down his cheek. The little whore had done that. No one had ever left a mark on his face, no one. The thought that Dawson's bitch had done it left a bad taste in his mouth. He leaned over and spit in the sea.

They were making good time, keeping the boat right on schedule. They'd be reaching Cabo San Lucas today, heading in for another fuel stop. This time Dawson had better keep the little bitch quiet or he would do it himself.

Bobby wasn't afraid of Jake Dawson. He wasn't afraid of anyone. But the money was big on this job—once he got paid. And that wouldn't happen until they reached Belize, and even then, not without Dawson. General Valisimo needed Dawson's hotshot weapons expertise. The deal wasn't going down without it.

Bobby slid the cigarette between his lips, inhaled another deep drag, and slowly blew it out. He would put up with Dawson until he got the money, then he'd take care of the bastard—and his little whore.

Bobby got hard just thinking about what he'd do to the bitch before he offed her. Anticipation was part of the thrill.

Maybe it wasn't so bad he had to wait.

They reached Cabo San Lucas early in the afternoon. Jake let Bobby and Luis go ashore for an hour or so while the boat was being refueled. He gave them a list of the food and supplies they needed, enough for their last two days on board, and told them to take an hour or so for themselves. He figured they'd calm down a little if they had a couple of tequila shooters, maybe even got laid.

Jake stayed aboard. He wasn't taking any more chances with Allie, who was tied up and locked in the head. Two hours later, they set off on the last leg of their sea voyage, crossing the mouth of the Sea of Cortez to the Mexican mainland. Day after tomorrow, they would arrive at a secluded cove south of Matzatlan near a little inlet called Teacapan, where they would rendezvous with the general's men.

As soon as the boat was underway and moving toward the open sea, Jake went below. He let Allie out and untied her, brought her up on deck for a breath of fresh air. "I'm sorry I had to do that, but you have to admit you gave me no choice."

Allie cast him a surly glance. "You don't think I should've tried to escape?"

Jake smiled. "I didn't say that. If I were in your shoes, I'd have done the same thing."

Allie stared off toward the shoreline, which grew smaller and smaller with each passing minute.

"Hey, Jake," Luis called down from the bridge. "Take a look at this gauge, will you? I think that pump is acting up again."

"Don't go 'way," he said to Allie, whose look turned even more sour. Ignoring a flicker of amusement, Jake left her standing beside the rail and climbed the ladder to the bridge.

Don't go 'way. Allie watched the retreating coastline, still fuming at Jake's parting words, trying to gauge the distance between the mainland and the yacht. The boat was running a little southwest, maybe as far as a mile offshore. It was a long haul, but the water was warm and she was a very good swimmer. Chrissy's smiling face rose into her mind. They had both tried out for the swim team, but only Allie had made it. She'd stayed on the team all three years she'd been at San Diego State.

A shot of adrenalin kicked her pulse up. She could do it. She could swim that far. She glanced around, saw the men were all occupied somewhere else. If she went over the side right now, by the time they realized she was gone, it might be too late to stop her.

Her heart raced, pumping extra courage into her veins. Saying a prayer that the men wouldn't see her—and the water wasn't full of man-eating sharks—Allie tore off her windbreaker and jerked off her Reeboks, shoved them behind a deck box out of sight. Then she slipped over the aft rail onto the swim step, took a deep breath, and disappeared into the churning water.

Not daring to risk a glance back, Allie started stroking hard for shore.

"The packing around the drive line's got a leak," Jake said to Luis. "No big deal, but the bilge pump's still running hot. We'll get it fixed before the boat heads back to San Diego." Which wouldn't be for a while, not until they were finished in Belize. If all went as planned, Jake wouldn't have to worry about going back on the boat. He would be flying home to L.A.

"Hey, man!" Roberto's frantic shout cut into his thoughts. "You better get down here, quick!"

There was something in Roberto's tone that made him think of Allie and alarm bells went off in his head. He hit the ladder to the deck and ran over to where Bobby stood at the rail.

"What's going on?"

"Your bitch—that's what's going on. Take a look out there." He pointed toward the shore. "You see that little orange speck?"

Jake's hands tightened on the rail. "Goddammit!" Yelling up to the bridge, he pointed toward where Allie swam toward shore, and Luis swung the yacht in that direction, cranking the engines up to full speed. Jake watched in disbelief as the little orange speck that was Allie kept going, plowing through the waves as if she had gills.

"She's spotted us," Roberto said. "There's a boat off to her left. She's turning in that direction."

Sonofabitch! That was all they needed, a boat full of rich American fishermen trying to save a damsel in distress. Toeing out of his deck shoes, Jake dragged his T-shirt over his head and unzipped his cutoff jeans. He wore his Speedo underneath, having planned to enjoy the sun a little, maybe take a nap on deck that afternoon.

The yacht across the way, a big fifty-five-foot Hatteras, hadn't spotted Allie yet. He didn't intend to let them. As soon as they were close enough, Jake dove into the water and started swimming. The ocean was warm, the swells only two or three feet.

He had nearly caught up with her before she spotted him. Once she did, she realized he would get to her before she could reach the boat and started waving and yelling at the men on the yacht.

Damn! Desperate to shut her up, the instant he reached her, he clamped his hands on her shoulders and simply shoved her under the water. Allie started fighting to get free, but he didn't release his hold, just held her there until she quit struggling, then dragged her up.

Allie broke the surface, sputtering and gagging, fighting to drag in a breath of air.

"Take it easy. I'm not gonna hurt you." She had swum a good long ways and he thought that she must be exhausted, which was the reason he didn't expect her to fight him, much less try to kick him in the balls and swim away.

Sonofabitch! She hadn't hurt him. The water was too much of a buffer for that. He started swimming again, amazed that her strokes were still so strong.

She'd done that a lot, he realized—amazed and surprised him with her courage and her strength. He couldn't help admiring her, couldn't help wondering where she had learned to swim like a damnable fish, wondering a lot of things he shouldn't want to know.

Wishing he didn't have to bring her back at all, he caught up with her and shoved her under again, holding her down a little longer this time. She couldn't get away from him, and the men on the fishing yacht hadn't noticed them, but he wasn't taking any more chances. He had underestimated her too many times already.

When he felt her struggles weaken, he dragged her to the surface, holding her up as she gasped and coughed, thrashed around like a drugged seal, and spit up a mouthful of water. Her strength was nearly gone. She fought him only briefly as he rolled her onto her back, slid an arm around her neck, and started towing her back to the boat.

The exhaustion she was fighting set in by the time they'd reached it. It took Bobby's and Luis's help to haul her aboard. Jake followed her up on the swim step and together they helped her over the rail onto the deck. Allie stood there shaking, staring at Luis and Roberto with a mixture of hatred and fear.

Afraid she would collapse, Jake eased her back against his chest, which was probably the worst thing he could have done.

"What's the matter with you, man?" Roberto taunted. "You let this little *puta* walk all over you and you don't do nothing about it? You say she belongs to you, but you don't make her behave."

"Yeah, man," Luis put in. "She's been trouble from the start."

"I say we get rid of her right now," Roberto said. "As soon as it gets dark, we throw the body over the side."

Allie straightened away from him, shaking even harder.

"He's right, man," Luis agreed. "You can't keep her in line, we gotta get rid of her."

Allie stared at the men and he could see the fear she fought to hide. He had tried to warn her, tried to make her understand. Now he'd have to do it in the most brutal manner.

He spun her toward him, slapped her hard across the face. "You heard what Luis and Bobby said. You're more trouble than you're worth. You try anything else, I'll let them have you. You understand?"

She just looked at him, her hand pressed to the growing red mark on her cheek. Tears welled in her eyes, and for the first time since they had found her aboard, she looked defeated.

Jake's chest tightened. He couldn't imagine what she must be thinking. He straightened, towering well above her, grabbed her shoulders, and shook her—hard. "You understand?"

"Yes . . ." she barely whispered, the sound so pitiful it made the knot in his chest ache.

"Good. Now get your ass below."

She started to walk, but her legs were shaking so hard he didn't think she could make it. He wanted to lift her up and carry her but he knew he didn't dare. Instead he waited, watching helplessly as she gathered the last of her courage and crossed the deck to the salon. As she disappeared inside and started down the stairs, he breathed an inward sigh of relief.

"You're right," he said to the men. "What happened is my fault." He gave them a cocky grin. "Amazing what a man'll do for a piece of tail."

Luis broke into a howl of laughter.

Bobby barely smiled. "You gonna take her all the way to Belize, man?"

"Nah. I doubt the general would approve. I'll get rid of her myself when we get to the mainland."

Bobby made no comment, but his shoulders seemed to relax.

Luis looked disappointed. "You said we could have her when you were through."

"If we've got time enough, you can. Right now, I'm going down and give her another lesson in what will happen to her if she doesn't behave."

Chapter Eight

Dripping wet, exhausted clear to the bone, Allie sank down on the chair in the cabin.

Jake had hit her. So what did she expect? The man was her jailer, not her friend. With a trembling hand, she touched the deepening bruise on her cheek. It was ridiculous to feel so hurt, so betrayed. Jake Dawson was a criminal, a kidnapper. She must have been insane to believe he was different from the other two men.

Her stomach felt suddenly queasy. Perhaps for the very first time, she realized how alone she really was.

And how close she had come to dying.

Dimly, she heard the door open and close. Looking up, she saw Jake coming down the stairs. His jaw was set, his expression grim. He looked as hard and dangerous as he had the day she had first come aboard, and for the first time in days, she was very much afraid of him.

Jake stopped right in front of her. His big hands were balled into fists, and a shiver of fear ran through her, making her tremble again. For long moments, he said nothing and her fear kicked up another notch. When he reached toward the bruise on her cheek, Allie flinched away from him and heard Jake curse.

He sank down on the edge of the bed a couple of feet away, raked wet black hair away from his face. Bracing his elbows on his knees, he leaned toward her.

"Look at me."

Allie blinked, tried to ignore the ache that was building in her chest. She didn't want to meet that intense blue gaze that seemed to look inside her, that could make her forget she was his prisoner, make her want to trust him, and she knew now for certain she couldn't do that.

"Look at me, Allie . . . please?" The softness in his voice drew her like a beacon.

"I'm sorry I hit you."

Yeah, right. Allie glanced away.

"Look at me, dammit!"

She did, but she wished she hadn't. Tears started running down her cheeks.

Jake released a shuddering breath. "Please don't do that. I hate it when you cry."

"I'm not crying," she said, hoisting her chin as she wiped away the wetness.

"I'm sorry I slapped you. I've never hit a woman in my life."

Allie said nothing.

"I had to do it. I know that sounds like a crock of bull, but it's the truth. At the time, it was all I

could think of to do. They would have killed you—
or have you forgotten that part?"

Allie sniffed. "I haven't forgotten."

"You don't trust me now, do you?"

"I never trusted you."

"I think you did. I think you knew I wouldn't
hurt you. I tried to scare you, but I never really
succeeded. That's why you weren't afraid to try to
escape."

"I tried to escape because I want to live."

"I'm the only one who can help you do that,
Allie."

She didn't answer. She noticed he was staring at
the red mark on her cheek.

"I never wanted to hurt you." His expression
held so much regret her chest started aching again.
His features shifted, his gaze probing, as if he
assessed her in some way.

Allie came to her feet. "What is it? Why are you
looking at me that way?"

Jake stood up, too. "I'm trying to decide if you're
smart enough to handle what I'm about to tell you.
I'm trying to convince myself to risk putting my
life in your hands."

"What are you talking about?"

"I'm talking about telling you the truth. If I do,
and you screw up, both of us are dead."

Allie wet her lips, unsure she wanted to hear
more. "I don't understand."

"I'm sure you don't. The hard fact is, if I don't
tell you the truth, I can't let you go. And if I don't
let you go, sooner or later, Bobby or Luis is going
to kill you—or worse."

Allie crossed her arms over her chest, fighting
the chill that swept over her skin. "Why would you
take that sort of risk?"

"Because I don't have any choice. And I've come to believe I can trust you. Today I saw how much grit you have. How much determination. You're a whole lot tougher than you look and a helluva lot smarter."

She wasn't sure if she had just been complimented or insulted. "I'm listening."

"I'm not working for Baranoff. That is, I am, but I'm also working for Uncle Sam. I'm an undercover agent, Allie. I've been in deep cover for nearly a year. We've been after Baranoff longer than that, but this is the first real chance we've had to nail him. If we can pull this off, we can stop him once and for all."

Allie's legs felt suddenly weak. Dear God, could she possibly be that lucky? An undercover agent, just like on TV? Did she dare believe he was telling the truth? Her thoughts returned to those moments up on deck. Her cheek still throbbed where he had hit her. But he was right in what he'd said. If he hadn't done something totally convincing, the other two men might have killed her.

At least he had bought her a reprieve.

She felt his hand, feather-lightly touching the red mark on her cheek. "Dammit, I tried to hold back, but I had to make it look good. If I had a lick of sense, I'd hit you again, just to be sure those guys are convinced."

Allie's eyes shot to his face.

"Don't worry, I feel sick just looking at what I did to you the first time."

He was telling the truth. She could see it in his eyes. "You really . . ." She swallowed. "You really are one of the good guys?"

Jake actually grinned. Reaching out, he pushed

a lock of her wet blond hair back from her·face. "Yeah. I'm a regular Dudley Do-Right."

She didn't know how it happened. One minute she was standing there looking up at him, afraid to hope, desperate to believe he was telling her the truth; the next thing she knew, she was crying against his shoulder, her arms around his neck, her body pressed against him.

"Easy, baby. Everything's gonna be all right." He held her tightly, one of his big hands stroking over her hair. She was soaking wet, her tank top clinging to her breasts, her nipples pebble-hard and poking into his chest. Wearing only the little red Speedo that barely covered his male parts, Jake was all but naked. Her mind screamed a warning. Allie didn't listen.

Jake wasn't a criminal. He was a cop and he was going to save her. She was going to see her family again. She was going to see her friends. She was going home to Whiskers.

She felt the heat of his long, hard body soaking through her clothes, felt the muscles expand in his chest and the friction of his curly black chest hair rubbing her nipples through the tank top. The attraction she had been fighting rose up with near-violent force. She wanted to dig her fingers into the sinews across his shoulders, wanted to drag his mouth down to hers, wanted to kiss him and kiss him and never stop.

It was lust of the hottest sort, and she had never felt anything like it.

Jake must have felt it too. The muscles across his chest strained with tension. His skin felt hot and damp, and when she looked up at him, his mouth crushed down over hers.

Allie made an odd little keening sound and her

fingers dug into his shoulders. His tongue stole into her mouth while the little Speedo and all it contained pressed like a hot rod into her belly.

The bottom dropped out of her stomach and Allie swayed toward him. A roller coaster ride had never been so exciting. The kiss went on and on, his lips as soft as she remembered and even more insistent, his tongue plunging into her mouth, tangling with her own, sweeping out and then in again. Her hands moved over his chest, testing the width, absorbing the texture, the hardness. His skin felt smooth, his muscles so tight they quivered. She brushed a flat copper nipple and heard him groan.

It was time to stop. They were strangers. She didn't let strange men make love to her.

She didn't let familiar men make love to her.

Allie started to pull away, but he kissed her again and she kissed him back. His hand covered her breast, massaged it roughly, tugged on the end. She gasped as he jerked her wet tank top over her head, bent, and took a nipple into his mouth.

Ohmygod! Her damp skin steamed. Her body burned. Her legs nearly collapsed at the heat roaring into her stomach, the ache that throbbed lower down.

It was past time to stop. What if he was lying? What if this was all an act just to get her in bed? Jake Dawson wouldn't be the first man to con her.

He reached for the zipper to her khaki shorts and zipped it down, slid his hands inside her panties to cup her bare bottom. He lifted her, pulled her more snugly into his groin, and nothing had ever felt so good. She was hot all over, aching and burning and on fire. Any minute, he would have her on her back and he would be inside her—exactly where she wanted him to be.

Ohmygod!

A memory arose of the last time she had made love, of the burning humiliation she had suffered when it was over. What if Jake treated her that way? What if he laughed at her, made fun of her? At least with David, she'd been able to avoid him. Here she was a prisoner. There was nowhere to go, no way to get away from him.

Jake kissed the side of her neck and his warm breath fanned over her skin. Her legs were shaking so hard, any minute she would collapse in a heap on the bed.

"Jake?"

"It's all right, baby. Just let yourself go."

"I don't . . . this isn't . . . please stop, Jake."

For an instant he seemed dazed, unable to move.

"Jake? P-please let me go."

His muscles tightened, strained toward her as he battled the same hot lust that still pumped through her. She wondered if she had let him go too far, if maybe he would simply continue. If he did, she wasn't sure she could resist.

Instead, he lifted his head from the hollow between her neck and shoulder, and a regretful sigh whispered past his lips. Jake sank like a stone down on the edge of the bed. Long tanned fingers raked through his wavy black hair. "I didn't mean to do that."

Allie reached down and grabbed her soggy tank top off the floor, pulled it on with hands that trembled. "Neither did I."

"We're just . . . we're both under a lot of stress. And living in such close quarters . . . sometimes things just happen."

"Yes . . . of course . . . such close quarters." But that wasn't it. She had never behaved like that in her entire twenty-eight years. It was Jake. There was something about him, something she had been drawn to almost from the start. He was big and tough, not the sort she should have found attractive. But Jake was a cop, there to save her, not hurt her, and the truth was he was a hottie.

Perhaps it was simply that she had ignored her sex drive for so long.

He stood up again and she saw that he was still hard. In his tiny swimsuit, there wasn't any way he could hide it. He caught her staring and his mouth curved up. "You might pretend not to notice."

Her face turned as red as the mark on her cheek, masking it completely. "I don't think I can. That's the smallest bathing suit I've ever seen."

Amusement flickered in his eyes. "I started wearing them in the Army. You get used to the freedom."

Allie fixed her gaze very carefully on his face. "You said you were going to let me go. Did you mean it?"

"We'll be at our rendezvous point day after tomorrow. Teacapan is the closest village. There's another little town called Caimanero that's not too far away. You can catch a commercial flight at the airport in Matzatlan. It's about sixty miles to the city. I know you speak pretty good Spanish, so that won't be a problem. I'll give you some money, but as soon as you're free, you'll be on your own."

"I'll make it to the airport. When I get there, I'll need to call my parents, let them know that I'm all right. They're bound to be worried sick."

"As long as you don't tell them where you are."

"I won't tell them anything except that I'm safe and on my way home. By the time I get there, I'll have thought of a story they'll believe."

Jake nodded. "After you reach the States, there's a man I want you to call. His name is Martin Biggs. Biggs is my direct superior, the head of the department in L.A. I'll give you his number. Don't talk to anyone else. If you do and my cover gets blown, I think you can guess what will happen."

Allie shivered, thinking of Roberto and Luis. She could all too easily imagine.

"I'm going back up on deck. You'd better stay down here, let things cool off a little."

Allie nodded. She could stand a little cooling off herself.

"I'll be back later. I'll bring you a tray for supper."

Allie watched him walk away, thinking about what had happened. Thinking that the back of him looked nearly as good as the front. She didn't see him again until he brought down the dinner tray—sandwiches and a bowl of soup—but he didn't stay. She waited nervously for him at bedtime, imagining all sorts of torrid scenarios, telling herself she wasn't about to let any of them happen. In the end, she needn't have worried. Jake never appeared.

In the morning, he came down to shower and change, then went up to the bridge. It was obvious he was avoiding her, and Allie was glad. If Jake was telling the truth, tomorrow they would reach their destination. Jake would let her go and she would return to San Diego.

She would never have to see Roberto and Luis again.

She would finally be out of danger.

She would never see Jake again.

Allie ignored a ridiculous twinge of disappointment and told herself how lucky she was that she was about to go home.

* * *

Seated at the end of the long oak bar at the Raucous Raven, Dan Reynolds sipped his beer and watched Barb Wallace at work. He hadn't noticed her much before—not that she wasn't pretty. With her shoulder-length black hair and fair complexion, Barb was extremely attractive. She was maybe five-foot-four with a curvaceous little body. She was also too outspoken for his taste and, after her bitter divorce, a notorious man-hater.

Dan glanced toward the door, wondering what was keeping Archie Hollis. After eight days of searching for Allie's car that included a screw-up with the security company that had towed it away and somehow misplaced the records, they had finally located her fluorescent, lime green Beetle. There were no signs of violence, nothing out of the ordinary inside.

The only thing interesting about the car was that it had been parked at the marina—in an area near the slip where Felix Baranoff docked his impressive company yachts.

Barb finished with her customer and returned to his end of the bar.

"I knew it," she said, referring to what he'd told her about the car. "I swear to God, I knew she was going to get in trouble when she started messing with someone as powerful as Felix Baranoff."

"Take it easy. As far as we know, Baranoff hasn't got any connection to any of this. A lot of people visit the marina. You said yourself it was Allie's day off. Maybe she just likes the ocean."

"Yeah, and maybe you and the SDPD have your noses so far up Baranoff's butt you can't see what's right in front of your eyes. I read the papers. I know he's in tight with the chief of police. I know he was a big contributor to the district attorney's campaign, but that doesn't make him lily-white in all of this."

Irritation trickled through him. Barb Wallace had a way of doing that to him. "No one said he was. I'm just telling you we haven't found any connection."

"Forgodsake, Chrissy's dead, Dan. Allie was convinced that she was murdered, now Allie's turned up missing. The two of them must have found out something Baranoff doesn't want them to know."

His irritation inched upward. "Chrissy Chambers wasn't the only one who got killed on that boat, you know, and as far as we can tell, it was an accident. We haven't got any reason to think Felix Baranoff had anything to do with it."

"Well, maybe it isn't him. Maybe it's someone else in the company. Has anybody talked to him? Asked him about any of this?"

As a matter of fact, that's exactly what he intended to do, if Hollis ever got there. "Look, Barb. Anything could have happened to her down there. With so many odd jobs for hire, the marina is crawling with lowlifes. Boat bums are a notorious bunch of drifters, and some of them have rap sheets you wouldn't believe. We've been working that angle, interviewing anyone who might have seen or heard something."

"And so far you've come up with zilch, right?"

Dan's jaw tightened. He hated a smart-ass and a smart-ass female was worse than the rest. "Not yet, but we haven't finished talking to everyone."

"This wasn't some boat bum, Dan, and unless you're stupid enough to believe in a million-to-one coincidence, you don't think so, either."

Dan clamped hard on his tongue, though the truth was he agreed. "I've said all I'm going to. This is police business, Barb. We're doing everything we can to find Allie Parker. We won't stop until we do."

Barb stood there for several long seconds, then she dragged in a shuddering breath. It surprised him to see the sparkle of tears in her eyes. She blinked until they disappeared. "I'm sorry. I know you're doing your best. I'm just so worried. Her mother calls me every day. Mr. and Mrs. Parker are beside themselves."

"I know. I've talked to them a couple of times."

"I know it doesn't sound like it, but I'm glad you're the one who's working on Allie's case."

Surprised again, Dan cleared his throat. "Like I said, we won't give up until we find her." She nodded, began to mop up the bar, though it was already spit-shine clean.

Dan fiddled with his empty iced-tea glass. "What time do you get off work?" he heard himself ask, surprising himself this time.

"Five-thirty." She eyed him with a hint of suspicion. "Why?"

"I thought maybe you might want to have dinner."

She started to shake her head, which annoyed him all over again. "Don't get me wrong. I thought we could talk about Allie, maybe come up with some angle that might have been overlooked."

She relaxed, even managed a smile. He thought she might feel better if she believed she was doing something useful, and for some ungodly reason he didn't like seeing those tears in her eyes.

"All right. That sounds like a good idea. I'll write some things down, try to think of anything I might have forgotten. I'll have to feed my boys first, but that won't take very long.''

"Say seven, seven-thirty?"

"Seven-thirty would be fine."

"What's your address?"

"It's 988 G Street. It isn't far from here."

Dan jotted the address down, along with Barb's phone number, which she seemed hesitant to give him, and she took off to wait on a customer at the opposite end of the bar.

Just then Archie Hollis walked in.

"You're late," Dan said, glancing at his wrist-watch.

"Yeah, well, this ain't the only case I'm working, you know."

"I want to talk to Baranoff. I thought it might be better if we both went in together."

"Now, hold on a minute. The captain know about this?"

"He knows where we found the car. Considering the fact Allie's roommate was killed on one of Baranoff's yachts, I don't think it's out of line to speak to him."

"And I think you're asking for trouble. You better get the captain's okay before you take it on yourself to include Felix Baranoff in your suspicions."

"Fine, then I'll go by myself." Slapping a couple of dollars on the bar for his iced tea, Dan came off the stool and started toward the door.

Hollis dogged his heels. "You're that determined?"

"I just want to ask him a couple of questions."

Hollis shrugged. "It's your ass, buddy," he said as they headed out the door.

* * *

Allie lay curled on her side, sleeping peacefully, when Jake finally arrived in the cabin for a couple of hours of badly needed rest. Late in the afternoon, the weather had turned nasty and the boat pitched and swayed. Flat black clouds hung over the water, and whitecaps rode the crest of each wave.

Allie slept undisturbed. Jake thought of Roberto and what could have happened to her, and his jaw knotted. Tomorrow they would reach the rendezvous point near Teacapan and he would send her home. He had worked out a plan he hoped would free her without blowing his cover.

And he hoped like hell, once she was safely away, she would do exactly what he had told her.

He tossed a glance her way as he stripped off his T-shirt and popped the snap on his cutoff jeans. Telling her the truth was risky, but he hadn't had any choice. As soon as he'd been convinced she had nothing to do with Baranoff or was involved in this in any way, he was obligated to protect her. It was just part of his job.

He had waited longer than he should have, trying to figure a way to get her to safety without blowing his cover—and maybe get both of them killed.

He hadn't expected the explosive attraction that had flared like a rocket between them, and since then he had avoided her, but he could only do it so long before the other two men got suspicious.

Or demanded he turn her luscious little body over to them.

The thought stirred a memory of how that sweet little body had felt pressed against him and Jake went rock-hard. Damn, how could he ever have believed she wasn't sexy? That her body was too slender, her breasts too small? His hands still carried the imprint, like the twin halves of a soft, ripe peach. Her hips were slim, but her bottom was round and perfectly curved, the muscles firm, like the ones in her long, long legs.

God, he hated blondes.

Why was the blonde upset when she got her driver's license?

Because she got an F in the box marked sex.

Jake grimaced as he kicked aside his cutoffs and toed out of his deck shoes. If they did give grades for sex, Allie would probably get an A. He couldn't remember being that turned on in years. Christ, he'd had one helluva time convincing himself to stop, that he couldn't just drag her into bed and bury himself to the hilt.

But God, he had wanted to. He still did.

Jake sighed as he lifted the sheet and climbed in beside her. She was wearing one of his T-shirts, he noticed, instead of her shorts and tank top. Now that she knew he was a cop, she trusted him again.

Jake thought how easy it would be to lift the T-shirt, spread those pretty legs, and slide himself inside her.

She thought she could trust him?

God, what a fool she was.

Chapter Nine

A shaft of early-morning sunlight speared through the clouds and came in through the port-holes above the bed. The weather was clearing, the temperature climbing again. Allie burrowed deeper into the pillow. Her head felt muzzy, her muscles soft and liquid, relaxed in a way they hadn't been since she had come aboard. At first she wasn't sure why she had slept so deeply, then awareness began to creep in. She realized she wasn't alone.

For a moment, she froze, knowing it was Jake and that she lay very, very close to him. Her heartbeat quickened and her breathing went faster. Her skin felt hot. Her fingertips tingled where they nestled in the curly black hair on his chest. The sheet was shoved down. One of her legs was entwined with his and her body pressed intimately along his entire right side.

For several long second she lay still, completely unable to move. She felt the rise and fall of his breathing and relaxed a little, knowing that he was asleep.

Her gaze drifted, moved over the indentations of his ribs, down his flat belly. It skimmed over his navel, followed the dark line of hair that disappeared inside the waistband of his shorts to the spot where his heavy sex rested.

Only it wasn't at rest.

Allie gasped at the thick ridge straining against his white cotton briefs and realized he was fully aroused.

"You're playing with fire, honey. If you don't want to feel that inside you, I'd suggest you unwrap yourself and get back on your own side of the bed."

Allie squealed and scrambled away, bolting out of the bed as if it were in flames, backing away until her shoulders hit the wall of the cabin.

Jake chuckled, then she thought she heard him groan.

"I—I need to use the head," she said, hurrying in that direction. Feeling a little bit safer knowing that Jake was a cop, she had washed her clothes last night and hung them in the bathroom to dry.

"You might as well shower while you're in there. I'll need a cold one myself, once you're done."

"Yes . . . yes, I could see that." Quickly closing the door, she climbed into the shower and leaned against the wall, trying not to think of herself wrapped around Jake Dawson like a python. Trying not to think of his incredible body, of how big and hard he was—all over.

The shower calmed her some. She dressed

quickly and returned to the cabin. Jake went in as she came out, showered and dressed in jeans, canvas boots, and a short-sleeved blue oxford cloth shirt over his usual khaki T-shirt. He was meeting someone this morning, she knew, once they reached their rendezvous point—and he was freeing her from her luxury prison.

She hoped.

"So how do we do this?" she asked a little nervously as he slid a belt through the loopholes of his jeans.

"I figure the best way is for me to take you off somewhere and shoot you." Jake buckled his belt and glanced up to see her face had gone utterly pale.

"Forgodsake, I'm not gonna do it for real. Once Bobby and Luis think you're dead, they'll stop worrying about you. If we're lucky, they won't give either of us any more trouble."

Feeling slightly silly, Allie breathed a sigh of relief. "When will you do it?"

"As soon as I get the chance. You'll have to stay hidden until after we leave, then you can be on your way." He opened a drawer, took out an envelope. Walking over to the desk, he grabbed a pen and scratched a phone number on a slip of paper. He handed the envelope and the paper to her.

The envelope was full of money. Allie counted the bills and stared up at him. "There's two thousand dollars here."

"The plane fare won't be cheap. Not without more notice. You'll need some clothes and you'll probably want a room."

"What if some of this is left over?"

He shrugged. "The agency uses confiscated drug

money. Buy yourself something pretty. You certainly deserve it after what you've been through."

That was the truth. Allie tucked the wad of bills deep in the pocket of her khaki shorts.

"Oh, and before I forget . . ." He returned to the desk and jerked open the bottom drawer. "I brought these down last night. I figured you would want them." He handed back her pocketknife, her emergency Bic, the miniature screwdriver set, and the rest of the stuff he had taken from her purse. Yesterday, he had retrieved her windbreaker and Reeboks from where she had left them on deck before her ill-fated swim, and she had already put them on.

"How long till we get there?"

"Another hour or so. Even with the storm last night, we're within our allotted time."

Jake returned upstairs and Allie paced the cabin. Watching the brass ship's clock on the wall, the hour and a half it took for them to reach the rendezvous point seemed to take forever. Eventually, she felt the engine vibrations slow, looked out the porthole, and saw the boat easing closer to shore.

They entered a small, sheltered cove south of a promontory that kept the yacht out of sight. A sun-bleached wooden dock jutted out in the water and a dark-skinned Mexican man stood near the end. He grabbed the lines Roberto tossed him as the boat approached and secured the yacht to the rickety wooden dock.

Jake climbed down from the bridge and joined the Mexican. She couldn't hear what they were saying, but they were smiling and nodding and she thought that must be good. The minutes dragged. She was sweating, her nerves on a razor's edge.

She bit the end of a fingernail, caught herself, and shoved the offending hand behind her back.

She continued to peer through the porthole, watched as four more men appeared on the dock and began carrying stacks of long, rectangular wooden boxes off the boat. It was the last thing she had expected.

Uncertainty rose with the speed of a tropical storm. Why would Baranoff be smuggling drugs *into* the country? He wouldn't be, of course. Which meant he was smuggling something else. Which meant Jake Dawson wasn't an undercover agent with the Drug Enforcement Agency, as she had believed.

Sweat broke out on her forehead. Allie told herself not to panic, that she had simply misunderstood. Jake hadn't actually said he was DEA, but it was always on TV and she'd just assumed that since Baranoff was involved in illegal drugs . . .

But obviously he wasn't. Or at least not in this particular case. Allie fought to stay calm, tried to think clearly.

She tried *not* to think that if Jake had lied, she might very soon be dead.

At that moment he appeared in the doorway, grim-faced and looking like the jailer he had been and not the least like the sympathetic cop he was supposed to be.

''Get up here.''

Her pulse leaped up another fearful notch. *Stay calm,* she told herself, grabbing her canvas bag as she headed for the spiral stairs. *There's bound to be an explanation.*

She noticed the automatic pistol shoved into the back of his jeans and felt a sudden tightness in her chest. Outside the salon, Luis stood near the rail, but Roberto was nowhere in sight.

"Hey, baby—" Luis grinned. "How 'bout you and me doin' The Nasty a couple of times before we go?" He made a lewd gesture with his hands that Allie ignored, keeping her attention focused on Jake.

"Sorry," Jake said. "We haven't got time. There's another weather front moving in. The plane is loaded. We need to get the hell out of here."

"Come on, man. You promised."

"You can have all the pussy you want when we get to Belize."

"I like blondes, man. I've had a hard-on for this one since the first time I saw her."

"Yeah, well, I hate blondes. And this one's nothing but trouble. I'm getting rid of her before she has time to cause any more."

"Wait a minute, man."

But Jake wasn't waiting. His hand wrapped like a band of steel around her arm and he started jerking her forward. Across the deck, up and over the port rail, and off the boat. She could barely keep up with him as he hauled her along the dock toward the heavy growth of jungle that lined the shore.

"Keep walking," he said, giving her not the slightest glance. It occurred to her that if he was playing a role, he was doing a very good job. Allie shivered, trying to ignore the fear creeping up along her spine. Until she knew for sure that Jake was lying, he was still her best chance of getting out of this mess alive.

"Wait a minute!" she said, deciding to play along

with him, digging her heels in and skidding to a halt on the wooden dock. "Where are you taking me?" She tried to jerk free, but not too hard. Luis was back there waiting. "I'm not going anywhere with you. I'm staying with the boat."

Jake jerked her off-balance and started walking again, dragging her toward the jungle at the edge of the shore, her feet barely touching the wooden planks. In the distance, she could see a break in the dense vegetation and behind it a long thin slice of open land that served as an airstrip. A twin-engine plane sat near the end, and the man she had seen on the dock stood next to the cockpit door.

Jake stepped off the dock and turned in the opposite direction, passing a battered red Ford pickup that had brought the four men who unloaded the boat. She thought maybe he was going to drive her off somewhere in the truck but instead he kept walking, dragging her on toward the jungle. He had taken only a couple strides past the pickup when Roberto stepped out from behind it.

He held a big ugly automatic pistol and he smiled as he pointed it at Jake.

"Where you going, *amigo*?"

She could feel the tension that swept through Jake's body. "I'm taking care of a problem—remember? I'll be back as soon as I'm finished."

Ignoring Bobby's weapon, he started walking, coming to a halt when he heard the deadly click of the action sliding back.

Jake slowly turned. "What the hell are you doing, Roberto?"

Bobby lifted the automatic, pointed it directly at

Jake's chest. "You aren't going nowhere, man."
Stepping forward, Bobby reached behind Jake's
back and dragged the pistol from the waistband of
his jeans, then reached into his pocket and relieved
him of his heavy folding survival knife.

"Are you crazy? We've got to get rid of her and
get the hell out of here."

"We're leaving, all right. Only she's going with
us." Bobby flashed a cold smile, reminding Allie
of the retribution he had promised for humiliating
him as she had. "I got plans for her when we get
there."

Allie's stomach sank like a stone in a bottomless
pit.

"Not a chance," Jake said, still gripping her arm.
"I should have done this sooner. We both know
that. Now give me my gun and let me take care of
this."

Roberto shook his head. "Either she goes with
us, or I screw her right here—and I do her real
slow when I'm finished. What's it gonna be?"

Allie started trembling.

Jake looked at her and there wasn't an ounce of
compassion in his face. "Fine, she goes. You can
have her when we get to Belize." He returned his
attention to Bobby. "But we have to get out of here
now. That storm won't wait and Baranoff will see
all of us dead if we blow this so you can get your
kicks offing some dumb blonde. Give me back my
gun."

Allie was too frightened to take umbrage to the
jibe.

Bobby's look turned hard. "You don't get it,
amigo. From now on, I'm running the show. You
get the gun back when we get to Belize."

Jake said nothing. But the look on his face could

have frozen water. "You sure you want to do this . . . *amigo?*" The words were spoken with a softness that was far more menacing than if he had shouted.

Something flickered in Bobby's eyes, but his hold on the gun didn't waver. "Get going. Like you said, that storm isn't going to wait."

Jake started walking, his hold a little gentler as they turned toward the runway and headed for the plane.

Allie's legs started shaking. The trembling moved up her body until she shook all over. "Take it easy," Jake said so softly no one else could hear. "We're a long way from Belize."

And getting farther and farther away from the States. Tears burned the backs of her eyes. She thought of her mother and father, imagined what she must be putting them through, and cursed herself for ever stepping foot on the *Dynasty II.* Surely by now her father had called the police, but what good would it do? No one knew where she was, or even where to start looking. They would probably search for her car, but she had parked in a two-hour parking zone at the marina, and it would have been towed to some lot long ago.

Allie stumbled and Jake steadied her to keep her from falling.

"Watch where you're going, you stupid bitch." Roberto shoved her so hard she sprawled in the dirt. A twig jabbed into her leg and she scraped the skin off both of her knees.

"Leave her alone," Jake warned. "You might be enjoying yourself, but I don't want to deal with a crying woman for the next eight hours."

Bobby just grunted. Jake helped Allie to her feet, his jaw clamped so hard a muscle bunched in his cheek. They climbed into the plane and she saw that Luis and the man on the dock, apparently the pilot, were already aboard. She didn't know what kind of plane it was, but there were military-style web seats in the back and the interior was filled with the heavy wooden boxes that had been hidden in the hull of the *Dynasty II*.

She wondered what was in them, wondered what would happen to the yacht once they were gone, then figured someone was undoubtedly looking after it. The men probably planned to return to the States the same way they had come.

She ducked her head as she moved around in the cabin. It was hot inside the plane, the metal skin heating up in the tropical sun. She sat down in one of the hanging web seats and Jake settled himself beside her. She kept hoping he would look at her, but even when he did, there wasn't a trace of emotion in his face.

She glanced at Roberto, saw him smirk, and her stomach rolled with nausea. It took all of her courage not to cry but she managed to hold back the tears. She wasn't giving up, not yet. She thought of what Jake had said. *Take it easy. We're a long way from Belize,* and took heart in the words.

For some insane reason she still trusted him.

Perhaps it was because she didn't have any other choice.

Felix Baranoff hit the button on the intercom on his desk. "All right, Eve. You may show the officers in." He watched them walking toward him. The younger man, brown-haired, probably mid-thirties, was dressed in an inexpensive dark brown sport coat and tan slacks, but he had wide shoulders and the coat fit him well. Women probably never noticed the quality of his clothes.

The second man he knew, Detective Archie Hollis, red-haired, early forties, a tacky dark green checkered coat and wrinkled slacks.

Unconsciously, Felix smoothed the lapel of his navy blue, Bijan pinstriped suit, appreciating the expensive fabric, grateful he was no longer forced to wear clothes from J. C. Penney's, as he had done in his early years.

He smiled at the men. "Detectives Reynolds and Hollis, I believe. My secretary informed me you were here to see me earlier in the week. Unfortunately, I was out of town on business." The sort he preferred on occasion, a few days in Vegas with the big-busted redhead who was his current mistress. He didn't gamble much—he didn't like to lose—but he enjoyed the screwing and the shows. "So what can I do for you?"

"We're sorry to bother you, Mr. Baranoff," Hollis answered before the younger man could speak. "This is just routine, you understand. We're looking for a woman named Mary Alice Parker. She turned up missing over a week ago and hasn't been seen since."

"And in what way may I help you?"

"Ms. Parker's car was found in the parking lot at the marina," Detective Reynolds said. "Near where your company yachts are docked. She may have gone there in the hope of finding information on the explosion that killed her roommate, Christine Chambers."

For the first time, Felix actually gave them his attention. "What sort of information? I thought the explosion that killed the Chambers girl was an accident."

"Everything we've uncovered points to exactly that, Mr. Baranoff," Hollis said. "But the Parker girl wouldn't accept that."

Reynolds took out a photo of a pretty blond woman with a pixie face and big blue eyes. "Have you ever seen her before?"

Felix examined the photograph closely. "No, I'm afraid I haven't."

"Then she never came here asking questions, or in any way contacted you?"

"No, why should she?"

Hollis spoke up. "The girl was upset about her roommate getting killed. She was convinced it had something to do with smuggling drugs and that you were somehow involved."

He smiled, felt himself relax. "I presume you assured her that wasn't the case."

"I told her she was way off base, Mr. Baranoff, but Dan thought maybe she might have come here, or you might have seen her around someplace."

"I'm afraid not, gentlemen. I'm sorry I couldn't be more help."

Reynolds stepped forward, extended the photo. "Do you think you might keep this? Circulate it among your staff, see if any of them might have seen her?"

Felix accepted the photo. "Of course. I'd be more than happy to do that. And if there's anything else I can do to help, don't hesitate to let me know."

The men left the office and Felix tapped the photo he held in his hand. He had told the truth. He had never seen the woman, but he would indeed ask around. He didn't like loose ends and apparently this was one. Of course the woman's disappearance near the place his yachts were docked could simply be coincidence.

Felix set the photo very carefully on his desk beside the phone. Unfortunately, he had never been a believer in coincidence.

Chapter Ten

The roar of the engines and vibrations of the plane drowned out any attempt at conversation. Jake thought it was just as well, since there was nothing he could say to Allie to make her feel any better.

Damn, he had hoped by now she'd be on her way back home. No such luck. Maybe he should have taken Roberto out when he'd pulled the gun. In Special Forces, he'd been trained to disarm an enemy in a dozen lethal ways, but there was always an element of risk, and with Allie just inches away, he didn't want to chance getting her killed.

He should have kept a closer eye on Roberto. The guy had always been a little off-key, along with paranoid and probably schizophrenic.

Jake glanced around the inside of the cabin. They were flying in an old DeHavilland Twin Otter, a slow but reliable airplane designed to take off and land on short runways. Though the Otter was built to carry as many as nineteen passengers, the inside of this one had been gutted for hauling cargo, and the engines had been souped up to make better time. There was a toilet in the rear, which was good, since it was an eight-hour flight to Valisimo's camp in Belize, just across the Mexican border.

The day moved sluggishly past, drifting into late afternoon. After seven hours of flying, they were less than a hundred and fifty miles from their destination. Three hours ago, they had made their scheduled fuel stop, but Roberto had refused to let Jake leave the plane, keeping watch on him at gunpoint.

Something wasn't right and Jake was very much afraid he knew what it was.

He glanced at Allie, saw that she was staring out the small round window at the jungle below, saw that Luis was asleep.

His jaw was hard when he spoke to Roberto. "All right, Bobby. It's time you stopped playing games. I want my gun back and I want it back now."

Bobby gave him an unpleasant smile. Coming out of his seat, he pulled his 40mm Smith and Wesson from the shoulder holster he'd been wearing since they boarded the plane. Jake's gun, a 9mm Glock, had been stuffed in Bobby's suitcase.

"I told you," Roberto said, "you get your pistol back when we get there."

"You stupid sonofabitch. Valisimo is going to be suspicious if I get off this plane at gunpoint. You blow this deal, and if he doesn't kill you, Baranoff will."

Roberto lifted the pistol, pointed it in Jake's face.

"Do you think I'm a fool? Did you really believe I wouldn't notice the way you protected the girl? You weren't even screwing her, were you? When the satellite phone went out, I figured you were up to something. The day you dragged her out of the ocean half-drowned, I went out on the aft deck and opened one of the hatches. I could hear you, man. I know who you are—a stinking, lying scum-sucking pig. If Valisimo didn't need you, you would already be dead!"

Jake didn't wait to hear more. He erupted out of his seat like a volcano, slamming Roberto's arm up in the air, wrenching it so hard he yelped in pain and pulled the trigger. Allie screamed as the gun exploded, blowing a hole through the metal ceiling above their heads. The oxygen in the cabin began to rush out through the bullet hole, sucking anything loose along with it. Scraps of paper, bits of dirt, and straw all flew through the air toward the fifty-cent-size hole.

Allie must have realized their air supply would soon be gone, and at fourteen thousand feet it would be difficult to breathe. She fished inside her purse and jerked out a little compact, broke off the curved, mirrored top and slapped it over the hole. The suction drew it up tight, sealing off the opening.

It plugged the leak, but while she worked, Luis jumped into the fray.

Jake had Roberto down, wedged between rows of wooden boxes as they struggled for the gun. It should have ended quickly, but the cramped position and worry for Allie's safety threw Jake off. Luis jumped on his back, wrapped an arm around his neck, and started to choke him. Jake tried to drag in a breath of air, but he couldn't let go of

Roberto, and the wiry brown arm at his throat was like a vise, cutting off his air supply.

Black spots danced in front of his eyes. His vision grew dim and the cabin began to spin.

From the corner of his eye, he saw Allie leap on Luis's back and start banging him on the head with her hairbrush, trying to knock him off before Jake lost consciousness. Bobby took advantage of the confusion, twisted and freed his gun, then swung it toward Jake.

"Look out!" Allie screamed. Jake knocked the hand away and Bobby fired again—right though the curtain that closed off the cockpit.

For an instant, the plane climbed upward and the floor rushed up, then it slowly nosed over. The engine noise grew louder as the plane began a sharp descent.

"You idiot!" Luis yelled. "You shot the pilot!"

"Sonofabitch!" Jake slid toward the cockpit and all of them piled on top of each other. Jake wrenched the gun away and shot a hard punch into Roberto's jaw, knocking him unconscious. Allie picked up a greasy foot-long wrench from beneath the row of webbed seats, slammed it down on Luis's head, and he slumped against the wall.

Bracing himself against the pitch of the plane, Jake ducked behind the curtain and saw the pilot slumped over the controls, a neat little bullet hole dripping blood from the back of his head.

The ground was coming up fast. Jake jerked the pilot away and slid into the seat. Gripping the controls, he pulled back as hard as he could, fighting to get the nose up, praying he could get the plane leveled out before it was too late.

"Get back there and buckle yourself in!" he shouted to Allie, who scrambled to do as he said.

He could tell she was terrified, but so far she hadn't panicked. For a blonde—hell, for anyone he knew—she wasn't short on nerve.

The ground raced toward them at two hundred forty miles an hour. Two fifty. Two sixty. The whine of the engines roared in his ears. Just when Jake thought there was no way in hell he could possibly get the plane to respond in time, the nose began to tip up. He kept pulling back, kept praying, and at the last possible instant, the plane leveled off. They started to climb again, but they were less than two hundred feet off the ground.

Still, they might have made it if it hadn't been for the low ridge of jungle-covered hills that sprang up right in front of them. There was no way they could clear the trees at the top of the ridge.

"Hold on!" Jake shouted, strapping himself in the pilot's seat. "We're going in!" He lowered the flaps and reduced the engine speed as much as he could. Scanning the ridge, he picked a narrow opening between two clumps of trees, waited till the last possible second, then cleared the board, turning off all the electrical switches.

The jungle rose up and a flash of green rushed past. He felt a sudden, bone-slamming jolt, then a series of smaller painful jolts. The sound of grinding metal filled his ears and he knew the wings had just been sheared of. Leafy jungle foliage rushed past the windows. He braced himself, put his head down in his arms as the windshield splintered and glass flew into the cockpit. Shards of glass and metal sliced into his skin and scalp, and a trickle of blood ran down his forehead.

The wheels hit heavy jungle foliage and ripped away, and the fuselage slid through the wet, leafy undergrowth like a sled in a snowstorm. The plane hit hard once, bounced, hit again, shuddered violently, and the whole left side tore away.

He must have been knocked unconscious. He couldn't remember what happened in the next few seconds. When he opened his eyes, an eerie silence surrounded him and the plane sat dead calm in the middle of the jungle. The cabin roof above his head was gone, the cockpit so full of leaves and branches it was hard to move.

Jake shook his head, trying to clear away the cobwebs, fighting a rush of dizziness. Then he thought of Allie, unbuckled his seat belt, and started to move.

"Allie!" At first he didn't see her and his heart pinched sharply. With the left side of the belly ripped open, there was a good chance she had been thrown out. He started lifting boxes, praying he would find her, knowing any minute the fuel leaking out of the tanks could erupt in a deadly explosion. He spotted Luis, his body crumpled oddly, his head canted off to one side. One of the boxes must have slammed into him and broken his neck.

Jake took a deep breath, praying Allie hadn't suffered a similar fate.

He lifted away another couple of boxes and saw her wedged underneath. His hand shook as he reached for her, gently touched her cheek.

Her eyes fluttered open. "Jake . . . ?"

Relief filtered through him. "Take it easy. I'm right here. How badly are you injured?"

"I'm not . . . not really sure."

She moved her legs, then her arms, neck, and torso. "Nothing's broken, I don't think."

"Good, because we have to get out of here.

There's fuel leaking all over the place. This thing could go up any minute."

She tensed, drew herself up a little unsteadily. "What are we waiting for?" Rummaging through the rubble, she yanked up her big canvas purse and threw it over her shoulder, started scrambling toward him over the debris. He wiped a trickle of blood from his eyes and took her hand.

"What happened to the others?" she asked as he led her toward the opening in the fuselage. He glanced around, looking for his canvas pack, but it must have been thrown out of the plane. He spotted Roberto's black Samsonite suitcase, jerked it out from under a box that had broken open, and kept on moving.

"The pilot and Luis are dead," he said. "I don't know what happened to Roberto and we don't have time to find out." He reached the jagged tear in the belly of the plane and jumped to the ground, reached up, and swung Allie down.

Her cheek was cut and there were nicks and cuts on her forehead and neck, but other than that, she seemed all right.

He took her hand again and they started running, climbing over downed trees, making their way through the wet vines and leaves, trying to get far enough away so they'd be safe if the plane blew up.

He pulled her down behind the thick trunk of a tree and they leaned back against it, both of them breathing a little too fast. Allie watched the plane for several long minutes, both of them waiting for the roar of an explosion, Jake keeping watch for any movement around the perimeter or coming from inside. If Roberto was still alive, he was armed.

And his first order of business would be to kill them.

Minutes ticked past. Allie turned toward him, the realization of what had happened beginning to set in. Her face as pale as cotton, she started to tremble. She wrapped her arms around herself but the shaking only grew worse.

Damn, he wished none of this had happened, that somehow he could have saved her from all of this, but regrets were useless now.

"Easy," he said, moving toward her. "Everything's going to be all right." He eased her into his arms and she let him, her body pressing into his warmth. "The plane's down, but we're alive. That's all that matters."

She nodded against his chest. "I know. I'll be all right in a minute. I just . . . I can't seem to stop shaking."

He tightened his hold, wishing again he could somehow have protected her. Eventually, the tremors begin to fade, and her body slowly relaxed. She took a deep breath and stepped away, then frowned at the blood that wept from the cut on his forehead.

"You're hurt."

"Just a few cuts and scratches. Nothing serious." Allie, of course, ignored his assessment. Turning, she grabbed her canvas purse, reached in, and pulled out one of those little packages of Kleenex women always seem to carry. She used one of them to wipe away the blood on his forehead and examined the slice in his skin just below the hairline.

"It isn't that bad," he said again. "Head wounds always bleed a lot."

She didn't answer, just gently wiped the blood off his face then pressed the Kleenex against the cut until the bleeding began to slow and finally stopped altogether. Wadding up the Kleenex, she dug a neat little hole in the dirt and very carefully buried the bloody tissue.

Jake grinned. "Environmentally conscious, even way out here."

Allie bit back a smile and returned her attention to the plane. "How long do we have to wait until we know for sure it isn't going to blow up?"

"The more time the better. But we'll have to go back pretty soon. It'll be dark before long. We need to salvage what we can and get out of here."

"Do you think the radio still works?"

He shook his head. "The entire front of the cockpit is nothing but broken glass and crumpled metal. It's a miracle I got out of there in one piece."

Her features shifted, seemed to close up. She swallowed, looked up at him. "You aren't with the DEA, are you?"

Jake let his head fall back against the tree trunk, scrubbed a hand over the late-afternoon shadow of beard along his jaw. "No."

"Then you're not . . . not really . . ."

He glanced up, saw the worry she couldn't quite hide. "It's not what you're thinking. I work for the ATF—Department of Alcohol, Tobacco, and Firearms. I've been with them for the last five years."

Her eyes closed in relief while her cheeks brightened with anger. "Why did you lie?"

"I didn't. You thought Baranoff was involved in illegal drugs. I just let you continue to believe it."

"Why?"

"Because I thought the less you knew, the safer you'd be." Her chin angled up. She wasn't the least bit happy with his deception, however vague it was, and he really couldn't blame her.

"What's in those boxes, Jake?"

He turned, looked back toward the crumpled remnants of the plane, still saw no movement inside. If Roberto was in there, he had to be injured. Dead would be better, of course. "Portable, shoulder-fired missiles. The Stinger-Hornet RRLRM. That's Rapid-Response Long-Range Missile. It's the most sophisticated transportable surface-to-air missile that's ever been produced."

"God."

"You can say that again. While you're at it, maybe you could put in a word for us. Right about now, we can use any help we can get."

Her lips curved a little. He thought it was a good sign. Then she returned her gaze to the plane. "So how did Baranoff get them?"

"He stole them from a Raytheon missile plant in Tucson, Arizona . . . or at least someone did, and Baranoff managed to wind up with them. And it isn't the first time. The ATF's been after him for the past two years. That's how I got involved in this."

She stared at him, her expression so solemn it made his chest feel oddly tight. "Don't lie to me again, Jake—not even by omission. My life's at risk here, just the same as yours. I want your word that from now on—no matter how bad it is—you'll tell me the truth."

Jake said nothing. It wasn't his way to say more than he absolutely had to. But Allie was right. Her life was on the line, just the same as his. And she had earned the right to know.

"Fair enough," he finally agreed. "Anything you want to know, I'll tell you."

"Are you married?" The words seemed to come out of nowhere and she flushed the moment she said them. "I'm sorry. I realize it's hardly important, under the circumstances, and you don't strike me as a marrying kind of guy, but—"

"But we nearly wound up in bed and you'd like to know whether or not I've got a wife and kids back home."

The color deepened in her cheeks. "Do you?"

"No, I'm not married. I'm divorced. In fact, I'm a two-time loser. Fortunately, I've learned my lesson. I'm not stupid enough to make the same mistake again."

Something flashed for an instant in her face, then she glanced away, sinking back against the trunk of the tree.

"While we're clearing the air, I think it's time you told me your name."

She sighed, rubbed a spot on the side of her head. "Allie Parker."

He cocked a questioning eyebrow.

"All right," she said. "Mary Alice Parker, if you really have to know."

Jake grinned. "Alice?"

She scowled. "Call me that and you'll wish you hadn't lived through that plane crash."

He chuckled but didn't test her. Besides, she didn't look like an Alice to him.

"How are we going to get out of here?"

Jake gazed into the dense tropical rain forest that surrounded them. "Walk, I'm afraid. They'll start looking for the plane when it doesn't arrive, but there's a lot of jungle out there. When Bobby shot the pilot, we veered way off course, and an Otter isn't all that big. They might not find it for weeks."

"How far till we come to a town?"

"From the last fix I got on our position, we're maybe eighty miles—"

"Eighty miles!"

"More or less. The village of Tikal in northern Guatemala is probably the closest."

"You're telling me we have to walk eighty miles through the jungle with no food and one canteen of water before we reach any sort of civilization?"

"You were the one who wanted the truth, remember?"

Allie bit her lip and glanced away. Even pale and shaken, with nicks on her forehead and a scratch on her cheek, she looked pretty. She had washed her hair that morning and it gleamed like gold in the hot late-afternoon sun. His body tightened. Sitting in the middle of the jungle, cut, bruised, and beaten all to hell, a jillion miles from nowhere—and he wanted her. He could hardly believe it.

Damn, he hated blondes.

He shifted a little, forced his mind off sex, and tried to get comfortable in his now too-snug jeans.

"Water won't be a problem," he said. "In this part of the country, it rains more than eighty inches a year. There are plenty of rivers and streams, even underground springs. And there's plenty of food if you know how to get it. It just so happens I do. I know very well how to survive in a place like this. We'll make it, Allie, I promise you."

She blinked up at him. "They teach you jungle survival in the ATF?"

He smiled. "Army Special Forces. I served eight years, most of it at Fort Davis in Panama. I was a weapons specialist for the Seventh Group. Central and South America was the area we specialized in."

"That's why they picked you for this assignment."

"Valisimo wanted someone who could teach his men to operate the new, more sophisticated Stingers that Baranoff was selling. Our inside man brought me in as the guy who could fill the bill."

"So what were you back then, a lieutenant or something?"

"Major." He returned his gaze to the Otter. It was time to go back in, salvage what they could, and try to find out what had happened to Roberto. "We've waited long enough. Hopefully, we'll find something useful in the plane. The bad news is my bag went out through the rip in the belly. I carry basic survival gear, but the wreckage is strung out for more than a mile, and as dense as the ground cover is, there's not much chance we'd be able to find it."

He turned, flipped open the locks on Bobby's suitcase, felt among the stacks of shirts and pants, and found his pistol, the Glock he felt naked without, and his heavy folding survival knife.

"At least we've got these." He stuffed the knife in his pocket and the gun into the back of his jeans. He searched through the bag, looking for the spare clip, but didn't find it. Fifteen shots, counting the one in the chamber. Not that many in a place like this. He rummaged through the suitcase, looking for anything else that might be useful.

"Knit shirts and shorts, a set of khaki fatigues, and a pair of hiking books." He tossed all but the camouflage fatigues away, since the stuff was too big for Allie and too small for him. He crammed the fatigues into his pack, though he didn't figure he could talk her into wearing them just yet.

Allie reached into the suitcase, pulled out a white

cotton T-shirt and a plastic container of sunscreen, which she stuffed into her purse, then dragged out a can of bug spray. "Here's a winner."

Jake grunted. "They say it takes one to know one. Cockroach that he is, Bobby wanted to be prepared." He pulled out a carton of cigarettes and a baggie that held marijuana. "Look at this crap."

"Not much that's helpful, is there?" Allie fished through Bobby's shaving kit, pulled out a tooth-brush, disposable razor, nail clippers, a little travel soap, and a fingernail file. "Still, you never know what might come in handy." She stuffed them into her purse. "Maybe we'll have better luck in the plane."

"Let's hope so."

"Think it's safe to go back?"

"As safe as it's going to get. You stay here. I'll go see what—"

"I'm going with you. Two of us searching are better than one."

Jake shook his head. "Bobby's armed. If he's alive, he'll be waiting for us. You'll be safer if you stay right here."

"I haven't been safe since I set foot on the *Dynasty II*. I'm going with you."

"You're staying, dammit. I've kept you alive so far. I intend to keep it that way till I get you back to San Diego."

Allie tossed him a mutinous glare, but didn't argue.

Silently cursing all stubborn women and espe-cially pretty little blondes, Jake dragged his gun from the back of his jeans and set off for the plane.

*   *   *

Allie watched Jake pick his way through the heavy leaves and vines and disappear inside the damaged fuselage of the Otter. Hearing no sounds of a struggle, she assumed that Roberto was either dead or had been thrown out when the fuselage tore open.

Around her, the sounds of the jungle began to creep in, the zeet-zeet of insects, the shrill cry of a bird, the sound of water trickling over the damp, mossy earth. She had seen pictures of a jungle, but she could never have imagined the sounds and the pungent smells, the profusion of colors, bright red hibiscus, some sort of blue jungle morning glory, huge purple orchids. For a minute she lost herself in the beauty, then the hot jungle sun glinting on silver caught the corner of her eye and she returned her attention to the plane.

And to Jake.

Are you married? A fresh wave of embarrassment washed over her. God, how could she have blurted it out that way? They had just survived a terrifying plane crash, for heaven's sake. His marital status was hardly high on the list of priorities. What an idiot!

At least she'd found out he was single, though why it mattered so much she wasn't sure. It was even less important, now that she knew his feelings on the subject.

She fixed her thoughts on what was going on in the plane. Still seeing no signs of trouble, she left her place behind the tree, staying low, and carefully made her way toward the open side of the plane. Jake wasn't the only one being forced to cross miles of dangerous, unchartered jungle. She might find something she could use to make the task a little easier.

Stepping over a decaying log, she crept toward

the fuselage and levered herself up inside. It was hot and dim and smelled of some sickly sweet vine that protruded through a broken window. She scanned the interior for Jake or any threat from Roberto, but saw no sign of either. Then a hand clamped over her mouth and another slid around her waist, jerking her back against a solid male body, and she almost leaped out of her skin.

"I thought I told you to stay where you were." The softly spoken words rumbled up from deep in a wide, hard chest, sending a little tingle across her skin.

Allie peeled Jake's hand away from her mouth. "If you're trying to scare me to death, don't waste your time. I'm sure there are more than enough creatures out there in the jungle to do it for you." He was hard as a rock and handsome as sin, even with the cuts on his face. Her heart kicked up annoyingly and she stepped a little away.

"Did you find Roberto?"

Jake shook his head, dislodging a lock of wavy black hair that fell across his forehead. "He must have been thrown out. If he was, he's almost certainly dead."

"Are you going to go back and look for him?"

"No."

"What have you found so far?"

"A compass and a half-used package of matches, an old canteen, a machete, some rope, a couple of cups, and a few sheets of plastic. But I'm not finished yet." He returned to his search and Allie turned away as he plucked a pair of broken reading glasses from the pocket of the dead pilot's shirt. Fixing her mind on the task she had come for, she did a quick prowl around, making her way toward the rear of the plane.

She grinned when she found a sleeping bag on a luggage rack near the john. Next to it was a half-empty first aid kit and a green wool army blanket, not that she would need it to keep warm. It was pushing ninety in the plane and definitely uncomfortable. As she moved around what was left of the fuselage, she tried not to look at Luis, crumpled like a rag doll against the wall. She tried not to wonder how rapidly his body would decay in the humid jungle heat.

She tried not to worry that the same thing might happen to her.

Instead, she returned to the opening in the side of the plane to wait for Jake, who joined her a few minutes later.

"Not bad," he said, eyeing the bedroll and blanket. "Looks like you've redeemed yourself." He was carrying a backpack that must have belonged to the pilot or Luis. He had emptied it out and refilled it with the items he had salvaged.

"I see you found some maps," she said, spotting them on the top of the pack."

He nodded. "They'll definitely come in handy."

They jumped to the ground and Jake took the bandages and ointment she had salvaged from the damaged first aid kit and added them to the pack. He held up a small bottle of iodine she gave him. "We can sure as hell use this. We won't have to waste time boiling water. The iodine will do the trick."

He tied the sleeping bag and blanket onto the backpack, then paused for a moment beside one of the flattened tires. Using his big folding knife, he hacked off small chunks of rubber.

"What are you doing?"

"It's hard to find dry tender for a fire. This stuff helps it along."

Finished with the task, he stuck the bits of rubber into a side pouch, slung the pack across his shoulders, and led her away from the plane.

He took a last glance at the Otter. "Stay here. I want to take one more look around."

He was gone longer than she thought he would be, and when he finally reappeared, his expression was grim.

"What did you find?"

"Nothing."

"That's good, isn't it?"

"Probably. I'd feel better if I'd found some trace of Roberto. The good news is, he must have been thrown out, and even if by some miracle he lived, he's probably badly injured. He'll have wild animals and hunger to contend with. A guy like Bobby . . . there's not much chance he'll make it." He took her hand. "Come on. It's time we got out of here."

Allie let him lead her into the deep shade of the trees, then stopped and turned. "I've been thinking, Jake."

"I've warned you about that before."

"Roberto figured out you were a cop, right?"

"So?"

"Do you think he told anyone?"

"No. I think he wanted to wait till we reached Belize. He wanted the glory of personally turning me over to Valisimo. He thought if he waited, he might get something out of it for himself."

"That's what I figured, too. Is Valisimo the man who was buying the missiles?"

"He's the leader of what he calls The People's Revolutionary Army. They're a group of Mexican rebels opposed to the National Action Party. They want Vincente Fox overthrown. I think Valisimo has visions of leading the country himself. That's why he wants those missiles so badly."

"I still don't get it. I don't understand how the ATF was going to tie—"

"The plan was to catch the general receiving stolen goods and force him to incriminate Baranoff."

She stared off toward the jungle, looking in the direction they had started to travel. "So how far do you think we are from Valisimo's camp?"

"Sixty, maybe seventy miles, but that's just a calculated guess."

"So we're closer to the general's camp than we are to the nearest village."

Jake took hold of her shoulders. "I don't like the look I see on your face. What are you getting at, Allie?"

"I don't think we should head for the village. I think we should go to the camp."

"No way. Not a chance. You've already been through hell. I'm not about to risk—"

"Listen to me, Jake. For the most part, those missiles are still intact, right?"

"They're packed to withstand an airdrop, so yeah, they're still intact."

"No one knows you're a cop except Roberto, and you said yourself he'll probably never make it out alive, and even if he did, it wouldn't be in time. If we head for Valisimo's camp, you could still deliver the missiles, just the way you planned, and we could still catch Felix Baranoff."

Jake shook his head. "I might do something like that if I were alone, but I sure as hell can't take you with me and I'm not about to leave you here."

"You *can* take me with you. I've been pretending

to be your paramour since we left San Diego. I'll just keep doing it. Believe me, now that I know you're not going to kill me, it'll be a whole lot easier.''

"No."

"Why not?"

"Because you're my responsibility. I'm getting you back to San Diego and that's the end of it."

Allie sat down in the middle of the trail and drew her legs up under her chin.

"What the hell are you doing?"

"If you want me to go back to San Diego, you'll have to carry me, because the only direction I'm walking is toward Valisimo's camp."

Jake made a sound of frustration in his throat. "You are the most hard-headed, irritating female I've ever had the misfortune to meet."

"Felix Baranoff killed my best friend. I want to see him pay for it."

"The hit was made on Donny Markam. He was trying to horn in on Baranoff's territory. Your friend just happened to get in the way."

"That doesn't make any difference. Baranoff killed her. I want him to pay."

Jake frowned, opened his mouth to argue, slammed it closed again. "This isn't a good idea, Allie."

She came to her feet, brushing leaves off the seat of her shorts. "Come on, Jake. We've come this far. Let's finish it."

Jake looked over her shoulder back at the plane. It was all but hidden in the deep green foliage. Only a faint glint of silver appeared now and then through the heavy vines and leaves.

"I must be crazy for even thinking about this."

"It's the right thing to do—you know it is."

"Christ." He ran a hand through his hair, shoving it back from his forehead. "All right, but you may not be so keen on this by the time you've walked sixty miles in the bush."

That took the smile off her face.

"And forgodsake while you're doing it, be careful. There are jaguar and puma in these jungles, to say nothing of poisonous toads, crocodiles, spiders, and snakes. Watch where you're walking and keep your eyes open." As Jake stalked off into the trees, following a narrow game trail leading east and obviously unhappy with his decision, Allie summoned her courage and hoisted her purse onto her back, using the straps that made it a backpack but until now had been mostly for decoration.

Sixty miles through a hostile, humid jungle only to reach a camp full of rebels who wouldn't hesitate to slit their throats if they had an inkling of why the two of them were there.

Allie shivered in the hot jungle heat. *I must be out of my mind.*

Chapter Eleven

I must be out of my mind. The minute he realized his cover had been blown, Jake had given up any notion of pursuing his objective. From that point on, he'd just been trying to keep himself and Allie alive.

Now, at her insistence and his own reluctant agreement, they were forging ahead once more. Swearing softly at the situation he found himself in and just because he felt like it, he stepped over a downed tree, careful not to get stuck on the thorny branches, and held them away from the path as Allie stepped over behind him.

For the first half-hour, he had continued to glance over his shoulder, worried that the going would be too tough and she wouldn't be able to keep up. But those long legs of hers just kept moving forward like beautiful, suntanned pistons, carrying her determinedly along the trail.

It was hot in the jungle but not unbearable, the way it would be later on in the year. April in the southern Yucatan got maybe two or three inches of rain, and the temperature reached the mid to high eighties. Still, some of that rain, had fallen earlier in the day. It was humid as hell and it felt a whole lot hotter. The last time he had turned to check on Allie, he saw that she had stripped off the windbreaker she had worn as a protection on the boat and tied the sleeves of the jacket around her waist.

He wished she'd left it on, hot or not. She was braless underneath her orange tank top—thanks to him—and a picture of those round, upturned, pointy little breasts jiggling beneath the thin cotton immediately burned into his brain. Every time he closed his eyes, the erotic image appeared and he got hard.

Not the most comfortable way to walk through a jungle. *Sonofabitch.*

The going was slow. Traveling mostly through deep shade beneath hundred-foot trees that formed a canopy above their heads, they fought their way through dense vines and foliage dripping with water from the brief tropical storm. If he hadn't spotted the game trail, it would have been nearly impossible to make any progress at all.

As it was, they had to stop time and again while he used the machete to chop his way through downed or rotting foliage then search again for the game trail.

Still, they traveled maybe four miles before the sun began to sink behind the trees. Jake needed to find a safe place to camp before it got dark and finally chose a small clearing on a rise not far from a meandering, overgrown stream. So far the bugs hadn't been too bad and the animals they had encountered had been small and harmless, mostly monkeys and a few colorful parrots.

He turned to look at Allie. "This is far enough for today. We're on a small rise and the ground is dry and fairly clear. We'll make camp here for the night."

She sank down right where she stood, her face flushed as she closed her eyes and collapsed against the trunk of a tree. He realized she had been pushing herself far harder than he had believed, and inwardly he cursed himself.

"You should have said something, dammit. We could have stopped sooner."

She gave him a weary smile. "I'm fine. I've always loved hiking—though this isn't exactly the terrain I'd choose. I used to go out to Point Loma all the time before I got so busy. I guess I'm a little out of practice."

"You did just fine," he said gruffly, meaning every word. Allie stretched, tried to work the kinks out of her back, and he tried not to notice her breasts. They were apple-round and just as firm beneath the bright orange tank top, and he remembered exactly the way they fit in the palm of his hand. He cleared his throat, looked off into the trees. "You'll feel better after a good night's sleep. Tomorrow we'll slow the pace a little."

Allie just nodded.

He let her rest while he gathered wood for a fire. When he returned, he spread out a sheet of plastic, unzipped the sleeping bag, and spread it open to form a mattress for the two of them. It was cooler in the evenings this time of year, but the army blanket would be enough to keep them warm.

Jake didn't think he'd need anything at all. He got hot just thinking about sleeping beside her. He could almost feel that tight little bottom nestled into his groin, the flutter of her hair against his cheek. It occurred to him that the circumstances between them had changed. He wasn't her captor any longer. She was his partner now, a willing participant working toward the same objective. They were both unattached and attracted to each other. As long as Allie understood he wasn't interested in anything but a physical relationship, maybe they could—

He stopped himself before the thought could completely form. He was a cop. And he was on the job. Allie was a civilian and he was supposed to protect her. Screwing her was hardly part of his assignment. He glanced at Allie, whose eyes were closed, her breathing even and deep. He watched those small pert breasts rise up and down and went hard in a heartbeat.

Christ, what the hell was the matter with him? Allie might be a blonde and he'd always had a yen for them, but she wasn't his usual sort. He liked them hot and brassy, the kind of woman who could keep up with him in bed, but aside from that, pretty much did what he said. Allie was stubborn and hardheaded, willing to fight him at every turn. She was also smart and brave and, he was fairly sure, naïve as hell when it came to men.

She deserved a marrying kind of guy, the kind who could give her a home and family. Those things were not for him, though there was a time he'd wanted them very badly. It wasn't going to happen, and Jake had accepted the fact long ago.

He thought of his ex-wife Marla and their little boy, Michael, five years old the first day of June. He thought of the divorce he hadn't wanted and how much he missed his son. He wondered where the boy was, wondered if he was well and safe, and looked down to find his hand balled into a shaking fist. He took a deep breath and visibly released it, forcing the painful thoughts away as he had taught himself to do.

As he had said, one thing was clear—marriage wasn't a mistake he intended to make again.

Felix Baranoff lifted his private cell phone from the top drawer of his desk and pressed it against his ear. He heard the general's gruff voice, listened to his words, and the skin went white around his mouth.

"What do you mean, the plane never arrived? Where the hell is it?"

"We believe it went down in the jungle between here and Santo Emilio. That was its last scheduled fuel stop. We have helicopters out searching now. So far they have found no sign of it."

Baranoff cursed, wondering if Valisimo was telling him the truth or if he had simply confiscated the weapons to avoid paying for them. "That plane belonged to you. I'm holding you responsible for whatever may have happened to it. As far as I'm concerned, the delivery has been made. Whether or not you find the cargo, I'll expect to receive payment in full."

"You may expect whatever you choose," Valisimo said, "but the agreement was for you to provide the . . . cargo . . . along with the expertise that is needed to use it. You will not receive a single *centavo* until I have both of those things.''

Felix clamped hard on his jaw. On the opposite end of the phone he could hear the general breathing. He tempered his words, choosing them carefully now. ''Then I would suggest very strongly, General Valisimo, that you find that missing plane.'' Felix hung up, his fingers almost painfully tight around the leather-covered phone.

Valisimo might believe he was the one in control of this situation, but Felix had friends in high places. A couple of batches of weapons were hardly enough to win a revolution. If the general wanted to continue doing business in the arms world, he would have to pay his debts.

Felix's expression hardened. Valisimo owed him and he intended to collect. The general had something he wanted, something even more precious than money. Once Felix had verified its existence, he had been obsessed with owning it. And nothing, especially not a zealot like Alejandro Valisimo, was going to stand in his way.

Still, it would be better for everyone involved if the plane was simply found and the missiles recovered. Felix would give the man the benefit of the doubt and a little more time before he took the next step.

The intercom buzzed on his desk. He hit the button and his secretary, Eve Holloway, informed him, ''Ron Marvin's on the phone. You said if he called I should—''

''Yes, put him through.'' Marvin was a troubleshooter of sorts, a man you could count on for answers. He wasn't cheap, but he was worth it.

Felix picked up the receiver. ''What have you got, Ron?''

"Just this—some old guy who was working on the *Imperial Dynasty* says he saw the girl down on the docks the day she disappeared. She was asking questions about your yachts, but she didn't stay long and she left, as far as he knows."

"Has he spoken to the police?"

"Not so far. He wasn't there the day they came snooping around asking questions, but apparently someone gave him a description and he remembered seeing her there."

"Is he sure she left the dock?"

"He says she was there one minute and gone the next. That's all he remembers."

"What time was that?"

"About noon, I guess."

Just before the *Dynasty II* left the harbor. Surely it was coincidence—another in the series—a fact that didn't set well. But she couldn't have boarded the yacht. Dawson would never have risked it. On the other hand, those two idiots Valisimo had hired were capable of anything. If they'd wanted a female along, they might have simply taken her, hidden her aboard.

He returned his attention to the phone. "Warn the old man to keep quiet. Tell him if he wants to keep his job, he'll forget he ever saw Allie Parker."

"Will do, Mr. Baranoff."

Felix hung up the phone, wondering if his instincts might be correct. If they were, and Allie Parker had been taken aboard the *Dynasty II,* by now the men would have had their fill and the girl would be dead. Even if Valisimo found the plane and the deal went down the way they'd planned, she wouldn't be returning with the *Dynasty II.* Dawson was smarter than to let the girl live.

Felix felt the pull of a smile as he leaned back

in his chair. Unless something new turned up, as far as he was concerned, Allie Parker was no longer a problem.

Barbara Wallace marched up the wide front steps, jerked open the heavy glass doors, and marched into the San Diego Police Department. A beefy black sergeant sat at the front desk and she walked straight in that direction.

"I want to see Detective Dan Reynolds," she demanded. "Tell him Barb Wallace is here."

The sergeant made a call, nodded into the phone as if the person on the other end could see him, then returned it to its cradle. "Reynolds is out of the station. If you'd like to speak to someone else—"

"No. I . . . I'll just leave him a message, if you don't mind."

"Sure."

She had started to give the man her name when she heard Dan's voice coming from over her shoulder. "I don't suppose you're looking for me?"

A little tingle moved down her spine as she turned to face him. That he could do that with just a few words irritated the hell out of her.

"Actually, I was." But she damned well wished she wasn't. He was too darned good-looking. Just plain too sexy. She'd found that out the night they had gone out to dinner. The last thing she wanted was to be attracted to a man—any man. She knew what they wanted, what all of them wanted, and it had nothing to do with what *she* wanted.

Nothing at all.

"I need to know what's going on with Allie. You

haven't been in the bar for a couple of days. I figured I might find you here."

Dan gripped her arm and started leading her toward the door. "Let's go outside. It's a nice sunny day and we'll have a little more privacy out there."

She let him guide her, trying not to notice the long, strong fingers that wrapped around her arm. She pulled away from him the minute they reached the bottom of the stairs but followed him to a spot on the grass. "All right, now tell me what the police are doing to find Allie Parker."

Dan sighed. "I'll tell you, but you aren't going to like it."

"Why not?"

"This is a missing persons case, Barb. It's handled by the homicide division, which means it isn't at the top of the priority list—homicide is. The minute there's a body down, that takes precedence over everything else. Unfortunately, we've got a kidnap-murder and the dead girl is Fred Mortensen's daughter."

"So who's Fred Mortensen?"

"Fred Mortensen—as in the San Diego Chargers star quarterback."

"Oh. That Fred Mortensen. Now that you mention it, I heard something about that on the news."

"We've all got heavy caseloads to start with. Since this happened, we've been putting in overtime. Allie's case has been shoved to the back burner."

Barb's eyes narrowed. "They can't do that. You can't let them."

"I know the way you feel, but the truth is we've done everything we can. Allie's been entered in the NCIC. Maybe—"

"What the hell is the NCIC?"

"It's the National Criminal Information Center,

a highly computerized information system. They
keep records of stolen vehicles, felony warrants,
missing persons, and a thousand other things.
They're the guys the dispatch calls when a cop
pulls you over.''

"So other states know to look for her?"

"That's right. Unfortunately, so far nothing's
turned up. Unless it does or a lead comes in from
somewhere else, there's nothing more we can do.''

Tears suddenly burned. Mrs. Parker had called
her just that morning. Her husband was so upset
that the doctors had put him on high blood pressure medication. Barb felt so terribly sorry for
them. And Allie was her friend. Since the divorce,
she didn't have all that many.

She felt Dan's arms go around her and realized
she was crying. "Hush," he said softly, holding her
against his chest. "We both know you're too tough
to cry.''

He felt so solid, so warm. She wanted to slide
her arms around his neck and just hang on. In all
her thirty years, she had never had a man she could
lean on, someone she could count on to stand by
her when she needed him. Her husband, Mal, had
certainly not been that kind of guy. Oh, he was
handsome enough, and he could be charming, but
good looks and charm only went so far. Barb had
married him thinking he was her knight in shining
armor, the man who would rescue her from a
drunken mother and a father who knocked the
hell out of his wife and his daughter whenever he
felt the urge.

But Mal was no knight. He was a user, a leech,
and a womanizer who cheated on her every day of
their marriage.

Since the divorce, she had told herself she would

never need another man, and until Dan Reynolds came along, she had been almost completely convinced.

Barb sniffed and pulled away. "You're right, of course—I'm way too tough to cry. I don't know what I was thinking."

Dan looked at her the way he had the night he had taken her to dinner—as if he wanted to ask her out again.

As if he hated himself for wanting to.

"What are you doing later tonight?" His voice sounded gruff. The words seemed to tumble out against his will. Barb wished he hadn't said them almost as much as he did.

Tell him you're busy, a little voice warned. *You've known men like him before, men who can charm you, make you fall in love with them. Men like Mal, who left you with a stack of bills and two little kids and never looked back again.*

But Dan Reynolds wasn't Mal Wallace. And she wasn't the same weak woman that she had been before. "It's a school night. I planned to stay home with the boys."

Dan smiled. "I like kids. How about if I bring over pizza?"

Don't do it! "All right."

"Good. I can't stay long. I've got work to do later, but I can get away for a couple of hours. Seven o'clock about right?"

Barb just nodded. The voice inside her head was swearing, calling her an endless list of names.

"Fool" topped the head of the list.

Chapter Twelve

Allie told herself this was all just a crazy, horrifying dream. She was sleeping in the comfortable bed in her apartment in San Diego, not on a sleeping bag in some humid Mexican jungle sixty miles from nowhere.

For a minute or two, she could almost make herself believe it, but the night sounds were too real, the dampness clinging to her skin too sticky and uncomfortable. Earlier, after their march through the jungle, she had been nearly too tired to eat, would have been if the succulent smell of roasting meat hadn't penetrated her exhausted slumber.

She awakened long enough to decimate one of the pair of plump, juicy doves Jake had trapped and cooked on a spit over the fire, then went immediately back to sleep. Unfortunately, once it got dark, she awakened once more, her adrenalin pumping at the unfamiliar jungle sounds in the thick, impenetrable undergrowth. The blood-chilling screech of a cat, somewhere in the distance, the eerie shimmer of leaves as an animal moved silently through the foliage just a few feet away. Even Jake's big hard body lying next to her on the sleeping bag wasn't enough to calm her jittery nerves.

In fact, knowing he was there made sleep even more elusive. She wanted to snuggle closer, to feel the warmth of his skin, the strength of his body wrapped protectively around her.

What would it be like making love with him? To feel those steely muscles moving above her, to absorb all that barely leashed power and strength?

A memory arose of the day he had kissed her, of his big hands cupping her breasts, and a syrupy warmth slid into her stomach. She could only guess what it might be like if they made love, but just the thought was enough for moisture to collect between her legs.

Stirring restlessly on the sleeping bag, Allie forced the dangerous thoughts away. She had never lusted after a man before, and this certainly wasn't the time to start. Instead, she listened to the rasp of an insect on a branch above her head, heard the whisper of rustling leaves at the edge of the clearing, and tried not to imagine some great jungle beast padding toward them in the darkness.

Eventually, the fatigue in her weary muscles spread out through her aching limbs and she drifted into a fitful slumber. She wasn't sure how long she slept. Not nearly long enough, she thought tiredly as some strange sound intruded and her eyes snapped opened.

In the first faint light of dawn sifting down through the branches and leaves, she could just make out the clearing that held their makeshift camp. Beside her, Jake lay sleeping on his stomach, his head turned toward her, black hair falling into his eyes, one big arm serving as a pillow. The blanket rode down at his hips, and while she had made use of Roberto's T-shirt, Jake slept in his jeans, his feet and torso bare.

Her gaze moved over those incredibly wide shoulders, so smoothly muscled and darkly suntanned. Enjoying the view, she indulged herself and glanced downward, over the ridges of sinew across his back and—

Allie gasped aloud. *Ohgod, ohgod, ohgod.* Jake's eyes popped open, though she hadn't said the words aloud, and she realized how lightly he'd been sleeping.

"What is it?" he asked without moving even an inch.

"S-spider. Big s-spider." In fact, it was huge. A thick, black, hairy-legged tarantula of some kind at least eight inches long! Allie started to shiver. "What . . . what should I do?"

"It probably isn't the poisonous kind." His voice sounded calm, matter-of-fact even. As if having a dangerous spider crawling across his body was an everyday occurrence. "Can you find a stick or something to get it off with?"

She nodded, noticed that he still lay absolutely still. Whirling around, her mind flew over the contents of her purse and Jake's backpack. When nothing useful came to mind, she searched the ground around the clearing, spotted a sturdy branch with a Y-shaped fork at the end, and grabbed it up, then returned to where Jake still lay frozen on the ground. The spider had crawled a couple of inches farther, placing it squarely in the middle of his back.

Allie took a deep, steadying breath. "If you had any idea how much I hate spiders ..." Inching closer, working to keep her hands from shaking, she moved the branch in its direction. The tarantula must have noticed, for its furry legs bunched beneath it, pushing it a little bit higher in the air, and what must have been its head came up.

Ohmygod, ohmygod.

Danger signals went off in her head. It was going to bite him any minute.

"Just go slow," Jake said softly. "Try to ease the branch underneath it."

She nodded, though he probably couldn't see her, then wiped the sweat from her palms and tried to do exactly as he said. Inching the branch closer and closer to the spider, hoping not to alarm it any more than it was already, she slid the branch under the front legs, letting the giant insect get the feel of the damp wood, then sliding it a little farther. The instant she felt she had enough of the branch underneath, she jerked upward and swung with all of her strength, flinging the tarantula across the clearing like a flyweight hockey puck.

She was breathing hard, her stomach rolling with nausea when she saw Jake push himself up on an elbow and start to grin.

"Not bad for an amateur. You can play on my team anytime you want."

"Very funny."

"Unless you're trying to score another goal, you can get rid of the stick now."

She glanced down, saw that her fingers still

clutched the branch in a death grip. She let it drop and sank down on the bedroll next to Jake.

"You okay?" he asked, seeing the sheet-white color of her face as he sat up cross-legged beside her.

"No. What if that awful thing had bitten you? What if you'd gotten sick way out here—maybe even died? What would I have done?"

Jake reached over and caught her fingers, trapped them between his big hands. "Like I said, it probably wasn't the poisonous kind, but even if it had been and I'd been bitten, you would have handled it. Just like you did just now."

Allie shook her head, not nearly as certain as Jake. Nervously, she moistened her lips. "I hope you're right."

When he made no reply, she looked up and found his eyes fixed on her mouth. For an instant, she couldn't talk, couldn't seem to breathe.

Seconds ticked past. She thought that he would kiss her, and God, she wanted him to.

Instead, he clenched his jaw, muttered an oath, and came to his feet. She might have believed he no longer desired her if it hadn't been for the huge bulge straining toward the zipper of his jeans.

"It's time we got moving," he said roughly, dragging a khaki T-shirt over his head. "We've got a lot of ground to cover today."

Allie made no reply, just turned and started packing up her things. Using some of the treated water from the canteen, they shared the toothbrush she had retrieved from Roberto's suitcase, since she had left behind the one she'd used on the boat. Jake refilled their water supply, adding several more drops of iodine while she rolled up the sleeping bag and tied the ends, securing it in an oblong bundle he refastened to his backpack.

Halving the last nutrition bar left in her purse, they set off through the jungle.

It was hotter today, the sun beating down with relentless force. She was lightly suntanned from the occasional day she spent lying beside her apartment swimming pool, but not nearly dark enough to keep her from burning. Though the shade was deep beneath the double layer of trees in the jungle canopy, there were other areas of bright, burning sunlight. She used the sunscreen she had found, applying it to the back of her neck and arms, and they set off at as brisk a pace as possible, following game trails again.

It was difficult going. Branches, thin-bladed grass, and thorny shrubs scratched her legs, roots and vines caught at her ankles. She was sweating as she walked behind Jake, fighting the little gnats that buzzed around her face, cursing herself for the impulsiveness that had gotten her into this mess in the first place.

Jake seemed impervious to the discomfort. His steps never faltered, and except for the times he looked back to make certain that she was all right, he just kept walking. Sometime around midday, they reached a spot in the rain forest so dense it was nearly impassable, but Jake merely peeled off his T-shirt and began to hack away with the machete.

Allie watched the powerful muscles working beneath his skin and her breasts began to tingle. It was insane to be thinking of sex out here in the middle of the jungle, but she couldn't seem to help it. Sweet God, the man was beautiful, so sexy he gave a whole new meaning to the word.

Jake cleared a path that led down to a narrow stream, and they traveled for a while along the banks. The water ran east, the direction they were heading, toward the sea, and for a short distance the going was easier than it had been.

Still, her body was aching, her legs beginning to tremble, by the time Jake called a halt for the day.

"We'll stop here. I've spotted a couple of landmarks I think I can find on the map. I should be able to figure out where we are and the best way to get where we're going."

"How will you do that?"

"By using triangulation." Grabbing a stick, he drew a picture on the ground, marking the two landmarks and the angle from each to their current location. "Of course, this would be a whole lot easier if I had my GPS."

Allie leaned back against a tree, her feet aching and her body covered with sweat. "That stands for Global Positioning System, right?"

"Yeah. It can tell you exactly where you are anyplace in the world."

"I got my dad one last Christmas. We used to go backpacking together. He loves electronic gadgets and he was always a little paranoid we'd get lost." She smiled. "He'd be nuts right now if he knew I was out here in the middle of the jungle." The smile slid off her face as she thought how worried he and her mother must be.

"With any luck, Allie, this'll all be over soon and you'll be back in San Diego."

"I wish I could call them, at least let them know I'm all right."

"Yeah, well, my satellite cell phone was in my bag along with the GPS and everything else I had with me."

Burying thoughts of family and friends back home, Allie watched him roll out the maps, scratching a mosquito bite on the back of her leg, though fortunately the breeze last night had kept most of the bugs away. Wistfully, she glanced off toward the stream. It wasn't all that deep, knee-high maybe, but it looked cool and inviting.

"Do you think it would be all right if I took a bath while you're working?"

He looked over at the water. "It's moving good and fast. Let me take a quick look around first." He walked the bank on both sides, searching for wild animals, then returned to where he had spread his maps on the ground. "It looks okay. Just don't wander too far away."

She surveyed the stream, saw a small swirling eddy behind a cluster of big leafy plants that were just out of his line of vision. "Don't worry, I won't go far."

But she couldn't wait to wade in, to wash off the bug spray and sunscreen, to rinse her hair and perspiration-soaked skin. While Jake continued working with his maps, Allie stripped off her clothes and sloshed into the knee-deep water.

Determined not to think of Allie splashing in the stream just a few yards away, Jake used the pen he'd retrieved from her purse and his belt as a ruler to plot their location in the jungle. Assuming his calculations were correct, they were closer to Valisimo's camp than he had first thought. Three or four days of hard travel would put them in the vicinity. Odds were, even if they didn't find the exact location of the camp, Valisimo's watchdogs would probably find *them*.

Satisfied he had done the best he could, Jake rolled up the maps and set off to check on Allie. She'd been in the water long enough. He didn't want to leave her there alone and he needed to find something for them to eat before it got dark. Jake opened his mouth to call out to her just as she unleashed an unearthly scream.

Shoving through the undergrowth like a madman, he burst through the tangle of plate-sized leaves and stopped dead in his tracks.

Allie was standing in the water up to her knees, grinning at a green and yellow turtle that had climbed out on a log to sun itself. Apparently, the turtle had taken her by surprise.

Now the tables were reversed.

Allie gasped and dropped down to cover herself, but it was already too late. "I—I'm sorry," she stuttered, her arms wrapped protectively across her breasts. "He startled me is all. I didn't mean to scream."

It took all of his will to turn his back, and even when he did, the picture of her standing there naked burned like a red-hot brand into his brain. *She's a natural.* It was all he could think of. Allie Parker was a natural blonde. Of all the women he had screwed and even the two he had married, he had never been to bed with one. It was a secret fantasy that had ended in disappointment every single time.

Sonofabitch!

Standing stock-still a little downstream, he listened to her splashing toward the bank, heard the rustle of fabric as she dragged on her clothes.

"Your legs are pretty scratched up," he said, forcing the words past a too-dry throat, hoping they sounded bland and indifferent, that she couldn't tell how much he wanted to be inside her. "I think it's time you set aside your female vanity and put on Roberto's fatigues."

His mild tone must have eased her embarrassment. Dressed once more, she sighed and walked up behind him.

"I figured you had some diabolical reason for bringing those along. Much as I hate the idea, I guess you're right. I should have put them on this morning."

He kept his back to her and started walking. "I'll get them for you." He had a hard-on the size of an oak tree. God knew what she would think if she saw it. Damn, she was driving him crazy.

Allie followed him into the camp and waited as he pulled the camouflage pants from his backpack. Roberto wasn't all that big. The pants were several inches too long for her and too big around the waist, but her belt kept them up without a problem. Using the machete, he cut off the excess length, leaving enough material to tuck into her high-top Reeboks. When he was finished, he stepped back to survey his handiwork.

Damn, how could a woman possibly look good in a pair of baggy fatigues? But the belt showed off her tiny waist, and those pert little breasts jiggling beneath the tank top left no doubt that she was a woman.

An image returned of her standing buck-naked in the middle of the stream, the triangle of gold at the base of her legs glittering with tiny beads of water.

"We need to eat," he said gruffly, fighting a second arousal. "I'll be back as soon as I can find something edible."

He strode out of the camp, grateful for the

chance to bring his body back under control. Walking the banks of the stream, he returned to the spot where Allie had seen the turtle. The creature still sat there in the mud at the edge of the water. Jake pulled off his T-shirt to use as a net, caught it neatly, dispatched it with the Swiss Army knife, cleaned it, and returned to the camp.

Turtle soup was a delicacy that could be cooked right in the shell, which could be used as a bowl again later.

For the next half hour, he gathered wild tubers, rose apples, tamarind, and palm shoots. Satisfied with his cache, he made his way back to the clearing.

Allie was waiting when he got there, the camp laid out just the way he had done it the night before, the bushes cleared away to avoid insects and snakes, the sheet of plastic laid down as protection against the damp, the sleeping bag unzipped and spread out on top of it, the blanket neatly unfolded.

His body tightened as he looked at it. Damn, how many more nights could he sleep beside her and not touch her?

"Dinner won't be long," he said, dragging his eyes away from their sleeping pallet, putting himself to work making the soup.

"I hope it doesn't take too long," Allie said, walking up beside him. "I'm starving."

So was he, but not for food.

They enjoyed the soup an hour later, sitting in front of the fire in the darkness. Even without any salt, it tasted delicious.

"I have to admit you're a pretty good cook." Next to him on the bedroll, Allie took a sip from the tin cup he had filled for her. "I guess you learned to make turtle soup in the Army."

His mouth edged up. "Kinda comes in handy when your airplane crashes and you find yourself stranded in the middle of the jungle."

Allie grinned. "That's a fact. Is that also when you learned to fly?"

He nodded. "I figured if I was jumping out of the damn things, I ought to know how to fly them."

"So why did you join the Army? Was it something you always wanted to do? Did you enlist straight out of high school?"

"I graduated high school a year early then went on to USC."

A dark gold eyebrow hiked up. "No kidding— USC? That's impressive."

"My mother died when I was sixteen. My older sister got married and that left me pretty much at the mercy of my father. Dad wanted me to go to SC. He said he wanted a better education for his son than he'd had when he was a kid. Of course, after I graduated, he expected me to go into the family business. He had high hopes that someday I'd take over the company."

Allie tipped up her cup and swallowed a mouthful of broth. "I gather you weren't interested."

"My family is in the dry-cleaning business, Allie. Do I look like the kind of guy who'd be happy running laundries?"

She laughed. "Not exactly."

"Just before graduation, my dad and I had a bad fight about it. We'd never really gotten along anyway, not after my mother died. I figured it was time I went off on my own. That's when I joined the Army."

Allie bit into a chunk of turtle meat and chewed with obvious relish. Jake had no idea why he was telling her all of this stuff. He rarely talked about himself. Maybe it was that she looked sincerely interested. Or maybe because they were in the middle of nowhere, with a somewhat nebulous future, and it just felt good to talk to someone.

"From what I've heard," she said, "there's the Army and then there's Special Forces."

Jake grinned, thinking of how rough SF training had been. "Yeah, well, that's what I found out, too." One of his buddies, Pete Varner, had wound up with a broken arm during a parachute jump. Charley Hanks and Willie Lewis had dropped out after a forty-mile march through a Panamanian jungle when they found their bodies covered with leeches. "The truth is, I liked the challenge, and I found out I was good. Very good. After I got out, with the skills I'd developed, being a cop seemed the logical choice."

"What about the ATF? Do you like what you're doing for them?"

"I like law enforcement but I'd rather be on my own. Someday I hope to own my own security company, maybe do a little private investigation work on the side. The money'd be good and I think the challenge would be enough to hold my interest."

Allie sighed. "I've never figured out what I want to do. I've tried a jillion different things, but nothing ever feels quite right."

He studied her there in the firelight, sitting cross-legged on a sleeping bag in the middle of the jungle, eating turtle soup with her fingers. His ex-wife Marla couldn't go on an afternoon picnic without complaining about the ants and the heat.

"What about a husband and family?" he asked softly. "That's what most women want."

Allie glanced up at him and smiled. Damn, she

had the prettiest smile. "I love children. Someday I'd love to have a family of my own. But I'd want the kind of husband who would help with the parenting, and I'd want to be a working mom. I don't think staying home full time would be enough for me." She shot him a grin. "I once considered a job as an assistant to a biologist doing research in rain forest ecology. Thank God I didn't take it."

Jake laughed. "Oh, I don't know. You seem to be doing a pretty good job of surviving out here. Look how you helped me find that turtle we're eating."

Color washed into her cheeks as she remembered the stream and that he had seen her naked. "Don't remind me."

Jake's light mood faded. Dammit, why had he mentioned the turtle? Now all he could think of was soft curves, long legs, and blond hair—everywhere it should be. His groin thickened, swelled until it throbbed.

Allie said nothing more, and they finished their soup in silence, fishing the tender chunks of meat out with their fingers, then setting the empty cups at the edge of the fire. Jake glanced at Allie, dressed in her baggy fatigues, and tried not to think of the golden blond curls nestled beneath them. He tried not to imagine how those curls would tease his fingers.

Tried not to wish he was having Allie Parker for dessert.

Chapter Thirteen

They broke camp a little after dawn. While Allie brushed her teeth, Jake used Roberto's disposable razor to rid himself of three days' growth of beard. Allie had kind of liked the pirate look it gave him, but Jake said it was hot and itchy and gave the bugs a place to hide.

Another day of marching east took them into a dense rain forest, then an area of sunshine, tall, dry grasses, and low, thorny shrubs. They followed a trail that ran along the edge of a creek, where they stopped to gather berries and bunches of finger-sized bananas for lunch. In the trees above their heads, little black howler monkeys chattered and showered leaves down on their heads. Yellow-billed toucans swooped through the branches, and a crimson parrot sassed them while they ate, sucking berry juice off their fingers.

It was unbearably hot by midafternoon, the humidity growing though the trail led them back into the deep shade of the tropical canopy.

"God, what I wouldn't give for a nice cool shower," Allie mused with a wistful sigh as they continued along the trail, ducking low branches and stepping over downed trees, dodging sticky vines and sharp-bladed leaves. Jake made no reply, just kept striding forward, pressing her harder than he had the day before.

The sound of rushing water somewhere ahead kept her spirits up and her feet moving in that direction.

"Oh, my God." As they rounded a corner in the trail, Allie stopped dead in her tracks at the sight of the magnificent waterfall cascading down from a huge rock outcropping twenty feet above. Two wide granite ledges, one above the other, each worn smooth by years of relentless pounding, caught the brunt of the water that roared down from above.

"You wanted a shower," Jake said with a grin. "I'm happy to oblige a lady whenever I can."

She stared at the frothy white foam bubbling up in a pool at the base of the falls. "You couldn't have known this was here."

"No, but I figured from the noise that it might be something like this."

"It's beautiful. I think we've stumbled onto a little piece of paradise."

He glanced at the lush green foliage surrounding the falls. "Paradise in a place like this can still be deadly. Let me take a look around before we go any farther." He studied the area where they stood, then moved off toward the pool at the base of the waterfall. It was worn into solid rock, about six feet deep and twenty feet across. Giant leaves and plants grew at the edge of the water, cloaking it in greenery. Clusters of red and yellow hibiscus and a pink flower that looked like an azalea clung to the jagged granite walls rising nearly straight up to the plateau above.

"Looks okay," Jake said, walking toward her, reaching out to take her hand. "Come on. Time for that shower you wanted."

Allie let him guide her to the edge of the slick rock pool and for several minutes they simply stood there admiring the beauty that surrounded them, letting the cool mist float over them. Then she heard a rustling in the trees above her head and looked up just as something fell off an overhanging branch and landed across her shoulders.

Allie screamed. Jake whirled at the same instant and a big hand shot out, clamping hard behind the head of an olive-skinned snake with hourglass markings along its back. He jerked the snake away and whacked off the head with his machete so fast she almost missed it. The vicious-looking jaws were still working, the black tongue flicking in and out, as he hurled the head into the bushes a safe distance away. He tossed the four-foot body a few feet off the trail.

Trying to calm her madly racing heart, Allie stood there shaking, rubbing her arms up and down to banish the chill that came from inside her. "What . . . what kind of snake was it?"

Jake's face looked grim. The shadow of an afternoon beard already forming along his jaw made him look downright fierce. "Fer de Lance. Some species live in trees."

Allie blinked, swallowed hard. "It had a shovel-shaped head. I always thought . . . I thought that meant it was poisonous."

His jaw flexed. "Deadly. The venom destroys the red blood cells. Victims bleed from the nose and mouth. There's swelling, vomiting. The body goes into shock. You could have been dead in a couple of hours."

She started shaking harder, and the next thing she knew she was wrapped in his arms. A shudder moved through Jake's big body.

"It's all right," he said, running his hands up and down her back. "It's over and you're safe."

Allie looked up, into that strong, handsome face and thought how glad she was that he had been there. How grateful she was simply to be alive. Adrenalin still pumped through her and her heart refused to slow. Her fingertips rested on the muscles across his chest, and a long-boned, powerful thigh pressed intimately between her legs. Her pulse kicked into a roar, and something hot and liquid sank into her stomach.

Her eyes locked with his and she saw the pupils contract, the area around them glittering like cut blue glass.

Allie moistened her trembling lips. "Will you . . . kiss me, Jake?"

His nostrils flared. A heartbeat passed that seemed like an eternity. Then his mouth crushed down over hers.

Allie moaned and her arms slid around his neck. Her body swayed toward him of its own accord and he dragged her hard against him. His kiss was hot and fierce, his tongue plunging in, ravaging the inside of her mouth. He caught her face between his hands and turned her head, kissing her first one way and then another. Deep, ravenous kisses made her head spin. Scalding, white-hot kisses turned her knees to jelly and her brain to mush.

It wasn't enough.

She wanted to touch him, to have him touch her, wanted to feel his hot, damp skin against her own. Her hands flew to the hem of his T-shirt and she shoved it up, dragged it off over his head. He groaned as she kissed his collarbone, planted small moist kisses at the base of his throat. She felt Jake's hands sliding beneath her tank top to cup her breasts, his thumbs brushing over her nipples. Heat and need washed over her. Desire sank into her bones.

Her fingers ran over his chest, testing the ridges of muscle, the curly black hair that arrowed toward his navel. Instinct guided her, urging her toward a flat copper nipple, circling it, feeling the end bead into a tiny bud.

A shudder rippled through him. Jake caught her mouth and kissed her deeply. Allie trembled as he pulled the tank top over her head and his lips began to move along her throat. He trailed warm kisses over her shoulders, down to the slope of her breast, then took the fullness into his mouth. Sensation roared through her. Allie clung to his powerful shoulders, her legs shaking so badly she could barely stay on her feet.

Still, it wasn't enough. Her hand strayed to the snap on his jeans. She popped it and reached for his zipper, desperate to remove the barrier that remained between them. Jake caught her fingers as she started to slide the zipper down.

"You do that and I won't be able to stop. Not this time." Fierce blue eyes, brimming with hunger, spoke of a need that matched her own. "I want you too damned badly."

Allie gave him a tremulous smile. "Life is so short, so precious. I don't want to waste a moment more."

It was all the encouragement he needed. Jake made a low sound in his throat and in seconds he had stripped away her clothes and his own, leaving them and his pistol in a wild tangle at their feet. Allie's gaze skimmed his body and she blanched at the size of his erection, so big it arched away from his flat belly, apparently too heavy to stay upright.

"We'll take it easy," he promised, seeing her trepidation. "I'll take care not to hurt you."

Allie closed her eyes as Jake lifted her up and carried her over to the edge of the pool, laying her down on the wet, slick rocks among a cluster of ferns and big white ruffled orchids.

Jake came down beside her, all sleek muscle and dark-tanned skin. Angling his body over hers, he kissed her, teasing the corners of her mouth, nibbling her bottom lip then taking her deeply with his tongue. Long dark fingers caressed her breasts, pinched her nipples into tight little peaks that he abraded with his thumb. Damp fire slid into her core and her legs moved restlessly, searching for something more. She knew little of making love and yet instinctively she believed that this was right, that making love with Jake was exactly what she wanted.

Wild kisses followed. Wet, hungry kisses. Raw, erotic kisses that set her on fire. Warm lips captured a nipple, and her stomach contracted as he began to suckle there, nipping and tasting, laving her with his tongue. She could feel his erection pressing against her thigh, and the heat and the rock-hard length made her shiver.

She wanted to feel him inside her, wanted to feel that hard male body pressing her down on the slippery rocks.

"God, I want you," he whispered, long fingers moving across the flat spot below her navel, through the tangle of blond curls at the juncture of her legs. He paused for a moment to touch her there, looking down at her body almost with reverence. Allie gasped as he slid a finger inside and began to gently stroke her. Pleasure rippled through her in softly building waves, and the air seemed to thicken around her.

"You're hot and wet," he said gruffly, sliding another finger in, stretching her to accommodate his larger-than-average size. "You're as ready as I am, but dammit, you're tight."

She arched upward, pressing herself more fully against the skillful, probing hand that was doing such incredible things to her body. "I'm not . . . not a virgin, Jake."

He laughed softly, stroked the aching bud at her cleft, and she bit down on her bottom lip. "You're a grown woman, honey. I didn't think you were."

"But . . . but you probably ought to know . . . I've only had sex one time."

He paused in kissing her neck, barely raised his head. "You've only been to bed with one guy?"

"Well . . . yes. And we only did it once."

She felt his muscles tighten, and terror rolled through her that he meant to pull away. "Oh, God, Jake, please don't stop. It doesn't matter, does it? I want you to make love to me. I want—"

Jake silenced her with a hungry kiss. "Baby, I know what you want." With that he moved between her legs, parting them with his knee, found the entrance to her passage, and began to ease his hard length inside her.

Allie moaned as he went deeper, slowly stretching, filling her inch-by-inch until he was embedded completely.

"You all right?" he asked softly. "I'm not hurting you?"

She shook her head, not quite able to speak. It felt so good to have him there, his hardness warming her from the inside out.

"I'll try to go slow," he said, but she could see the effort it cost him in the tension coiling through his limbs. Jake started to move and her nails dug into his shoulders. Little tremors of heat radiated out from the place they were joined, and an ache throbbed there. Allie arched upward, taking him deeper, desperate to soothe the ache.

"Easy," he whispered, sliding himself out, kissing the side of her neck, then driving himself inside her once more. The tempo increased and her body responded, moving with the rhythm, meeting each of his deep thrusts. His breathing grew more ragged, his chest rising and falling, the muscles in his buttocks tightening beneath her palms.

Her skin burned. Her pulse throbbed. Faster, deeper, harder, until she thought for certain she was going to fly apart.

"Come for me, baby." Jake's deep voice rolled over her like a caress, and for once she did exactly as he commanded, her body clenching, then shattering into a million pieces.

Ohmygod! She had never felt anything like it. She knew what an orgasm was, of course, but she couldn't have guessed it felt anything like this. Like the world had just exploded and she was soaring off the planet into space. Like a thousand firecrackers had all gone off at once. And the pleasure . . . good Lord, the pleasure was so intense it was almost unbearable.

Jake's climax followed a few seconds later, his powerful body straining, the muscles so taut they quivered. With a low groan, he braced himself on his elbows until the tremors finally faded, then slowly he relaxed and lowered himself into the shallow water flowing over the rocks at her side.

For long moments, neither of them spoke. Allie's throat ached with a thick lump of tears she hadn't expected. What had happened had been incredible. Earth-shattering. It was unlike anything she had been prepared to handle—and she knew in her heart that what she was feeling was love.

You're in lust, not love, her practical side pronounced. *You're a grown woman who's ignored her sexual needs for years. It's past time you did something about it.*

The voice of reason made her feel better and she snuggled closer to Jake, allowing her eyes to drift closed. Then they snapped wide open again.

"Oh, my God! Jake—we didn't use protection! I can't believe it. I never even thought—"

"I did."

"You did what?"

"I did think of it and we did use protection."

"We did?"

"Yes, we did."

"But how . . . where did you get it?"

"Them," he corrected. "A whole box, in fact." He flashed a wicked grin. "I found them in Roberto's suitcase. Like you said, you never know what might come in handy."

"You . . . you were planning to seduce me?"

He looked a little embarrassed. "Actually, I was

doing my very best not to. But I wasn't sure exactly how much willpower I had."

Allie laughed. She couldn't help it. He might have been prepared for this to happen, but the fact remained—she was the one who had done the seducing. And she wouldn't mind doing it again.

Lying in the shallow water running over the rocks, Jake listened to Allie's soft laughter. Making love to her had been amazing, far beyond anything he had imagined. Her body was a turn-on, slender and smoothly muscled, yet soft in all the right places and incredibly feminine. She was sensuous and responsive, sexually his equal, but it was more than those things. He felt a connection to Allie he had never felt with a woman.

Maybe it was all they had been through together. Or the fact she wasn't afraid to stand up to him. Whatever it was, it scared the living hell out of him—and it made him want her again.

And it made him curious about her.

He plucked a purple-throated orchid that grew over the stream and set it in the middle of her palm. "How old are you, Allie?"

She bent her head and inhaled the subtle fragrance. "Twenty-eight last February third."

"So how come you've only made love one time?"

With a sigh, she sat up on the rock, a little stream of water running over her legs and feet, washing away the musty scent of sex. "Because it was pretty much a disaster." She fiddled with the orchid, gently touching the petals. "His name was David Carlson. I met him when I was a sophomore at San Diego State. On weekends and after school, I worked for a veterinarian named Dr. Meyers. I like animals. For a while I thought maybe I'd enjoy a career in that field."

"Another dead end, I take it."

She nodded. "I always cried when the animals had to be put down or were badly injured or—"

He chuckled. "I get the picture."

"At any rate, David had this beautiful brown and white collie named Venus. He brought her in for her shots, and about a week later she cut her foot and he brought her in to have stitches. David and I talked and he asked me out. He was a good-looking guy, in the graduate program at UCSD. I really liked him. I thought he liked me."

"So you went to bed with him."

"Not right away. We dated for a couple of weeks. We spent a lot of time together and I really thought we had something special together. David kept pressing me for sex. He said it was the next logical step in developing our relationship. I was twenty-one years old. I figured I'd waited long enough."

"So what happened?"

"We went to dinner one night, and after we came back to my apartment, I invited him to stay. We had sex and he left as soon as he was finished. I never heard from him again."

The anger Jake felt surprised him. "You mean the bastard never even called?"

She glanced away and he could see it was still a painful subject. "I was embarrassed and hurt. The sex hadn't been anything to write home about so I figured I must have done something wrong. Later I found out David was a major player, severely into the numbers game. He just wanted to add me to his list of conquests." She toyed with an orchid petal. "I was so humiliated at being a one-night stand, I swore I'd never make love to another man until I was sure I could trust him."

Allie's gaze came up to his face. "I trust you, Jake."

There was such sincerity in her eyes that his chest squeezed almost painfully. "Maybe you shouldn't, Allie. You know I'm not a marrying kind of guy. You know what I do for a living. Whatever is happening between us, it isn't going to last. Once we're finished here, you'll go back to San Diego and I'll go back to L.A. We'll start our lives again, right where we left off. That's just the way it is."

She stared down at the beautiful orchid, then back into his face. "I know that, Jake. But I could have died today—or four days ago in that plane crash. From now on, I'm going to take what I want from life. I'm going to savor every moment and not have a single regret."

For long seconds he just looked at her, sitting there in the mist beneath the falling water, holding an orchid in her hand. Knowing he shouldn't, that it would only complicate matters more than they already were, he reached for her, pulled her into his arms, and simply held her.

She was so alive, so full of life. That was part of what attracted him so strongly, that spark of life that seemed to glow inside her. He had felt it as they had made love, felt it as he had been inside her. He wanted to feel it again.

Desire filtered through him, pooled thick and heavy in his groin. He felt her tremble, saw the need in her eyes, and knew she wanted him, too.

They made love again, more slowly this time, then showered in the water spraying down from the rocky ledge above the pool. They dried a few minutes in the sun, and he resisted an urge to make love to her again, though that was exactly what he wanted. He had hoped, once he'd sampled her delectable little body, that his fascination with her would fade.

He glanced in her direction, felt his body tighten, and muttered a curse. There wasn't a snowball's chance in hell he was going to be that lucky.

Chapter Fourteen

Sitting down on a moss-covered fallen log, Allie pulled on her Reeboks, her body throbbing pleasantly in spots that had never throbbed before. She carefully shook out her shoes, as Jake had warned her to do, tucked the ragged hem of Roberto's fatigues into the tops, then glanced at Jake, who was already dressed except for the T-shirt he was dragging over his head.

"You ready?" he asked.

"As I'll ever be, I guess."

He smiled as he stuffed his pistol into its usual place behind his back in the waistband of his jeans. Allie had just reached down for her big canvas bag when a series of shots rang out from the deep shade of the trees, spraying into the dirt and foliage all around them, careening into the rocks, knocking chunks into the air and missing Jake's head by inches.

"Get down!" Shoving Allie behind a thick-trunked tree, Jake followed her down, covering her with his body, pulling his pistol as he moved, sliding back the action, sending a bullet into the chamber.

Allie tried to calm her pounding heart and keep a firm hold on her fear. "Is it . . . is it Roberto?"

"Damn near gotta be." Two more shots and still Jake didn't return fire. Allie knew his ammunition was limited. He had to make every bullet count.

"He must have been following our trail," Jake said. "Christ, I hoped he was dead."

"If it's him, why didn't he try to kill us before this?"

"Probably just caught up with us. We've been covering a lot of ground. And he may be injured."

"Or maybe he's just weak. He probably hasn't been eating as well as we have."

Jake cast her a glance. "I think that's a compliment." Another shot rang out, this one splintering a branch above their heads and knocking down a shower of leaves. "I need to get closer, but I hate to leave you here."

Allie stared toward the place in the jungle where the bullets were coming from. "I wish I had a gun."

A black eyebrow arched. "You know how to shoot one?"

She shrugged. "I always hit the targets at the carnival. I've got half a dozen teddy bears to prove it."

Jake's mouth twitched as he shook his head. Another shot slammed into the tree.

"I'll be all right," Allie said, reading Jake's indecision. "Go get him."

Another blast echoed through the jungle, com-

ing from a different angle, slamming into the tree
from the left.

Jake worked a muscle in his jaw. "Just stay down.
I won't be gone long, and I'll have my eye on you
the whole time."

He fired a shot at Roberto to keep him pinned
down, then slipped silently off beneath the leafy
plants, camouflaging his position, disappearing
into the shadows of the jungle.

Allie thought of the gun she didn't have. She
needed to distract Roberto long enough for Jake
to get a shot. Then again, there were other ways to
distract someone without using a pistol. Glancing
down, she spotted a palm-sized rock, eased over,
inch by inch, to pick it up. Pressing herself flat
against the tree, she tossed the rock into a cluster
of ferns a few feet away, making the lacy branches
dance.

Shots echoed, thudding into the moist ground
among the ferns, and she heard the sound of Jake's
pistol off to the right, two quick shots, then Roberto
firing off another round.

Silence fell. There was only the sound of her
heartbeat thundering madly in her ears. The
stillness stretched eerily. Seconds turned into minutes. Not even the chirp of a bird, or the rustle of
a leaf. The minutes lengthened and Allie's worry
grew in proportion.

Maybe Jake was hurt. Maybe one of Roberto's
bullets had hit him. Maybe he was lying out there
dying, desperately needing her help.

Worry gnawed at her, making her palms begin
to sweat. She realized she had started to chew on
one of her nails and jerked the end of her finger
out of her mouth.

She stared into the foliage where Jake had disappeared. She couldn't just sit there. She had to do something! She waited another five minutes that seemed like twenty. Straightening her spine, determined to find out what was happening, she started into the foliage, careful to keep low and out of sight, following the course Jake had taken. She had gone only a few paces when the rumble of his voice, coming from directly in front of her, stopped her in her tracks.

"I thought I told you to stay where you were."

Her gaze traveled from his canvas boots up a pair of long, jean-clad legs, across a brawny chest to his face. "I thought you might be hurt. I couldn't just leave you out there."

His features stayed hard. "The next time I tell you to do something, you do it. Understand?"

Irritation trickled through her. She straightened to her full five feet five inches. "Whatever you say, Major Dawson. Next time, I'll leave your bones to rot out there in the jungle."

His posture slowly shifted, began to relax. He raked back a lock of his wavy black hair. "Sorry. You didn't deserve that. I just don't want you getting hurt."

"Well, I don't want you getting hurt, either. But if I think you might be, I'm probably not going to sit around and do nothing about it."

His wide grin surprised her. "I guess I can live with that."

"What happened out there?"

Jake put the safety on his pistol, shoved it into the back of his jeans. When he did, she spotted the patch of fresh blood beneath his right arm.

"You've been shot!"

He shrugged. "As they say in the movies, 'It's only a flesh wound.' "

"It needs to be cleaned and bandaged. With the bugs and disease out here, that's important."

"Yeah, I know." He led her behind a cover of rocks, sat down, and pulled his T-shirt off over his head.

"So what happened?" Allie asked as she rummaged through her bag for the gauze, tape, and antibacterial ointment she had found in the damaged first aid kit in the airplane.

"It was Roberto, all right. I got a good look at him when you distracted him with that rock." He smiled. "That was pretty quick thinking, by the way."

"Thanks."

"I got a couple of shots off. I hit him. Thought I killed him at first, but unfortunately he's still alive. I found blood drops leading into the jungle, but I lost his trail in the water above the falls."

"What if he makes it to Valisimo's camp before we do?"

Jake stared off into the heavy green foliage. "I'm betting he won't make it at all. He's shot and he's bleeding pretty badly. Pretty soon he'll be too weak to travel. He'll have animals and insects to worry about. Odds are he's done for this time. But I underestimated him before and it damned near got us killed. I'm not going to do it again."

Using some of the treated water in the canteen, Allie cleaned the wound, a tear through the flesh where the bullet had creased Jake's side and just missed shattering some of his ribs. Pressing a pad of gauze over the injury, she tied it neatly in place, wrapping strips of gauze around his chest.

"You're pretty good at this."

"I told you I worked for a veterinarian."

He chuckled. "So you did."

They retrieved their gear and set off, but instead of heading east, Jake turned south, shoving through the tall sharp-bladed grass until he bisected a game trail that led in the direction they needed to travel. He made two other turns, carefully wiping away their tracks with a palm frond or covering the trail with leaves and twigs as they walked along. The terrain was less hospitable, but at least Roberto wouldn't know which way they had gone.

"It's possible," Allie said when they paused for a drink of water, "Roberto might forget about us and just head straight for the general's camp. He's hurt. He'd be able to get help there."

"Yeah, but Bobby's got no idea where the camp is. At least we've got maps and a few good landmarks to point us in the right direction."

"Still, he might get lucky."

Jake screwed the lid back on the canteen. "Yeah, he just might."

Both of them were quiet as they entered another area of shadowy rain forest. There was no sign of Roberto and they continued on, making slow but definite progress. Allie was hot and tired by the time Jake decided to make camp in a clearing on a knoll surrounded by rocks that provided cover and a good vantage point of the surrounding area.

Earlier, before they left the pool, Jake had skinned the snake he'd killed, rolled it in leaves, and stuffed it in his backpack.

"See how handy you are?" he teased as he skewered the meat on a stick and held it over the very modest campfire he had made to avoid the possibility Roberto might see it. "This is the second night in a row you've helped me get supper."

Allie laughed, thinking of the turtle and her

apparent bad luck for reptiles. Though her stomach rumbled, making it clear the bananas and nuts they had eaten during the day weren't nearly enough, she accepted her share of the meat without much enthusiasm. Taking a tentative bite, she discovered the meat was firm-textured and slightly sweet, a cross between lobster and chicken, she told herself, but wasn't really convinced.

They ate in the darkness, the fire already doused, exhaustion making her eyelids heavy. By the time they crawled onto their sleeping pallet, she was sure they were both too tired to think about having sex. But the minute she stretched out next to Jake, he reached for her. Allie's fatigue fell away and they made sweet, unhurried love.

Afterward they slept curled together until they fell asleep—or at least she fell asleep.

Allie awakened several hours later to find Jake sitting up, his back propped against a rock, the pistol close at his feet.

"Go back to sleep," he said softly. "You've got a couple more hours before it's time to get up."

"What about you? You need to rest, too."

"We're getting close to the camp. I'll sleep when we get there."

"But—"

"I'm used to this, Allie. Go on now, go back to sleep. I want you rested in the morning."

Allie did as he said, her slumber deep and untroubled, strangely secure with Jake watching over her.

Eight o'clock Saturday evening, Dan Reynolds sat at a wobbly oak table in the kitchen of Barbara Wallace's small apartment. He jiggled the rickety table, watched it sway back and forth. "You ought to let me fix this thing for you."

Barb paused as she pulled a tray of garlic French bread out of the oven. They were having spaghetti tonight, a specialty, Barb had told him when she had invited him over. "You'd do that for me? You wouldn't mind?"

"It's no big deal. It just needs a little glue and some wood clamps to hold it until it dries. Next time I come over, I'll bring the stuff with me."

Barb looked stunned. He didn't know if it was because he had implied he would be coming back or if she was amazed he knew how.

"No one's ever fixed anything for me," she said. "Not unless I paid them." She cast him a wary glance. "Or maybe you had something other than money in mind."

Irritation hardened his jaw. "Dammit, Barb, you're the most cynical female I've ever met. If the dinner you're cooking tastes half as good as it looks, that'll be more than payment enough, okay? Like I said, it's no big deal."

Barb looked a little embarrassed. "Sorry. I guess I've come to expect the worst out of people. Especially men."

"I'm the one who's supposed to be cynical. Being a cop has a way of doing that to a guy."

"So does being married."

"I suppose it could. I guess it would depend on the person. I take it your ex-husband wasn't much."

"You might say that." For a moment, he didn't think she would continue. In the end, she told him about Mal Wallace, even told him about her dad.

"When I was little, I used to hide from him under the house. I was afraid of spiders, but not as scared as I was of my dad. Then I figured out that when he couldn't find me, he'd take it out on my mother and I couldn't stand that. From then on, I just tried to stay out of his way."

Dan carefully masked a look of pity. He knew Barb would hate that. "My folks were divorced. I didn't have a really great childhood, either, but it was nothing like yours."

"I guess that's why I'm so wary. It isn't anything personal."

But it felt damned personal to Dan. He was coming to like Barbara Wallace, sharp tongue and all, and he was more than a little attracted to her. Lately, he'd been fantasizing about taking her to bed. He wondered what she'd say about that.

Just then the door to the kitchen burst open and her two sons, Pete and Ricky, came rushing in. Their faces were flushed with exertion, their clothes damp with sweat.

"Hi, Detective Reynolds," Pete said.

"What's for supper, Mom?" said Ricky.

"Spaghetti." Barb smiled at their whoop of joy over a favorite meal. "But you don't get to eat until you go wash your hands."

"Aw, Mom."

"Come on, guys." Dan slid back his chair and came to his feet. "We'll get that spaghetti a whole lot quicker if we make your mother happy."

The two boys grumbled but followed him into the modest bathroom. Like the rest of the apartment, it was neat and clean, with homey little touches like the pink embroidered doily that sat beneath the spare roll of tissue, things Barb had done to make the otherwise bland apartment seem like home.

"I need some soap," Ricky said. Dan handed him a bar of Dial and watched him work the soap into a lather. Ricky was seven, black-haired like his mom, thin, and wiry. Pete was six, red-haired, and usually grinning. They were great little kids. It was obvious their mother was doing a good job raising them.

He handed Pete the soap while he helped Ricky dry his hands. Dan washed his own, then they all returned to the kitchen.

The table was set by the time they had returned, but only two plates rested on the kitchen table.

"Tonight you boys can eat in front of the TV. I'll bring your plates in there."

Barb returned a few minutes later, having settled her sons at the coffee table and clicked the remote to the Disney channel.

"Thanks for coming," she said as they sat down to eat. "I figured you'd be busy on a Saturday night, but I thought it was worth a try. I've been wanting a chance to talk to you."

Dan felt a shot of irritation. For some insane reason, he had actually thought Barb had called because she wanted to see him.

"If that's all you wanted, you could have dropped by the office. You didn't have to go to so much trouble."

At the sharpness in his tone, Barb glanced up from her steaming plate of food. "I was thinking of having some posters printed with Allie's picture on them. You know . . . the kind they use for lost kids? I thought we could put them up around town. Maybe someone would see them and remember something useful."

The *we* mollified him a little. Maybe she had just wanted an excuse. And dammit, why did he care?

"They're pretty expensive," he said, wishing he had made at least some progress in the case, that the hope of finding Allie Parker, alive and well, wasn't getting slimmer every day.

"If we do them in black and white, it'll cost about two hundred dollars, but my boss let me put up a sign in the bar and we've already collected over fifty."

"That's great." He reached for the bottle of Valpolicella he had brought and already opened, then poured each of them a glass. "I'll be happy to make a donation, and once you get them printed, I'll help you get them out. I'm sure the guys in the department will do their part, too."

The spaghetti was delicious, the salad crisp and cold, the French bread hot and crunchy. He was nearly finished when his cell phone started to ring. Swearing, he tugged it out of his jacket pocket and answered the call.

It was Archie Hollis, his partner since the Parker girl had disappeared. "Okay, great. I'll be there as quick as I can." He pushed the End button and returned the phone to the pocket of his coat.

"What is it?" Barb asked.

"We got a break in Allie's case. Some old man who works on boats down at the marina came into the office. He says he saw Allie Parker the day she disappeared."

Barb gripped her wineglass a little tighter. For the first time he realized they were empty jelly jars. "Why did he wait so long to come forward?"

"Apparently, he was warned not to talk, but his conscience wouldn't let him keep quiet any longer."

"Warned not to talk by who?"

Dan dragged his coat off the back of his chair, his mind already moving toward the answers he hoped to get. "Felix Baranoff," he said.

*   *   *

Captain Tom Caruthers paced the floor behind the desk in his office, his mind on the two men who had approached him in the room three weeks ago, FBI agents Morris and Duchefski.

The men had come to see him after the explosion of the *Dynasty I,* the yacht that had killed Donald Markham and Christine Chambers. Morris and Duchefski had informed him their department was in the middle of a high-priority undercover investigation and warned him in no uncertain terms not to rock the boat with Felix Baranoff. Tom had been told not to divulge the information even to his own men. Fortunately, from all accounts, the explosion appeared to be an accident and the inquiry was dropped.

Then his own men, Detectives Reynolds and Hollis, had interviewed Baranoff regarding the missing Parker girl, and he'd gotten a second call, this one from a district agent with the Department of Alcohol, Tobacco and Firearms, a guy named Martin Biggs. Apparently Baranoff was under surveillance, and agents had spotted the detectives entering the Dynasty Corporation headquarters building overlooking the bay.

Biggs had warned him in even stronger terms not to step on Baranoff's toes, and Tom had reprimanded his men, warning them that unless they had solid evidence, they had better leave a man as influential as Felix Baranoff alone.

Tom was sure they thought he was sucking up to the wealthy importer and acting like a regular prick.

Now the old man who worked for Baranoff down at the marina had come forward and Tom was going to have to play the role again. Worse than that, the Parker girl was still missing and there was no way in hell they could follow their only lead.

Shit. This had really been a sucko day.

Standing in front of his captain's battered desk, Dan Reynolds could hardly believe his ears. "What do you mean the old man's statement doesn't change anything? The day she went missing, Allie Parker was spotted on the exact dock where Baranoff keeps his yachts. She suspected he was somehow involved in her roommate's death. She was down there trying to dig up evidence. The old man's story gives us a direct connection."

"Allie Parker thought Felix Baranoff was involved in smuggling drugs. We've never turned over a shred of evidence that he is anything but a first-class citizen. The old man's story just confirms what we already knew—that she disappeared from the area near the marina. For chrissake, her car was towed from the parking lot! The fact somebody physically saw her there doesn't change a single thing."

Dan's jaw felt tight. "If Baranoff isn't involved, why'd he try to keep the old man quiet?"

"Because he doesn't want any more bad publicity. You can hardly blame him for that."

"Where's the old man now? I want to talk to him."

"He's already left. You can read his statement. I put it on your desk."

Dan clamped down on his tongue. He'd always respected Tom Caruthers. He never would have believed the captain would roll over for Baranoff or anyone else, just because the guy had bucks. Of course, Tom was probably getting pressure from upstairs. The mayor and the district attorney were always on Baranoff's exclusive party list.

"So that's it, then, boss?" Archie Hollis scratched the red hair on the back of his head. "We just leave it alone?"

"Hell no, you don't leave it alone. There's a woman missing out there somewhere. It's our job to find her. Just do it without involving Felix Baranoff."

Dan didn't argue. He knew the captain well enough to know it wouldn't do him an ounce of good. But he was going to find the old man and talk to him. If he dug up any new information, he would approach the captain again.

If he had to, he'd go directly to Baranoff—and worry about the consequences later.

Chapter Fifteen

By the fifth day of their journey, the matches were gone and Allie's Bic lighter was empty. Jake used the broken reading glasses he had taken from the dead pilot's pocket as a magnifying glass to start the fire for their evening meal.

Allie checked the wound in his side, which was healing nicely, and changed the bandages, then Jake set off to find food. Thanks to a snare he'd set up on a well-used trail leading down to the river, they were having roast peccary, a small wild pig that lived in the rain forest.

Allie had gathered some plants that Jake had pointed out as edible—cattail shoots, pokeweed, and wild figs, which were steaming in leaves beneath rocks at the bottom of the fire.

The meat was surprisingly good, though the cattail was stringy and the pokeweed pretty tasteless.

Nutritious, though, and that was all that mattered. When they finished, Allie leaned back against Jake, cradled between his long legs, her head against his chest.

"Okay, I told you about David Carlson. It's only fair you tell me about your ex-wife."

He grunted. "Which one?"

"How about the first one?"

He sighed, rightly figuring she wouldn't stop pestering him until she knew. "Her name was Cindy Stengal. She was a cheerleader."

She swiveled around to look at him. "In high school?"

"Yeah."

"For heaven's sake, how old were you?"

"Cindy was a junior. I was a senior."

"A senior in high school—and a big jock, no doubt."

He grinned. "Captain of the football squad."

She nestled back down against him. "So how did you end up married? Wait a minute—let me guess. Cindy the cheerleader got pregnant."

"You got it."

"And you, being one of the good guys, had to do the right thing and marry her."

She felt his shoulders lift in a shrug. "It seemed like the only option at the time. Her father and mother were against it though. As soon as Cindy confessed that she wasn't really pregnant, they annulled the marriage."

She came up again, turned around. "What? She lied just to get you to the altar?"

"Like I said, she was only a junior in high school."

"Sounds to me like her parents did you a favor."

"Considering how young we both were and the

fact that we were never really in love, I guess they did.''

"So what about wife number two?''

His demeanor shifted. She was surprised at the tension that crept into his features.

"Her name was Marla Stevens. She was a big, blowsy blonde I met in a bar called the Alley Cat in Fort Bragg.''

"A big, blowsy blonde? Does that mean what I think it does?''

"It means she was a hot item, or at least I thought so at the time.''

"I'm not sure I like your taste in women.''

His mouth edged up. "Except for you, of course.''

She grinned. "Except for me.''

"At the time, I thought she was great. I'd been in Panama for over three years. Marla was terrific in bed and all the other guys had the hots for her. When she started talking marriage, I thought, what the hell? You're twenty-seven years old. It's time you settled down and started a family.''

"Did Marla want that, too?''

"She said she did. She wanted me to leave the Army and I guess I was ready. I took a job with the ATF and they transferred me back to L.A. Unfortunately, Marla didn't like being a cop's wife any better than she did having a husband in the service. Then she got pregnant and—''

"Pregnant!'' This time she scooted out from between his legs and turned completely around to face him. "You never said you had a child.''

His jaw, roughened with nearly a week's growth of beard, faintly tightened. "A boy. Michael Jacob Dawson. I always called him Mikey.'' There was something in his eyes, something so bleak her stomach knotted.

"Why didn't you tell me you had a son?" she asked softly.

"Because I don't." His features turned hard. "Not anymore. I came home from work one day and found Marla in bed with Carter James, one of the guys in the department. I filed for divorce the next day. Two weeks before it was final, Marla split. She took Mikey with her and I haven't seen him since."

"Oh, God, Jake." The pain on his face made her ache inside. Suddenly it seemed hard to breathe.

"I tried to find them. I hired a private detective. I spent every extra nickel I had, but they never found even a trace." He looked down at her, then glanced away, his throat moving up and down. "Mikey will be five years old the first of June and he probably doesn't even remember what his father looks like."

Allie caught his hand and pressed it against her lips. "I'm so sorry, Jake. I can't imagine what it might be like to have a child and not know where he is, or whether or not he's safe. It must be terrible for you."

A long breath whispered into the darkness. "I try not to think about him. I can't stand it if I do. Marla never was a particularly good mother. I spent more time with Michael than she did. I think maybe that's why she took him. She knew how much my son meant to me. She just wanted to get back at me for filing for divorce."

Allie leaned toward him, slid her arms around his neck. "I wish there was something I could say to make you feel better but I know there really isn't."

Jake pulled her tightly against him. For long minutes he just held her. Then she looked into his face and their eyes locked. His lips moved over hers, and as always, heat flared between them. He took her there on the bedroll, pounding out his pain and heartbreak, replacing it with pleasure.

When they were finished, he curled her against his side, but he didn't fall asleep. In the morning, she found him watching over her as he had done the night before.

This time, she knew it wasn't thoughts of Roberto that kept him awake. It was worry for his son.

Jake pored over his maps, checking current landmarks, rechecking their location in relation to Hacienda Curazon de la Selva, Valisimo's headquarters, appropriately named House in the Heart of the Jungle.

According to what Baranoff had told him, the general's camp was, at present, located on the Belize side of the Mexican border about twenty miles southwest of a little village called San Rafael, not far from the New River. If Jake's calculations were correct, they were somewhere within five miles of the camp.

"We're getting close, aren't we?" Allie asked him when they stopped to take a breather late that morning.

"Yeah." He must have been frowning, because her hand came up to touch his cheek.

"You're worried about Roberto. You're afraid he might have beat us to the camp."

He glanced up the overgrown path they'd been following. "It's got to be a million to one he could make it there at all, but it's possible. If he did and he's convinced the general I'm a cop, we won't last ten minutes."

"What do you think we should do?"

"Forget this whole crazy idea and go straight to San Rafael."

"And if we do, Baranoff gets off scot-free."

"There'll be other chances to catch him."

"In what—another two years? Come on, Jake. We know Roberto's wounded. You said yourself the odds are a million to one in our favor. I say our luck's been holding so far—let's go on the way we planned."

Jake looked down into her upturned face. The sun had brightened her cheeks, and anticipation sparkled in her eyes. She smiled, her pretty lips pink from the berries they had eaten. Longing stirred in his chest and he had to look away.

"All right," he said a little gruffly. "We'll go forward the way we planned. But I want your word that once we get inside the camp, you'll do exactly as I say. That means when I tell you to do something, you do it—no questions asked."

She grinned. "Whatever you say, Major. Your word is my command."

"I'm not joking, Allie."

The grin slid away. "All right, I promise I'll do what you say."

He grunted. He didn't really believe her, but giving her word might slow her down enough to think.

They moved forward through the jungle, stopping to hack their way through vines and low-growing foliage, traveling slower than they had been. Jake's side ached, but the bleeding had stopped. Allie's bandaging job and replacing the bloody T-shirt with the blue oxford cloth shirt he'd been wearing when the plane crashed managed to keep the bugs away.

Jake swore as it began to rain. Not a light misty drizzle, but a full-blown tropical downpour.

"Damn, I guess this was bound to happen, sooner or later."

"Actually, we've been pretty lucky so far."

He smiled. The cup was always half-full for Allie. "I suppose you're right."

"What do we do? I don't see anyplace dry where we could wait it out."

"Neither do I. All we can do is keep going."

So they did, sloshing through the mud and wet leaves, their clothes soaking wet and plastered to their skin, hair stuck down, water dripping into their eyes as they trudged relentlessly along.

It rained for more than an hour. A hot, drenching rain that made the jungle steam. By the time it ended, they were standing in sticky black mud several inches deep, a humid mist rising up around them. Jake glanced at Allie, who walked up beside him looking like a drowned cocker spaniel. Grinning at the disheartened expression on her face, he bent and stuck his finger in the mud, then reached over and smeared a streak down the bridge of her nose, placing a dot on the end.

For a second she just stood there. Then, very calmly, she reached down and picked up a handful of mud. She drew a line across his forehead, marks on his nose, and lines on each side of his face, making him look like an Indian war chief.

His grin went wider. Picking up another glob of mud, he caught her by the front of her tank top and pulled her against him, then drew patterns on her cheeks and a zigzag line on her chin.

Allie smiled sweetly up at him. Grabbing a fistful

of mud, she drew circles around his eyes, a thick line down his nose, and rubbed a muddy blob on his chin.

Jake scooped up a handful of mud and pulled open her tank top. Catching sight of her pretty little breasts with their tight pink nipples, he paused.

"You do that," Allie warned, "and I'll have to retaliate—and believe me, I won't stop until you're one big giant mud ball. Unless we find another waterfall, or it starts to rain again, we could be wearing this stuff for days."

Jake started laughing. He was hot, wet, and miserable. He hadn't eaten a real meal in days; his back ached from hours of wielding the damn machete; and he was laughing. He let the mud slide through his fingers, dragged Allie closer, and took her mouth in a scorching hot kiss. She was all wet, warm female and his body went rock-hard.

Allie must have felt the size of his erection. With a moan, she went up on her toes and her arms slid around his neck. He cupped her bottom and lifted her into his hardness, letting her feel how badly he wanted her. The kiss grew wilder, hotter, breaths mingling, tongues plunging in and out. Desire burned through him, so hot that beads of sweat broke out on his forehead. He wanted to drag her into the mud, jerk down those baggy fatigues, and bury himself inside her. He wanted to make love to her until neither of them could move.

He stopped kissing her long enough to glance around. Everywhere he looked he saw wet plants and muddy earth. Thunder rolled and the sky opened up again. *Sonofabitch.* He clamped his jaw, trying to control himself, to convince himself there was no way in hell they were going to have sex, when he realized his shirt was unbuttoned and the little tugs of pleasure/pain were Allie's teeth nipping into his chest.

"We need a bed," she whispered, shoving the shirt off his shoulders, down his arms, and tossing it over a bush. "God, Jake, what are we going to do?"

"Christ . . ." He kissed her hard again, searching frantically for anyplace that might serve their needs. Spotting a block of granite protruding out of the foliage just a few feet away, he spun her in that direction. "Grab hold of that rock."

She blinked up at him over her shoulder.

"Do it, baby. I promise this'll be good." As he worked the buckle on her belt, she bent and grabbed hold of the stone. Jake unfastened her water-logged fatigues and jerked them down around her ankles. Her little white bikini panties went next, leaving her naked, bent over among the wet green leaves. The sight was so erotic his erection began to throb.

He set his gun on the rock beside her and unzipped his soggy jeans, freeing himself as he moved behind her. He cupped a small, soft breast, kneaded it gently, and plucked the end, felt goose-bumps rush over her skin. His hand smoothed over her bottom, each globe so firm and round it made him nearly crazy to be inside her. Reaching between her legs, he stroked the wetness building there and felt her shiver.

"Cold, baby?" he whispered against her ear as he eased her legs a little wider apart.

"Hot," Allie countered, wetting her lips and tilting her head back to give him better access to her throat. "So hot."

His body tightened. He dragged a condom out of the pocket of his jeans and hurriedly put it on, grateful he had put one within easy reach. He nipped her earlobe, kissed his way down her neck, then with a single deep thrust, he was inside her, buried to the hilt.

A heavy shudder rippled through him. For a moment, he just stood there, absorbing the feel of her slender body gloving him so sweetly, as if she'd been created just for him. She felt so damned good, so warm and tight. A flood of heat poured through him and he had to clamp down on his body to keep from losing control.

Allie shifted her hips, taking him deeper still, and he bit back a groan.

"God, what you do to me," he said.

"You feel . . . so . . . good."

"Lady, you have no idea." But he intended to show her. Gripping her hips, he began to drive himself in and out, thrusting hard and deep. He wasn't gentle. Their existence out there was raw, primitive. It was the way he took her, demanding more from her than he ever had before. Allie willingly gave it, demanding an equal share for herself.

They climaxed together, their wild cries muffled by the hot rain and rustling leaves. For long moments, he held her against him, their bodies still joined, the heavy sheets of water pouring over them, cleansing away the sweat and mud, and the sticky-sweet musk of sex.

The echo of thunder rumbled and the wind whipped the branches on the trees. Allie shifted a little, and Jake tightened his hold around her. Tilting her head back, she looked into his eyes, went up on her toes, and kissed him very softly on the mouth.

There were moments in his life, he thought, that he would remember forever. Standing half-naked in the jungles of Belize holding Allie Parker in his arms would be one of them.

He looked down into her big blue eyes, and his throat felt thick. His chest was squeezing, and he didn't know why.

Uncomfortable with the emotions he was feeling, he bent his head and kissed her one last time, then knelt and set himself to the task of rearranging her clothes.

The rain began to lighten. The screech of a howler monkey sliced through the humid air, breaking the lethargy that had enveloped them, jerking them back to reality. She looked down as he drew her panties back over her hips and color washed into her cheeks. She wasn't completely accustomed to her own sexuality yet, which Jake found somehow charming.

He pulled up the fatigues and began to rebuckle her belt. "I can do it," she said, her color still high as she finished the job while he pulled on his shirt.

Stuffing his pistol into the back of his jeans, he started up the trail, and Allie fell into step behind him, staying with the pace he set. They trudged through the wet green foliage, Jake pausing far too often to hack away with the machete, grateful for the work in a way, since it kept his mind off the woman behind him and emotions he couldn't afford to feel.

Fortunately, less than half a mile later, they stumbled onto a limestone path, the first real break they'd had since their plane had crashed in the jungle.

"What in the world is this doing here?" Allie asked.

Jake studied the open trail stretching out in front of them. "It's Mayan. Tikal isn't all that far away.

There's Chan Chich, La Milpa, El Posito, and recently they found the ruins of two more ancient cities in this area. Undoubtedly there are more."

"This path looks pretty well used. Do you think the general—"

"Mayan families, descendants of the ancient tribes, still gather in the ruins for religious celebrations. Their journeys take them over the old stone paths. Of course, Valisimo's men undoubtedly use them, too."

They started along the path, both of them grateful for the open, easy-to-travel route, the first since their journey had begun. It wouldn't be long before their presence alerted Valisimo's men, Jake knew, and it was only minutes later that three armed soldiers in camouflage uniforms stepped in front of them. He heard Allie gasp as the men took aim with their weapons and another four moved in from the rear.

"Buenos dias," Jake said to them, giving the men a friendly smile. *"Me llamo* Jake Dawson," he went on in Spanish. "We're looking for General Valisimo." He slid an arm around Allie's waist, marking her as his possession. "The plane the general sent for us in Teacapan went down and we're the only survivors."

The barrels of their AK-47s slid down and their grim frowns gave way to smiles. *"Sí,* Major Dawson," said a short, dark-skinned man standing in the middle of the group. "General Valisimo, he has been searching for you. He will be very glad to know you are still alive. Come. We will take you and your woman to the camp."

Jake caught Allie's hand and gave it a reassuring squeeze. "So far so good."

She returned the smile a bit nervously. "Let's just hope our winning streak holds a little longer."

Jake nodded and they started up the trail, surrounded by Valisimo's men.

Chapter Sixteen

Hacienda Curazon de la Selva was the general's name for the secluded farm he was currently using in the Orange Walk District of Belize. This was explained by a short Mexican soldier, a sergeant named Rodriquez.

Rodriquez took them to a big white, two-story colonial-style house built several feet off the ground that actually looked more Caribbean than Spanish. Constructed of wood and surrounded by porches, it had louvered shutters and a slightly rusted, corrugated metal roof. The farm itself, a *finca*, it was called, had literally been hacked out of the jungle. Sometime back, it had fallen into disuse, the fields that had once produced sugar cane now sitting idle and heavily overgrown.

An area off to the left and some distance away from the house provided a clearing for equipment, tents, and supplies. This was where about thirty soldiers were encamped, the general's elite guard, the sergeant proudly told them.

"I thought there would be more of them," Allie said.

"It's safer for the men not to be located all in one place. The PRA has a number of secret locations in the jungle."

As they approached the wood-frame house and walked up the wide front porch steps, Allie expected the interior to be as rustic as the outside, but when Sergeant Rodriquez pulled open the screen door and escorted them into the entry, she was surprised to find cream silk sofas, Oriental carpets over polished hardwood floors, and expensive European antiques.

Valisimo walked out of a wood-paneled study that opened into a wide, high-ceilinged hall. Dressed in a perfectly tailored olive drab uniform with red and gold braid and flashy gold epaulettes, the general was a man of medium height and build, with dark brown hair, silvered at the temples, and very dark skin.

Except for the uniform and his particularly large, beak-shaped nose, he was fairly unimposing. Then he turned his nearly black eyes in their direction and Allie glimpsed a spark of fire in them that seemed to burn.

He smiled as he extended a hand to Jake, but the glance he cast Allie held obvious disapproval. "Major Dawson. Fate has been kind to you, it seems."

"Yes. The lady and I escaped unharmed. Unfortunately, the others weren't so lucky."

"All of them were killed?"

"I'm afraid so, sir."

"What of the cargo?"

"Still intact. If you've got a helicopter we can use, we can pick them up whenever you're ready."

The general's whole demeanor relaxed. "That, at least, is a relief."

"There's something you ought to know, General."

"Yes?"

"The plane crash . . . it wasn't mechanical failure, pilot error, or anything like that. One of the men you hired in Los Angeles, Roberto Santos, attempted to divert the plane away from its projected course. In the fight that ensued, his gun went off, I was wounded, and the pilot was shot and killed." It was the story they had concocted to explain the bullet wound in his side and the dead pilot they would find with a hole in his head.

"*Por Dios.* What were the man's intentions?"

"I'm afraid I don't know. I imagine he wanted the missiles. Sixty stingers, worth in the neighborhood of two hundred twenty thousand apiece. Maybe it was a temptation he couldn't resist."

The general shook his head. "The men were highly recommended by a contact in Los Angeles. But it is difficult to find men of honor these days." He gave Jake a moment of silent regard, then shifted the subject to Allie. "I wasn't told you would be traveling with a woman."

Jake tossed her an intimate glance. "This is my . . . traveling companion . . . Ms. Parker. Allie, our host, General Alejandro Valisimo."

The general's smile was stiff as cardboard. "And what exactly is Ms. Parker's role in all of this?"

Jake's mouth edged up in a man-to-man smile. "I like a woman in my bed. I didn't think there'd be much chance of that happening way out here."

Valisimo didn't spare her another glance. "As long as you succeed at what you came for, I do not suppose it will be a problem."

"Thank you, General."

"I am sure you are both exhausted. I will have my housekeeper show you to your rooms."

"One will be sufficient," Jake said, and Allie fought a rush of embarrassment. Jake's eyebrows slanted faintly together, a reminder she had better remember her role or both of them were in trouble.

"As you wish," the general said curtly. "I will see if we can find something a little more appropriate for your . . . for Ms. Parker to wear."

"Thank you," Allie said a little stiffly. "That's very kind of you, General."

He simply nodded. "We have a medical officer here among the soldiers. When you are ready, he can look at your wound."

"Thank you," Jake said.

"Now if you will excuse me, Major, there are some calls I need to make. Dinner is served promptly at eighteen hundred." Turning, he walked back down the hall to his study.

The housekeeper appeared, a black woman, very round and broad-hipped, with big dark assessing eyes.

"I am Mrs. Wilkerson. If you will please come with me."

They followed the woman, who had a vaguely British, slightly Caribbean accent, up the stairs and down a long hall to a large airy room at the far end of the east wing of the house.

"I will see what I can do about your clothes," the black woman said.

"Thank you." Jake closed the door behind her,

and Allie glanced around. The queen-sized bed in the center of the room brought a wistful sigh to her lips. It was swathed in netting, with big feather pillows, white islet sheets, and a lightweight white islet spread. There were mint green accents throughout the sunny room, and white wicker furniture; a dresser, nightstands, and an old-fashioned rocker added extra charm to the room.

"The general has very good taste," Jake said.

"Yes, he does," Allie agreed as she made her way into the bathroom. It wasn't completely modern, but there were big, fluffy white towels, a basket of lemon-scented French hard-milled soap sitting on the back of the pull-chain john, and an old claw-foot tub that made her yearn to climb in.

Jake smiled indulgently. "Go ahead. You've definitely earned it."

She grinned. "I have, haven't I?" Allie started to ask what he planned to do next, but the look on his face discouraged any serious conversation. It occurred to her that the room might be bugged and someone might be listening. Until they were sure it wasn't, it was safest simply to stay in character.

Turning her back, Allie stripped off her dirty orange tank top, the fabric stained with berry juice, mud, and God only knew what else. "You sure you don't want to join me?" she asked over her shoulder.

Jake's voice sounded gruff. "I'm sure I do, but I think I'd better pass for the moment."

Holding the tank top over her breasts, she turned to close the door and the hungry look on his face sent her confidence up a notch. Playing the role of his sex-hungry bedmate might be easier than she had imagined. And maybe not all that far off the mark. She had to admit, whenever she looked at Jake, she wanted to devour him, even if they had just made love.

The thought didn't sit well. She was growing too attached to him, getting too involved. She worried about him, enjoyed just talking to him, and she lusted after him to a mortifying degree. Considering that with any luck at all they would be home in less than a week and she would probably never see him again, her growing dependence on Jake was frightening.

Now that she had known him, spent weeks with him under the most difficult conditions—she couldn't imagine what her life would be like without him.

Empty, she thought. *Dull and boring. And miserably, unbearably lonely.*

Allie bit her lip, something painful squeezing inside her chest. The implication of what she was feeling hit her like a blow.

Dear God, I'm in love with him! She waited— prayed—for the practical side of her nature to convince her it wasn't the truth, but not a whisper came from that region of her brain.

She was in love with him. Head over heels, completely off the deep end in love, and the knowledge made her slightly sick to her stomach.

God above, she was in love with a man—for the first time in her life—and in less than a week she was going to lose him.

Allie leaned back against the sink, the smooth white porcelain cool against her fingers. Swallowing past the lump that formed in her throat, she shoved the terrible knowledge away. There wasn't time to feel sorry for herself. Not while they were still here, not when one wrong move might cost one or both of them their lives.

Determined not to think anymore about Jake, Allie started the water, discovered it was actually hot, climbed in, and settled back against the rim. When she found a package of bubble bath on the ledge beside the tub, she squealed so loud that Jake burst through the door on the run.

At the sight of the pistol he gripped in his hand, a guilty flush warmed her cheeks and she slid farther down in the tub. "Sorry. It just sort of slipped out."

A corner of his mouth twitched. "You're back in civilization now, honey. I'd appreciate a little reserve."

Allie grinned. "I'll do the best I can."

Jake said nothing, just stared down at the water in the tub. Allie realized the bubbles had parted enough to show the tops of her breasts, but instead of sinking lower, some little demon made her sit up even straighter in the tub, giving him a glimpse of her nipples. His expression altered. His gaze turned so hot she was sure the bubbles would simply melt away.

"Lady, you are asking for trouble."

From the look on his face, Allie didn't doubt it. Her nipples began to tingle as those hot blue eyes looked their fill, and beneath the water, she squirmed. She might have gotten more trouble than she could handle if a knock hadn't sounded at the door.

Grumbling beneath his breath, Jake walked across the bedroom to answer it. She heard the housekeeper's Caribbean accent, then the sound of Jake's canvas boots striding off down the hall.

Wishing she could stay in the water and simply

enjoy herself, Allie climbed out and dried off instead, her worry resurfacing again.

What if Roberto had made it to the camp? What if something else had gone wrong?

Even the pretty red and yellow striped skirt and embroidered white peasant blouse she found laid out on the bed couldn't ease her mind. Open-toed sandals sat next to the skirt, along with two sets of clothes for Jake. There were slacks, a clean white shirt, and shoes, a set of army fatigues and a pair of high-topped, lace-up leather boots.

A tray of food sat on the table: cold meat and cheese, a stack of flour tortillas, and a carafe of red wine. Her stomach growled and she turned in that direction, helping herself to the meat and cheese until she felt pleasantly full.

She glanced toward the door, wishing she knew what was happening downstairs, but interfering at this stage of the game was probably not a smart thing to do. Returning to the bathroom, she dried her hair with the blow-dryer she found under the sink and took out the little makeup kit she carried in her purse. Dressing in the clothes the house-keeper had brought, she ran a comb through her freshly washed hair, crimping it a little with her fingers to make it curl, then she pulled on the open-toed sandals.

A quick look in the mirror had her smiling. She hadn't looked this good since she left San Diego. With the color in her cheeks and her sun-lightened hair, probably not even then.

She chewed her lip, wishing Jake would return, wondering again what was happening downstairs. She didn't dare go down there. Did she?

But he hadn't actually told her to stay in the

room, and if something had gone wrong, they might need to make a run for it.

Taking a fortifying breath, Allie opened the door and headed down the hall.

The rain had started again, pounding on the tin roof, the wind whipping the branches of a nearby tree against the windows. Standing behind the polished mahogany desk in his study, the general handed his satellite phone to Jake.

"Your employer, Señor Baranoff, wishes to speak with you, Major." Apparently Valisimo had called the Russian importer to inform him the missiles had arrived, his man was still alive, and the deal could now go down as they had originally planned. "I will wait outside to give you some privacy."

Jake took hold of the small black cell phone, waited until Valisimo closed the door, then pressed the receiver against his ear.

"Dawson."

"So, you managed to stay in one piece. That's fortunate for us both."

"Yes, and you'll be happy to know the missiles are still intact as well."

"So the general tells me. When will you be picking them up?"

"As soon as Valisimo can get a helicopter ready. Tomorrow I imagine."

"Good. General Valisimo also informs me you are traveling with a blond woman named Parker."

"That's right."

Something shifted in the air at the opposite end of the phone. "I find that an interesting coincidence. You see, a woman named Mary Alice Parker turned up missing from the marina here in San

Diego on the same day the *Dynasty II* headed out of the harbor for Mexico."

Jake's stomach went cold. It never crossed his mind that Baranoff would make the connection between a missing woman named Parker and his trip on the *Dynasty II*. He had figured if no one tried to stop the boat within the first two days, he was in the clear. No one knew Allie was aboard. There was no way to trace her disappearance to his departure on the yacht. But maybe he'd been wrong.

"Have the police posed a problem?" he asked, knowing a denial was useless and deciding the best strategy was to stay as close to the truth as possible.

"Not so far. There's no evidence linking the girl's disappearance with the yacht."

Then how the hell did you know? Jake silently asked. But Baranoff was a brilliant man. His brains and determination had taken him from an impoverished childhood in the Ukraine to the ownership of a Fortune 500 company and the cream of American society.

"What about the girl?" Baranoff asked. "I don't know how she came to be aboard my yacht and I don't want to. What I want to know is why you haven't gotten rid of her?"

Jake pushed a note of arrogance into his voice. "The girl isn't a threat—at least not here. She does what I tell her and that's mostly to keep me happy in bed. After her bout with Santos and Lopez, she thinks I'm her savior. She's developed a sort of attachment, if you know what I mean."

"You realize you can't bring her back to the States. She knows too much."

"That won't be a problem. Once I'm through with her, I'll see she disappears."

The pause was less than a heartbeat. "General Valisimo may not approve."

"Valisimo won't say a word. He doesn't want his secrets exposed any more than you do."

Another brief pause. "The *Dynasty II* won't be coming back either. The woman's fingerprints will be all over it. There's DNA evidence to worry about. I don't want this girl connected to me in any way. I'll arrange for another boat to pick you up at the rendezvous point. Just let me know when you expect the transaction to be completed."

"Yes, sir."

"You're certain there won't be any more problems?"

"Once the missiles arrive and the instruction for their safe operation has been completed, I'll take payment in the form you specified and return with it to the rendezvous point for transportation home."

For a moment Baranoff said nothing. "This sale had better go down exactly the way we planned—do you understand what I'm telling you?"

Jake knew, all right. One wrong move, one word to Valisimo, and he and Allie would both be dead. "I won't let you down, Mr. Baranoff."

"Good. Then I should expect your arrival at the rendezvous site in less than a week."

Jake hung up the phone and realized he was sweating. He should have known that sooner or later the police would be sniffing around the marina, asking questions about Allie. Her car would have been parked somewhere near or someone might have seen her. Still, it was a far stretch to connect her disappearance with the *Dynasty II*, even if Felix Baranoff had managed to do it.

Jake took a deep breath as he started for the door

of the study, grateful the Russian had accepted his story. The truth was Baranoff wanted this deal to go through. He wanted the prize he was getting for the missiles.

Something he couldn't get anywhere else in the world.

The ancient Mayan treasure, the Mask of Itzamna.

Jake knew all about it. Itzamna, the celestial dragon, was the male figure worshiped by the Maya as the god of creation. He was the god of agriculture, writing, and the calendar. The eleven-hundred-year-old mask, if it truly existed and Baranoff was sure that it did, was made of jade and solid gold, a treasure of immeasurable worth.

And Felix Baranoff was determined to possess it.

Jake paused as he reached for the doorknob, thinking of the Russian and his obsession with the mask. The ATF wasn't the only department with its sites on Felix Baranoff. The FBI wanted him, too. Using a Landsat satellite and airborne sensors, the Mexican government had discovered the location of two new Mayan cities. The satellite, able to discern both natural and man-made features, had turned up evidence that the structures in the nearly buried city were being looted.

Sources linked Valisimo to the stolen art objects, along with Hector Chavoyas, the dealer who fenced the goods for the PRA, and Felix Baranoff, who made his trades directly, cutting out the middleman.

In an unusual cooperative effort between the two American groups and Mexican *Federales*, Jake had been working to achieve their separate goals.

The ATF hoping to stop the ongoing sale of weapons.

The FBI and Mexican authorities trying to put at least a dent in the antiquities-smuggling trade.

Jake thought of Ramon Perez, the Mexican government's inside man and his contact here in the camp, his next order of business. Then he pulled open the study door, and all conscious thought flew right out the window.

Looking prettier in her red and yellow skirt and simple peasant blouse than he had ever seen her, Allie stood in front of the door talking to a man Jake recognized from photos he had been shown. Enrico "Rico" Valisimo was the general's eldest son, the man in charge of the illegal antiquities operation, the means the general was using to bankroll his war.

Though right now, from the scorching look Rico was giving Allie, antiquities were the last thing the man had on his mind.

"I hope I'm not interrupting." Jake tried to make the words sound less threatening, more friendly, but somehow his voice refused to cooperate.

Allie glanced up at him, but he couldn't read her face. He wondered if she was trying to hide her attraction to Rico's dark good looks and chiseled features. Immaculately dressed in white linen slacks, a flowered silk short-sleeved shirt, and expensive alligator shoes, he would undoubtedly be attractive to any number of women.

That Allie might be one of them irritated the hell out of Jake.

To make matters worse, there he stood, still wearing his rain-damp, filthy jeans and dirty blue oxford shirt.

"Señor Dawson. It is a pleasure to meet you." Ignoring Jake's grubby appearance, Rico extended a hand, though he didn't look any too happy about

it. Jake noticed the man's neatly trimmed, buffed-
to-a-sheen fingernails, thought of the mud beneath
his own, and gripped the man's hand a little harder
than necessary.

"The pleasure's all mine," he said with a phony
smile.

"Señorita Parker and I were just getting
acquainted." He cast her a glance that carried a
little too much heat. "It is a shame her trip has
been marred by such terrible tragedy, but now that
she is here, I personally intend to make certain
she receives every comfort."

"Thank you, Señor Valisimo," Allie said. "That's
very kind of you."

"Please . . . you must call me Rico, as my friends
do."

Allie gave him a sunny smile. "Only if you'll call
me Allie."

"Allie," he said, pronouncing the *A* as a Spanish-
sounding *Ah* and making the name sound almost
poetic. "It is a very lovely name."

"Where we come from," Jake said rudely, "an
alley is a dirty little street."

Allie's surprised gaze flew to his face. Her smile
looked a little uncertain. "I'm afraid Jake has never
much liked my name."

It wasn't the truth. He thought it was kind of
cute and it fit her far better than Mary or Alice,
but what the hell? Right now he didn't much care.

Rico turned his attention to Jake, his black eyes
running over the filthy jeans and rain-soaked shirt
that had partially dried and stuck to his skin, reveal-
ing the bandages around his chest.

"Forgive me, Señor Dawson. I should not have
kept you. Unlike the lady, I can see you have not
had a chance to bathe and change."

"No, I haven't. I'm sure my mood will be greatly improved once I'm wearing clean clothes again." He turned a hard look on Allie. "You coming?"

Allie lifted her chin. "Señor Valis—Rico—has offered to show me his father's orchid collection."

The edge of Jake's mouth barely curved. "Then by all means, you should see it."

"Dinner is served at six," Rico said, repeating what the general had told them as he turned to lead Allie away.

Furious, Jake stalked up the stairs.

Chapter Seventeen

Allie didn't see Jake until dinner.

As soon as she could politely excuse herself from Rico's company, she had returned to their room to rebandage the wound in Jake's side, but he wasn't there. There was water all over the bathroom floor and the slacks, shirt, and shoes were missing from the bed. Perhaps he had gone to see the camp physician. Allie hoped so.

She knew he was angry, but she wasn't quite sure why. They were there to do a job and she was trying to do her share. She wished she could have talked to him.

At ten till six, Allie left the bedroom and made her way downstairs. Rico, dressed now in tan slacks and a short-sleeved cream-silk shirt, was waiting in the living room, a glass of white wine in his hand.

"Señorita Parker. Please come in. May I pour you a glass of wine or perhaps some sangria?"

"Wine would be nice. Thank you." She accepted the chilled glass and took a sip, closing her eyes at the cold, crisp flavor. "You can't imagine how much you appreciate the simple things in life after five days out in the jungle."

"I am sorry for all you have been through," he said, moving closer. His hand caught hers and he brought it to his lips. "I hope I can find a way to make it up to you."

He was looking at her the way he had that afternoon, and she wasn't so naïve she didn't recognize the gleam of desire in the nearly black eyes so like his father's.

Ignoring a jitter of nerves, Allie drew her hand away just as Jake walked in.

"I'm sorry," he said with a smile that didn't reach his eyes. "I always seem to be interrupting."

"Not at all," Rico said smoothly. "Señorita Parker and I were discussing the hardships posed by the jungle. What may I offer you to drink?"

"Tequila," he said. "Straight up." Freshly shaved, dressed in the black slacks and white short-sleeved shirt she had seen on the bed, he looked devastatingly handsome, and so sexy a tug of heat pulled low in her belly.

Allie watched him take a hefty sip of the tequila, saw the way his mouth flattened out when he looked in her direction, and nervously moistened her lips. What on earth was the matter with him? She hadn't done anything to make him look that way, at least nothing she knew of.

She risked a glance at Rico, saw the man's confident smile, and realized with a start that Jake wasn't mad—he was jealous!

She chewed on the thought for several seconds, flattered in one way, irritated in another. Good Lord, did he actually believe she was interested in the smooth-talking Mexican? The man was a revolutionary, a criminal who dealt in stolen weapons, maybe worse. Then again, with his perfectly barbered short black hair, strong features, dark eyes, and olive skin, he really was a good-looking man.

A little thrill shot through her. She wasn't the least bit interested in the general's son, but knowing it might matter to Jake, she couldn't suppress a feeling of elation.

Jake tossed down his drink and passed the glass back to Rico, who casually refilled it. She was relieved to see him drinking it a little more slowly this time.

"You went to see the physician?" Rico asked. "My father mentioned the problem with Santos on the plane."

"A scratch only. Dr. Hernandez says it's healing very well."

"Thank God," Allie said, greatly relieved.

Footsteps sounded near the arch leading into the living room. "Good evening, gentlemen. Señorita Parker." General Valisimo walked toward them through the opening, his uniform white this time, though it sparkled with the same red trim and gold braid on the shoulders.

"Good evening, General." Jake shook the man's hand. Whatever his face had revealed when Jake looked at Rico was gone, replaced with a look that was definitely all business. He set his half-finished glass of tequila down on a nearby table while the three men exchanged pleasantries and the general asked after the injury in his side.

"Not a problem," Jake repeated.

"I am glad to hear it," Valisimo said. "I only wish this Santos were still alive so that I could deal with him myself."

Allie ignored the little creepy-crawly that moved over her skin at the thought of Bobby Santos showing up at the hacienda.

"I believe supper is ready," the general said. "I am sure, after your ordeal, you and your . . . lady . . . could use a decent meal."

"Anything beats the hell out of snake-on-a-stick," Jake said, and Valisimo laughed.

The dining room was as expensively furnished as the rest of the house. A long, ornately carved wooden table sat in the middle of the room. It was big enough for twelve and set with silver-rimmed porcelain plates and stemmed crystal glasses. They dined on chicken simmered in a spicy red sauce, fresh vegetables, beans, rice, and tortillas. Allie ate with relish, enjoying every bite. She noticed that Jake did too.

When the meal was finished, the general set his linen napkin down beside his plate, and focused his attention on Jake.

"I have arranged for a helicopter to arrive here at zero six hundred," he said. "I presume you will have no trouble finding the spot in the jungle where the plane went down."

"No, sir. I charted our course as we traveled. There are some pretty good landmarks if you know where to look. I don't anticipate any trouble at all."

"Good. Then if you would join me in my study, there are a few last-minute details I would like to discuss."

Jake tossed a glance at Allie, silently commanding her to return upstairs to their room.

"If you are concerned about your friend," the general added, "I am sure my son will be happy to keep her company."

Rico smiled. "It would be my pleasure."

A muscle knotted in Jake's jaw. Allie caught the dark glance he gave her as he turned and followed Valisimo out of the room.

Damned woman.

Half an hour later the meeting came to an end and Jake left the study in search of Allie, alternately cursing, then worrying about her. She might be attracted to Rico Valisimo, but dammit, she was playing with fire.

Did you hear about the blonde who stood in front of the mirror with her eyes closed?

She wanted to see what she looked like asleep.

Another time he might have laughed. Now worry kept the frown firmly fixed on his face. Allie was naïve when it came to men. She had no idea what the general's son was capable of, but Jake had read the man's dossier. Raised by a father who was rarely there but indulged him in every way, Enrico Valisimo was a far more ruthless man than his idealistic sire or either of his two younger siblings.

And where women were concerned, far more dangerous.

Jake found them on the terrace, Rico standing a little too close, Allie gazing up at the huge silver disk of a moon that shined down on the jungle canopy at the edge of the abandoned farm.

Rico caught her chin and turned her face to

him. Allie's eyes widened in surprise as he leaned forward to kiss her.

"Nice night," Jake said through gritted teeth. He wanted to ram a fist into Rico's pretty-boy face. He wanted to turn Allie over his knee and paddle her until she came to her senses.

She smiled a little uncertainly, stepped away from Rico, and walked toward him.

"Miss me?" he asked, an edge to his voice.

Allie just smiled. "A little." She slipped her arm through his. "Señor Valisimo has been showing me around."

"I could see that."

She continued smiling up at him, ignoring the note of sarcasm in his voice. "It's been a very long day," she said. "Why don't we go up to bed?"

His eyes ran over her in a burning glance that left no doubt what he meant to do to her when they got there. "Yeah," he said. "Why don't we?"

Allie's face flamed, but to her credit, she stayed in character, and the welcoming smile remained in place. She turned to Rico. *"Buenas noches,* Señor Valisimo. Thank you for keeping me company."

"Good night, Allie."

Jake's fingers tightened around the hand she had rested on his arm, keeping it firmly in place as he led her toward the door.

"The helicopter will arrive here at six," Rico called after him.

"I'll be there." He grinned at Allie and winked. "No matter how entertaining the night might prove to be." His hand slid over her bottom and gave it a proprietary squeeze. He knew he had pushed her too far, and by the time they reached their bedroom, he could feel the simmering anger sliding off her in waves.

Which was fine.

His own ire was twice as hot.

The minute he closed the door, he swung her around to face him. "What the hell do you think you're doing?" He wasn't worried about anyone hearing them. He had checked the room for bugs, and there wasn't anyone else in the rooms in this wing of the house.

Her eyebrows shot up. "What am I doing? I'm doing exactly what I'm supposed to be doing. Acting like I'm your plaything and trying to be polite to our host. What do you think *you're* doing?"

His jaw clamped. "Trying to keep you out of trouble. The same thing I've been doing since the day Bobbie Santos found you aboard that damned yacht."

"Is that right?"

"Yeah, that's right."

"What exactly do you want me to do? Be rude to the general's son?"

"Well, you sure as hell aren't doing that. You've got Rico Valisimo panting all over you. Do you have any idea what kind of man he is?"

"So far, he's been a perfect gentleman. Unlike you, who is acting like a jealous fool."

"Jealous? You think that's the reason I'm mad? Because I'm jealous?" It was true—which only made him madder. He was in the middle of a highly sensitive undercover operation, one Allie was now involved in up to her pretty little neck. It was his job to keep her safe. He had to stay calm and in control—for both their sakes.

But he hadn't counted on Rico Valisimo—or Allie's attraction to the man.

"That's it, isn't it?" she pressed. "You're jealous of Rico."

His jaw clamped so hard he could barely speak. He stared into her angry blue eyes, his own glittering with fury. "You're damned right I am." Jake reached out and caught both her arms.

And the control he had been fighting so hard to maintain completely and utterly snapped.

Allie gasped as Jake pressed her up against the wall and his mouth crushed down over hers. She could feel the fury in every muscle and sinew of his big hard body. His chest rose and fell as if he had run a race, and his eyebrows slanted nearly together. She had never seen him so angry, so totally out of control, and in some remote corner of her mind, she wondered why she wasn't afraid.

The hard kiss deepened and heat rushed over her. He jerked the string on her peasant blouse and shoved it down, baring her breasts, and everywhere he touched, her skin seemed to burn. She moaned as he cupped the fullness, bent his head, and took her nipple into his mouth. She was shaking when she felt his hands beneath her skirt, pushing it up around her waist. He paused when he realized she wasn't wearing any panties and his eyes gleamed in silent accusation.

"I—I only have one pair," she stammered. "I rinsed them out and hung them up to dry in the bathroom."

For an instant, the tension in his shoulders seemed to ease, then he kissed her savagely again.

Heat crawled through her, erupting in goosebumps on her skin. His hand slid over the flat plane beneath her navel, found her softness, palmed her there, and a long finger slid inside her. Allie squirmed and arched against him, her body aching and hot all over. He had never been so fiercely possessive, so determined to have her, and it sent her up in flames.

"You think Rico can make you feel like this?" he taunted, those skillful fingers stroking her deeply again.

Allie trembled as he lifted her up and wrapped her legs around his waist. Jake found her wetness, stroked her, then drove himself hard inside. A soft moan escaped and Allie clung to his neck, but Jake didn't pause, just drove into her hard and deep, sending her pulse into orbit. She could feel the heavy thrust and drag of his shaft and her nerve endings splintered.

"You think he can make you come like I can."

Allie bit back a whimper, the pleasure so intense she felt light-headed. She could see the anger in his eyes and there was something more, a yearning she was afraid to hope was real.

"I don't care about Rico," she said. "I only care about you."

He grunted as if he didn't believe her, then surged deeply inside her again. In the back of her mind a memory returned of Jake and the wife who had betrayed him, the woman who had slept with his friend and stolen his son. For the first time she realized where his anger was coming from, that the old pain had never really left him. She understood what he was feeling, and love for him swelled inside her.

"I don't care about Rico," she repeated as he filled her deeply again. "I'm not Marla. I'd never betray you, Jake."

His whole body tightened. Something flickered in his eyes. Then it was gone. Jake kissed her roughly, yet there was something tender in the hot mouth moving over hers. He thrust into her again, and Allie started coming. She didn't think she was ever going to stop.

Jake's hard release followed, a deep, shuddering climax that had his muscles straining and his arms tightening almost painfully around her. Eventually, the tremors began to ease and finally subside completely.

The silence of the room engulfed them. Allie reached up and laid a hand against his freshly shaven cheek. "I meant it, Jake. I don't give a damn about Rico Valisimo or anyone else." *You're the man I love.* "You're the only man I care about. Only you."

His head dropped down until his forehead came to rest against hers. "I'm sorry. I don't know what the hell came over me." And he didn't look any too happy about it.

"I was just playing a part," Allie said. "I wanted to help you in some way. I thought maybe I could learn something useful and I did."

His head came up. "What did you learn?"

"Rico was bragging about the business deal he'd just made. He says he's got half the missiles sold for nearly what they paid for the whole load."

Jake let go of her legs and they slid down his body. He dealt with the condom he had put on sometime during their lovemaking. "Did he say who he'd sold them to?"

"Eduardo Ruiz. He's Colombian, the leader of a group called the National Revolutionary Army."

"I know who he is. He heads a communist narco-guerrilla operation down there." He leaned down and very gently kissed her. "You did good. As far as that thing with Rico . . . like I said, I don't know what came over me."

"You've got to trust me, Jake. The way I trust you. I won't let you down if you do."

He reached down and touched her cheek. "Funny thing is, when you put it that way, I realize I do." Allie smiled as he pulled her blouse back over her breasts and very carefully tied the drawstring. "I trust you more than any woman I've ever known."

"I'm sorry you misunderstood. Rico is—"

"Rico is a dangerous son of a bitch." His face went hard again. "The man's a killer, Allie. He thinks no more of pulling the trigger than swatting a fly. He's credited with the death of at least six of his own men, people he no longer found useful or in some way displeased him. The guy has no conscience. He'll do whatever it takes to achieve his ambition."

"Which is?"

"Make himself filthy rich. By most men's standards, he already is, but for Rico it isn't enough. He's ruthless when it comes to getting his way. You give him the least encouragement and he won't bat an eye at taking what he wants. He might try it anyway."

Allie shivered. He hadn't seemed all that bad a man, but she knew Jake wouldn't lie about something so important. "I promise I'll be more careful."

Jake just nodded. With each passing second, she could feel him withdrawing and she was afraid she knew why. Every time they made love, they grew closer and Jake gave up a little more of himself. He was getting more involved than he had ever intended.

And it was the very last thing Jake wanted to do.

* * *

Jake joined Allie in bed a little while later and she snuggled down beside him. Her body warmth seeped into him and her hair felt soft as silk against his shoulder. Even though they had just made love, a curl of desire tugged low in his belly.

Jake ignored it.

Something had happened since their arrival at Hacienda Curazon de la Selva. Seeing Allie with another man had affected him in a way he hadn't expected. He wasn't the kind of man to share a woman, but he had never become a raving lunatic over one before, not even Marla. He had never let a woman interfere with his job, never let one make him lose his highly valued control.

But Allie had accomplished both those things without even trying.

He heard her breathing deepen as she lay beside him and knew that she was asleep. When had she come to mean so much to him? How had he allowed it to happen? He was in the middle of a critical mission. Circumstances had dragged Allie into it with him. He had to stay calm and he had to stay completely in control.

If he didn't, he could wind up getting them killed.

Lying beneath soft folds of mosquito netting that draped over the bed, Jake punched his pillow, wishing he could fall asleep. That afternoon, after his visit to the doctor, he'd been approached by Ramon Perez, the Mexican agent who was his contact in the camp. Perez had a satellite phone encrypted with a Department of Defense code. With the right phone number and code word—in this case *Ixchel,* the Rainbow Lady, Mayan companion to Itzamna—the caller could go directly to a secret DOD frequency and wouldn't have to worry about being intercepted.

Perez had already made contact with the arrest team and everything was in place. As soon as the missiles arrived and the soldiers had been given instructions for their proper use, the exchange would be made.

High-tech Stinger missiles for ancient Mayan treasures, the mask alone valued by collectors at more than seven million dollars.

Jake stared up at the white gauze netting above the bed. Once the antiquities were traded, agents from all three cooperating groups would swoop down on this place like coyotes on chickens, and Alejandro Valisimo and his son would be arrested, squelching the deal with the Colombian, Eduardo Ruiz.

Hopefully, in exchange for leniency, they would give evidence against Felix Baranoff, who would also be arrested.

In less than a week, if everything went down according to plan, Jake would be back in L.A. Allie Parker would be back in San Diego and he would be free of his growing, unwanted attachment to her. In the meantime, he had to stay away from her.

It shouldn't be that tough, he told himself. He only had to last three days.

Jake looked at Allie, her shiny hair tousled, her pretty lips softened in slumber, and his body tightened until he went rock-hard.

Who was he kidding? It was gonna be a hellish three days.

* * *

Barb took an order for a Heineken and a glass of white wine and carried the drinks down to the couple sitting at the end of the bar. She didn't mind her job at the Raucous Raven, but once she'd completed the computer courses she was taking, she could get a higher-paying job, provide the boys with a better future.

She was thinking about the extra money she would make once she passed her classes, when she saw Dan Reynolds shove through the etched glass doors. He moved with a confidence most men lacked, and watching him sent her heart kicking into a clatter.

Damn, damn, damn, every time she saw him, her attraction grew stronger. He paused in front of the bar, sat down on a stool in front of her, and for the first time she noticed his face.

Grim was way too pale a word.

"Oh, God—is it Allie?"

He glanced up as if he had only just noticed she was there, saw the fear in her eyes, and quickly shook his head. "No, no, it's nothing like that."

Barb sagged with relief.

Dan raked a hand over his face, rubbing his eyes as if he hadn't gotten enough sleep. "I need a beer."

Watching him with a surreptitious sideways glance, Barb opened the cold box, dragged out a frozen mug, and set it on the bar. "Bud all right?"

"Fine."

She held the mug under the tap and filled it to the brim. "So what's going on? You look like you lost your best friend."

He sighed. "In a way, maybe I have."

"What do you mean?" She set the beer in front of him and Dan took a hefty drink.

"I've been working on that break we got in Allie's case—the old man down at the marina?"

"I've been wondering what happened."

"Captain Caruthers thought it was another dead end. He told us to drop it, said it was a waste of time, but I just couldn't let it go. I went over to the old man's house, a shabby little apartment not far from the marina. I'd read the statement he gave the day he came in. What he told me when I went to see him was pretty much the same, but—"

"So what did he say?"

"That he was doing some woodwork on Baranoff's fancy new yacht, the *Imperial Dynasty*. He said Allie asked him a couple of questions about the boat and about the *Dynasty I*."

"That's the boat Chrissy Chambers was killed on."

He nodded. "Then he mentioned something that wasn't in his statement. He said there was another Dynasty Corporation boat in its slip that day, the *Dynasty II*. He said he pointed it out to Allie. She was headed in that direction when he went back to work. That was the last time he noticed her around."

"I don't get it. You think her disappearance had something to do with Baranoff's other boat?"

"Maybe. The old man also said the *Dynasty II* took off for Mexico twenty minutes later."

Barb stopped wiping up the bar. "Twenty minutes? You don't think . . . ?"

"I don't know, but I'd sure as hell like to find out. I went back to Caruthers and told him what I'd learned, but he wouldn't budge. He says Baranoff uses those yachts to impress his wealthy clients and the fact Allie happened to be wandering nearby that day didn't mean a thing. He says he'll take me off the case if I don't leave Baranoff alone. I never thought Tom Caruthers would back down from anyone. Looks like I was wrong."

"I can't believe this."

"Believe it."

"This is crazy. How could asking the man a couple of questions cause that much trouble?"

"I don't know."

"Surely there's something we can do."

"Maybe, but I can't talk to Baranoff, not if I want to keep my job."

Barb untied the black and red apron she wore over her short black skirt, slipped it over her head, and tossed it onto the bar. "Well, I don't work for the police department or your Captain Caruthers. It's just about time for my lunch break and I can talk to anyone I want."

Dan swore foully as Barb headed for the kitchen to find someone to relieve her. When she walked out again, he caught her arm.

"You can't talk to Baranoff. Even if you managed to get in to see him—which you won't—what do you think he's going to say? That someone on the *Dynasty II* abducted Allie Parker and took her off to Mexico?"

"I don't know. Is the boat back in San Diego?"

"No."

"Then maybe that's where she is. We know she was right there on the dock just about that time. Maybe she went sniffing around the yacht, looking for information, and somebody caught her. Maybe they took her with them on the boat. Maybe they planned to get rid of her. Maybe they . . . they . . ."

Maybe they killed her and dumped her body into the ocean.

But she couldn't say the words. They stuck like a glob of peanut butter in the back of her throat.

Dan caught hold of her shoulders. "I know what you're thinking, but we don't know that happened. We can't assume anything yet. As far as Baranoff goes, there's nothing you can do. I'll talk to Caruthers again. Maybe I can get him to at least find out where the *Dynasty II* is now."

Barb just nodded. The lump in her throat was starting to ache. She had called Allie's mother just that morning. Mr. and Mrs. Parker were still holding out hope that Allie would be found alive and well, but that hope was getting slimmer every day. Barb looked at Dan Reynolds, a foot taller than she was, so strong and sure of himself, the kind of man who made you believe you could count on him. She wished she could slide her arms around his neck and just hold on to him.

She wondered if her thoughts might have shown on her face, for Dan moved closer and his arms went around her. "Don't give up," he said softly. "Not yet."

Barb held on to him hard, knowing she shouldn't, that people in the restaurant were staring. "Thank you," she whispered, forcing herself to let go and back away. "For everything."

Dan reached out and caught her chin. If the room had been empty, she thought he might have kissed her. "I won't let this drop. I promise."

She nodded, mustered a smile. "Why don't you finish your beer?"

"You said it's your lunch hour. Why don't we sit down at a table and have something to eat?"

Barb nodded, though she wasn't really hungry. She was determined to speak to Felix Baranoff. Maybe, if Allie was on the yacht, the man wasn't even aware of it. Maybe he would help the police if he understood how important it was.

Before she left work, she would call Suzi Johnson, her next-door neighbor, and ask her to pick the boys up from school. She would stop at her apartment to change out of her uniform then drive down to the Dynasty Corporation building to see Felix Baranoff.

And she wasn't going to leave until he answered every one of her questions.

Chapter Eighteen

The weather cleared, leaving the jungle to dry beneath an unrelenting sun. The mud began to congeal and it wasn't long before a hard black crust covered the barren ground where the soldiers were camped.

Hearing the rustle of clothes as Jake dressed in the camouflage pants and shirt that had been left for him the day before, Allie awakened just before dawn. She rubbed the sleep out of her eyes and sat up in bed, watching him pull on the heavy lace-up boots.

"Looks like the clothes fit okay," she said, appreciating how good he looked in them, tough and masculine, the ex–Special Forces major that Valisimo expected him to be, the same look he wore on his face.

He pulled on a second boot and snugged up the

laces. "The boots are a little too tight, but I'll live with it."

"You know what they say about men with big hands and feet."

His mouth curved faintly, then the smile slid away. "I'll be gone most of the day. Valisimo's got an old Vietnam-era Huey Five Hundred out there. It'll only carry about seven hundred pounds. It'll take three trips to get those missiles back here." He walked to the side of the bed, sat down in a small white wicker chair beside it. Such a dainty piece of furniture, by contrast, made him look even bigger and tougher than he did already.

Jake reached over and caught her hand. "There's a man named Perez," he said softly. "He knows who we are. If anything should happen while I'm gone, you find Captain Perez. I've asked him to keep an eye on you, so he won't be far away. If anyone can get you out of this place in one piece, it'll be Perez."

"You think Roberto might show up?"

"It's possible. If he does, just stick to the story I told. It'll be his word against ours."

He stood up from the chair, picked up a leather holster he must have commandeered somewhere in the camp, and buckled it around his waist. He looked like the soldier he once was, and for the first time she realized he was telling her what to do in case something happened to him.

Holding the sheet up over her breasts, Allie swung her legs to the floor. "You don't . . . don't expect trouble out there?"

"No, but these men are fighting a war. In war, you never know what might happen."

Allie stood up, dragging the sheet along with her. "Promise me you'll be careful."

He gave her a fleeting smile. "I'm always careful."

"But you'll be especially careful this time."

He paused, stared at her for several long moments, then nodded. Turning, he started walking away.

"Jake?"

He stopped and turned.

"Kiss me goodbye."

The muscles in his throat moved up and down. He strode toward her, dragged her hard against his chest, and kissed her so fiercely her legs nearly buckled beneath her. Allie sagged down on the bed as he turned and walked out of the room.

It took several long minutes for her heart to slow, several hours more before she was showered and dressed in her clean-again khaki shorts and orange tank top, ready to go downstairs. She wished she were wearing a bra, or even her windbreaker, but it was hot outside and her part as a mercenary's woman didn't allow her that kind of modesty.

Instead, she finished the chocolate-filled tortillas, sliced mangos and bananas, and thick black coffee that arrived on a tray for her breakfast, then made her way downstairs. She was hoping she wouldn't run into Rico, and as luck would have it, he was nowhere to be seen. No one stopped her as she wondered out of the house, down to where the soldiers were encamped, their tents, hidden under camouflage netting, stretched across the overgrown fields all the way to the edge of the jungle.

Men in camouflage uniforms milled about, others bent over cooking fires. A group of men at the edge of the field were engaged in target practice and she wondered how a small private army could afford to waste the ammunition.

"*Hola*, señorita!" Allie turned at the sound of the little boy's voice. "I am Miguel," he said brightly, introducing himself in surprisingly good English. "You are the major's woman, yes?"

She laughed. "Yes, I'm the major's woman." Funny, for the first time she realized it was true. All along, she had told herself she was playing a part, but the fact was, she belonged to Jake Dawson, had for some time, whether he wanted it that way or not.

"You are very pretty," he said.

"Thank you." He was no more than six years old, thin to the point of skinny, and covered with dirt. He wore a frayed pair of pants at least three inches too short that hung on his bony hips. No shoes, no shirt, his coarse black hair hacked off as if someone had used a machete, his rib bones protruding through his chocolate brown skin. Incongruously, a small white orchid rode above one ear.

"The major left in the chopper," he said. "I saw them fly away this morning."

"He's picking up cargo from the airplane that crashed in the jungle."

"*Sí*. He has made two trips already."

"He's got several more loads, I think."

Miguel looked up at her with huge, velvet brown eyes. "Would you like to see my puppy?" he asked with a child's rapid change of subject.

"I love puppies. I'd love to see him."

Miguel took hold of her hand. "Come, Poco is in the supply shed. His mother and brothers are there."

Allie followed the child into an old wooden shed

that was hot and dim inside, stacked high with bales of straw. Shafts of sunlight slanted in between broken boards, and in the corner she spied a black and white mongrel dog. The animal was panting, her tongue lolling out as six tiny black and white spotted puppies tugged at her nipples for milk.

"That's Poco. He's the smallest. That's why I chose him. It's hard being the smallest."

Allie squeezed his hand, imagining how hard it must be for a little boy to survive out here at the edge of the jungle, wondering where his parents were, if perhaps his father was one of the soldiers in the camp.

"How did you learn to speak English?" she asked.

His thin chest puffed out. "My father was a *Zapatista*. He was a very important man. He and my mother, they taught me to speak English just as they did."

Zapatistas, she had learned from Rico, were Mayans who protested mistreatment by the government. Apparently, General Valisimo was partially of Mayan descent.

"Where are your parents now?"

Miguel glanced down at his dirty bare feet and simply shook his head. When he glanced up, the look in his eyes was so bleak Allie didn't press him any further. Surely he wasn't alone out here? But he didn't look at all like the well-cared-for child of loving parents, and Allie wondered again what might have happened to them.

He let her hold the puppy, whose big brown eyes looked remarkably like his own, then he returned it very carefully to its mother. Watching his tender care, Allie fell a little bit in love with him. She had always adored children and somehow she sensed this one was special.

They spent the next hour wandering the camp, Miguel proudly showing her some of his favorite places: a spot at the edge of the rain forest where clusters of orchids grew in thick, colorful sprays, branches that sheltered colorful parrots, and a grove where monkeys chattered in the limbs above their heads.

There were women in the camp, she realized, mothers and wives of the soldiers, and prostitutes who sold their favors to the men.

It was to one of these that Miguel introduced her. *"Hola,* Conchita. I have brought someone to meet you."

"Where have you been?" the woman scolded. "There is work to be done." She was short and dark, like most of the people in the camp, maybe mid-twenties, heavily built, with massive, swaying breasts.

"I will do the work," Miguel promised. "I have been taking care of the major's woman."

Conchita just grunted and Allie realized that everyone in the camp must have been expecting Jake's arrival.

She smiled and extended her hand. *"Buenas dias,* Conchita. Are you Miguel's mother?"

She wiped her hands on the apron tied around her waist. "Miguel, he works for me and I take care of him."

"I see." But she didn't, not really. There was little affection in the woman's dark eyes when she looked at the boy, though it was obvious that Miguel yearned for the slightest kind word.

Allie left him late in the afternoon and returned to the house just in time to see the chopper appear above the trees. Hoping to see Jake, she started toward the spot where the helicopter set down, stirring up a cloud of dust and leaves.

The minute Jake jumped through the opening, nearly a foot taller than most of the other men, something happened to her heart. It set up a racket like a kettledrum and it was hard to draw in a breath. There was something about a man in uniform, people said. Allie had never given it much thought, but she had to admit, no man had ever looked more masculine that Jake did in his dusty fatigues, or more completely in command. He was in his element, she realized, and her rapidly thudding heart squeezed painfully.

In a few more days, she would return to San Diego. She would have her life back again, but Jake would no longer be part of it. Their wild adventure would be over and he would be gone, but there was really no other choice. Not for either one of them.

She watched the men unload crate after crate of missiles. It was obvious Jake knew what he was doing and the soldiers obeyed without question. It seemed certain the way of life he had chosen for himself was the right one for him. Allie knew how hard it was to find your calling in life. Jake had found his, and even if he came to love her, there wasn't any place in that life for a wife and family.

Allie blanched at the unexpected thought. Was that what she expected? Did she see herself as married to Jake? Did she imagine the two of them raising children? Well, it wasn't going to happen. Jake had already suffered two failed marriages— even if the one to his conniving high school sweetheart didn't really count. He wouldn't take the chance again.

Her throat felt suddenly tight. Allie turned and started walking, no longer so eager to see him. Maybe it wouldn't be so difficult if she hadn't slept with him. Maybe the hurt wouldn't be so bad.

If only she hadn't fallen in love with him.

But she didn't think there was anything she could have done to stop it. And there certainly wasn't anything she could do about it now.

The heat of the day was beginning to dissipate by the time Jake made his final run to the crash site and returned with the last load of missiles. After arranging for the officers to begin instruction at oh-six-hundred the following morning, he went upstairs to shower and change.

Allie wasn't in the bedroom. He didn't know where she had gone, but at least she wasn't with Rico; he had seen the man leaving camp after the first chopper run that morning. According to Captain Perez, Rico traveled several times a week to the ruins in the jungle that contributed so heavily to his own personal fortune and his father's military campaign.

Jake paced the room for a while, restless, though he could have probably used some sleep. Realizing a nap wasn't going to work, he gave up and went downstairs. He found Allie in the living room, dressed for supper in her pretty yellow and red skirt and white blouse, speaking to General Valisimo, who was smiling instead of frowning at her today. Which didn't really surprise him. Allie had a way of winning people over.

The meal was pleasant and typically Mayan: chicken tamales; *calabazas,* a kind of squash; beans and tortillas. The general seemed pleased with the safe arrival of the missiles, and eager for the officers' training to start. Some were already there; the rest would be in by late that night.

Rico missed dinner but arrived in time for brandy and fat black Cuban cigars, which the men smoked out on the terrace. Allie joined them, sipping a glass of sherry the general brought her.

"These missiles," Valisimo said, leaning back in his chair, "they will do everything Señor Baranoff has promised?"

The general probably knew almost as much about the Stinger as Jake did, but it was obvious he wanted his money's worth—and to be certain the man Baranoff had sent was capable of teaching his men.

Jake set his cigar down in a crystal ashtray on the glass-topped table they were sitting around and prepared himself for the show. "They're everything he promised and more. The Hornet is the most advanced portable, shoulder-fired missile in the world. It's designed to counter high-speed, low-level ground attack aircraft, which it does by employing a unique Rosette Scan Pattern image-scanning technique that allows it to discriminate among targets—including flares and background clutter. It also uses a sophisticated TAG system, enabling the missile to orient itself toward vulnerable portions of the aircraft, maximizing the hit."

The general took a long draw on his cigar, waiting for the pièce de résistance—the reason he wanted the missiles so badly.

"But as I'm sure you know, General, the Hornet goes one step farther. Not only is it a heat-seeking missile like its predecessors, but the Hornet's computerized SET system allows it to follow the contours of the land, making it nearly impossible to detect the location from which it was fired. It's this latest improvement that's made it so top secret."

And worth thirteen million in Mayan treasures.

It was the missile's capabilities along with the quantity being purchased that had both the ATF and Mexican authorities worried. They believed that the true intent of the People's Revolutionary Army might be to destroy civilian aircraft, along with Mexican military planes, as a means of forcing the government to acquiesce to its demands.

The general sat forward in his chair. *"Muy bien,* Major Dawson. I believe my men will be in very capable hands."

"Thank you, sir."

"How many days will it take to complete the training?" Rico asked, rolling his cigar between fingers tipped with manicured nails.

"Not long. According to the general, the men have already been taught the basics. We'll only be dealing with the specific differences between the Hornet and the standard MANPADS system. I'd say two days at most."

Rico set the cigar in the crystal ashtray. "If that is the case, you may count on payment for the missiles Friday morning. We'll have a plane ready to return you and Ms. Parker, along with the specified cargo, to the rendezvous point in Teacapan."

Jake nodded. "Friday it is."

The general slid back his chair. "Dawn comes early for most of us. Perhaps it is time we retired."

"Suits me," Jake said, also coming to his feet.

Rico stood up too. "I'm afraid I am not yet sleepy. I think I will stay up for a while." Jake caught the look he flashed Allie. "Since Ms. Parker is not a soldier, perhaps she would like to join me."

Allie's gaze flew to Jake's, then slowly returned

to Rico. "That's very kind of you, but I'm afraid I'm tired as well." She gave the Mexican a grateful smile. "Perhaps another time."

Rico looked none too pleased. "Another time then," he agreed.

They dispersed in different directions, heading toward different parts of the house, Jake leading Allie upstairs. Funny. Tonight even Rico's blatant invitation hadn't fazed him. Allie had made her feelings clear and he knew how honest she was. As he had said, he trusted her. More than any woman he'd ever known.

Still, he was in too deep already where the lady was concerned.

When they reached their room, he made no move to touch her, just stripped off his clothes, climbed into bed, and pretended to fall sleep. Fortunately, he was tired enough that he actually did. When he awakened just before dawn, he ignored the painful tent his erection made beneath the sheets.

Two more nights, he told himself. Two more hellish nights and this whole damned thing would be over. For the first time in weeks, he was actually looking forward to going home.

Chapter Nineteen

With Jake off teaching in the soldiers' camp, Allie wandered out of the house, looking for little Miguel. She didn't have to go far. She thought that perhaps he had been watching for her to come out.

"Señorita Allie!" he shouted, for they were already well past the formal stage of their relationship.

"Good morning, Miguel. I hoped I would find you."

"*Sí*. I have been waiting for you. I wish to show you the wild pig I caught."

She rounded her eyes at him. "You caught a wild pig? How on earth did you do that?"

He shrugged his bony shoulders. "He has been bothering some of the women, rooting around in their gardens and stealing food. Conchita says she is going to make supper out of him, but I kind of like him. He has little tiny eyes that look sort of sad.''

He took her hand and led her to a pen that he had made out of brush to enclose the pig. The animal was bigger than Allie had thought it would be, remembering the little peccary that Jake had snared and cooked for dinner.

This pig was feral, maybe twice the size of the peccary, with tusks that curled up around his nose.

"I named him Arturo because he looks like Señora Lupe's husband.''

Allie stifled a laugh. He was such a darling boy. She would miss him when she left the jungle.

They wandered away from the pig's pen and started toward the wooden supply shed to check on Poco. The puppy was fine, asleep when they arrived and sleeping again by the time they turned to leave. They started out of the shed when a shadow appeared in the open doorway, cutting off some of the light streaming in.

"Conchita needs you, *muchacho*," Rico said. *"Andele. Pronto!"*

Miguel hesitated, cast Allie an uncertain glance, obviously not wanting to leave.

Allie wasn't too happy about it herself, since she would be alone with Rico. She forced herself to smile. "It's all right, Miguel. You had better go see what she wants.''

Reluctantly, he moved past the shadowy figure in the doorway, who cuffed him on the side of the head. "Next time you do what I tell you. *Comprende?*"

"*Sí*, señor.'' The boy left the shed rubbing his injured ear and Allie fought to hold on to her temper. Since it wasn't a good idea to make Rico angry, she simply waited until the boy had left and followed him out the door. She was relieved when Rico did nothing to stop her.

"There is something I wish to show you," he said, taking a firm grip on her arm.

Allie glanced around, trying to think of a polite way to refuse him, but he was already leading her away. As they moved farther from the encampment, she spotted a tin-roofed cottage in the distance, a smaller version of the big house where Valisimo lived.

"Where are we going?"

"I told you . . . there is something I wish you to see."

She let him lead her toward the cottage, her nervousness continuing to build. Jake had warned her about the man. Now here she was, getting farther and farther from the house where she had no protection from him, and she couldn't think of a way to escape.

She stopped him at the bottom of the stairs leading up to the porch. "What place is this?"

The hard smile he gave her twisted her stomach into a knot. "This is my house. Did you think I would be living under the same roof as my father—under the general's thumb?"

"No, I—" His grip tightened on her arm and he started up the stairs, forcing her to follow.

She hung back when he opened the door. "I don't think this is a good idea. Jake wouldn't like it and . . . and you've never seen how mean he can be when he's in a rage. He—he might hit me or—"

He jerked open the door. "Get inside. I am tired of playing games with you."

The well-mannered Rico was gone. In his place

was the ruthless man Jake had described. Allie stiffened her spine. "I've got to get back to the house,"
she said, jerking free of his hold.

Rico shoved her through the door so hard she
stumbled and went sprawling on the hardwood
floor. She groaned as a sharp pain shot into her
knee and turned just in time to see a little brown
dynamo come racing up the front porch steps.

"Let her go!" Miguel slammed into Rico so hard
the man lost his balance and slammed into the
door frame.

"Miguel!" Allie screamed as the child began
flailing his small fists at Rico, who slapped him so
hard he flew backward across the porch and rolled
down the steep wooden stairs. Ignoring the pain
in her knee, Allie stumbled to her feet and ran for
the door. By the time she'd reached it, Miguel was
back on his feet and attacking Rico again.

Allie screamed as Rico hit him with his fist and
sent the little boy tumbling backward down the
steps again, then he grabbed hold of Allie's hair
and yanked her hard against him. She remembered
the day Bobby Santos had attacked her on the boat
and desperately tried to recall the moves she had
learned in her self-defense class. Stomping down
hard on Rico's shin, she jerked free, whirled, and
brought her knee up hard into his groin.

Unlike Bobby, Rico blocked the blow, but it gave
her the time she needed to race past him down
the stairs. Miguel's small body lay in a crumpled
heap on the ground a few feet away. Dear God,
she couldn't just leave him! With shaking hands,
terrified of what Rico would do next, she knelt
beside him, reached out, and smoothed back the
little boy's hair. He moaned and his eyes slowly
opened.

"Are you all right?" Expecting Rico to come after them at any moment, she heard the soft thud of footfalls coming from the direction away from the house and glanced up to see a pair of heavy boots topped by camouflage fatigues standing right behind her.

"Is the boy all right?" Jake's deep voice rumbled toward her and Allie nearly fainted with relief.

"I'm not . . . not really sure."

"How about you?" He didn't move and she realized he was staring at Rico, who still stood on the porch.

"I'm fine . . . thanks to Miguel." She helped the child to his feet, and though he swayed a little, he seemed able to stand on his own.

"Let's go." With a last hard glance at Rico, Jake swept the child up in his arms and the three of them started walking away from the cottage. Jake carried the boy directly to the tent belonging to Dr. Hidalgo, the camp physician.

"Nothing seems to be broken and I do not think he has suffered a concussion."

"Thank God," Allie said, feeling a wave of relief.

"Still, it would be best if the boy rested for the balance of the day."

"I'll make certain he does." Jake said nothing of how the "accident" had happened and the doctor didn't ask. Jake returned the boy to Conchita, who at Jake's insistence and after receiving a handful of *pesos* for her trouble, allowed him to skip his usual chores and rest for the afternoon.

That night Rico didn't join them for supper. His father made no mention of where he might be, and Allie didn't ask.

As he had done the night before, when they reached their room, Jake went straight to bed. Allie knew he was avoiding her, but she also knew why. Their time together was almost over. Distancing themselves was the best thing for both of them.

Still, she didn't sleep very well and she didn't think Jake did either. The following morning, he set off for the camp to complete the officers' training, which meant tomorrow they would be leaving.

In a few more days, her life would be her own again.

Allie felt like crying at the thought.

Barb still hadn't managed to see Baranoff. It hadn't been until early that morning that she was able to arrange for Suzi to take care of the boys after school so she could make her self-assigned call at Dynasty headquarters.

By dressing in her only decent suit, a soft pink linen she wore with a string of faux pearls, and making her visit seem personal instead of business, she made it past the security guards at the front desk and arrived on the top floor of the building, where, she discovered, the importer's private offices were located. There she ran into a far more formidable obstacle, a woman named Eve Holloway, or so the sign on her expensive teakwood desk read.

"Excuse me, Ms. Holloway," Barb said to her. "My name is Barbara Wallace. I would like to see Mr. Baranoff."

The woman looked at her over a pair of sleek, black, rhinestone-studded half-glasses. "And you would be . . . ?"

"I'm a friend of his. Mr. Baranoff and I met briefly at a benefit for the Cancer Society last month." Barb knew he had been there. She had seen the article and his photo in the *San Diego Union Tribune.*

"Do you have an appointment, Ms. Wallace?"

"Not exactly. I live in Los Angeles, you see. Felix suggested I drop by the next time I was in town."

Eve Holloway assessed the pink linen suit with an eye for its value, and Barb was glad it was a passably good knockoff of a designer label. And pearls, these days, took an even more discerning eye.

"I'm sorry, Ms. Wallace, Mr. Baranoff isn't in. In fact, he's out of town until tomorrow. If you'd like to leave a message, I'll certainly see that he gets it."

Barb bit her lip, wondering if the woman was telling the truth. Glancing down at the calendar sitting open on her desk, she saw today's date blocked out in red ink.

"Thank you, that won't be necessary. I'll be in town for a couple of days. I'll give him a call on Friday." Not hardly. But she would definitely be dropping back in.

Barb left in the elevator, made her way through the lobby, and stepped out onto the street. The minute she walked through the electronic glass doors, a hand clamped on her arm and she was dragged around the corner.

"I can't believe you really did it." Dan Reynolds was furious, his grip on her arm like a vise.

"Actually, I didn't. Baranoff won't be in until tomorrow."

His hold relaxed, but he didn't let her go. "What the hell did you think you were going to accomplish? You're not a detective, Barb. You don't know a damned thing about police work. That's my job, remember?"

"I remember. Do you?"

He clamped down on his jaw. "We're doing the best we can." He glanced up and down the street. "Where's your car?"

"Just down the block."

"Fine. Let's go."

She went, but somewhat grudgingly. This was a free country, after all. She had every right to talk to Felix Baranoff or anybody else.

"I don't know why you're so damned angry. Even if I'd gotten in to see him, there's nothing wrong with that."

"Nothing's wrong with it—except you'd be asking him questions that involve confidential information you got from the police department." He stopped, spun her around. "Information you got from me!"

Barb blinked up at him. She hadn't thought of it quite that way. "Oh."

"Oh? That's all you've got to say?"

She had never seen him this angry. Crazy thing was, even shaking with fury, he looked so sexy she wanted to go up on her toes and kiss him until he couldn't breathe. The thought was so amazing she nervously wet her lips and just stood there staring up at him.

"Christ." Whatever she had been thinking must have been stamped on her face. Dan hauled her into a nook in the side of the building and pressed her up against the brick wall with his body. His kiss was so scorching she had to grab hold of his shoulders just to stay on her feet.

When he'd finished, he didn't say a word, just started dragging her off toward her old blue Toyota. He took the keys out of her shaking hand

and opened the door, then practically shoved her behind the wheel.

"I'll be over tonight at nine. Make sure the kids are in bed when I get there."

"W-why?"

He caught hold of her chin. "I think you damn well know why." Then he turned and walked away, leaving her staring after him.

A good five minutes passed before Barb was able to start the car. She wouldn't be there when he got to the apartment, she told herself. She couldn't afford to get involved with Dan Reynolds or any other man. She had her kids to think of. She'd learned her lesson where men were concerned. She wasn't making the same mistake again.

She had eight more hours to convince herself.

She was going to need every one of them.

The Thursday afternoon sun was beginning to set by the time Jake had concluded his class and dismissed the men. Standing inside the tent that had been set up for his use, Jake checked his watch, waiting for Captain Perez to arrive.

Ramon Perez was a small, wiry man with leathery dark skin and shrewd black eyes, a mercenary working for the Mexican government under deep cover as a captain in the PRA since two months after Valisimo had first formed his army.

Though Perez wasn't Mayan, many of the soldiers were, some of them former *Zapatistas* who had survived the revolt in '94, but had never given up their struggle for change. They were fighting for improvements in health care and better schools, and for land reform. After a thousand years of persecution, Jake was sympathetic to their cause but not at the cost of hundreds, maybe thousands, of military and civilian lives.

He looked up as the captain lifted the tent flap and walked toward him.

"The timetable is set?"

"It's coming down tomorrow morning. Are the teams in position?"

"The men will be ready to move in as soon as you give the command."

"When you see me getting into the Jeep to leave for the plane, give them the signal to go."

He nodded. "They will arrive within ten minutes."

Jake rubbed a hand over his face, tired after a night of restless sleep. "Let's hope this comes down as smoothly as we planned."

"*Sí*, for everyone's sake." Straightening his slouch hat, Perez left the tent, and a few minutes later, Jake followed him out.

It looked as if, at least so far, everything was going as scheduled. Tomorrow, as soon as he received payment for the missiles, choppers full of FBI, ATF, and Mexican *Federales* would swoop down on the general's quarters. Rico and the general would be arrested as quickly as possible and removed from the area while a separate group of men would arrive at the tent where the missiles had been stored and disarm the soldiers who guarded them.

Their orders were to avoid the rest of the military compound and hopefully a small-scale war. The missiles would be disarmed and later transported back to the States.

As for Valisimo's soldiers, without leadership and financial support, the People's Revolutionary Army would be nothing but a disorganized bunch of ragtag farmers and mercenaries. They would scatter like ants in a stepped-on anthill.

At least for the present, the threat they posed would be over.

And Jake would be on his way home.

The notion wasn't as pleasant as it should have been. Jake knew why.

It didn't matter. There was no room in his life for Mary Alice Parker or any other woman, no matter how tempting she might be. He was a failure when it came to marriage and family. His work just didn't allow enough time to fulfill that kind of commitment, or perhaps he just wasn't much of a husband. After Marla, he knew that only too well. Soon Allie would be gone from his life, and it was undoubtedly the best thing for both of them.

Still, he found himself walking back to the house, more eager than he should have been to see her. As he neared the front steps, he couldn't help thinking of yesterday and how damned lucky she was that he had gone to look for her.

But he had never trusted Rico, and when Jake couldn't find Allie and Rico also seemed to be missing, his sixth sense had kicked in and he'd gone in search of her. When he had seen her running down Rico's front porch stairs, the little boy lying unconscious on the ground, he had guessed what must have happened. It had taken sheer force of will not to pound Rico Valisimo into the dirt, but considering their nebulous position, it wouldn't have been a very smart move.

Jake shoved open the door and stepped into the high-ceilinged entry. When he walked into the living room, he was relieved to see Allie right where he'd warned her to stay—in no uncertain terms— safely inside the general's house, which was heavily staffed with servants. He was, however, surprised to find the little boy who had defended her so bravely, sitting on the sofa beside her.

Miguel jumped up as Jake approached and very smartly saluted. *"Buenas tardes,* Señor Major Jake."

Jake saluted him back. *"Buenas tardes,* Private Miguel." The little boy grinned and a memory appeared of his own son, now nearly Miguel's age. They were playing ball back then, he recalled. Michael had caught it neatly between his legs, and the grin on the little boy's face made Jake feel like the proudest father on earth.

He thought of his son and worry hit him as it always did, fear that something might happen to him and he wouldn't be there. He forced the terrifying thought away.

"Thank you for taking care of Allie while I was gone," he said to the boy.

"She is my friend," the child said simply. "But now that you are home, I must go. Conchita will be angry if I do not help her with the laundry." He flashed another grin. *"Adios,* Señorita Allie."

"Adios, Miguel."

As soon as the screen door slammed, Allie turned in Jake's direction. He recognized the look in those big baby blues and figured he wasn't going to like what she was about to say.

He walked over to an ornate antique sideboard to pour himself a drink. "Go ahead, spit it out. What are you dying to say?"

"I want to take him home with me."

The glass jerked in his hand. "What?"

"I said—"

"I heard what you said. The answer is no."

"He doesn't have any parents. The housekeeper says his father was a *Zapatista* sympathizer who was killed by members of a group called the Red Mask. His mother died a couple of years after her husband."

Jake carried his drink, a rum and Coke, over to the sofa and sat down beside her. "Listen to me, Allie. Even if we got him back to the States, it wouldn't be legal."

"Once we got there, I could adopt him. I could—"

"You're a single woman, Allie. Even if the authorities would grant you custody of the boy—which they might not—it takes a lot of money to accomplish a foreign adoption."

Allie blinked and he could tell she was trying not to cry. "I hate to think of just leaving him here."

Jake slid an arm around her shoulders. "Listen, honey. There are thousands of kids in Mexico like Miguel. You can't take all of them home."

She brushed at a tear that had escaped down her cheek. "I don't want to take all of them home. I just want to take Miguel."

Jake kissed her forehead. "You're really something, Mary Alice Parker. You know that?"

Allie turned and slid her arms around his neck, and for a minute he just held her. He had to force himself to let her go.

"I've got to go up and change for supper," he said. "I'll be back as soon as I'm finished."

Allie nodded and glanced away, her expression sadly resigned.

Jake sighed as he climbed the stairs, understanding her pain all too well. He had a child he loved and worried about. He wanted to be with him. Allie had fallen a little in love with Miguel and she wanted to protect him.

Tomorrow they would leave and it was going to be tough on everyone. On Allie, little Miguel—

He glanced back into the living room to where Allie sat, and realized, for perhaps the first time, how hard this was going to be on him.

Chapter Twenty

"The captain wants to see you in his office."

Dan Reynolds nodded to Elaine Sawyer, the young blond street cop who had brought him the news. "I've got a couple of phone calls to make. Tell him I'll be there as soon as I'm finished."

"Captain Caruthers says now."

Dan looked up from the stack of messages he had been thumbing through on his desk. "Fine," he grumbled. "I'll go right now."

Elaine arched a finely plucked eyebrow and walked away, leaving him feeling guilty. It wasn't her fault he was in such a crappy mood, but he hadn't slept very well last night and he was pretty much still pissed at Barb Wallace about it.

Frigging women. The lights had been off at Barb's apartment when Dan had arrived last night. He'd gone up and knocked anyway, even though he

could see she and the boys weren't at home. With
the reason for his visit more than clear, it was obvious that she had run from him. Maybe he shouldn't
have been so pushy, but dammit, he knew she
wanted him just as badly as he wanted her, and he
was tired of letting her hide from her feelings.

Then again, maybe it was just as well. The last
thing he needed was to get involved with a ball
buster like Barb. God must have been looking out
for him last night.

Tired and grouchy from his lack of sleep, Dan
jerked open the door to the captain's office before
he noticed the two men standing on the other side
of the big glass windows.

"Glad you could make it, Reynolds," Captain
Caruthers said sarcastically.

Dan flicked a glance at his partner, Archie Hollis,
who sat in a chair in front of the captain's battered
desk, then turned his attention to the two men
dressed in dark suits, legs slightly splayed, hands
folded in front of them, looking exactly like the
government agents they undoubtedly were.

"What's going on?"

"Detectives Reynolds and Hollis," the captain
said by way of introduction. "Meet Special Agents
Morris and Duchefski, FBI."

Wondering what the hell FBI agents were doing
on his turf, Dan shifted his gaze to his captain then
stiffened at the hard look on Tom Caruthers's face.

"Detective Reynolds. Did I or did I not give you
a direct order to leave Felix Baranoff alone?"

Inwardly Dan winced, his anger at Barb Wallace
heating up again. "Yes, sir, you did."

"Then why were you observed outside his building yesterday afternoon?"

Dan glanced at Archie, who was glaring at him nearly as hard as the captain. "Observed by who?"

"Both the ATF and FBI are involved in surveillance of the building. The question is what were *you* doing there?"

Dan straightened uncomfortably in his chair. "I discovered a friend of mine had gone to see Mr. Baranoff. She wanted to ask him some questions in regard to the disappearance of her friend, Mary Alice Parker. I was trying to head her off before she caused any trouble."

"Then you had nothing to do with the woman's visit?"

"Not directly, no."

"How about indirectly?"

Dan took a steadying breath, wishing he could wring Barb's pretty little neck. "I might have mentioned that Ms. Parker had been seen near one of Felix Baranoff's yachts the day she disappeared. I believe my friend thought there might be some connection."

"So she was taking it upon herself to find out? Considering what a formidable man Felix Baranoff can be, I'd say that took a fair amount of guts."

"If there's one thing this particular lady isn't short on, sir, it's guts." At least she always managed to stand up to him.

"Actually, there *is* a connection between the two," the captain said, surprising him. "The day she turned up missing, Mary Alice Parker was aboard the *Dynasty II*. The yacht left San Diego Bay headed for Mexico. You'll be happy to know that at this moment, Ms. Parker is alive and well, the guest of a man named Alejandro Valisimo at his home in Belize."

Dan felt a swell of relief so big a lump formed in his throat. "That's really good news, sir."

"Unfortunately, it isn't news we can release. Not at this time. Through their contact in Belize, the ATF has learned that the lady has become an integral part of a highly secret operation that should be concluded sometime today. Once it is, she'll be able to phone her parents and assure them she's all right. Until then, word of this has got to be kept top secret."

Archie Duggan scratched the thin red hair on his head. "You guys are saying this operation has somethin' to do with Baranoff, right?"

Caruthers nodded. "ATF and FBI agents are moving into position as we speak. The good news is, it won't be long before this whole damned mess is over."

Dan felt a second wave of relief. "That's the reason you stopped me from questioning Baranoff."

"I'd been warned off the case in no uncertain terms. Now that I know the Parker girl is safe, I feel a whole lot better about it."

Dan did, too. He couldn't wait to tell Barb the good news. He smiled as he walked out the door. Maybe she'd be grateful enough to invite him over for dinner again. Maybe she would ask him to stay after the kids went to sleep.

Damned if he didn't hope so.

Praying her nervousness didn't show, Allie descended the stairs dressed once more in her khaki shorts and tank top, prepared to leave for the return trip to the rendezvous point, though if Jake's bust went down as planned, she wouldn't be leaving on Valisimo's plane. Jake wore his fatigues, his automatic pistol casually strapped to his waist. Rico and the general waited at the bottom of the stairs.

"I have spoken to Colonel Fernandez," Valisimo said. "He is more than satisfied with the training you have provided our officers in the use of the missiles. It appears, Major Dawson, this phase of your assignment has been successfully completed." He turned to Rico. "Since that is the case, I will leave it in the capable hands of my son to arrange payment, as previously agreed."

Valisimo extended a hand and Jake shook it. "Perhaps in the future, our paths will cross again," Valisimo said. "Have a safe journey home, Major Dawson." He made a slight nod in Allie's direction. "Señorita Parker."

Rico stepped forward as the general turned and headed down the hall and disappeared into his study. "I imagine you will wish to examine the merchandise."

"Mr. Baranoff has instructed me to do so, yes."

So far no mention had been made of the awful scene yesterday with Rico in front of his house. Though he was far cooler to her than he had been, the general's son behaved as if the encounter had never occurred. Allie imagined he preferred to ignore any kind of failure, especially that of a personal nature.

"The items are ready," he said. "If you will please follow me . . ." Rico led them into a sunny room at the back of the house where several wooden crates sat open on the floor, each oozing handfuls of strawlike packing material. Wondering what the boxes were for, Allie sucked in a breath at the sight of the long antique oak table in the center of the room that glittered with an incredible array of pre-Columbian artifacts.

She tossed a glance at Jake, but he revealed no surprise. Allie had assumed that payment for the missiles would come in the form of gold or perhaps Mexican or American currency, not illegal antiquities. Apparently Jake had known from the start. He simply walked forward and began to look over the valuable objects on the table, picking up a statue of a man about eight inches tall carved in soft gray stone, turning it into the light to examine it more closely.

There were a number of similar small statues, some of the figures sitting, others standing, all recognizable as Mayan and probably from somewhere nearby. One stood out from the rest, a cube of stone maybe ten inches square, reddish in color that looked like the head of a dog. Its teeth were bared in a soundless snarl and its eyes protruded ominously. Jake studied the piece, then set it back down and picked up a lovely jade figurine, one of half a dozen.

The opposite end of the table held fine examples of Mayan pottery, and there was a rectangular piece of granite that had been carved into a calendar of some sort. But it was the objects made of gold that were most impressive, necklaces, earplugs, something that might have been worn as a crown.

"I'm not an expert," Jake said, "but it looks genuine to me." It went without saying that if it weren't, the general would have Baranoff to deal with and no more weapons of any sort would be available for future purchase.

"You may be certain they are exactly what they seem."

"And the mask?"

Rico walked over to one of the crates, knelt, and lifted something out. Unlike the thin, pounded gold used to fashion the exceptional pieces on the table, this was heavy, a mask created in solid gold and rich green jade. As Rico set it on the table in front of Jake, Allie saw that the mask was carved to look like a dragon.

"The mask of Itzamna," Rico said. "The celestial dragon, over a thousand years old. Many think it does not exist. Those who believe it does would pay a fortune to own it."

Jake carefully lifted the mask into the light, and sunshine glittered off the brilliant, heavy gold. Whichever way the mask was turned, the eyes, carved of purest green jade, seemed to remain on the beholder. The teeth were also of jade as well as the inner portion of the ears. It was exquisite. The most magnificent piece of artwork that Allie had ever seen. No wonder Felix Baranoff was willing to sell his soul in order to own it.

Jake handed the mask back to Rico. "Everything appears to be in order. As soon as these are packed and ready to load, our business will be concluded."

Rico didn't reply, just walked into the hall and snapped his fingers. Several servants came on the run. Rico motioned for them to pack the objects on the table, and then Jake and Allie watched as the task was carefully completed.

A few minutes later, the crates were carried to the front of the house, where a Jeep was waiting to haul passengers and art to the plane. From the

corner of her eye as she stepped out onto the
porch, Allie saw Rico draw Jake a little away. Instead
of heading for the Jeep, she eased back out of sight
beside the door so she could hear what they were
saying.

"The woman," Rico said. "She knows more than
my father would like."

"The woman's my responsibility. If she poses a
problem, I'll take care of it."

She could almost see his jaw harden, as it had
yesterday on the porch. "You had better see that
you do."

Jake started walking, and at the approach of his
heavy boots, Allie turned and started down the
steps to the Jeep, wondering how many people
wanted her dead. Baranoff, certainly. Now Rico
and his father.

She shivered as she climbed into the back of the
Jeep.

Standing in a pay phone in the coffee shop across
the street from the police station, Archie Hollis
dialed the private number he had been given but
knew better than to use except in the gravest emergency.

A man's deep voice answered at the opposite
end. "Yes?"

"Your deal went wrong. There's ATF and Feds
all over the place. Get out if you can."

The phone clicked off without a reply. Hollis
doubted the guy could get out of the building
without getting busted, but Baranoff was the type
who'd be prepared for any emergency, and Archie
was regularly paid some very big bucks, at least by

his standards, for a tip-off just like this. If the guy got away, Archie imagined he'd be well rewarded.

He hung up the phone and ambled over to the counter. "Give me a hot dog and a couple of Diet Cokes to go." He paid for them with a pair of wadded-up dollar bills he found in his coat pocket and carried the bag back to his office, stopping to leave one of the soft drinks on Dan Reynolds's desk as he passed.

Archie wondered if Baranoff would get away, thought of the abrupt end an arrest would mean to his extra monthly dough, and hoped like hell that Baranoff got lucky.

Jake settled into the Jeep next to a young corporal named Nuñez, who was their driver, and the short Mexican cranked the engine. They had just started up the driveway when Jake noticed a group of soldiers making their way toward the house. They were carrying a litter, he saw, and cold dread slipped down his spine.

"Roberto . . ." Allie said softly from behind him, the word laced with fear.

"Keep going," Jake told the driver. "We've got a plane to catch." Corporal Nuñez pressed the accelerator, his neck craned toward the group of men. They had almost made it past when one of the soldiers shouted for the driver to stop.

He was speaking such rapid Spanish, Jake lost part of the conversation but he heard the word *policia* and knew Bobby Santos was saying that he was a cop.

"I am sorry, Major," the driver said. "But Lieutenant Ortega is my superior and I am ordered to stop."

Jake flashed a quick look at Allie. "Ten minutes," he said in English. "That's all we need." Then he climbed out of the Jeep and walked over to talk to the men.

"We found him about ten kilometers from the camp," the young lieutenant said. "He has been shot."

"That's right," Jake said evenly. "I'm the one who shot him. Roberto Santos is the man who caused the general's plane to crash. He was trying to divert the aircraft and steal the cargo. The general is well aware of what this man has done."

"He . . . he's lying," Bobby panted. "He's . . . police." Bobby was covered in blood, his shirt ripped in so many places it hung by a few thin threads from his shoulders. The wound in his chest smelled putrid and crawled with maggots, his arm had gone purple with gangrene.

Jake drew himself up, exuding the cool authority that came with the years he'd spent in the service. "As I said, the general is well aware of this man's actions. We both believed he was dead. It's a miracle he isn't, and equally obvious he soon will be. Whatever you want to do with him, that's your business. In the meantime, we have an appointment in Mexico to keep. Would you like to be the one to explain to the general why we're not there when we should be?"

The lieutenant seemed uncertain, his eyes darting from Jake to Roberto and back again. He glanced toward the airstrip in the open fields behind a row of trees where a twin-engine Cessna sat with the engines idling.

"I am sorry for the delay," the lieutenant said. "Please proceed, Major Dawson."

Jake turned and swiftly walked back to the Jeep.

He wanted Allie away from the house when the choppers arrived and they would be there any minute. The Jeep had almost made it to the airfield when the radio erupted with static and instructions for their return to the house blared over the speaker.

The driver glanced up just as Jake pulled his pistol. "Sorry." He slid back the action on the Glock. "You can go back if you want, but the Jeep stays here."

"But my orders—"

"Pull over. Now."

One glance at the gun Jake pressed against the base of his skull behind his ear and the driver did as he was told. As soon as the key was turned off, Jake reached over, popped the snap on the holster the corporal was wearing, and jerked out his pistol. It was the same new Heckler-Koch .45 caliber he had seen a number of the officers wearing, the latest model weapon worn by the U.S. Special Forces. Jake wondered where the general had gotten the guns and how many smuggled antiquities it had taken to pay for them.

Jake heard the distant whop, whop, whop of choppers. "You can go, but I'd advise you to do it quietly." He pointed the gun in silent warning, and the corporal climbed out of the Jeep and backed away with his hands in the air. *"Vámanos!"* Jake commanded. *"Pronto!"*

The soldier took off running back toward the house and Jake quickly jumped out of the Jeep and slid behind the wheel.

"Where are we going?" Allie asked.

"Over there behind those trees. We need to find some cover." By the time they'd reached the safety of the trees, the heavy thud of rotor blades filled the air. Jake rounded the Jeep and helped Allie down. "Just stay low. We should be safe here."

Five armed helicopter gunships arrived within seconds of each other, and the minute Allie realized some of them were heading toward the military compound, she shot to her feet.

"Oh, my God, I never thought about them attacking the camp! What about Miguel?"

Jake glanced in that direction, his own thoughts turning to the boy. "The women's tents are at the edge of the compound. The men won't be headed in that direction. Miguel should be safe there." But he could hear rounds of ammunition being fired and a stray bullet might hit the child. One glance at Allie's terrified face and his decision was made.

"Give me your word you'll stay right here and I'll go after the boy."

She nodded, her eyes a little frantic. "I promise. I won't move a muscle." Her hands were trembling as he pressed the Heckler-Koch into her palm.

"You got any idea how to use this?"

"I've never shot a pistol, but I've watched the way they do it on TV and I've seen you do it. I think I know how it's done."

He slid back the action and took off the safety. "If you have to shoot, keep your arms straight out in front of you. Just aim and pull the trigger." He showed her once quickly. "And forgodsake—don't hit me when I'm on my way back."

Hoping she wouldn't need the gun, he headed into the trees. On the opposite side of a clearing up ahead, he saw a group of armed men moving silently into the jungle toward the missile tent. Retrieving the Stingers was a top priority and it was obvious the men sent to accomplish the task were an elite, well-trained force. As he started toward the airfield, hoping to skirt the encampment and reach the area where the women's tents were set up, Jake watched the men moving with efficient, deadly speed, spreading out until the tent was completely surrounded.

Clearly outnumbered, the general's soldiers tossed down their weapons without ever firing a shot.

Jake kept moving, careful to stay low and out of sight, staying just at the edge of the rain forest. Behind him, two of the choppers landed in an open field behind the general's house and in minutes the structure was surrounded. Uniformed men rushed in through the front and back doors. Jake heard several bursts of gunfire coming from inside the house. A series of shots returned, then silence.

He paused long enough to see the general, hands on his head, walking at gunpoint out the front door, followed by half a dozen heavily armed men, most of them *Federales*, several others that appeared to be FBI or ATF.

Rico was nowhere to be seen.

Jake continued toward the military camp. The officers who had arrived for the missile training had disbursed to their home bases last night, leaving only the original force of PRA men. At the sight of the gunships and realizing the missiles had already been seized, most of the soldiers, clearly the inferior force, fired a few feeble rounds and disappeared into the jungle.

Jake kept moving toward the tents he could see in the clearing up ahead. Most of the women had fled into the rain forest. Those who remained crouched behind downed logs or hid behind overturned wooden tables. He glanced around, hoping to spot the boy. Sporadic gunfire echoed in the distance and he prayed the child hadn't run in that direction. Moving between two canvas tents, he came out the other side, his pistol gripped in his hand. One of the women screamed and started running, disappearing into the foliage. Then he saw the boy.

"Señor Major Jake!" The child ran toward him, his thin little legs moving like pistons across the hard-packed earth. Jake knelt and scooped Miguel into his arms, and the little boy clamped on to his neck. He could feel the small body trembling, the narrow shoulders vibrating with his effort to hold back tears. Jake smoothed the boy's dark hair back from his dirty face.

"It's all right, son. No one's going to hurt you. This isn't going to last much longer."

Still, the little boy clung to him like a monkey to a tree, and Jake found himself hating the idea of leaving the child behind nearly as much as Allie did. Still, they couldn't possibly take him back to the States, and Miguel's presence was only going to make the parting more difficult for Allie.

Returning the same way he had come, Jake made his way toward the airstrip and finally reached the Jeep.

"Miguel!" Allie dropped the pistol down on the seat of the Jeep and started racing toward them. As soon as she reached them, Jake pressed the child into her outstretched arms.

"He's all right. Just a little shook up is all."

"You're safe," Allie crooned, holding the little boy tightly against her, stroking the child's dark head. "The fighting's almost over."

Miguel didn't answer, which was a statement in itself. Jake knew he was trying very hard not to cry.

Allie looked off toward the encampment. The gunfire had stopped, and through a break in the trees, Jake could see uniformed Mexican *Federales* prowling the camp, looking for any of the PRA soldiers who might still be around.

"What will happen to Valisimo's men?" Allie asked, cradling the child against her shoulder. "Will the Mexicans go after them?"

"I don't think so. Eventually Valisimo's men will join up with the rest of his army, but without leadership and finances, their effort won't last long."

"It's kind of sad," Allie said, hugging Miguel a little tighter. "They only wanted a better way of life."

"There are people at home who want a better life. They work for it through peaceful means. That's what has to happen here."

"I know, but . . ."

Jake reached over and grabbed her hand. "Come on. Let's finish this and get out of here." He helped her into the Jeep, settled Miguel in her lap, and went around to the driver's side to fire up the engine.

It didn't take long to get his passengers and cargo of priceless antiquities back to the general's house, which buzzed with *Federales*, FBI, and ATF agents.

One of them, a lanky man with thick gray hair, walked toward him. "You Dawson?"

"That's right."

The man stuck out his hand. "Inspector Carmine."

"Nice to meet you, Carmine." He motioned to the woman beside him. "This is Allie Parker."

Carmine smiled. "We know all about Ms. Parker.

We were told she was the one who uncovered the PRA's connection to Ruiz and his Colombian narco-guerrilla operation. Their missile deal is dead in the water now, but we'll be keeping a closer eye on them from here on out, thanks to you. Nice to meet you, Ms. Parker.'' He reached out and shook Allie's hand. ''Looks like you both did a damned good job here.''

Jake surveyed the activity around them. ''Any casualties?''

''None of our guys. A couple of the general's men were wounded. They're being looked after now. Rico Valisimo is dead.''

Beside him, Allie's head snapped up. She set Miguel on his feet and took hold of the child's small brown hand.

''He try to shoot his way out?''

''Looks that way. He went up against three of our best agents. I guess he found out the hard way he wasn't invincible.''

Jake thought of Rico knocking a defenseless child unconscious, of his intention to force himself on Allie. ''Not much of a loss. What happened to Roberto Santos?''

''They're flying him out with the wounded, but the guy's in pretty bad shape. Hard to tell if he'll make it.''

''And the general?''

''They're questioning him now. Odds are good he'll testify with you and Ms. Parker against Felix Baranoff in exchange for a deal.''

Jake nodded. ''Valisimo's a patriot. Rico and the Russian are the bad guys here.''

''Yeah, that's what we figured.'' He turned his

attention to Allie. "I imagine you're anxious to call your folks, let 'em know you're okay."

"Yes. I know how worried they must be."

"As soon as we get word the operation in San Diego has been completed, you can use my satellite phone."

"Thank you. I'd appreciate that."

The next half-hour was spent mopping up. Jake had a lengthy report to write but no one seemed in a hurry to get it. He spoke to Carmine about Miguel, and the agent promised to speak to the Mexican authorities.

Allie was still standing next to the boy when Agent Carmine reappeared with one of the Mexican officers. "This is Colonel Fuentes. He's come for the boy. He says he'll personally see the child is placed in a home where he'll be well looked after."

Allie's fingers tightened around the little boy's hand. "I—I'd be willing to take him, if you could arrange it. I realize there would be a number of complications, but—"

"I am sorry, Señorita Parker." The colonel's face showed obvious regret. "There are procedures for this sort of thing. When you return to your country, if you are still interested in adopting the boy, I'm sure Agent Dawson would be able to help you discover the best way to proceed."

Allie's eyes filled with tears. "Are you sure you couldn't make an exception just this once?"

"I'm afraid it is out of the question. As I said, I am sorry."

Jake slid an arm around her waist. "There's nothing you can do, Allie. Try not to make it any harder on the boy."

She bit her lip and glanced away, fighting not

to cry. "You're right. I'm sorry." Forcing herself
to smile, she knelt beside little Miguel. "You were
really brave today. Did I tell you that?"

He slowly shook his head.

"I was so proud of you, Miguel."

The child looked up at her shyly and smiled.

"You were a brave boy today, and now, for a little
while longer, you have to be brave again." She
turned to the colonel, a tall, imposing, dark-
skinned man with sympathetic eyes. "This is Colonel Fuentes. He's going to find you a new home,
so you won't have to live in the jungle anymore."

"I like living in the jungle."

"I know you do, but you need a family, Miguel,
someone who will take care of you."

"You could be my family."

Her throat worked as she swallowed back a lump
of tears. "I'm sorry, sweetheart. I'd love to take
you home with me, but I can't. You have to stay
here."

"But I want to go with you."

She blinked hard and swallowed. "The colonel
is going to take very good care of you." She drew
the child close and hugged him. "But I promise
I'll never forget you." She swung her canvas purse
down from her shoulder, dug inside, and drew out
her wallet. Her hands trembled as she pulled out
her driver's license and handed it to the boy.
"Here. This is for you." Miguel accepted it with
small, grubby brown hands. "Now you have a picture of me so you won't forget me either."

The little boy clutched the license to his chest
as if it were made of Mayan gold. "I won't forget
you, Señorita Allie. I promise."

Allie hugged him hard and the boy clung to her

neck. Both of them were crying when she pulled away.

Miguel looked up at Jake. He swiped at his tears with a fist, leaving streaks in the dirt on his cheeks. "Goodbye Señor Major Dawson."

Jake rested a hand on the little boy's dark head. *"Vaya con Dios, Miguelito."*

The colonel hoisted the boy into his arms and started walking away. Miguel watched them over Fuentes's shoulder, his black eyes glistening with unshed tears. He didn't say anything, just waved over the colonel's shoulder until both of them disappeared out of sight among the trees.

Jake looked at Allie, who still stood waving though Miguel could no longer be seen. Jake turned her into his arms and held her while she cried.

"I'm sorry," she said. "He's just . . . he's just such a sweet little boy."

"It's all right. If more people felt the way you do, there'd be a lot less suffering in the world."

She clung to him a moment longer, then drew a little away, brushing the tears from her cheeks. "I wish things could be different."

"I know." Having lost a son the same age as Miguel, Jake knew only too well what she was feeling. But there was nothing he could say that would make her feel any better. Only time could do that.

He was glad when Inspector Carmine reappeared, forcing their thoughts in a different direction.

"We're just about finished here," Carmine said. "They picked up Hector Chavoyas, Rico's fence, about ten minutes ago in Mexico City."

"Nice work," Jake said. He watched the last of

the men leave the house. "What'll happen to the Mayan artifacts?"

"They'll be turned over to the government of Belize. That was the deal we made when they agreed to let us into the country." Jake nodded, glad such incredible antiquities would be shared with the descendents of the people who had created them in the first place.

"We've got a chopper ready to fly you out," Carmine said to Jake, casting an assessing glance at Allie. "Question is, would you rather go to Belmopan and head straight back to the States or spend the weekend on the beach in Belize City. You've certainly earned a couple of days R&R, and the government will foot the bill. But it's up to you, of course."

Jake looked at Allie, and for the first time, it hit him that this was all really over. Once they got back to California, the feisty little blonde he had come to admire would no longer be part of his life. In the past few days, he had done his best to distance himself, to prepare both of them for this very moment. Now that it had finally arrived, he wasn't nearly ready to give her up.

His chest squeezed. God, he was going to miss her. Damn, why did life have to be so full of difficult turns?

He looked down at Allie's shining blond head and knew if the decision were his, he would grab every moment he could get with her. But it wasn't fair to Allie. Sooner or later, their relationship would come to a very dead end. It would be less painful for both of them if that end happened now.

Allie glanced up, straight into his eyes. Her own held a look of uncertainty. "I can't speak for Jake, but I . . . I could use a little time on the beach."

The tightness in his chest slowly eased. He reached out and took hold of her hand, wanting these last few days more than anything he could remember. "So could I."

"Then it's settled." Carmine turned and started walking. "Grab your gear and follow me."

Chapter Twenty-one

After a teary phone call to her parents telling them she was safe and coming home in just a few days, checking on Whiskers, who was doing just fine, and receiving their promise they would call worried friends, Allie set off with Jake for their much-needed R&R.

The weekend they'd been promised in Belize City turned out to be three glorious days on Ambergris Caye, an hour's boat ride from the city. The caye was a narrow strip of land twenty-five miles long and four miles wide with incredible white sand beaches and water such a beautiful bright blue-green it made your eyes hurt to look at it.

They stayed in a thatched-roof cottage surrounded by palm trees, nestled in the sand at the edge of the sea. Allie flung her canvas purse into a bamboo chair just inside the doorway and flopped down on the queen-sized bed with a big grin on her face.

"I can't believe this. I've never seen anything more beautiful."

Jake came down on top of her, bracing himself on his elbows. "Neither have I . . . except maybe you."

Allie slid her arms around his neck. "What do you think we ought to do first? Explore the town, go snorkeling, or just take a walk on the beach?"

Jake stared down at her as if she had lost her mind. "Not even close," he said, bending his head to take her mouth in a deep, toe-curling kiss.

Allie kissed him back, agreeing with him completely. In the last few days, she had missed their lovemaking. In the time since they had first come together at the base of the orchid-strewn waterfall, she had begun to crave Jake's touches, his kisses, having him inside her. If these days on the beach were the last they would ever share, she meant to enjoy every one of them.

She was in love with Jake Dawson. Perhaps the only man she would ever love. But she wasn't so naïve as to believe that loving someone was enough to conquer every hurdle. The life Jake had chosen held no place in it for her, and Allie was determined to accept that. In the meantime, they had three whole days. She refused to let anything spoil them.

Certainly that incredible afternoon was one of the best days she could remember. The sex was as great as it always was, maybe better, since neither of them had thought they would ever be together this way again. It was several hours later, both of them sated and lazily content, that they roused themselves enough to explore the little village of

San Pedro, deciding they would enjoy the balance of the day at a leisurely pace.

Before leaving Belize City, they had bought a few essentials: bathing suits—Jake's no more than a scrap of yellow cloth, her own purple-flowered cotton not much bigger—shorts and T-shirts, tennis shoes for Jake, and a pair of darling silver sandals to go with the backless blue sundress Allie found in a cute little open-air boutique.

Allie wore a T-shirt with an angelfish on the front as they wandered barefoot through the white sand streets between colorful clapboard houses, poking their heads into the tourist shops. San Pedro had three thousand inhabitants, Allie learned, reading one of the signs at the outskirts of the village, the occupants, it seemed, mostly *mestizo*. With Spanish the local language, they had no trouble getting around, and the island people seemed cheerful and friendly.

As the afternoon wore on, they stopped at a cantina called the El Serape for tall tropical rum drinks with chunks of pineapple and tiny paper umbrellas on top. The music of a steel band echoed from down the street and they wandered in that direction, winding up in a small seafood restaurant for dinner, then wandering back to the cottage, where they made love two more times and drifted into a deep, refreshing sleep.

Allie awakened the following morning with more energy than she had felt in days, nudging Jake awake with a kiss that led to more interesting things. After a traditional caye's breakfast of fried jacks, eggs, and bacon accompanied by a tall glass of soursop juice and thick black, Caribbean-style coffee, they decided to prowl the beach.

Later in the day, they rented a thirty-foot sailboat,

which Jake claimed Allie had a natural talent for crewing. Allie figured that meant he liked the part where she let the boat drift and they made love on the deck beneath the warm, saturating sun.

Allie wore her sundress that night, and after a supper of succulent grilled snapper, conch, and shrimp, they slow-danced in the sand to the distant music of a reggae band. Allie could feel the weekend slipping away, but she refused to think about it. *Tomorrow,* she silently told herself. *Just be happy you still have one more day.*

That day arrived all too quickly. Their last morning on Ambergris Caye, they went scuba diving, a sport Allie had learned when she worked on the cruise ship.

"They were giving lessons in one of the pools," she said with a shrug. "I thought it might be fun. Since then I've only tried it a couple of times. The water's pretty murky around San Diego and a whole lot colder than here."

Grinning, Jake shook his head. "I'm beginning to think there isn't anything you can't do."

"Well, I'm hardly an expert, but I'm right about diving, aren't I? It is kind of fun."

Actually, it was more than just fun. It was incredible. In the crystal waters of a nearby reef, Allie saw tropical fish of every color, shape, and size, sting rays and skates, grouper, some sort of massive sunfish, and what Jake told her were harmless nurse sharks, though there was a very good chance he wasn't telling her exactly the truth.

It was dark by the time they finished an early supper and returned to the cottage, the plan, by unspoken agreement, to spend the evening alone in the cozy seaside cottage. A storm was rolling in.

And it was their last night in Belize.

Fresh out of the shower, Allie looked over at Jake, who stood in front of the window with a towel around his hips, staring out at the clouds and lightning. His hair was still damp, and the light from the lamp beside the bed shimmered on beads of water that still clung to his shoulders. The muscles there seemed taut, a subtle tension that hadn't been there until tonight.

Allie's gaze ran over his magnificent body, the harshly beautiful profile of his face. She thought how much she had come to love just looking at him, watching him smile, or simply walk across the room. She thought of how empty her life would be without him, and her throat closed up.

They would be leaving in the morning. It was over between them. She couldn't ignore reality any longer.

"Jake . . . ?"

He turned at the sound of her voice. Though he tried to muster a smile, a darkness lurked in his eyes that hadn't been there before. "It's been three terrific days, hasn't it?"

She worked to smile in return. "Absolutely. The very best."

"I'll never forget this place." He started walking toward her. "Or you, Allie."

She went into his arms and they closed around her, encircling her in his warmth. "L.A. isn't that far from San Diego," she said softly. "Maybe we could see each other . . . once in a while."

"Yeah, maybe we could." But the regret in his voice said they never would. He would be off somewhere, working undercover again. She might not see him for months at a time, and worrying about him would be torture.

She looked up at him, blinked against the sudden burn of tears. "It's over, isn't it, Jake?"

His gaze drifted off to the window above the bed. Distant lightning flashed in a turbulent sky and thunder rumbled as the storm moving toward the island. "You knew it would be . . . sooner or later."

She rested her head on his chest and felt the brush of his jaw against her hair. "Yes . . . I knew."

"Once I get back, I'll be given a new assignment. I'll disappear again. God only knows how long I'll be gone this time. That kind of life isn't what you need, Allie. You deserve something better than that."

She glanced up. "What about you, Jake? Don't you deserve more, too? Don't you want more out of life than just a job?"

He sighed into the shadows of the room. "I make a lousy husband, Allie. I've tried it, remember? I won't risk that kind of failure again—especially not with someone I care about."

Her throat was hurting. She didn't want to cry but she was afraid she was going to. "I'm going to miss you, Jake."

His hold tightened around her. He cradled the back of her head against his chest. "God, honey, I'm going to miss you, too. More than you'll ever know."

Her heart hurt. She had known it would be hard to lose him, but she hadn't expected the pain to start so soon. "Make love to me, Jake. I don't want to think about tomorrow. I don't want to think about anything at all. This is our last night together. Tonight I just want to feel."

The blue of his eyes seemed to darken. There was a turbulence in his expression that somehow matched the storm. Framing her face in his big

suntanned hands, he bent his head and very gently
kissed her. Allie kissed him back with all the love
in her heart.

"Jake . . ." she whispered, hoping he wouldn't
hear the faint note of anguish. Perhaps he did, for
his mouth crushed down over hers. It was a wild,
taking, plundering kiss. A scorching, soul-numbing,
heart-stopping kiss, and yet there was so much tenderness, so much yearning, it made the lump in
her throat expand. She reached toward him, slid
her arms around his neck, felt the hot, wet glide
of his tongue and the brush of his fingers beneath
the underside of her breast.

His mouth moved along her throat and over her
shoulders. He drew the towel from her body and
let it drop next to his in a soft white heap on
the floor. She wanted to touch him, kiss him. She
wanted to know the line of ridges that marked his
spine, the curve of muscle across his chest, the
indentation of his navel. Her hands moved over
his skin, testing each of those things, memorizing
them.

Jake kissed his way along her throat and shoulders. Very gently, he cupped a breast, his fingers
stroking slowly over her nipple, making it swell and
distend. Damp black hair brushed her skin as he
lowered his head and took the tip into his mouth,
began to suckle the fullness. Allie arched toward
him, trembling, her knees turning pliant, barely
holding her up. Outside the window, she could
hear the sea washing up on the beach, the soft
suction of sand being swept back into the water.

Jake's hands skimmed over her body, gliding
down to her waist, over her hips, her bottom, sepa-
rating and cupping each globe as he kissed her
again, lifted her, and pressed her into his hardened

sex. He was thick and rigid, incredibly hot, and she wanted to feel that heat inside her.

A soft little mew escaped from her throat, but it was muffled by the rumble of thunder and Jake's mouth coming down over hers. Her hand trembled where it rested on his chest and she could feel his heart beating like the wings of a gull trapped in the storm. He trailed soft kisses along her throat and over her breasts, his fingers sifting through the damp curls at the juncture of her legs, sliding between the hot, wet folds of her sex. The sigh of the wind through the palms mimicked the sound she made as he gently began to stroke her.

"Jake . . ." she whispered, aching for him now, needing him like the island needed the rain. Her eyes slowly closed as he lifted her up and carried her over to the bed, gently lowered her to the center of the mattress. He reached over and turned out the light, leaving the room in shadows, then followed her down, his hardness nestling between her legs.

A tender, erotic kiss followed. Thunder rumbled, rattling the windows, mixing with the thunderous cadence of her heart. She opened to the hot, probing pressure of his tongue and felt a surge of love for him as raw and powerful as the storm. Warm, moist kisses trailed across her shoulders, breasts, and belly. Damp, steamy kisses slid over the flat spot below her navel. Jake moved lower, kissing the inside of her thighs, making her stomach contract and her heart tremble.

He eased her legs farther apart, pressed kisses into the soft blond curls above her sex then found the rigid bud at the entrance and took the sensitive flesh into his mouth. Allie bit back a sob as sensation hit her. Lightning flashed, a jagged fork of gold that illuminated her face and betrayed her pleasure. Jake watched as she began to climax, hot desire in his eyes. Allie cried out his name as a second climax shook her. She laced her fingers in his hair, her body quivering beneath his determined assault.

For moments she simply lay there, throbbing with newly spent desire, the patter of the rain against the thatching on the roof forming a soft cocoon around them. Jake kissed her gently as he came up over her, sliding his hardness inside with a single thrust. It felt so good to have him there, so perfectly right.

I love you, she thought. *I love you so much.* But they were words she could not say.

Instead, she told him with her body, opening herself to him, taking him even more deeply, giving him all that she had. Jake took possession of her mouth, kissing her fiercely, rekindling the passion that she had felt before. With each of his driving thrusts, shivers ran over her skin and a violent need for Jake seemed to rise from her very core.

They reached the pinnacle together, a powerful climax that left them both breathless and shaking, a sheen of perspiration on their skin. A bolt of lightning flashed, illuminating the darkness, casting shadows over the bands of muscles across Jake's chest, the hair-roughened sinews in his legs.

He's so beautiful, she thought, *and for a short, sweet time, he was mine.*

But the few tender memories she carried of Jake were all she would ever have of him. She snuggled closer, felt his arm go around her, and fought to hold back tears.

* * *

They left the island by boat the following morning, then caught a cab in Belize City for the airport. All the way there, Jake was silent and Allie felt even less like talking. They were strangers again, heading back to their separate worlds. Their adventure together was over.

On the plane next to Jake, who had managed to get them seated in the exit row, giving his long legs a little more room, Allie leaned back in her seat, trying not to think that in a very short time, she would likely never see him again.

American Airlines Flight 1724 carried them safely to Dallas, where they boarded a flight to LAX. From there, Allie was scheduled to catch the six o'clock shuttle to San Diego.

"We've got an hour to kill," Jake said with a glance at his watch. "You want something to eat?"

Allie shook her head. "Listen, Jake. I know you must be anxious to get home. You've probably got a jillion things to do. It's only an hour until my flight. There's no sense staying out here with—"

His eyes blazed. He dropped the canvas bag that held his island-purchased clothes, reached out, and gripped her shoulders. "What the hell are you talking about? I've dragged you thousands of miles away from your home. I nearly got you killed half a dozen times. Do you really think I'm going to leave you in some frigging airport in the middle of L.A.?"

She had never seen him quite so shaken. "I'm sorry. It's just . . ." She swallowed past the lump in her throat, wishing it wasn't so hard to breathe. "This is really hard for me, Jake. I just . . . I don't want to make a fool of myself."

He hauled her hard against him, wrapped her tightly in his arms. "You could never do that, honey." He kissed the top of her head. "If anyone's a fool, it's me."

She didn't press him to explain. She didn't want to know. She just wanted the aching in her heart to end, but it didn't look like that was going to happen anytime soon.

They walked the length of the concourse holding hands, then sat down in a row of seats in front of the window. Dressed once more in his faded cutoff jeans, Jake dug into the front pocket and pulled out a small piece of paper.

"I wrote down my phone number and address, just in case you need them. My office number is down there, too. If you have a problem and you can't get ahold of me, ask for Inspector Biggs. He knows who you are and he'll do whatever he can to help you."

Allie accepted the scrap of paper. "I won't be needing this, but thank you for the thought."

She hesitated a moment, then dug into her purse and pulled out a cocktail napkin she had taken from the plane, just in case she might need it. She wrote her address and phone number down, and the number of the Raucous Raven.

"I want you to have this, but please don't call me, Jake. Not unless it's an emergency." She handed him the napkin, hoping her hand didn't shake.

Jake swallowed, then nodded, accepting that a clean break was better for both of them. Folding the napkin very neatly, he tucked it into the pocket of his jeans.

The loudspeaker sounded, calling Flight 440, the

shuttle to San Diego. Allie picked up the canvas bag Jake had bought her in Belize, exactly like his black one, only hers a bright blue.

"Time to go." She forced herself to smile, but her mouth barely curved. "Have a good life, Jake."

He glanced away, the muscles in his throat moving up and down. He looked into her face. "Goodbye, Allie. I hope you find what you're looking for."

I already have, she thought.

She hoped that he would kiss her. When he didn't, Allie went up on her toes to press a kiss on his cheek. She could feel the roughness of his late-afternoon beard and unconsciously her hand came up to touch it, her fingers trembling against his dark skin.

Jake moved so swiftly, she didn't realize what was happening until she was crushed against him, his mouth on top of hers, his kiss hot and fierce. Allie clung to him, her body pressed into his, aching for him, desperately in love with him.

As swiftly as it had started, the fierce kiss ended. Jake turned and started walking, his long strides carrying him rapidly away. Allie started walking in the opposite direction, her legs shaking, her throat so clogged with tears she couldn't swallow. She didn't realize she was actually crying until the flight attendant at the gateway asked if she wanted a Kleenex. Allie accepted the tissue and started down the ramp, trying not to think of Jake and how much she would miss him.

She should be happy, she told herself. She was heading back home, her terrible ordeal at an end. She would see her family, her friends, see Whiskers again. Her life was finally returning to normal.

Allie had never been more miserable in her entire twenty-eight years.

Chapter Twenty-two

It was Monday night. Barb Wallace parked her dented blue Toyota in the lot behind a little restaurant called The Hamlet in the Gaslight District, not far from the Raucous Raven. Her neighbor, Suzi Johnson, was staying with the boys. As soon as Barb got back, she was making them all homemade pizza. Suzi was bringing dessert—her famous chocolate chip cookies.

The parking lot of The Hamlet was more than half-full, but she didn't see Dan's dark brown unmarked Chevy. She made her way to the front of the old brick building, pausing for a moment in the entry to collect herself. She had never been to The Hamlet, which was small and simply furnished with round wooden tables and maple captains' chairs, but it was clean and close by, and Dan had said it was important that he see her. He said it had something to do with Allie.

It was Dan who had called her on Friday to relay the good news. In a very businesslike voice he had said that Allie was alive and safe and would soon be back in San Diego. By then Mrs. Parker had already called, but Barb appreciated Dan's concern, though she could tell he was still pissed at her for standing him up the night before.

She felt kind of bad about that. She shouldn't have been such a coward. Instead of running out of her apartment like a thief in the night, she should have just told him she wasn't interested. Unfortunately, where Dan was concerned, she didn't trust herself.

One thing was sure—after that kind of treatment, he wouldn't ask her out again. Barb sighed at the thought. At least he had cared enough about her feelings to call with the news about Allie.

After all these weeks, Allie Parker was alive and apparently unharmed. It seemed all of the prayers people had said for her were answered. It was amazing, really, the story Mrs. Parker had told, that Allie had been hiding aboard the *Dynasty II* when it took off for Mexico, that the boat had been involved in some kind of weapons smuggling, but that one of the men on the boat had turned out to be an undercover agent.

"They got off the boat in Mexico and then there was this plane crash," Mrs. Parker had said. "And Allie was lost in the jungle and then—well, you know how she is—she just had to help that nice man who saved her and so they decided to catch the men who were smuggling the weapons and that's what they did."

Barb found herself grinning. Leave it to Allie to

wind up in some incredible adventure, though Barb doubted it was quite the cakewalk Allie had led her mother to believe. Barb's grin slid away. If Allie was all right, why had Dan insisted on this meeting? It certainly wasn't because he wanted to see her. Since the night she'd stood him up, he had called only the one time, and except for the relief she could hear in his voice when he talked about Allie, the call had not been friendly.

Typical male. If a woman didn't put out, a man wasn't interested. She knew better than to expect anything else, but it hurt just the same.

Steeling herself against feelings for Dan she was determined not to have, Barb surveyed the interior of the restaurant. The walls inside the room were the same unfinished brick as the exterior. Round green glass lamps hung from a dark brown ceiling. She started forward, caught a hint of movement from the corner of her eye, and was surprised to see Dan standing a few feet away, his eyes trained on her face. If she hadn't known better, she might have thought he was glad to see her.

Dan started walking toward her and she tried to read his expression, but the light in the room was too dim.

"I'm glad you came," he said when he'd reached her, sounding as if he actually meant it. "I wasn't sure you would."

Barb fiddled with her purse as he took her arm and started leading her toward a table in the corner. "You said you wanted to talk to me about Allie." She paused in front of the chair he pulled out for her, trying not to look worried. "I thought she was all right. Her mother said she was on her way home. She said Allie would be back in San Diego sometime tonight."

"As far as I know, Allie's fine." He waited till she'd sat down then made his way to a chair on the opposite side of the table.

Barb set her purse on the Formica top, determined not to notice how good he looked in jeans and a short-sleeved pullover shirt. "If Allie's fine, why did you want to see me?"

Dan took a deep breath. He rubbed a hand over his face, looking more nervous than she had ever seen him. "First of all, I owe you an apology."

Her eyebrows went up. "You do?"

"I didn't realize it at first, but yes, I do. I don't normally press a woman so hard she finds it necessary to pack up her children and steal off into the night. It's just . . . to put it straight, I wanted you. So damned much I was thinking with my dick instead of my brain. I thought . . . I kind of got the idea you wanted the same thing I did, but I see now I was wrong, and like I said, I'm sorry."

She didn't contradict him. She didn't dare let him know how right he was, that Detective Dan Reynolds turned her on—big-time. She was divorced, a single mother with two little boys. The last thing she needed was a wild fling with a hot-looking cop.

"Maybe I overreacted," she admitted, feeling at least partly to blame. "I'm a big girl. I'm not really afraid of you." *I'm afraid of me.* "But I know what guys think. I'm divorced and I work in a bar. They think that makes me easy."

Dan stiffened. "I never thought you were easy."

"Maybe not, but the truth is, even if I happened to be attracted to you, I'm just not ready for a sexual fling."

Dan opened his mouth to respond, but the waitress arrived just then, a snappy little blonde in hip-hugger jeans and a yellow scoop-neck tank top that bared a perfect midriff.

"Can I get ya somethin' to drink?" she asked, popping a huge wad of purple gum. She was cute in an overage high school girl sort of way, but she wouldn't last five minutes with a boss like the one Barb had at the Raucous Raven.

"The lady'll have a glass of white wine," Dan said, remembering her usual drink. "And you can bring a Bud Light for me."

She walked away snapping her gum, wriggling a basketball-round bottom that amazingly Dan didn't seem to notice.

"There's another reason I asked you to meet me," he said. "But what I'm telling you has to remain strictly confidential."

"Bartenders learn in a hurry that the best way to keep their jobs is to keep their mouths shut."

"It's about Felix Baranoff. Undoubtedly you know he avoided arrest and now he's wanted on smuggling charges."

"Are you kidding? You'd have to be blind, deaf, and dumb not to know that. It's been on CNN every thirty minutes for the last three days. I guess Allie was on the right track. It just wasn't drugs the guy was peddling."

"The day you went to see him, the Feds had him under surveillance. I didn't know it at the time, but that was the reason Captain Caruthers wouldn't let me talk to him about Allie's disappearance."

"So he wasn't just kissing Baranoff's influential ass."

"He was trying to nail the guy, just like everyone else. The Feds had the bust set up for the following morning, and they thought they had every detail covered. The arrest should have gone down without a hitch."

"But it didn't."

"No, it didn't. What we all want to know is why."

The waitress appeared just then. She set the glass of wine and a mug of beer down in front of them, blew a bubble, and snapped it at Dan. "Anything else I can get for ya?"

"Not right now, thanks."

She sashayed away and Barb returned her attention to the man sitting across the table. "So what's that got to do with me?"

Dan took a swallow of beer, set the mug back down in front of him. "Probably nothing, but the Feds are working every angle. You went to see Baranoff the day before the bust went down. Is it possible you might have said something, done something that could have aroused his suspicions?"

"I told you, Baranoff wasn't in his office the day I went to see him." She took a sip of the ice-cold wine. "The only person I talked to was his secretary, and all I said to her was that Felix and I had met at a cancer benefit. As far as I could tell, she bought it hook, line, and sinker."

"Well, somebody tipped him, or he got on to the surveillance." Dan reached across the table and caught her hand. "The Feds are bound to question you, Barb. But I don't want you to worry. Just tell them the truth and you shouldn't have a problem."

She eased her hand away, though it wasn't really what she wanted to do. "I wish they'd nailed the bastard."

"We'll get him sooner or later."

She took another sip of wine, then shoved back her chair. "If that's all, then I guess I'd better be going. The kids will be wondering where I am. Thanks for the warning, Dan."

He stood up and rounded the table, waited for her to stand and collect her purse. "So what are you cooking?"

"Homemade pizza. Most of it's out of a box, but I add a little extra string cheese, some pepperoni, and whatever else I can find in the refrigerator."

"Sounds good to me. I don't suppose you'd invite me over?"

A little thread of warmth flared inside her, but Barb shook her head. She knew what he wanted, the only thing he wanted. "I don't think that's a very good idea."

"Not even if I left before nine?"

Her gaze searched his face. "You're that determined to get me in bed?"

"Maybe I just like being with you. You ever think of that?"

"Actually, I didn't." She studied his expression, read sincerity there. "You're scaring me, Dan. I'm afraid of what will happen if I start to believe you."

"I guess that's only fair—because, lady, you're scaring the living hell out of me."

She couldn't help a smile. She didn't think Dan Reynolds was scared of very many things. "We're out of milk. If you'll stop at the store and pick up a quart, I'll fix you dinner."

Dan smiled, looking oddly relieved. "For a slice of that pizza, I'll pick up a whole half-gallon."

Barb started walking and Dan fell in beside her.

She felt his hand at her waist, guiding her around tables and chairs as they made their way to the door, an old-fashioned, protective gesture, something you read about in romance novels but men didn't do anymore.

Or maybe some of them did. Was it possible for a man to be exactly what he seemed?

Don't even think about it, a little voice warned, and Barb very determinedly listened.

"What the hell's going on?" The door slamming behind him punctuated Jake's words.

Ever since he'd heard the news—in the backseat of a cab on his way home from the airport—he'd been fuming. Instead of heading for his apartment to try and get some badly needed sleep, he had come directly to the ATF headquarters building on South Figueroa. He wasn't all that surprised to find his boss still working.

"Why didn't you tell me the bust went wrong? I can't believe I had to hear it on the goddamned news!"

"Calm down, Dawson." His superior, Martin Biggs, a craggy-faced man in his fifties with thinning brown hair and a high-waisted, pear-shaped body, eyed Jake's wrinkled khaki T-shirt and faded jeans, the clothes he'd been wearing since early that morning when he'd left Belize. "In case nobody's mentioned it—you look like hell." He pointed to the chair in front of his desk. "You'd better sit down before you fall down."

Jake flopped down in the chair, weariness washing over him in waves. "I just came from the airport. It's been a long damned day." The scene with Allie had left him drained and oddly empty. Letting her board that plane had been one of the hardest things he'd ever had to do.

Afterward, to make matters worse, he'd discovered that all the months of work he had done to catch Felix Baranoff had gone right down the drain. "Why didn't you tell me the bust went bad when I was in Belize?"

"Because there wasn't a damned thing you could do about it and you needed a rest. Doesn't look like you got much of one—or did you?"

The question squeezed a knot in his stomach. "Yeah, I got one." More than a rest. Three days in paradise. The time he'd spent with Allie on Ambergris Caye was the best of his life. He ran a hand through his hair, trying to shove back the fatigue. "So what the hell went wrong?"

"The truth is, we don't have a clue. We figure Baranoff either spotted the surveillance, or someone on the inside tipped him off."

Jake sat up straighter in his chair. "One of our guys?"

"Maybe. But a captain with the SDPD and a couple of homicide dicks were also in the know. One of them, a guy named Reynolds, showed up outside the Dynasty building on Thursday. The woman he's involved with, a bartender named Barbara Wallace, also went to see Baranoff that day."

"They tell you why?"

"Seems both of them are friends of Mary Alice Parker. You remember her, don't you? Pretty little blonde? Likes to take extended boat trips out of the country?"

He remembered her all right. The question was, how was he going to forget her? "Yeah, I remember. What were they doing at Dynasty?"

"According to the woman, she was beginning to suspect the Parker girl's disappearance had something to do with the *Dynasty II*."

"Smart lady." And now that he'd had time to rouse his muzzy brain, he recognized the name. Allie had mentioned that Barb Wallace worked with her in a place called the Raucous Raven. Said she hoped Barb would take care of her cat when she turned up missing.

"Apparently Mrs. Wallace wanted to talk to Baranoff about Allie Parker's disappearance. Reynolds says he was there to keep that from happening, since his boss had put the kibosh on any contact with Baranoff until the bust went down."

"He knew about the surveillance?"

"Not at the time. According to his superior, a captain named Caruthers, Reynolds didn't find out about the surveillance until just before the bust went down."

"You think Reynolds and Wallace are telling the truth?"

Biggs shrugged a pair of rounded, slightly-gone-to-fat shoulders. "So far nothing's turned up that puts them in Baranoff's pocket."

Jake scratched his jaw, rasping his day's growth of beard. "According to the news, you guys had a small army outside that building. How the hell did the bastard get away?"

"Near as we could tell, he went out through the equipment room in the underground garage. We found a pipe tunnel that leads to the building next door. Looks like Baranoff had an escape route planned just in case."

"Sounds like him. You think he's still in the country?"

"If he planned an escape, he probably had a way out of the country."

"Probably."

"If he's still in the States, he's gone way underground. The media is having a field day with this." Biggs handed Jake a two-day-old copy of the *San Diego Union Tribune*. The headline read WEALTHY ENTREPRENEUR SUPPLIES GUERRILLA WAR. "Stuff like this is all over the news. Right now Baranoff's face is better known than the president's."

"I imagine you've covered all the bases."

He nodded. "Every major airport and harbor was closed within minutes after the raid. The guy would have had one helluva time getting anywhere. If he hasn't already left, odds are, he'll lay low for a while, give things time to cool down."

"Baranoff's got all the patience in the world. I've got a feeling that's exactly the way he's playing this. He won't try to leave until he thinks it's safe."

"I hope you're right. If he's here, we'll get him."

"So what do you want me to do?"

"Get some sleep for starters. After that, you can do a little nosing around. See if somebody in our department tipped him. I want to know how the sonofabitch found out we were on to him, and if it's one of our guys, I want him hung out to dry."

Jake's jaw hardened. He thought of the months he had spent in deep cover working to bring down Felix Baranoff and end his smuggling operation. If they didn't catch him, sooner or later Baranoff would get out of the country. As soon as he landed somewhere safe, he would set up shop again, and it would be business as usual for him.

As Jake left the office, he thought of the hot, humid days he and Allie had spent in the jungle, how close they had come to dying in the crash of Valisimo's plane, of Chrissy Chambers, dead at Baranoff's hands.

He wanted Felix Baranoff, and he would do damned near anything to get him. But the FBI wanted him just as badly.

Jake wondered what the Feds would be willing to do.

Allie spent her first night back in San Diego at the condo with her mother and father. They had been waiting when her flight arrived at the airport and insisted she spend the night with them in Escondido. Allie didn't argue. Now that her wild adventure was over, she was emotionally drained and at loose ends.

"I never gave up," her mother said as they walked toward the car, a five-year-old Buick Skylark her father kept so spotless it looked as if it had just rolled off the showroom floor. "I knew you'd be all right." She smiled and patted Allie's hand. "You always had a way of landing on your feet."

Miriam Parker had Allie's same blond hair, though at fifty-five, it had faded to gray and had to be artificially colored. She was the ultimate homemaker, plump instead of slender as she had once been, but still devoted to her husband and only child.

"Your mother and I . . . we were so terribly worried." Henry Parker, a retired accountant, was a gray-haired man, average in height and build, way above average in intelligence. "We're so thankful that you're safe." Her dad had cried when he hugged her. Allie had never seen him cry before and it made her cry, too. She had guessed how worried her parents must have been, but she hadn't really imagined that in some ways their ordeal had been worse than hers.

As she walked into the condo, she could smell fresh-baked biscuits, maple ham, and her mother's special, country-style green beans, one of Allie's favorite meals.

"Supper's almost ready," her mother said, rushing off to the kitchen to get the food on the table. "I'll only be a minute." Cooking for her family had always been her mother's way of showing how much she loved them. She had also baked Allie's favorite dessert, a three-layer chocolate cake with walnuts on top.

Though Allie wasn't really hungry, she didn't mind the cosseting. She was tired clear to the bone, and thoughts of Jake weighed her down, sapping even more of her strength.

She had just sunk down on the sofa, her eyes gritty, eyelids heavy, when she heard a familiar meow.

"Whiskers!" Allie laughed as the cat jumped up in her lap and began rubbing its head against her cheek. Allie hugged the animal against her, burying her face in Whiskers's soft orange fur. "I was so worried about you. I've missed you so much."

"We thought you'd want to see him," her father said over Whiskers's loud purring. "I picked him up at your friend Barbara Wallace's apartment."

She knew Barb had been keeping him. Her mother had told Allie when she had worriedly asked about the cat during her call from Belize.

"Barb's been a good friend, Allie." Her father sat down in his favorite brown vinyl lounge chair. "I don't think your mother and I could have made it if it weren't for her."

He went on to explain how Barb had been the

one who'd discovered her missing, how she had worked with some young detective hoping to come up with a lead, that she'd raised money to have posters printed and helped get them up all over town. "She's a good girl, your friend. She called your mother nearly every day."

Allie felt the sting of tears. She had lost her friend Chrissy and no one could ever replace her, but she was lucky to have found another terrific friend. "I want to thank her. I'll call her first thing in the morning. If she's not busy, maybe I can stop by and see her after she gets home from work."

Her mother bustled in just then. "I can't believe that awful man escaped," she said. "After all the trouble you and that nice Agent Dawson went to trying to catch him."

Allie stopped petting Whiskers. "What do you mean *trying* to catch him? You're not talking about Felix Baranoff?"

"Oh, dear, that's right. You probably haven't seen the news."

"Not since I left Belize. Are you saying Baranoff escaped?"

"I'm afraid so, dear."

Her father made a rude sound in his throat. "Guy got completely away and they haven't found a trace of him since."

Allie sat back, thunderstruck. "I can't believe it. After all we went through to catch him? It isn't possible."

"I'm afraid it's more than possible," her father said.

"I wonder why they didn't tell us. We thought everything went just the way it was planned."

Her mother reached down and patted her arm. "You mustn't worry, dear. I'm sure they'll catch him soon." She turned and started back toward the kitchen. "Come on now, you two, supper's on the table. It's time to eat."

Completely disheartened, Allie was even less hungry than she'd been when she got there. Though the meal was delicious, she mostly moved the food around on her plate. As soon as they'd finished and the dishes had been rinsed and put in the dishwasher, she returned to the sofa in the living room and asked her father to turn on CNN.

Eventually, the story of the raid on the Dynasty building, Baranoff's escape, and the current effort to find him came on. Allie couldn't help wondering what part Jake would play in the effort, but odds were she would never find out.

She watched the news off and on the next day, wanting to keep up with the story, thinking she might catch a glimpse of him. It was doubtful, since he worked undercover and would want to keep his identity secret. Then, in a midday telecast, his photo appeared on the screen. He was identified as the ATF agent responsible for smashing the Baranoff-PRA weapons and antiquities smuggling ring and retrieving more than fifty stolen, high-tech Stinger missiles.

Some astute reporter had apparently dug up the story. Jake's cover was blown and she wondered how that would affect him. Still tired from her trip and all that had happened, she curled up on the sofa and dozed for a while, then at three o'clock that afternoon, she reached for the remote and again flipped on the news. Jake's face came instantly into focus, and the minute she saw it, her heart squeezed into a painful knot.

He looked so incredibly good. A little too tired, she thought, seeing the faint shadows under his eyes, but good all the same. Briefly, he went over what had taken place in Belize but refused to answer questions about the failed attempt to arrest Felix Baranoff, since he hadn't been in the country at the time.

When an ABC reporter asked him if the rumors were true that a woman had been involved in the operation in Belize, he had replied that yes, that was indeed the case, but declined to mention the woman's name for privacy reasons. He did say she had shown exceptional bravery and that, without her help, his mission might have failed.

Allie discreetly brushed away tears and, as soon as the interview was over, clicked off the TV. With a sigh of resignation, she went up to the guest room, refilled the bright blue canvas bag with the clothes she had brought from Belize, and asked her father to take her and Whiskers home.

"Are you sure you're ready, honey?" he asked. Her mother hovered nearby, a worried look on her face.

"I've been gone an awfully long time, Dad. I just . . . I really need to go home."

Her mother leaned over and hugged her. "I understand, dear. If there's anything you need—"

"I'll be fine. I'll call you first thing in the morning."

She left the house, and her father drove her downtown. They arrived out front, and Allie stared out the car window at the white, two-story building that housed her apartment. "I've been gone so long I forgot to ask what happened to my car."

"It's parked in your carport out in the alley."

Her father pulled the Buick over to the curb. "That young detective friend of Barb's brought it back over the weekend. He said he'd leave the keys in your mailbox."

Allie leaned over and kissed his cheek. "Thanks, Dad."

Cuddling Whiskers against her chest, she waved goodbye as she climbed the stairs and walked along the open corridor to her second-floor apartment. She dug the key out of her purse, went in, and closed the door. Allie sighed and leaned against it, her gaze slowly traversing the dimly lit interior. The blinds were closed and there was a musty smell that hadn't been there before.

Once the apartment had felt so warm and cheery, filled with healthy green plants, her cat, and her very best friend. The plants were all dead now and a layer of dust covered the overstuffed sofa and chairs and the coffee table in front of them. The apartment seemed cold and empty, full of nothing but hollow memories.

Setting Whiskers down on the dark brown carpet, she moved around the room, opening the blinds and windows, letting in the ocean breeze. She needed to dust, but she couldn't seem to find the energy. It was depression, she knew, the letdown after such an emotional experience.

According to her mother, her boss at the Raucous Raven had kept her job open. She could go back to work whenever she was ready, but the prospect didn't hold much appeal. She had only taken the waitressing job until she could complete her Internet courses. Now she was nearly a month behind and starting again wasn't all that appealing.

Tomorrow, she told herself. Tomorrow she

would feel better. She would be back to her old self again.

Ignoring the blue canvas bag she couldn't summon the will to unpack, Allie sank down on the sofa and tried not to think of Jake.

Chapter Twenty-three

Allie didn't make it to Barb's apartment until Wednesday night. An hour after she had returned to her apartment, the lawn in front of the place was overrun by TV cameras, news crews, and newspaper reporters.

Apparently, someone had unearthed the truth of her whereabouts during the weeks she'd been missing, her return last night, and her connection to Felix Baranoff. The hordes had descended en masse, and she had escaped them only by packing an overnight bag, climbing out a window in the laundry room at the rear of the building, and racing her little green bug to a nearby Easy 8 Motel.

At least she got a halfway decent night's sleep. Being out of the apartment, she didn't think so much of Chrissy, or that her killer had gotten away.

Unfortunately, she did think of Jake. There didn't seem to be much she could do about that.

The following morning, she called Barb to thank her for all her help and support, and the kindness she had shown her parents. Allie asked if she could stop by to see her after work.

"Are you kidding?" Barb said. "I'm dying to see you. Your face has been plastered all over the TV screen. I saw the news crews outside your place. Do you want to stay over here?"

"Thanks, Barb, I really appreciate the offer but right now I need a little time to myself."

"Well, like I said, I'm dying to see you. I want to hear every gory detail."

Allie didn't think she was ready for that, but she was looking forward to seeing her friend and maybe it would be good to talk to someone. She volunteered to bring Chinese food, enough for the boys, and knocked on the apartment door at three minutes to six that night.

The moment she walked in, Barb enveloped her in a giant bear hug that left both of them fighting back tears.

"I still can't believe everything that's happened," Barb said. "Are you really all right?" She took a step back to survey Allie's slightly longer blond hair and the suntan that was a whole lot darker than it had been before she left.

Allie smiled, but it wasn't as easy as it should have been. "I'm fine. Sometimes I can't believe it happened either."

The boys spotted her just then and came racing up, stopping just inches away.

"Mom's been real worried," Pete said.

"I know she has. Your mom is a wonderful friend."

"She's says you're bringin' Chinese," Ricky said with an eye toward the bag she clutched in her hand. "I love Chinese."

She laughed. They were such darling little boys. "I brought these for you." Allie dug into the pocket of her jeans and held up the sand dollar and conch shell she had found on the beach in Ambergris Caye. "Close your eyes."

They did and she mixed up the shells, putting one in each hand.

"Okay, now each of you choose a hand." They each picked a hand and took one of the shells.

"Thank you," Pete said with a grin, reminding her so much of Miguel that a lump rose in her throat.

She thought of the little Mexican boy and all she had experienced in the weeks that she had been gone. Everything about her seemed to have changed since she'd left San Diego. She tried to think of the good things, the amazing people she had met, the parts of the world she had seen that few people ever would. She had experienced the adventure of a lifetime, but somehow losing Jake and little Miguel seemed to outweigh those things.

She saw Barb walking toward them, smiling down at the boys. "Okay, you two. Leave Allie alone. Go wash up and you can have some Chinese."

The children hurried away and Barb looked over at Allie. "There's something different about you. I'm not exactly sure what it is." She took the bag of Chinese food out of Allie's hand and started for the kitchen. "Come on. We'll feed the kids in front of the TV and we'll eat in the kitchen so we can talk."

It was ten minutes later that they actually sat down at the table, Barb sticking spoons in the paper cartons of chow mien, fried rice, and sweet and sour pork, then passing out paper plates and forks. They all loaded their plates and started to eat.

"So tell me what happened," Barb said. "Your mom told me you were on Baranoff's boat when it left for Mexico and that's how all of this started."

Allie sighed, remembering the day she had sneaked aboard the *Dynasty II*. It seemed another lifetime. "I was just going to take a quick look aboard the yacht, see if I might find anything that had to do with Chrissy's death. The next thing I knew we were pulling out of the harbor." For the next half-hour, Allie told her friend what had happened in the weeks she had been gone.

"It was amazing," Allie finished. "The most amazing thing that's ever happened to me."

Barb swallowed a mouthful of chow mien. "I can imagine. On second thought, I don't think I could begin to imagine." She took another helping of fried rice. "I saw that ATF guy, Dawson, on TV. He looked like a major hunk to me. Does he look that good in person?"

Allie shook her head. "Better."

"Wow."

"Yeah, wow."

Barb's blue eyes suddenly widened. "Oh, my God—that's it! That's what's different about you. You slept with him, didn't you?"

Allie didn't answer. It was hard to swallow the bite of sweet and sour pork that she had been chewing.

"You don't have to say anything. It's written all over your face." Eyeing her shrewdly, Barb leaned back in her chair. "You didn't fall in love with him, did you?"

The pork refused to budge. Allie thought of Jake and blinked back a sudden well of tears.

"Oh, my God, you did!" Barb reached over and caught her hand. "It's all right. You were abducted, mistreated, nearly raped by some L.A. thug. You survived a plane crash and a week of misery in the jungle. Jake Dawson was your only link to the outside world. If the guy was the least bit kind to you, you were bound to fall in love."

"They call it the Stockholm syndrome," Allie said grimly.

"Yeah, that's it."

"That wasn't it."

"Oh, God, you mean you *really* fell in love?"

She sighed. "I tried not to—I really did. But Jake's just so . . . he's so . . ." She shook her head. How did you describe a man like Jake? Maybe that was it. He was just so much man.

"Never mind. I think I know what you mean."

There was something in Barb's voice that pricked Allie's attention. "You do?"

Barb nodded. She wasn't the sort to blush but there was definitely a hint of color in her cheeks. "Not you, too?"

"Not yet, but I'm teetering on the brink. If I'm not careful, I'm doomed."

"Who is it?"

Barb started closing the half-empty cartons of Chinese food, enough for another meal for her and the kids. "Dan Reynolds."

"Ohmygod!"

"Yeah, that's what I said."

"But I think that's great. Dan's a terrific guy. When he was dating Chrissy, I sort of hoped it might work out, but Chrissy's taste ran more to the

Donnie Markham type of guy. If Dan's interested in you—"

"Aside from taking me to bed, I'm not sure what he's interested in."

"Unfortunately, I know what Jake Dawson *isn't* interested in. He's got a past and he's an undercover cop. He's made it clear we don't have a future, and I suppose he's right. But I miss him so much it's killing me. Every time I see him on TV, I want to bury my head under the pillow and cry."

"That bad, huh?"

"Worse. Being with him was like . . . It was like . . . It was heaven."

"Well, you can't cry forever."

She sighed and leaned back in her chair. "Believe me, I know. I figure if I fell into love with him, I can find a way to fall out. And that's exactly what I'm going to do."

"Good for you." Barb wiped her hands on a dishtowel. "Let's make a pact. Men are nothing but trouble. We'll find a way to get over them."

"Wait a minute. Are you sure you want to get over Dan? If I were you—"

"I'm too big a coward, Allie. I've got the kids to think of. I've messed up once already. I can't afford to take that kind of chance again."

"You sound a lot like Jake."

Barb pondered that. She picked up the dirty forks and serving spoons, put them in the sink, and turned on the water. "Dan owns a twenty-eight-foot sailboat. He wants to take me and the boys out on the boat this Sunday."

"What did you say?"

"I haven't said anything yet."

"Do it, Barb. Give Dan a chance."

"I suppose that's what you'd do."

"Darn right I would. If I thought there was a chance it would work, that's exactly what I'd do." But in Allie's case it wasn't going to happen. Jake had made that clear.

"What are you going to do about that army of newspaper reporters waiting outside your front door?" Barb asked. "They aren't going to just go away."

"I've been thinking about that. I wish I could tell them something useful, something that would help the police catch Baranoff, but unfortunately, I can't."

"They want your story, Allie. They're not going to let up until they get it."

"I know. I think the best thing to do is just get it over with. Tomorrow morning I'm going to call the local TV stations. Once I give them what they want, I think they'll leave me alone."

At least she hoped so.

The last thing she wanted was to dwell on the past. She wanted to forget the last three weeks and get on with her life. She wanted to forget Jake Dawson, and that was exactly what Allie intended to do.

Martin Biggs hung up the phone and uttered a dirty word. Nearly three weeks had passed since the failed attempt to arrest Felix Baranoff and, since then, nary a sign of him. The FBI was getting antsy and so was he. The difference was the length to which the Bureau was willing to go in order to catch him.

Martin took a drink of the lukewarm coffee on his desk and thought of the call he'd just received. He'd have to tell Jake. It was early. Jake was usually up by now, but Martin didn't think he'd been sleeping very well. It was the girl, he knew. Dawson had fallen hard for the lady, though he hadn't quite figured it out. Or maybe he just wouldn't admit it.

Martin had read his file. Jake had two failed marriages, though the first was more like breaking up and getting back his high school varsity ring. The second one had cost him his son.

Over the years, the department had kept an unofficial eye out for the boy, and he was listed in the NCIC, but no trace of him had ever turned up, which wasn't all that unusual in cases where one of the spouses was determined to disappear.

Martin's own son was grown, twenty-two years old, coming home next month after a two-year stint in the Army. The thought of losing him made Martin's stomach turn. Jake had suffered mightily over the loss of the boy, and the pain had hardened his heart.

Marriage and family weren't high on Jake's list of priorities—not the way they had been before—and with the job he had, a successful marriage was nearly impossible, even if they were.

Martin thought of Mary Alice Parker, Allie, she called herself. He had seen her on TV a couple of weeks ago, calm and composed, handling the reporters with competence, certainly not Jake's usual sort. Besides being damned good to look at, Allie appeared to be charming and intelligent, a woman who could take care of herself. She had proven that more than once in the past few weeks, first aboard Baranoff's yacht, then in that god-awful Mexican jungle, and even in Valisimo's camp.

It was easy to see why Jake had fallen in love with her. Under different circumstances, they would probably have been a good match. It was highly unlikely that was going to happen, but whatever Jake's intentions toward Allie, he wasn't going to like what the FBI intended to do.

No, Jake wasn't going to like it—not one damned bit.

Allie climbed the stairs to her apartment. After the miserable evening she had just spent, the door up ahead looked like the pearly gates to heaven.

"I hope you had a good time tonight," Richard Blake said.

Allie forced herself to smile. "It was . . ." *Dull and boring. The most awful evening I've spent in years.* "Enlightening."

"Yes, well, understanding the commodities market is certainly something everyone should be able to do. I hope I've been of some help in that regard."

Allie nodded. "You certainly know your soybeans from your pork bellies." She paused in front of her door and stuck out her hand. "Good night, Richard."

Richard ignored the hint and leaned closer, pinning her against the door with his body. He clamped his lips over her and kind of sucked. *Like being kissed by a vacuum cleaner, a Wet Vac,* Allie thought. When he jammed his tongue down her throat, her gag reflex kicked in, and for a second she was sure she was going to throw up on him.

Richard ended the kiss. *There really is a God.*

Allie fumbled with her apartment key and hurriedly unlocked the door.

"I'm a little sleepy," Richard said. "I could use a cup of coffee before I start driving home."

Allie's lips barely curved. "Maybe some other

time, Richard.'' *Like hell,* she thought, practically slamming the door in his face. She slid on the chain lock with a shaky hand, then leaned back against it. *Ohmygod, ohmygod, ohmygod!*

How could she have forgotten how awful it was to date? She'd been so determined to get over Jake that she had agreed to go out with Richard, though she had turned him down half a dozen times before.

But Richard was an attorney with Ford, Wilkins, and Blake, one of the most successful law firms in San Diego. He was nice-looking, in a stuffy sort of way, brown-haired, mid-thirties. He had always seemed pleasant enough, if not particularly exciting, a settled-down kind of guy, which, after the heartbreak she had suffered with Jake, was the reason she had finally agreed to go out with him.

She must have been out of her mind.

Allie's eyes filled with tears. She was so tired of aching for Jake, of missing him, and wanting him. But finding a replacement wasn't going to work. There wasn't anyone like him—not for her—and making comparisons with guys like Richard only made her feel worse.

Allie slid down the door, cradled her head against her knees, and gave in to the tears she had been fighting for weeks. God, she missed him. Dammit, why did he have to be so . . . so . . . Jake? But the truth was, she loved him exactly the way he was and she wouldn't want him to change.

If she meant to get over him, she would simply have to find another way.

Jake shoved through the door of Martin Biggs's office, turned, and closed it behind him. Biggs grunted in his direction and continued to peruse the document he was reading. Apparently satisfied, he signed the paper with a flourish then looked up at Jake.

"About time you showed up. Dammit, Dawson, where the hell have you been? I've been trying to get ahold of you since yesterday."

"Sorry. My cell phone went on the blink. I was down in Del Mar . . . enjoying a day at the races."

"I hope that's some kind of code for telling me you've turned up something on Reynolds or his girlfriend, Barbara Wallace."

Jake almost smiled. It would have been a novelty since he hadn't done much of that lately. "I didn't find anything on them, but I found out something very interesting about Reynolds's partner, Archie Hollis."

Biggs motioned for Jake to sit down and he sank into a chair on the opposite side of the desk. "Such as?"

"Such as, Archibald Hollis has a very expensive habit. He loves to play the ponies and his luck isn't all that good."

"Interesting. He in debt to the big boys?"

"Not that I heard. Word is, Archie always pays his debts."

Biggs set his ink pen down on the desk. "Which means he's got another source of income."

"Looks like. Archie's fairly predictable. He spends about two grand a month at the track, but his paycheck goes directly into his Wells Fargo bank account and it just about covers his monthly expenses, so the money's got to be coming from somewhere else."

"Like maybe Felix Baranoff?"

"That'd be my guess," Jake said. "You gonna

call SDPD and have Hollis brought in for questioning?"

"Not yet. I'd rather wait until we've got Baranoff."

Jake's interest shot up. "You got a lead?"

"Not exactly. The good news is the Bureau's got an idea how to catch him. The bad news is their plan involves your lady friend, Mary Alice Parker."

The name rolled over him like a breath of fresh air and his whole body tightened. Every day that she had been gone, he had missed her. At night he dreamed of her. Hot, embarrassing wet dreams more erotic than any he'd had as a teenage boy. In the morning he woke up thinking about her, remembering her toughness, her courage, how beautiful she had looked standing naked beneath the waterfall.

"What does Allie have to do with catching Felix Baranoff?" Jake asked, afraid to hear the answer.

"The Bureau wants to set up a sting. They think Baranoff might come out of hiding if the lure is strong enough."

Jake shook his head. "Baranoff's too smart for that. He'll stick to his original plan, stay hidden until it's safe to leave the country, assuming he hasn't left already."

"I agree with you—with one exception."

Jake frowned as Bigg's meaning grew clear. "The mask of Itzamna."

"That's right. The FBI knows how bad Baranoff wants it. The idea is to make him believe Allie stole it during the raid on Valisimo's camp and smuggled it back to the States. It wouldn't have been hard for her to get it through Customs, since she was traveling with you. Those guys aren't likely to hassle a Federal agent, and Baranoff will know that. Allie could have found out how much he wanted the mask. She could have stolen it, and planned on selling it to him when she got back to the States.''

Jake shook his head. ''No.''

''No?''

''That's what I said. They're not involving Allie— not again—not under any circumstances. She almost got killed the first time. They can't expect her to take that kind of risk again.''

''The FBI says she won't be in any danger. They just want her to make contact with Baranoff and arrange the meeting. They say they'll take it from there.''

''And exactly how do they expect her to find the guy when no one knows where he is?''

Biggs picked up his ink pen, began to doodle on the notepad in front of him. ''Maybe through Eve Holloway.''

A bitter taste rose in Jake's mouth. They were on the right track with Baranoff's secretary and former mistress, which meant they were well on their way to involving Allie in their scheme.

Biggs leaned toward him across the desk. ''You were the one who told us if there was anyone we should be watching it was Eve Holloway.''

''That's right. Felix is a businessman. He's got land holdings, merchandise, banking and financial interests, God only knows what else. He has to stay in contact with someone, and Eve Holloway is the likeliest candidate for the job.''

''We've tapped her phones, both at home and at the office, but Baranoff would undoubtedly expect that. Wherever he is, he's got some way of safely making contact.''

''Or she could call *him*. Hell, she could phone

him from the ladies' room at Nordstrom and there's no way we would know. Has anyone talked to her?''

"The FBI. They say she's clammed up tight. She's devoted to Baranoff and she's not about to help us bring him in.''

"Eve's smart and she's completely loyal to Felix. A couple of years ago, she had an affair with him. Baranoff broke it off, but somehow he managed not to destroy the close relationship he'd always had with her.''

Biggs wrote something on the notepad. "So the Parker girl gets to Eve, tells her you had mentioned her as a close friend of Baranoff's, and dangles the mask in front of him—with a hefty million-dollar price tag attached.''

"He'll call Belize. He'll have someone find out if the mask was missing from the items that were turned over to the government after the raid on the camp.''

"That's already been taken care of. The authorities down there want him caught as much as we do. They've loaned us the mask in case we need it. The Bureau's got it in San Diego.''

Jake wasn't sure if what he felt was excitement or worry. "I hate to admit it, but this just might work.''

"Yeah, it just might.''

"But no way does Allie make contact with Eve. One of the female agents can pretend to be her.''

"Sorry. Too late for that. One of them talked to her yesterday and she agreed. Said she'd do whatever it took to catch the man who killed her friend.''

"Sonofabitch.''

"Take it easy. The protection's already in place.

There's no way to know how far Baranoff will go to get the mask, so they're protecting her round the clock."

"Not good enough." Jake got up from his chair. "You want me, I'll be in San Diego."

Biggs just smiled. "Figured you'd say that. FBI won't like it, but what the hell?"

Jake turned back to him. "Thanks, Martin."

"I'll make the necessary calls. Just be sure you keep me informed."

Jake started walking.

"And take good care of the girl."

Jake made no reply. Allie Parker had been his responsibility since the day she stepped onto the *Dynasty II*. It was crazy, but he'd actually missed taking care of her. Worse yet, his heart was pounding like a trip-hammer at the prospect of seeing her again.

Jake bit back a curse. He wondered if Allie would be the least bit glad to see him.

Chapter Twenty-four

It was raining. May in San Diego usually meant blue skies and seventy degrees, but today flat gray clouds blanketed the city and rain fell in opaque sheets. Gutters brimmed and overflowed, creating huge brown puddles in the typically arid earth.

Standing next to the round table in the kitchen, Allie inhaled the aroma of fresh-brewed coffee, the second pot she had made that day. A half-empty box of doughnuts rested on the tabletop, but it was the padded, velvet-lined box sitting open beside it that had captured her attention.

She stared down at the glittering golden mask nestled in thick black velvet. Piercing jade eyes stared back at her from the haunting face more than a thousand years old. The celestial dragon, the sun god, Itzamna.

With a mixture of awe and reverence, Allie

reached down and touched the shimmering mask
of gold. She remembered the first time she had
seen it, at the general's house the morning of the
raid, and Rico's smug expression when he had
set the mask on the table in front of them. She
wondered how many dozens of priceless antiquities
he had stolen before he paid the ultimate price
for what he had done.

Allie thought of Belize, and memories of the days
she had spent there rose up with startling force.
Jake's image appeared, as she hadn't allowed it to
do for a few weeks, and her heart squeezed painfully. Silently she cursed him. Why had she ever
gotten involved with a man like Jake? She had
known from the start an affair with him would only
end in disaster. Still, she wondered where he was
and what he would say if he knew she had volunteered to help the FBI catch Felix Baranoff. She
wondered if he would approve.

"Ms. Parker?" She glanced up, saw one of the two
FBI agents who had come to talk to her yesterday
morning standing in the kitchen doorway. Special
Agent Duchefski was maybe thirty, brown-haired,
and dark-eyed. He wore the same overeager expression that had been on his face since he first
appeared. "You about ready?"

She sighed, nodded, then walked toward where
he stood in the living room next to another FBI
man, an agent named Eddie Morris. Morris was
probably five years older, with sandy blond hair
cut unbelievably short. He was wearing sunglasses,
even though they were indoors.

Agent Morris waited while she went into the bedroom to collect her raincoat. They had decided it
would be best to approach Eve Holloway in person,
figuring the woman might be more likely to believe

her that way, and Eve's routine was predictable enough that it was easy to initiate a meeting.

"What the . . . ?" Agent Morris turned at the sound of someone pounding on the door. Duchefski crossed the room to see who was making all the racket. He turned the knob and pulled it open, then stepped back out of the way as a tall familiar figure swept past him into the room.

Allie swallowed. "Jake . . ."

He was dressed in a long canvas rain slicker that fell open as he walked. Low-slung jeans, a pale yellow button-down shirt, and a tweed wool jacket flashed underneath.

She drank in the sight of him. She had forgotten the confident way he moved, how lean and darkly tanned he was, how incredibly virile he looked all over.

"What . . . what are you doing here?" She might have forgotten some things, but she knew that angry expression and the riveting blue eyes that drilled into her like laser beams.

"Are you kidding? You didn't think I'd show up when I found out you'd been dumb enough to volunteer as bait for Felix Baranoff?"

Of all the scenarios she had imagined might happen if she ever saw him again, this wasn't one of them. A rush of adrenalin shot through her. "What are you talking about? I volunteered to help catch him. I'm hardly bait!"

"It's all right, Ms. Parker," Agent Morris broke in. "Dawson, you're way out of line here. You've got no say in this. Your assignment is over."

A hard smile curved Jake's lips. "Wrong. My assignment is over when you catch Felix Baranoff. In the meantime, I'm taking charge of Ms. Parker's protection."

"Bullshit," Duchefski said.

"Call your superior. He'll tell you that as far as Ms. Parker is concerned, from now on you answer to me."

"No way." Morris strode toward him. "You can't just walk in here and—" He slowed when Jake turned that steely gaze in his direction.

"Actually, I can. Like I said, call your superior. I gather that when I got here, the three of you were on your way to make contact with Eve Holloway?"

Allie lifted her chin. "We were just about to leave when you started hammering like a madman on the door." Ignoring Jake's scowl, she dragged her raincoat on over the jogging suit and tennis shoes she wore.

"And where is this illustrious meeting supposed to take place?"

"The fitness center," Agent Morris answered. "Eve Holloway does aerobics on Mondays, Wednesdays, and Fridays during her lunch break."

"All right, that works for me." He turned his attention to Allie. "You're wired, aren't you?"

"Wired?"

Morris looked a little nervous. "We didn't think it was necessary at this stage of the game."

"Well, I think it is. I want to know exactly what's being said to her. Get the stuff here or she doesn't go."

"Shit," Duchefski grumbled.

"Do what he says," Morris told him. He returned his attention to Jake as his partner stomped away. "There's a Roto-Rooter van parked out front. It's got everything in it we'll need."

"Good. I'm sure there won't be a problem but I'd rather play it safe."

Liking his high-handedness less by the minute, Allie tossed him a glare. "I don't know why—"

"I don't care if you know why or not. Like I said, I'm in charge of your protection. From now on, you do exactly what I tell you or this whole thing is over."

Allie bit back a nasty reply and sank down on the sofa, grateful for the anger that masked the turmoil she felt inside. She had thought she would never see Jake again, and part of her didn't want to. She knew how much it hurt to love Jake and she didn't want to suffer that way again.

Now he was here and acting like the ultimate prick, which was just as well. If he said one kind word, she would probably throw herself into his arms and she was determined not to do that. In the weeks he'd been gone, she had tried to forget him. Ending their relationship was the right thing to do and she had finally resigned herself.

It's over, she mentally repeated as he hung his rain slicker on the coat tree beside the door. The pistol he wore in the shoulder holster beneath his arm was a harsh reminder of the job that kept them apart, along with the not-so-small problem of Jake's aversion to marriage.

One thing was clear: Jake Dawson wasn't the man for her, and as long as he acted the way he was right now, she could almost make herself believe it.

Allie was wearing a wire and ready to leave fifteen minutes later, returning the mask to the care of the FBI for safekeeping until it was needed. Climbing into the Roto-Rooter van along with her three male escorts, she sat back in her seat as the van headed for the Vim and Vigor Fitness Center on

A Street, just a short walk from the Dynasty headquarters building.

"Once you get inside," Jake said from his seat
on the bench next to Allie, "remember there isn't
any rush. Just take your time, pick a good place to
approach her. You're a thief. You want to reach
Baranoff, but you don't want to say anything to
Eve that might lead to your arrest."

Allie nodded. She had already discussed the
meeting with the two FBI men and made several
dry runs earlier in the day. She nervously fiddled
with the pale blue T-shirt she wore under the jacket
of her jogging suit. YOU'RE NEVER TOO RICH OR
TOO THIN, it said.

It was almost noon when the van pulled over to
the curb a couple of blocks from the gym. Allie
jumped out and started walking. Vim and Vigor
was an unimposing, two-story structure with blue-
tinted windows. Allie stopped at the counter inside
and paid for a one-day pass, put her gym bag in a
locker, then went upstairs.

She had studied Eve Holloway's photo. Allie recognized her immediately when the woman walked
in at her usual time, five minutes after twelve. In
her mid-forties, she had chin-length dark brown
hair, high cheekbones, and well-defined, aristo-
cratic features. In her navy blue running shorts
and white-piped navy tank top, she still looked fit
and trim.

While Eve did warm-up stretches, Allie worked
out on the weight machines, enjoying the exertion
she had missed since her return to San Diego. Eve
did a dozen sit-ups, then climbed onto a walking
machine. The machine next to her was empty. Allie
didn't waste any time.

Climbing onto the treadmill, she punched in a

five-minute walking program, choosing the same speed Eve had picked, and began to get into the groove. On the screen overhead, CNN replayed world news, masking whatever conversation they might have.

Allie flicked a glance at the woman beside her. "You're Eve Holloway," she said matter-of-factly.

The woman turned, a slightly surprised expression on her face. "That's right." Her voice was sophisticated, upper-class. From what Allie knew of Felix Baranoff, just the sort of woman he would choose.

"I was told by a former associate of your employer's that you're his personal secretary."

Eve continued walking, pacing herself on the machine. "I'm his administrative assistant, yes."

"Well, I'd like you to give Mr. Baranoff a message."

"Surely you've seen the news. I have no idea where Felix Baranoff is. Why would you possibly think I would?"

Allie kept pace beside her. "As I said, one of his associates mentioned your name. He said you and Mr. Baranoff were very close friends. I figured if anyone could reach him, it would be you. If you can, I strongly suggest that you do. I think your employer will be extremely interested in something that has recently come into my possession."

A fine line tightened around Eve's mouth. "How did you know where to find me?"

"You're fairly predictable, Ms. Holloway. And also very efficient, from what I hear. Tell Mr. Baranoff I'm interested in Pre-Columbian art. Tell him I'm especially interested in a deity called Itzamna."

Eve Holloway tripped on the treadmill and nearly fell. "I know who you are. You're that woman—

Mary Alice Parker. You were aboard the *Dynasty II*. I've seen your photograph in the newspaper.''

"That's right. And I think Mr. Baranoff will be very interested in talking to me.''

Eve took a couple more strides, taking the time to gauge her next words. "I told you—I have no information as to where Mr. Baranoff might be at this time. However . . . if that circumstance happens to change, I'll tell him you were looking for him. How would he find you?''

Allie handed her a piece of paper with her phone number written on it. She turned off the walker and stepped down from the treadmill. "Tell Mr. Baranoff not to wait too long.'' She gave Eve a casual smile. "Have a good workout, Ms. Holloway.''

Allie left the exercise room and returned downstairs. She retrieved her gym bag and left the building. The Roto-Rooter van was parked around the corner, but she didn't go directly there. Two blocks from Vim and Vigor, the van pulled over to the curb and Allie got in.

Duchefski actually smiled. "You did a great job, Ms. Parker.''

"Yeah,'' Jake grumbled. "Too damned good.''

"You really think he'll believe I've got the mask?''

"If Eve Holloway knows where he is,'' Jake answered though she'd asked the question of Duchefski, "and I'm betting she does—he'll believe you've got the mask. He knows you were in Belize. You could have found out how much the mask was worth and how badly he wanted it. You had motive—money. And opportunity—the chaos during the raid and a way through Customs without getting caught. He'll check to see if the mask is missing and find out it is, and he'll figure you're the one who stole it."

"How soon do you think he'll call?"

Jake stared out the window of the van. Thunder rumbled in the distance. The rain had slowed for a moment, but the clouds opened up again and a sheet of water slammed against the windshield. So far he had hardly looked at her, except to scowl. It was obvious he wasn't glad to see her. She told herself the feeling was mutual and tried to make herself believe it.

He turned to face her once more. "The call could come in anytime. Today, tomorrow. Not long, I don't think. If he thinks you've really got it, he won't risk losing it to somebody else." Jake turned his attention to the two FBI men. "We aren't sure what he'll do when he gets the message. We'll need to keep Ms. Parker covered, but I'm going to need some sleep. I'll want one of you to spell me from midnight to six and a man outside the apartment twenty-four hours a day."

Duchefski mumbled something beneath his breath.

"The van will be parked across the street," Morris said. "Someone on our team will be in it. Agent Duchefski and I will both take turns spelling you at night."

"That's it then. I'll take over from here."

Looking none too happy, the men waited as the door slid open at the curb. Allie and Jake climbed out of the van and headed for the apartment.

"You'd better keep us informed," Morris called after them.

"You'd better make sure you keep your eyes and ears open," Jake countered. "I don't want any screwups."

Grumbling, the men slammed the door of the van. Walking next to Jake, Allie climbed the stairs to her apartment. The minute the door was closed, Jake swung a hard look her way.

"So Mexico wasn't enough. You decided to stick your neck out again."

She gave him a saccharine smile. "It's nice to see you, too."

"The plan was *not* to see each other, remember?"

Her mouth thinned. "Screw you, Jake Dawson. Nobody asked you to come down here and stick your big fat nose in where it wasn't wanted."

He scowled, then the corner of his mouth inched up. Such a beautiful mouth, she thought, and a little shiver of remembrance ran through her.

"Big fat nose?" he said.

Her chin angled up. "You know what I mean. You didn't have to come here. We were doing just fine without you."

The amusement faded from his features. "Were you?" His softly provocative tone said the question had nothing to do with catching Felix Baranoff and everything to do with their days together on Ambergris Caye.

Allie moistened her lips. "Yes . . ."

Jake turned toward the window and stared out at the storm. "I'm glad to hear it," he said blandly. "But I'm running the show from here on out, and from now on, you do what *I* say, not Moron and Doofus-chefski."

Allie ground down on her jaw, wishing she could hit him. She wondered how she could ever have fallen in love with such an arrogant, maddening man. Determined to ignore him, she started for the kitchen to make a fresh pot of coffee. Just what she needed—another shot of caffeine to calm her already jittery nerves. It didn't matter. She needed an excuse to get away from him, and coffee was as good as any.

She continued into the kitchen, and all the way there, she could feel Jake's eyes on her. Or maybe it was only wishful thinking.

A warm fire crackled in the huge stone hearth. Outside the window, a late-spring storm scattered snowflakes across the rugged landscape. They melted as soon as they hit the earth, but Felix enjoyed watching them, along with the sway of the pines in the wind and the rustle of the branches.

Lounging in a deep brown leather chair in the den, he sipped the glass of cognac he cradled in his hand and studied the mountainous hillside outside the window. He had bought the big log house four years ago, though the title never went into his name. It was his place of refuge, the spot he had chosen for just this sort of emergency.

Nestled in the evergreen and sage-covered hills outside the quaint New Mexican town of Santa Fe, he could hide away here for weeks and never be discovered. He could live in relative luxury for as long as it took for his picture to disappear from national TV screens, for interest in his activities to fade, and he could safely leave the country.

As he did in most things, he had planned ahead for that, his route already chosen, his final destination set. Switzerland would serve him well in his business endeavors. Perhaps he should have moved there long before this.

Felix took a sip of the fifty-year-old Napoleon brandy that was a personal favorite then set the crystal snifter on the silver tray beside his chair.

He started to reach for the TV remote control when a soft knock sounded on the door.

"I am sorry to interrupt." The man, Viktor Ivanov, was former KGB. He and his wife, Irina, both Russian emigrants living illegally in the country, occupied a smaller house on the opposite end of the property. They looked after the main residence with its very private two thousand acres, and occasionally, when the need arose, Viktor did other, more demanding sorts of jobs for him.

The couple was deeply in his debt, completely under his control. Which was the only reason Felix trusted them.

"I vill be driving into town," Viktor said. "Is there anything you might need?"

"Not that I can think of. Thank you, Viktor." He was a big man, blond-haired, thick-chested, and strong, an intelligent man who appreciated all that Felix had done for him. Viktor closed the door, and several seconds later, Felix's cell phone rang.

Like the house, the phone he kept here was listed under another name, Douglas Preston, the same man who owned the house—a man who had been dead for the past ten years. Those sorts of things could be arranged if one had enough funds at one's disposal. Felix had more than enough.

He flipped open the phone and pressed it against his ear, certain of who was calling. He had given Eve the number several years ago. He needed some way to stay in touch, no matter the situation, and like Viktor and Irina, he knew he could trust her. Eve had been in love with him for years, the kind of love that transcended a mere physical relationship. In a way, he supposed he loved her, too.

"Yes?"

"The Parker woman came to see me this morn-

ing. She says she has something you want. She
mentioned the name 'Itzamna.' "

His whole body went on alert. "Go on."

"She was very careful. She didn't say anything
that might be used against her, but she gave me
her phone number."

Questions started running through his head.
"I'll take care of it. Thank you, Eve." He started
to hang up.

"Felix?"

"Yes?"

"Are you all right?"

"Of course, my dear, I'm fine. I appreciate your
concern." Felix hung up the phone. The next call
he made was to a connection of his in Belize. The
man called three hours later. The mask of Itzamna
wasn't among the items turned over to the authorities. Someone was thought to have stolen it during
the raid on the PRA compound.

Felix smiled as he hung up the phone, certain
now exactly who had done it. The Parker woman
had been meddling in his affairs for far too long.
This time she was going to regret it.

When the right time came, he would see she was
taken care of, but not until he had what he wanted.

Not until he possessed the mask of Itzamna.

Chapter Twenty-five

Allie ignored Jake for the rest of the afternoon, staying away from him as much as she possibly could. But it wasn't all that easy to avoid a six-foot-four, two-hundred-pound male in such a small apartment. Especially one who made your insides curl every time he glanced in your direction. Eventually she went into her bedroom, leaving Jake alone in the living room. The cozy room, done in shades of white and rose with ruffled eyelet curtains and a quilted rose bedspread with a dozen throw pillows on top, was usually a cheery retreat but today it seemed confining.

Through the open door, she could see Jake moving around. He wasn't watching TV as she thought he would.

"I need to be able to hear if anyone comes up the stairs," he said, picking up a magazine instead,

a *National Geographic* that contained an article enti-
tled, "Animals of the Rain Forest." One of the
girls from the Raucous Raven had given it to her
the day she had returned to work.

Allie hadn't read it. It reminded her too much
of Jake. She watched him thumbing through the
pages and a perverse little voice rose in her head.
*I hope he remembers making love by the waterfall. I hope
he winds up with an ache in his—* She silenced the
wicked thought and closed the door to her bedroom.

She had been working again at the Raucous
Raven for more than two weeks, but in her spare
time she was trying to catch up on her Total Training Solutions website administration course. Taking a seat in front of her desk, she flipped on the
computer, went to the TTS website, pulled up her
next assignment, and began to read. There were
questions at the end of the section, but her brain
seemed unwilling to work. After ten minutes of
reading the same words over, she hit the Exit button, left the website, switched off the computer,
and leaned back in her chair.

Allie sighed into the silence of the bedroom. She
knew what was wrong. After her amazing adventure, a computer job seemed dull and boring. She
had tried to convince herself that in time her
enthusiasm would return, but her heart simply
wasn't in it. Not anymore.

What am I going to do?

Ever since she'd finished college, she had been
trying to figure out what she wanted to do with
her life. Six years later, she felt no closer to finding
the answer than she had back then. She wished
she could blame her latest failure on Jake, but she
was the one who had hidden aboard the *Dynasty*

II, setting into motion an adventure that had completely changed her life.

Disgruntled and tired of being cooped up, she returned to the living room. Jake stood next to the window, carefully out of sight, but able to watch the street in front of the apartment. He turned as she walked in.

"It's getting late," she said. "I'm hungry. How about you?"

The muscles tightened across his shoulders. For the first time he really seemed to look at her. The moment their eyes locked, the air seemed to crackle between them. Jake jerked his gaze away and so did Allie.

"We'll have to send out for something," he said a little thickly. "How about Chinese?"

Allie moistened lips that felt suddenly dry, wishing it wasn't so hard to breathe. "Fine." But looking at Jake, who had stripped off his button-down shirt, leaving him in the khaki T-shirt he wore underneath, her appetite disappeared. The soft cotton curved over a set of pecs any muscle jock would envy and disappeared into butter-soft jeans that wrapped around his long, muscular legs. Her gaze traveled the length of them, then returned to the distinct male bulge in front she remembered only too clearly.

Her stomach muscles contracted. Oh, God, she wanted him! She was getting wet just thinking about it. Embarrassment burned its way into her cheeks and she hurriedly turned away.

"Th-there's a place called the China Palace not far from here. The food's pretty good. I'll go get the phone number." She rushed out of the room and into the kitchen, her hands shaking as she pulled open a drawer and lifted out the heavy San Diego phone book.

"Here it is," she called back to him. "The China Palace. Five-five-five, six-two-one-three."

She heard Jake dialing, heard him ordering enough food to feed Valisimo's army, then he hung up the phone.

The curtains were closed and he was sitting down by the time her cheeks were no longer on fire and she could casually return to the living room. She grabbed the remote to turn on the TV.

"Keep the volume low," Jake warned, but just then a knock sounded at the door and she never hit the On button.

Jake was on his feet in an instant. The delivery truck couldn't have gotten here that fast and he knew she wasn't expecting anyone. He grabbed his tweed jacket off the coat rack and pulled it on over his shoulder holster. "Get in the bedroom."

Allie didn't argue. She had no idea what Felix Baranoff would do if he believed she had the mask. Her address was listed in the phone book, and if he happened to be in hiding somewhere in the city . . .

She hurried into the bedroom, pulled open the top drawer of the nightstand, and took out the .38 snub-nosed revolver she had borrowed the day Agent Duchefski had approached her and she had agreed to the FBI's plan. Since there was a waiting period, she hadn't had time to buy one. One of her customers had loaned her the pistol for "protection," since she was a single woman living alone.

Harley Adams was a regular, an older man who read *Soldier of Fortune,* went to all the gun shows, and apparently had a closet full of weapons, just in case he needed them.

Holding the gun in both hands as Jake had taught her, she cracked open the bedroom door just in time to see him jerk someone into the apartment and slam him up against the wall.

Ohmygod!

"Don't . . . don't hurt me!" Richard Blake fumbled in the inside pocket of his expensive Italian sport coat. "Here, take my wallet—there's at least four hundred dollars in there!"

"Who the hell are you?" Jake asked, holding him up by the lapels.

"It's all right, Jake." Allie set the gun out of sight on a shelf in the bookcase and hurried across the living room. "This is Richard Blake. He's an attorney. Richard's a friend of mine." Well, not exactly a friend. More of an irritation, like a boil on her behind.

"I came to see Allie," Richard said, fighting to regain his dignity as Jake released his grip on Richard's coat. "I can see I should have called first. It was an impulse. There's a marvelous little Chinese restaurant just down the street. I thought the two of us might get something to eat."

Allie groaned. The thought of spending another boring evening with Richard was enough to keep her from ever eating again.

Jake looked like he wanted to wring the guy's neck. Richard's eyes darted around as if he were searching for a way to escape.

"I'm sorry, Richard," Allie said, "but as you can see, I've made other plans."

The doorbell rang again and Jake swore softly. "What is this place—Grand Central Station?"

"Most likely it's the China Palace. It's about time for our order to arrive."

"I think I'd better go," Richard said hastily.

"Good idea," said Jake. He peered through the peephole in the door, seemed satisfied, stepped back, and opened it. Richard raced outside as if the apartment had just caught fire.

Jake set the two big bags of Chinese food down next to the lamp on the end table, paid the delivery boy, and firmly shut the door. "Who the hell is Richard Blake?"

"I told you—he's a friend."

Hard blue eyes drilled into her. "Didn't take you long to find a replacement."

She shrugged as if his interest in the matter wasn't important, which she told herself it wasn't. "What do you care? If the FBI hadn't needed my help, you never would have seen me again."

"Looks like you didn't care much, either."

Several heartbeats passed. Refusing to wither under that piercing glare, Allie picked up one of the bags and started for the kitchen. Jake picked up the other bag and fell in behind her. They carried them through the doorway and set them down on the round oak table.

Allie turned to face him. "Like I said, Richard is a friend. To tell you the truth, I don't find him the least bit attractive."

Jake studied her a moment, reached out, and ran a finger along her jaw. "What about me? You still attracted to me?"

A little shiver ran over her skin. Allie tried to ignore it, but her heart was battering the inside of her chest. Just looking at all that hard male muscle made her mouth start to water, and it wasn't Chinese food that she wanted.

"The food's getting cold," she said, turning away. "I think it's time we ate."

Jake's hungry look said that was exactly what he'd

like to do. Then his careful control slid back into place. "Good idea. I'll get the plates."

Stretched out on one of the narrow twin beds in what was once Chrissy Chambers's bedroom, Jake folded the thin foam-rubber pillow into a wad and stuffed it under his head, hoping to get some badly needed sleep.

Out in the living room, Duchefski was spelling him for the next six hours, although no one really expected any trouble, at least not this soon. Still, he couldn't fall asleep. Every time he closed his eyes, he could remember the jolt that had hit him like a rock in the chest the moment he had stepped through the apartment door and seen Allie standing in the living room.

Christ, what was wrong with him? He'd had a hundred women, married two of them, but none of them affected him the way she did.

He was hard just thinking about her. He wanted to slam through her bedroom door and rip the clothes off her luscious little body. He wanted to spread those long, beautiful legs and bury himself as hard and deep as he could.

And he didn't believe for a minute she wouldn't like it. All he had to do was walk in there and haul her into his arms.

Jake cursed into the darkness. Allie might want him, but she was determined to forget him. In the weeks since they had parted, she had already started to date while he hadn't been able to look at another woman without feeling guilty. Without feeling as if he had betrayed the one woman who meant so much to him. Jake thought of Richard Blake, the stylish, obviously successful lawyer that

Allie had been seeing. He was just the upstanding kind of guy she deserved, wimpy little bastard that he was.

Well, starting as soon as he got back to L.A., Jake was going to get back into the swing of things himself. He'd find himself a big-titted blonde and screw her until she couldn't wiggle. It wouldn't take him long to forget Allie Parker.

Jake nearly laughed out loud at the thought. Who was he kidding? He'd been trying to forget Allie since the day he had left her at the airport. So far, he had failed miserably, and now that he was here, close enough to reach out and touch her, things would only get worse.

Sonofabitch.

The next day began as poorly as the last one had ended. Allie could feel Jake's presence like a tangible force. Whenever he was in the room, energy crackled like invisible lightning between them. *Ignore him,* a little voice said. *He'll be gone in a few days, and after the way he's been acting, this time you'll be able to get over him.*

She watched TV for a while, with the volume turned so low—thanks to Jake—she really couldn't hear it. She settled down with a sexy romance novel, but the hero reminded her of Jake—or at least the Jake she had had known in Belize—and that only darkened her mood. A little past noon, she made tuna sandwiches for lunch, which he thanked her for with little more than a grunt.

His surly attitude was driving her crazy. She was beginning to think the man she had fallen in love was a figment of her imagination.

Afternoon slid into evening. Being cooped up

made Jake's already bad temper even worse. He paced the room like a jungle cat, and by the time it was dark, he was barely speaking. Conversation had dwindled to one-word sentences punctuated by dark, brooding glares. Ignoring her growing irritation, Allie returned to the computer in her bedroom and flipped on the switch.

She went to Internet Explorer and the website prompt came up, but instead of typing in www.TTS.com and completing another computer lesson as she should have, she went to SEARCH, typed in JOB OPPORTUNITIES, and hit Return.

An endless list of possibilities appeared, none of which looked particularly interesting.

Allie thought of the exciting days she had spent with Jake and cursed him for making her want something more. As bad as their ordeal had been, those days they had worked together to catch Felix Baranoff were the most thrilling in her entire twenty-eight years. She had never felt so alive, so passionately involved.

So committed.

Every decision, every move she made was critical, crucial to the success of the mission they had undertaken. Allie glanced down at the keyboard and her fingers began to move almost of their own volition. She typed the words LAW ENFORCEMENT into the Yahoo search engine and hit the return.

A long list popped up.

www.copnet.org looked interesting. There was officer.net and lawenforcementonline.com. She clicked on www.copcareer.com, began to study the options that appeared on a bright blue screen, and with every word she read, her heart seemed to beat a little faster. She glanced toward the drawer that held the gun she had borrowed from Harley

Adams. She remembered the way Rico Valisimo had beaten little Miguel and knew, under the right set of circumstances, she wouldn't be afraid to pull the trigger.

It's probably just a whim, she thought. *How many jillion jobs have you already tried?* But it didn't feel like a whim. It felt as if, for the first time in her life, she might have actually found the path that would lead to her true calling. She clicked on *Do You Have What It Takes?* and read the list of qualifications, none of which seemed daunting.

She was smart enough. Though she had dropped out of college, she had eventually gotten a degree in liberal arts. She was athletic and she could be tough when it counted. She had discovered that about herself when she was in the jungle. Though she couldn't see herself working as a street cop, there were dozens of different careers in the field and a number of them looked appealing.

It was something to think about, an idea that intrigued her more than any she had ever considered before. She wondered what Jake would say about it, and some perverse little demon goaded her to ask him.

Exiting the website, she escaped Internet Explorer and closed down the machine.

She found Jake in the kitchen, making a fresh pot of coffee.

"I can see you're busy," she said with a hint of sarcasm and an obviously phony smile, "but I was hoping to get your opinion on something."

"Yeah, like what?"

"An idea I've been mulling over for a while. I think I mentioned when we were in Belize that I've been working since the first of the year on computer training courses."

"You said you were interested in putting together websites. You said the pay was good."

"That's true enough. But now that I'm back home and at it again, I don't think that's what I want to do with my life."

"Why not?"

"Too boring."

He grunted. "No kidding." Turning, he twisted the handle on the water faucet and filled the glass pot to the brim. "So what did you want my opinion about?"

She watched him empty the water into the top of the coffee machine and thought how big he looked in her tiny kitchen. "I've done a lot of soul-searching since I got back from Mexico and I've been thinking . . ."

"Uh-oh—I warned you about that before."

Allie clamped down on her temper, hanging on to it by a thread. "I'm considering a career in law enforcement. What do you think?"

For a moment, the empty glass pot hung suspended from his hand. Then a big grin cracked across his face. "You mean you want to be a cop?"

"Not a street cop, I don't think, but yes, something that involves that kind of work."

He burst out laughing, the glass pot waving precariously. Allie grabbed it out of his big, clumsy hand before he smashed it against the counter.

"I don't see what's so funny. I didn't do too badly when we were in Belize."

He wiped tears of laughter from his eyes. "Being a cop is dangerous work." He grinned again. "Do you know when it's legal to shoot a blonde in the head?"

"No, why don't you tell me?"

"When you have a tire pump to reinflate it." He

laughed again, setting her teeth on edge, and it took all her control not to punch him.

"So you think I'm too stupid, is that it?"

"I never said that. It was only a joke."

"Well, I've got a joke for you, buster. How does a big, dumb undercover agent keep from getting a coffeepot cracked over his head?"

He glanced down at the glass pot she gripped like a weapon and the grin slid off his face. "Don't even think about it." He plucked it out of her fingers, shoved it into place under the drip mechanism, and flipped the switch.

"You know what you are, Jake Dawson?"

"I imagine you're going to tell me."

"A fake. Everything I thought you were is a lie. You're no different from the rest of the men out there. You're just another obnoxious jerk like Richard Blake."

Allie started to walk away but Jake caught her wrist. He turned her around so fast she nearly stumbled, and yanked her against his chest. "You think I'm like that little prick Richard Blake?"

Allie stared up at him, a red haze of anger appearing at the edge of her vision. "Yes!" she hissed into his face.

"By God, that'll be the day!"

Allie gasped as he bent his head and caught her lips in a red-hot searing kiss. She had pushed him too far, she realized, futilely shoving at his chest. Then his tongue was in her mouth and she no longer cared.

Ohmygod! Ohmygod! Allie swayed against him, gripping the front of his cotton T-shirt to stay on her feet. She could feel the kiss all the way to her toes, and her body zinged with pleasure, turning all soft and damp. She moaned into Jake's mouth, slid her arms around his neck, and her nipples went diamond-hard against his chest.

Jake groaned as Allie wildly returned the kiss, grinding her hips against him, sucking on his tongue, pushing her fingers into his wavy black hair.

She tried to tell herself she didn't want this to happen, but it was the world's biggest lie. Jake was holding her, kissing her—it was exactly what she wanted. She was in love with him. She had missed him with every heartbeat since the day he went away.

Jake deepened the kiss, ravaging her mouth, finding her breasts, palming them, pressing her hips into the kitchen table. She could feel his erection, thick and hard at the front of his jeans, rubbing into the vee between her legs. Allie squirmed, pressing even closer, her body in flames.

"Jake . . ." she whispered, fighting to shove his T-shirt out of the way, her fingers trembling as they slid into his curly chest hair.

A shudder ran through him and he grabbed the front of her blouse, started fumbling with the buttons on the front. He couldn't get them unfastened quick enough and the last two tore free and went flying across the kitchen floor.

He dragged the blouse off her shoulders, dispatched her bra, and his fingers closed over a breast. "God, I've missed you," he said, kissing the side of her neck. "Every day you've been gone has been a living hell."

"Worse than hell," she whispered, going for his zipper. She tugged it down and reached for him, wrapped her fingers around his shaft. He was big and hot—hard as steel—and she ached to feel him inside her. Jake was just as eager. He lifted her up on the round oak table, unbuttoned her jeans, and tugged them down to her ankles. He jerked them off then pulled down her white lace panties and tossed them away.

"I've got to be inside you. I've waited too long already."

"Yes . . . oh, God, yes, please." He was between her legs, spreading them wider, stroking the wetness that collected there, sending little sparks of heat shooting into her stomach. Then he drove himself deeply inside.

For an instant, he braced himself above her. "I've dreamed of this," he said softly. "Every damned night." Allie kissed him and a shudder ran the length of his body. Then he started to move.

Allie moaned at the pleasure that tore through her. She could feel him deep inside, filling her like a piece of herself that had been missing. His big hands cupped her bottom, lifting her against him as he set up a rhythm, sliding out then stroking deeply again, taking her hard, exactly the way she wanted. Her body quivered with each powerful thrust, and her womb clamped around him like a fist.

When the first climax struck, Jake didn't even slow, just kept on pounding into her until she came again, her body quaking with the force of it. A few seconds later, he reached his own release, his muscles going rigid, the tendons in his neck standing out, perspiration beading on his forehead.

Allie clung to him as they began to spiral down, afraid he would pull away. Afraid he would return to the hard, distant man he had been before. But as he eased himself from the warmth of her body, he drew her gently into his arms.

"God, honey, I'm sorry. I know I've been a jerk.

I was trying to stay away from you. I guess I figured as long as we were fighting, I wouldn't give in to temptation. I should have known it wouldn't work."

Relief swept through her. She reached up and gently touched his cheek. "I'm glad to see you—the real you, I mean. I've really missed you, Jake."

He sighed, shook his head. His hold tightened a little around her. "What I said about you being a cop . . . I didn't mean any of it. If that's what you want and you're sincerely committed, I think you'd be great in law enforcement."

"You do?"

He brushed back a strand of her hair, looped it over an ear. "Yeah. And one more thing—I really do like your name. I always meant to tell you that."

Allie laughed, remembering now why she had fallen in love with him. She almost wished she hadn't.

"Jake?"

He paused as he finished zipping up his jeans, his gaze returning to her face.

"I don't think you remembered to use a condom."

The color leached from his face. "Christ!"

"It's all right. Your timing's pretty good. I don't think it'll matter."

"Damn, I was so damned hot for you, I never even thought about it."

"To tell you the truth, even if I did get pregnant, I wouldn't care. I'd love to have your baby, Jake."

Several different emotions flashed across his face. One of them she recognized as pain. He had lost one child. He didn't want to chance another.

He cleared his throat, looked over the top of her head. "Let's just hope it isn't a problem." Bending toward her, he lifted her into his arms, his eyes running over her naked breasts. "I think it's time we went to bed. This table is way too hard for what I've got planned for you."

"But what about—"

"We'll leave the door open so we can hear if anyone comes up the stairs." He was good at that, she knew from the days they had spent in the jungle.

"Sounds like a plan to me." Allie clung to his neck, her body already throbbing as he carried her into the bedroom. Jake came down on top of her as he settled her in the middle of the bed and for the next two hours they made wild, insatiable love.

It was eleven o'clock when he returned to the kitchen to collect their discarded clothes before one of the FBI men arrived to spell him, then he returned to his post in the living room.

Warm and sated, Allie curled contentedly beneath the covers and enjoyed the most restful night's sleep she'd had since she left Belize.

Chapter Twenty-six

It was the jangle of the phone ringing in the living room that roused her from slumber. Allie groped for her blue terry cloth robe and dragged it on, her stomach fluttering with nerves at the prospect it might be Felix Baranoff. She hurried to the door and caught Jake's warm smile as she walked into the living room.

"Remember," he cautioned, "if it's Baranoff, try to keep him talking so we can trace the call, but don't make it obvious. You don't want to say anything that'll make him suspicious."

She nodded as he turned away from her to pick up the extension phone the FBI had installed. His arm brushed her shoulder and electricity jolted through her. How could he do that? she wondered. But her eyes loved the sight of him, and her body knew exactly how good he could make her feel when they made love.

Standing next to the phone a few feet away, Jake counted to three and both of them answered.

"This is Allie Parker. How can I help you?"

"Martin Biggs. I need to speak to Dawson."

Both relieved and disappointed, she cast a glance at Jake, who began to speak to the man on the other end of the line. When Jake hung up the phone a few seconds later, there was something dark in his expression that put her on alert.

"What is it?"

He released a weary sigh. "My father died. He had a heart attack early this morning. He was DOA at Cedar Sinai Hospital at three twenty-three A.M."

"Oh, Jake, I'm so sorry."

"The funeral's set for Sunday afternoon. I guess somebody decided I might want to go." He turned away from her and walked over to the window, by habit being careful to stay out of sight. "We haven't spoken in years," he said softly. "Not since Michael disappeared."

Allie came up beside him. "What happened? I know the two of you didn't get along, but I didn't realize you were completely estranged."

Jake ran a hand through his hair, still a little too long but shorter than it had been in Belize. Though his expression was carefully controlled, she didn't miss the turbulence beneath his surface calm. She wished she could wrap her arms around him and give him some sort of comfort, but the look on his face said it wasn't what he wanted.

"After Marla took off with Michael, I did everything I could think of to find her. I spent every penny of my savings on private detectives, but none of them came up with anything useful. I was desperate. I thought maybe if I set aside my pride and asked my father for help, he might agree. I figured, since Michael was his grandson, maybe he'd be interested in finding the boy as much as I was."

"What did your father say?"

"He said that I was a fool to marry a bitch like Marla in the first place. He said, dumb as she was, the kid was probably just as dumb and not worth the effort. I slammed out of the house and never saw him again."

"Oh, Jake."

"It's funny. I didn't think I cared if he lived or died, but I do. I keep remembering when I was younger, before my mother died. We were close in those days. We did all kinds of things together. Dad taught me to ride a bike and he bought me my first pair of skates. Every summer the two of us went camping up at Arrowhead. We looked forward to those trips all year."

"Maybe your mother's death changed him in some way."

"Yeah, I suppose it did. He was never the same after Mom was gone. He just worked all the time, and when he wasn't working, he was a real son of a bitch."

The pain on Jake's face brought a lump to Allie's throat. "The funeral is four days away. If we're lucky, all of this will be over by then."

"Even if it is, I'm not going. I haven't seen my father in years. Just because he's dead doesn't change what happened between us."

Allie reached over and caught his hand. "You've got to go, Jake. Deep down inside you love him. He's your father. You'll always love him."

"I don't know, Allie . . ."

"Listen to me, Jake. You have to go for the good

memories you carry, the happy times the two of you shared. Because if you don't, you'll regret it for the rest of your life.''

Jake seemed to ponder that. His gaze remained intense. ''If we've got Baranoff by then, I'll think about it. But I'm not leaving you before this is over. Not for my father or anyone else.''

Something warmed inside her. Jake had always been protective. It was one of the things she loved about him. Allie leaned forward and kissed him, not the scorching kiss that usually erupted between them but a sweet, gentle, tender kiss that told him how much she cared.

''You'd better get dressed,'' he said gruffly. ''If we get lucky, maybe the next call you get will be from Baranoff.''

Allie nodded and started toward her bedroom. She knew Jake was hurting but there was nothing she could do. She would be crushed if one of her own parents died. But Jake had a job to do and she knew he would do it, no matter what sort of pain he was going through.

Allie closed the bedroom door, aching for him. She had promised herself she wouldn't get involved with Jake Dawson again. How could she when Jake gave her no hope for the future. She'd been down the miserable path of loving Jake, and after he left, she knew how much it was going to hurt.

But love was like a runaway freight train, and trying to stand in its way was just about as useless. As she showered and changed into jeans and a lightweight pale blue sweater, her body still deliciously sore from the hours they'd spent in bed, she wondered if her heart would be crushed completely by the time Jake left again.

* * *

The call they had been waiting for came in a little after noon. Halfway through the tomato soup and bologna sandwiches she had made them for lunch, the phone began to ring. Leaping up from the table, Allie raced into the living room.

"Take it easy," Jake said, walking in behind her. He stopped at the extension phone on the table next to the lamp. "If it's him, just remember, he wants what you've got as much as you want him."

Allie nodded and took a deep breath. She carefully lifted the receiver on the count of three, the same moment as Jake, and pressed it against her ear. "Hello?"

"Mary Alice Parker?" Her heart kicked up at the faint Russian accent she heard in the man's deep voice.

"Yes?"

"I believe you have something I want."

"Yes. I think you'll be very interested in—"

"There's a phone on the corner of Fifth and Maple. Be there in five minutes." The line went dead and Allie's gaze flew to Jake.

"Sonofabitch. He's worried about a trace. We won't have time to set one up at the pay phone."

"This doesn't change anything. You knew you might not be able to trace the call."

"It sure would have made things easier."

Allie scoffed. "Nothing's ever that easy."

Jake glanced toward the door. "Dammit, I don't like this. This is exactly the kind of thing I was afraid of." His radio crackled to life. It was Morris. He was in the van across the street. They had monitored the call and were waiting for Allie to leave.

"The van will tail you," Jake said to her when

the men had finished speaking. "I'll go out the window in the kitchen. You won't be able to see me but I won't be far away."

Allie just nodded. "I'd better get moving if I'm going to make it in time." With a last glance at Jake, who looked not the least bit happy, she headed out the door. The corner of Fifth and Maple was a five-minute walk away. She would have to run a little to make up for lost time. Her heart raced as she descended the apartment stairs and started along the sidewalk, adrenalin pumping like a drug through her veins. It suddenly hit her that she hadn't felt anything but numbness until the morning, four days ago, when the two FBI men had walked through her front door.

Today she felt alive in a way she hadn't since she and Jake had worked together in Belize. As she raced down the sidewalk, she couldn't help thinking that maybe catching men like Baranoff was exactly the sort of career that would suit her.

Jake watched Allie rush to the pay phone just in time to grab the receiver before it stopped ringing. She wasn't being tailed, not that he could see. Standing well out of sight behind a sycamore tree, he watched the Roto-Rooter van back into a parking space down the street. Allie nodded at something Baranoff said, gesturing with her hand though the man on the opposite end of the line couldn't see.

The FBI would be working with the telephone company, trying to discover where the call was coming from, but it wouldn't be as fast as a trace that had already been set up, and unfortunately, by the time it was done, Baranoff, wherever he was, was bound to be long gone.

Jake swore as Allie hung up the phone and started the return trip down the sidewalk back to her apartment. He followed, keeping out of sight until she was up the stairs and safely inside the closed front door, then he went around to the back, up the fire ladder, and in through the kitchen window.

"Baranoff's chomping at the bit," Allie said when he appeared. "I told him I wanted a million dollars for the mask and he agreed. The meeting's set for tomorrow night. Eight o'clock in Old Town."

"Old Town? No way. You were supposed to set up the meet for noon tomorrow in the back parking lot of the zoo." It was the safest place they could come up with. Ingress and egress could be controlled. Not too many people, but enough to allow agents to move freely without being noticed.

"Baranoff wouldn't go for it. Like I said, I'm supposed to meet him in Old Town. A boutique called El Caballito."

Allie headed for the bedroom and Jake followed her in. He paced over to the window, then back to where she stood beside the bed. "This is exactly the reason I didn't want you involved in the first place."

"Well, I am involved so you'll just have to get used to it." She pulled open a drawer in the nightstand, took out what appeared to be a .38 caliber revolver, and set it down on the mattress.

Jake's eyes narrowed. "Where the hell did you get that?"

"I borrowed it from a friend. I plan to take it with me."

"You've never shot a pistol. It'll only get you in trouble."

"I stopped by the target range the day I got it. I spent a couple of hours with an instructor." She grinned. "I didn't do too badly, if I do say so myself."

"I don't like it."

Allie brushed a light kiss over his mouth and he felt the familiar pull deep in his gut. "I'm glad to hear it," she said. "I like it when you worry about me."

Jake caught her arm as she walked past him. "It isn't too late to back out. We can use a substitute, put a female agent in a short blond wig. By the time Baranoff figures out it isn't you, it'll be too late."

Allie shook her head. "I'm going through with this, Jake. This is the guy who killed Chrissy. I want him to pay for it. I have a chance to see that he does."

"You've also got a chance to get yourself killed."

She smiled and patted his cheek. "Not with you there, lover. I know you'll take good care of me."

Her eyes widened as Jake dragged her into his arms and very thoroughly kissed her. He didn't stop until her body was pliant against his, her wrists locked around his neck.

"Promise me you'll be careful," he said against her cheek.

Her reply sounded a little breathless. "I'm always . . . careful." Words he had once said to her.

"Even so, sometimes things can get out of control." He wasn't talking about the job anymore, he was talking about sex, and thinking about what had happened on the kitchen table made him harder than he was already. Damn, the woman

drove him crazy. Last night, he'd been so hot for
her he hadn't remembered to use a condom. He
hadn't done that since high school and look what
had happened to him then.

What if he got Allie pregnant the way he had
Cindy? He would have to marry her, of course. Just
like he'd had to do before. But Cindy hadn't really
been pregnant and he'd only been a kid back then.
He wasn't a kid anymore, and the thought of marrying Allie wasn't at all unpleasant. In fact, if the
circumstances were different—if his life were different—the prospect would sound damn good.

Jake thought of his parents' marriage, happy for
so many years. Then his mother had died and everything had changed. His father's death had stirred
up painful feelings of abandonment and betrayal,
but it was an old pain, dulled by the years of separa-
tion. He had dealt with the loss of his father long
ago. It was the early years he remembered now,
when they had been the kind of family Jake had
wanted for himself. Instead there was Marla and
losing his son.

Allie was different, he knew. She was sweet and
loving, strong, and a whole lot tougher than she
looked. Loving Allie would mean changing his life
again, risking another failure.

Deep down, Jake knew Allie was worth the risk.

He just wasn't sure he was man enough to take
it.

According to the FBI, everything was in place.
Thirty FBI and ATF agents in street clothes milled
the lanes and alleys of Old Town, San Diego. Allie
went there often with her parents—authentic Mexican food was a family favorite—but time had

slipped away and she hadn't been there in more than a year. She had forgotten how much she enjoyed the array of colorful flowers surrounding the marketplace, visible beneath jewel-like paper lanterns, the bright reds, yellows, and pinks that seemed to spring into view everywhere you looked.

The historic area was the oldest in San Diego, dating back to 1769. Besides the quaint adobe buildings, plaza squares, and museums, present-day shops, restaurants, and cantinas reflected the year-round air of fiesta. Huge crepe paper piñatas hung from ceilings draped with fringed serapes, and the music of mariachi bands urged even the most placid visitor onto the numerous dance floors.

It was a great place to visit, Allie mused, inhaling the aroma of spicy burritos and imagining the taste of a frosty margarita as she turned off the ignition of her little chartreuse Volkswagen and stepped out onto the street.

But not the place she would have chosen to meet Felix Baranoff.

Many of the lanes were narrow, little more than winding alleys, and the lantern light disappeared into darkness just a few feet off the pathways. The old whitewashed adobe buildings had been remodeled and added onto so many times there were dozens of entrances and exits. The area was overgrown with plants and shrubs, a colorful, noisy maze, with endless possibilities for escape.

Allie hoped the Feds were as prepared as they believed.

She studied the area around the parking space that had been chosen for her ahead of time and vacated by someone on the team as she drove up. Seeing nothing suspicious, she reached back inside the car and carefully pulled out the aluminum case that held the priceless mask.

"I've got it," she said into the microphone hidden in the locket around her neck. "Starting along the designated route." Though she couldn't hear them, the men could hear her, and her instructions were to keep in close contact. A van was parked somewhere near, she knew, recording her transmissions, and the men wore receivers in their ears. She felt a little safer knowing Jake and the FBI agents knew exactly where she was and what was happening around her. The Feds had argued against the pistol she carried in her small white over-the-shoulder purse, but she had been adamant.

In the end, Jake had surprised her by agreeing. "Odds are, she's already a better shot than you are, Dushitski."

An angry flush rose in his face. "Duchefski," he corrected. "And it doesn't matter how good a shot she is. She doesn't have a license to carry."

"Fine," Jake said, "we'll just pretend she isn't."

"Your ass is out a mile on this one, Dawson. Anything goes wrong and I'm going to have it."

Jake ignored him. He walked Allie to the door, a worried look on his face. "You're sure you're ready for this?"

"Ever since I figured out Felix Baranoff was the man behind Chrissy's death, I've been waiting for someone to catch him. Believe me, I'm more than ready."

He stared at her for several long seconds. Then he simply reached down and gathered her into his arms. Ignoring the FBI men, he kissed her very softly on the lips. "I want you to take care out there."

Allie clung to him, his hard strength bolstering her courage. "I will."

Instead of letting her go, his hold subtly tightened. "I'm crazy about you, Allie. I don't know if there's anything I can do about it, but I wanted you to know."

A thick lump formed in her throat. "I love you, Jake. You probably don't want to hear that, but just in case something goes wrong, I—"

"Nothing's going to go wrong," he said fiercely. "I'm not going to let it." He kissed her quick and hard, then stepped away. His expression turned inscrutable as his control fell back into place. "If anything goes wrong out there, get out. Your life's worth a whole lot more than Felix Baranoff's."

Allie shook her head at the memory as she walked along the grassy path and continued on to El Caballito. She couldn't think of Jake, not now. Not when there was so much at stake. Her fingers tightened around the handle of the shiny aluminum case she carried.

"Turning corner one," she said, barely moving her lips. She dodged a party of laughing tourists, stepped out of the way of a group of Mexican musicians dressed in tight black vaquero pants and short black jackets studded with silver conchos, and continued along her prearranged course.

"Approaching checkpoint two. About to reach the El Matador cantina." Agents were stationed the length of the route, dressed to look like tourists, in shorts or jeans and flowered shirts or T-shirts. She couldn't pick them out but she knew that they were there. Jake was among them. He had told her he would be with her all the way and she knew that, somewhere in the darkness, he gauged her progress. It felt good to know he was there.

"Just reached checkpoint three," she said, passing beneath an arch that led to the narrow lane in front of El Caballito. The Pony was a shop that specialized in Mexican pottery. The plan was to step inside, wait for Baranoff to appear, speak his name into the microphone, then get out of the way as FBI and ATF agents swooped in from all sides, surrounding the Russian before he could escape.

"El Caballito just ahead." Her palm felt clammy where it wrapped around the handle of the suitcase. She hoped Jake and the others were in position. She hoped everything went down exactly as planned. She hoped no one got hurt and they captured Felix Baranoff.

It was a helluva lot to hope for, she thought as she reached the door leading into the pottery shop.

Chapter Twenty-seven

El Caballito was a narrow, high-ceilinged structure with glass windows in the front filled with tasteful displays of pottery: a cluster of earthenware bowls in various sizes, vases full of bright straw flowers, jars, and cups, all of them arranged on red-fringed serapes.

"Walking inside," Allie whispered into the microphone, pausing a few feet into the room. Pottery dishes in blue, green, orange, and yellow lined the walls and sat on rough-hewn tables. Ceramic statues of birds and people, some of them replicas of pre-Columbian art, huddled in interesting groups on shelves along the walls.

Only two other people were inside the shop, a man and his wife, both in their forties, content, it seemed, just to browse. Allie figured they were agents and she was very glad they were there.

No sign of Baranoff. She glanced toward the back of the room. Behind a counter at the rear of the shop, a clerk wearing a white shirt and brown slacks glanced up from the stack of receipts he was counting. He wasn't an agent, she knew. Baranoff had arranged the meet. The shopkeeper might be in the Russian's employ, and replacing the man would put him on alert.

No one approached her, and Baranoff had still not appeared. Allie walked toward the clerk at the back of the shop.

"Excuse me. I'm supposed to meet someone here. My name is Parker."

The small man, brown-haired, with a mustache and glasses, smiled. "Yes, of course. The gentleman you're looking for came into the shop a little earlier this evening. He said you would be coming around eight o'clock. He asked me to give you this."

Allie reached for the folded-up square of white paper, her stomach suddenly queasy. "Thank you." Walking a few feet away, she opened the note and read it aloud so the agents could hear. "Come to the pay phone at the end of the block, next to La Tostada. Go out the back door and down the alley." She refolded the paper and tucked it into her purse. "I'm going there now," she whispered.

She didn't like it. Jake had told her—in no uncertain terms—that if Baranoff changed the plan, she should instantly abort. But it wasn't what the FBI wanted. And it wasn't what Allie intended to do.

She could almost hear Jake cursing.

"Sonofabitch!" Jake adjusted the tiny flesh-colored transmitter in his ear, wishing he hadn't heard correctly. Wishing Allie wasn't setting off on a new, uncharted course prescribed by Felix Baranoff.

"Take it easy, Dawson." Agent Duchefski hurried along in the darkness next to Jake as they made their way to the rear of the shop. "She's armed—thanks to you—and you're the guy who said she knew how to use it."

"Armed or not, I don't like it. Once she turns the corner, she'll disappear in a narrow alley between two buildings. We won't be able to get a visual again until she comes out at the other end of the block." He knew because he had spent the better part of the day checking and rechecking the route Allie would be using to get to El Caballito, as well as the lanes and pathways that honeycombed the surrounding area.

They reached a shadowy spot near the back door of El Caballito just in time to see Allie walk out carrying the aluminum suitcase. Dressed in jeans and an easy-to-spot bright orange T-shirt, she headed down a lane crowded with tourists, then turned down the narrow path between the adobe buildings that led to the pay phone next to the Mexican restaurant, La Tostada.

Jake squelched an urge to follow. If Baranoff spotted him, the man would be gone before they knew he was there. Odds were, Allie would receive a call from Baranoff at the pay phone, giving her a new location for the meet. He was playing it safe and Jake wasn't surprised.

Felix Baranoff was a lot of things, but stupid wasn't one of them. Unfortunately, the problem with surprises was, by their nature, they often came from unexpected sources.

Skirting the building, Jake caught up with a bus-load of German tourists, slowed his pace, and leisurely walked among them. The only transmission coming through his earpiece was the sound of Allie's breathing.

"I can see the lights of the restaurant up ahead," she finally said, and a fine thread of relief filtered through him. At least so far, she was all right.

He rounded the end of the building, broke away from the tourists, and headed for the end of the block, where he would be in position to spot Allie again. On the other side of the lane, he saw Duchefski do the same, weaving his way closer until he made his way up next to Jake.

He was sweating, Jake noticed as they lost themselves among another group of people, and his eyes kept darting toward the point where Allie was supposed to reappear.

"If anything goes wrong," he said, "I hope she's smart enough just to give him the case and get the hell out of there."

Alarm bells went off in his head. "That's always been the plan. What aren't you telling me, Duchefski?"

"Nothing. I just—"

Jake jerked him up by the lapels of his flowered shirt. "What aren't you telling me, Dushitski!"

"The mask isn't in the case. There's nothing inside but a couple of bricks."

"Sonofabitch!" Jake let go of Duchefski's shirt, mollified a little by the wrinkles he'd left behind. He wished he could wrinkle Duchefski's head.

"The mask was too valuable to risk," the agent said. "The government didn't want an incident with Belize if we lost it."

"But it was okay to risk losing Allie." Jake clamped hard on his jaw as he studied the narrow opening between the two buildings. "She doesn't show up in the next thirty seconds, I'm going in after her and this is over."

"You can't do that. You don't have that kind of authority."

Jake started counting the seconds sweeping past on the face of his wristwatch. "You just watch me." He looked back at the narrow opening, praying he would catch a glimpse of her blond hair.

But Allie never came out.

In the shadows of a doorway that opened onto the narrow alley, Felix Baranoff watched the young blond woman approaching. She was carrying an aluminum case as she walked past, and anticipation shot through him. He gave a quick nod of his head and stepped out of the way, allowing the big Russian, Viktor Ivanov, to move by him into the passage.

Viktor was efficient. He stepped behind the woman, clamped a hand over her mouth, slid an arm around her waist, and jerked her backward through the doorway out of sight. Felix closed it firmly behind them. Mary Alice Parker struggled for a moment, then spotted Felix standing in the shadows. He caught the subtle stiffening of her shoulders, then she forced herself to relax.

Viktor uncovered her mouth, but kept a thick arm locked around her waist. Her jaw tightened as he yanked a small white purse off her shoulder and tossed it away. Then he carefully removed the aluminum case from between her fingers.

The Parker woman gazed up at him. She surprised him with a slow, unflustered smile. "So, Mr. Baranoff, we meet at last." She surveyed the nearly dark interior of a room cluttered with Indian artifacts of the early California Spanish period. "What is this place? It looks like the back room of a museum."

Felix ignored her, knelt, and popped the latches on the suitcase. Excitement made his hands a little unsteady. He had waited for this moment for nearly two years, dreamed of it, savored it now. He slowly lifted the lid and stared down into the case, but instead of the glittering golden mask, the sight of two old bricks sent a jolt of fury shooting through him.

"You little fool! Who do you think you're dealing with?" He whirled the suitcase around, exposing the two bricks carefully nestled among the layers of rich black velvet, then slammed the metal case against the wall.

Wishing he could wrap his fingers around the woman's throat, he ignored her pale face and turned his attention to Viktor. "There isn't time. We'll have to take her with us."

"No way!" The woman jerked forward and at the same time kicked back, jabbing the heel of her Reebok into Viktor's shin. He grunted as she twisted, brought her elbow up hard beneath his chin, digging into flesh and bruising bone. Viktor hissed a Russian curse, but he still didn't release her. Catching a fistful of short blond hair, he jerked her around and slapped her across the face so hard she staggered and nearly went down. By the time she regained her balance, Viktor had a gun pressed in front of her ear.

"This isn't a good place to talk," Felix told her mildly, once more in control. "Until we do, one word and Viktor kills you—you understand?"

She flicked a glance at the door, then gave him

a shaky nod. An instant later, they were running down the stairs that led to the basement and his prearranged escape route, Viktor gripping the woman's arm, his gun—a big .45 caliber ACP—pressed carefully out of sight between her ribs.

Dodging dusty ancient weapons and woven baskets in various stages of repair, holding on to the briefcase that held the money he had brought in the event he actually had to pay, Felix used his flashlight to guide them across the basement through a door leading to a flight of outside stairs.

When they reached the top, they crossed a short stretch of lawn and went into another building, a former size X boutique that had gone out of business. On the far side of the structure sat a hundred-and-forty-year-old blacksmith shop and stable that, like the De la Guerra museum, closed at 6 P.M. Ignoring the smell of leather, burnt coal, and manure, Felix entered the stable and started across the dirt floor toward a door at the rear that led outside.

Once they had left the old wooden building, it wouldn't take long to reach the helicopter parked in a field three blocks away. A private jet would be waiting at the airport. He had planned to leave the country with the treasure that was meant to become the cornerstone of his European collection, but now that would have to wait.

Not for long, Felix thought, fighting a renewed burst of fury. He glanced over his shoulder at the woman Viktor dragged along at gunpoint. A few minutes with the ex-KGB man and she would tell him where it was.

And it wouldn't cost him a million dollars.

* * *

Jake raced down the alley like a madman, FBI and ATF agents swooping in behind him from every direction. Checking any possible exit from the narrow, high-walled lane, they slammed through doors and climbed up stairways.

Jake and three other agents headed straight for the back door of the De la Guerra Adobe, a museum of Indian artifacts that he had spotted during his earlier surveillance. Morris and Duchefski and six other men headed toward the front of the building to block Baranoff's escape.

Jake had a very bad feeling that it was already too late.

Weapon drawn, he slid to a halt beside the back door of the museum, waited a heartbeat, kicked it open, and ducked inside. His pulse was hitting at least two hundred and his mouth was so dry he couldn't swallow. He had heard Allie's last transmissions. She had been in the back room of the museum, had fought with one of Baranoff's men, but the only sound since then had been the soft pad of running feet.

Through an opening into the main part of the museum, Jake saw Morris, Duchefski, and a small army of men slam through the heavy oak front doors and sweep toward him. The wide plank floor echoed with the thunder of their feet. The lights went on, but there was no sign of Allie or Felix Baranoff, just the empty aluminum case she had been carrying and two broken bricks lying on the floor at the rear of the building.

Jake clamped down on a fresh jolt of fury. He didn't waste time looking through closets or searching side rooms. Instinct had him halfway down the basement stairs when he heard Morris behind him. Flattening himself against the wall, Jake found a light switch and flipped it on, spun into the room, gun gripped in both hands in front of him, but the basement was empty.

"No trace of them upstairs." Morris sauntered toward him. Jake thought of Allie, of the empty suitcase and what Baranoff would do to get the mask, and it was all he could do not to hit him.

"Baranoff would have had a way out," Jake said, forcing his attention to the problem at hand. "My hunch is, it's somewhere down here." He started searching, looking for an avenue of escape. It was easier to find than he'd expected, a door behind a woven Indian rug hanging on the wall.

Ducking beneath the rug, Jake kicked open the small wooden door and found a set of stairs on the other side leading to a grassy area south of the adobe.

"The building's surrounded," Morris said. "Unless he ducked into that building next door—"

But Jake was already moving in that direction. Morris motioned toward the group of FBI men behind him, and they started off toward the front, hoping to cut them off. Someone shoved a flashlight into Jake's hand and his fingers closed around it. He stepped into the empty building, three ATF agents close on his heels. He felt better knowing it was his guys behind him this time.

Maybe they wouldn't screw up.

Jake's stomach tightened into a worried knot. For Allie's sake, he prayed he wouldn't either.

Allie felt the barrel of the heavy automatic pistol pressing into her side as they crossed the dirt floor of the old wood-frame stable. She was desperate to communicate with Jake, but there was something in the man named Viktor's eyes that held her back, something that promised retribution for making him look bad in front of his boss.

But time was running out. She had to let Jake know where she was.

"What's going on?" she said with a quick glance around. "This place is a stable. Where the hell are you taking me?"

Allie winced as the gun stabbed with brute force into her ribs. "Mr. Baranoff told you to keep your mouth shut." He jerked her roughly against him, stared down into her face. His eyes were dark and hard and they never wavered. "Or I can kill you here."

Allie clamped down on a shot of fear. "You do and the mask dies with me."

"We'll be going for a short ride," Baranoff calmly explained. "You'll have one last chance to produce the mask. As you correctly assumed, I want it very badly. But I've faced other disappointments in my life. If you don't intend to cooperate, Viktor will be happy to shoot you right here."

Allie swallowed. She could smell anticipation oozing like sweet perfume from the big Russian's pores. "All right, we'll talk."

"A very wise decision," Baranoff said.

"I just wanted to make sure you'd brought the money."

He made no reply to that. If the money was in the briefcase he carried, he no longer planned to hand it over—assuming he ever had. He was the one in control. If she wanted to live, she would have to give him the mask.

Unfortunately, the FBI had somehow forgotten to put it in the suitcase.

Bastards.

No wonder Jake didn't trust them.

A few feet in front of her, Baranoff switched off his flashlight and carefully opened the door. He took a quick glance around, stepped out of the stable, and into the darkness. The Russian, Viktor, dragged her along behind.

They reached the corner of the building, and in the light of the moon that appeared between the clouds, Allie spotted a helicopter parked across the street.

It was surrounded by FBI agents, she saw at the same instant Felix did, and as she felt Viktor's big body go rigid and the gun press harder into her ribs, she wasn't sure she was glad to see them.

"This is the FBI!" The sound reverberated through a bullhorn somewhere in the darkness. "Put down your weapons. You are under arrest."

Allie's heart thundered. Viktor swore. Baranoff dropped the briefcase he had been carrying.

And all hell broke loose.

Baranoff jerked her in front of him and Viktor closed ranks, jamming the three of them together, Viktor's gun pressed once more against the side of her head.

"You want the girl to stay alive," Baranoff called out, "you order your men away from the helicopter."

A couple of seconds passed. "Not a chance, Baranoff," came the reply. "You aren't going anywhere." Though she couldn't quite see him, Allie recognized Jake's hard-edged voice coming from in front and to the left of them. He had worked for Felix Baranoff, knew him better than anyone else. He was exactly the man to deal with him.

"What about the woman?" Baranoff countered in his distinct, faintly accented English. "You want to see her dead?"

"The Parker woman stole the mask," Jake said offhandedly. "Either you kill her or she goes to prison. Doesn't much matter one way or the other to us."

Allie's pulse soared. Jake was gambling, hoping Baranoff would bite, that he would believe he had no options and simply surrender. She tried to read his profile. Would he buy the ruse? Believe she wasn't in on the bust?

"Sorry, Dawson. That isn't going to wash. It's obvious the woman set me up. I should have figured that out when I learned the two of you spent a cozy little weekend together in Belize. Now, get those men away from that chopper or she gets it right here."

Behind them and on rooftops in the distance, Allie caught the shadowy shapes of marksman taking up their positions, and a cold shiver ran through her.

"If she dies, so do you," Jake reminded him.

"I'm not going to prison. Not now or ever. The choice is yours. What's it going to be?"

Seconds passed. Nobody moved. Allie felt a trickle of sweat run between her breasts. Then the agents surrounding the helicopter slowly began to back away. She looked over her shoulder, saw another group of men moving into position behind the three of them, guns drawn and pointing in their direction, but they made no attempt to get closer.

"The chopper's yours," Jake said, motioning for the pilot to be released from custody and returned to the pilot's seat.

"I want a flight path cleared to the airport. I'll need clearance for the plane that's waiting for me there. Once I reach my destination, I'll set the woman free."

Jake didn't hesitate. "You got it." His voice rang with authority, yet Allie didn't believe for an instant he meant for Baranoff's jet to leave the country. Behind where Jake stood in the empty, weed-covered lot, the helicopter pilot started the engine and the blades slowly began to circle.

Baranoff turned to face her. "Make one wrong move and Viktor pulls the trigger." He reached into the right coat pocket of his suit and she glimpsed a small caliber pistol. "Or I will."

She nodded, moistening lips that felt like two dry sticks. Slowly, a single step at a time, they made their way through the grass toward the helicopter in the field ahead. The blades where whirling now, a blur she couldn't see. The roar of the engines made it nearly impossible to hear.

Allie thought about Baranoff and what he intended to do to her. He had lost the mask. As soon as he left the country, she was completely expendable. At the airport, dozens of FBI and ATF agents would be waiting, but once Baranoff had her in the chopper, who was to say what he actually planned to do. Even if he did have a plane at Lindberg Field, in the chaos that was sure to erupt, anything could happen.

As they neared the chopper, Allie saw Jake, his pistol raised and aimed at Viktor's head. For an instant she saw his eyes, saw the fear in them. Fear for her. It made her heart start beating even harder than it was already.

Then an odd sort of calmness settled over her. Jake was there. The team was in position. If she got the slightest opening—

Just then Viktor stepped into a depression in the dirt covered by a layer of weeds. His foot turned sideways and for an instant the gun left her temple. Allie dropped down, drove her elbow into Viktor's groin with all her strength, and slammed her shoulder into the hand that held the pistol, knocking it into the air. Viktor fired as Allie whirled away from him, out of the way. Jake fired along with half a dozen other men and the Russian went down like a brick.

His gun hit the ground a few feet away and Allie leapt for it. Allie grunted at the impact of Baranoff's weight as he followed her down, pressing her into the cold, damp grass. She was his ticket to escape, the only chance he had. Distantly, she could hear Jake yelling for the men to hold their fire and the sound of his feet on the pavement. Baranoff's hand plunged into the pocket of his coat and an instant too late she remembered the gun he carried.

Allie twisted, tried to grab his hand. Then he pulled the trigger.

Jake reached Felix Baranoff just as the gun went off, the shot echoing like cannon fire in his ears. He grabbed the Russian's shoulder and jerked him off Allie, ripping the fabric of his expensive silk and wool suit coat. He caught the hand that gripped the little .32 automatic, brutally shoved it upward, ignored Baranoff's hiss of pain. Felix pulled the trigger two more times, sending shots into the air, one of the bullets bouncing off the side of a nearby brick building, another whizzing into one of the chopper blades with a loud clattering twang.

Then half a dozen agents were on him, pinning him to the ground, ripping the pistol from his fingers. Moving away from them, Jake knelt in the grass beside Allie. Agents hauled Baranoff to his feet and Duchefski cuffed his hands behind his back, but Jake barely noticed.

His attention was fixed on Allie and the bloody wound in her chest. Her eyes were closed, her breathing shallow, a crimson stain spreading over her orange cotton T-shirt.

"We need an ambulance over here!" Jake shouted, though he knew one had already been called. He dragged in a calming breath and ripped open the T-shirt, exposing her pretty white lace bra, now drenched in blood, and the ragged hole just above her heart.

A chest wound in this area was always potentially deadly. This one looked bad, but he couldn't be sure.

One of the ATF guys ran up just then, an agent named Simpson, carrying a first aid kit with a big red cross on the top. He knelt next to Allie and flipped open the lid, took out a thick stack of gauze pads, and pressed them over the bullet wound.

"Ambulance will be here any minute," he said.

Jake just nodded. He prayed it got there quickly. If it didn't, he would commandeer the damned chopper and fly her the hell out of there himself.

He reached down, felt the pulse beating at the side of her neck, just to reassure himself. "Allie, honey, can you hear me?" A lump was sitting in his throat and it hurt to speak. He couldn't stand to see her lying there, couldn't bear to think of her hurting.

Her eyelids flickered, but didn't open.

"It's Jake, baby. The ambulance is on its way. It'll be here any minute. Just hang on until it gets here." He picked up her hand, noticed how limp and cold it felt, kissed the back, and wrapped his fingers around it as if it might help keep her warm. "You're gonna be all right. I promise. As soon as we get you to the hospital, you're gonna be fine."

He wasn't a man who prayed, but he said a prayer right then. He prayed that Allie would live, which was also a prayer for himself. He was in love with her. He didn't know when it had happened. He only knew that it had.

The moment he had heard her speaking to Felix Baranoff in the backroom of the museum and realized the jeopardy she was in, he had known exactly how much he cared. Though he'd tried to fight it, sometime during the weeks they had spent together, she had opened the nearly impregnable door to his heart and he couldn't imagine what his life would be like if that cold, heavy portal slammed closed again.

"Listen to me, honey. I'm right here beside you. I can hear the sirens in the distance. The medics will be here any minute. They'll take you to the hospital and I'll be with you all the way."

He looked down at her, his chest aching so bad it hurt to breathe. This was his fault. He shouldn't have let her get involved, should have flatly forbidden it. Jake shook his head. When had forbidding Allie ever stopped her from charging ahead?

He smoothed a trembling hand over her cheek, brushed strands of hair out of her face. He had lost his son. He couldn't lose Allie, too. "Somebody get a blanket over here!" He was terrified she would go into shock, but the lights of the ambulance were flashing just a couple of blocks away. In minutes paramedics would be there.

He swallowed past the knot in his throat, willing her to open her eyes, wishing he could turn back the clock and she would be well and safe. He was in love with her, crazy in love, the forever kind of love that he never thought to feel.

Her eyelids fluttered, slowly opened. "Jake?"

"I'm right her, baby." He lifted her icy fingers, pressed them against his lips.

"Did we . . . did we get him?"

"We got him, honey. You were terrific." And if Allie died and Baranoff lived . . . He swallowed, unable to finish the thought.

"It hurts . . . really bad, Jake. If I . . . if something happens to me—"

"Nothing's going to happen. You're gonna be all right." He squeezed her hand, told himself the wound wasn't as bad as it looked and she would be okay, but he was desperately afraid it wasn't the truth.

"But if it does, promise you'll tell my parents I love them."

He swallowed, nodded.

"Will you . . . take care of Whiskers?"

He tried to smile. Failed. "I'll make sure he's taken care of till you get home."

"What about you, Jake? If something happens to me . . . will you . . . take care of yourself?"

The words made his eyes sting. "I need you for that, honey. I need you so much."

"Promise you won't forget me."

Ah, God. "You aren't going to die, dammit." Her face began to blur and he realized his eyes were full of tears. "We've got a lifetime ahead of us. I love you, baby. I think I've known for weeks, but

until tonight . . ." He shook his head and the words
trickled away. Her eyes were closed and he didn't
think she could hear him.

Why hadn't he told her before? Now she might
die and she would never know how much he loved
her.

God, please don't let me lose her.

"All right, everybody—step back out of the way."
A stretcher appeared at the edge of Jake's vision
and relief mingled with a fresh onslaught of fear.

Then the medics shunted him aside, sliding into
position around her, removing the makeshift bandage Pete Simpson had been pressing over the
bullet hole, beginning the work that would enable
them to transport her to Mercy Hospital, just a few
miles away. In minutes they had wheeled her over
to the ambulance and loaded her aboard.

Jake climbed in beside her. He just prayed they
would get there before it was too late.

Chapter Twenty-eight

It was Sunday morning, two days later, when Allie opened her eyes in a private room at Mercy Hospital. She vaguely remembered being in the ICU after surgery, but apparently since then they had moved her somewhere else.

This morning she was lying in a stark white hospital room with gray linoleum floors. A television hung down from the ceiling over her bed. Next to it, a tray on rollers held a pitcher of water and a plastic cup with a straw in the top.

Her shoulder was throbbing. A shunt in her wrist hooked up to a clear plastic bag dripped liquid into her vein. When she looked down at the bandage taped around the needle, a movement beside the bed caught her eye and she turned to see Jake slumped in a chair far too small for his big frame.

He was sleeping, she saw, recognizing the signs

of exhaustion. Wavy black hair hung over his forehead, several days' growth of beard roughened his
jaw, dark circles shadowed his eyes, and his shirt
was so wrinkled it was obvious he had been wearing
it for days.

He must have felt her watching him, for his eyes
popped open and he came instantly awake in that
way he had done in the jungle. "Allie . . ."

She tried to smile, but her lips barely curved.
"Jake . . ." she said more thickly than she'd
intended, still groggy from whatever painkiller
floated through her veins.

He sat up straighter, raked a hand through his
hair. "How are you feeling? Dumb question. You're
probably hurting like hell."

Her mouth edged up, easier this time. "I'm alive.
Could be a whole lot worse."

"Yeah." The smile he gave her looked forced.
There were shadows in his eyes and she wondered
why.

She moistened her dry lips. Jake reached over
and picked up the cup of water, held it up so that
she could take a drink. She sipped through the
straw until she'd had enough, then set it back down
on the tray. "I'm going to be all right, aren't I?"

His smile was one of relief this time. "You're
going to be fine. The doctor says you were lucky.
The bullet went all the way through. He says it just
missed your heart, but that's good, because it also
missed hitting any bones or vital organs. The gun
was only a .32 caliber so it didn't do as much damage as a bigger weapon would have done. He says
you'll be out of here by the middle of the week."

She smiled with relief, let her eyes slide closed
for a moment.

"Allie?" His worried tone pulled her tired gaze back to his face.

"I'm all right. My shoulder's hurting a little and I'm kind of sleepy, that's all."

He reached over and pushed the plunger on the tube coming into her wrist. "There's an automatic release mechanism. Just push the plunger and you can send yourself a dose of painkiller anytime you need it."

She lifted an eyebrow. "An instant trip to La La Land?"

"Pretty much. Your mom and dad are here. They've been at the hospital most of the time since you were shot. They just went down to the cafeteria to get a cup of coffee."

She slowly nodded. Jake paced over to the window. She could tell something was bothering him. She was afraid to ask what it was, but it was worse not to know. "What is it, Jake?"

He turned to face her, his beautiful blue eyes full of turbulence. "I shouldn't have let you do it. I should have found a way to stop you."

She chuckled. She couldn't help it even with the pain in her shoulder. Maybe it was the drugs.

"What's so funny?"

"You are. You think this is your fault. Well, forget it . . . bucko. It was my decision to do this and I won't let you hog all the glory."

Her eyes closed again. When she opened them, Jake was looking at her the way he had the night she was shot. With so much love and tenderness her heart very nearly turned over. The first time he had done it, she had thought that she was dreaming.

"I love you, Allie," he said as she drifted off to sleep. She felt his lips very lightly brushing hers, and in the back of her mind, a memory arose of him saying those words before. She had wondered then as she did now if he meant them, and sank into slumber praying that he did.

Jake was gone, the sun going down outside the window, when Allie awakened again. The physician was in the room this time. He introduced himself as Dr. Charles Franklin, the surgeon who had worked on her injury. Briefly he explained what had happened to her and what he had done to fix her.

"You're a very lucky young woman," he said. "And the fact you are physically fit and mentally strong worked to our advantage."

"How long before I can leave?"

"If you keep recovering at the rate you have been, I'd say by the middle of the week."

She smiled. "I suppose I can make it that much longer." But she didn't like hospitals and she was eager to leave. Jake's assurances were one thing, but as protective as he was, she didn't completely trust him to tell her the truth.

As Dr. Franklin left the room, her parents walked in, the door swishing closed behind them. Her mother gave her a teary smile and dabbed at her eyes. Both Mom and Dad walked over and very gently hugged her. They asked the usual round of questions. How was she feeling? Was there anything they could do? Anything special she needed?

"We're taking care of Whiskers while you're getting well," her mother said. "Jake was very concerned about that. And Mrs. Chambers called. She wanted to thank you for finding justice for Chrissy. You're a real hero, dear."

She was feeling more alert this time, more able to put things together. "Baranoff's in jail?"

Her father nodded. "The man with him, Viktor Ivanov, was killed in the shooting. He was ex-KGB. He and his wife were living here illegally. The woman will undoubtedly be deported. Baranoff is facing a list of charges half a mile long. Jake says he won't see daylight for at least twenty years."

Obviously her parents had met Jake. Her father would like him, she was sure, and her mother would try to mother him, which would be really nice for Jake, since his own mother had died when he was still young.

Assuming he stayed around long enough to enjoy it.

"We don't want to tire you," her father said, watching the tiredness creeping into her features. "We'll be back in the morning if you need anything, dear."

Allie nodded, fighting to keep her eyes open.

"Jake said he would be back again tonight," her father added. "He's been here round the clock since you were shot."

"He's a very sweet man." Her mother leaned over and kissed her forehead. "I think he loves you very much."

Allie remembered Jake's words and prayed they were the truth.

Barb Wallace opened the door to Room 424 of Mercy Hospital. Beside her, Dan Reynolds held on to her hand. Barb had always hated hospitals. As far as she was concerned, being in one was the worst part of having a baby. She felt light-headed, her stomach was queasy, and her knees trembled just walking down the corridors. The blood had left her face the moment they'd shoved through the main doors into the lobby.

But Dan had insisted on coming with her to see Allie, and it wasn't nearly so bad with him holding on to her hand.

It was quiet in the room. Barb paused at the foot of the bed, took in the array of flowers on every possible surface: carnations, roses, tulips, daffodils. Mostly red roses. Allie had a lot of friends, and after the shooting, she was a local celebrity, but Barb imagined the roses were from the ATF guy who was obviously so crazy in love with her.

Barb had known it the minute she had seen him interviewed on TV, talking about what a true heroine Allie was, how cool and smart she had been in a tight situation, how much courage it had taken to face down Baranoff and his hit man.

"It looks like she's sleeping," Barb said, surveying the tube going into her wrist, the bandage around her shoulder peeking out of the sleeve of her hospital gown. Her hair needed washing and her skin was the color of the sheet. Generally she looked like hell, but the doctor had told them she was rapidly improving and it wouldn't be long before she could go home.

Allie's big blue eyes opened up just then. "Hi, guys."

They did the usual "how are you doing" stuff, and by the time they were done, some of the color had returned to Allie's cheeks.

"I saw Dan on the six o'clock news," Allie said. "Your partner was the guy who tipped Baranoff the day of the raid."

"That's right," Dan said. "Archie Hollis. They took him into custody about ten minutes after the shooting in Old Town. To tell you the truth, I never much liked the guy. We only started working together after you disappeared. We were constantly butting heads about the case. Now I understand why."

"I'm glad they caught him."

"You got that right," said Dan. "Nothing worse than a dirty cop. And speaking of cops, I met that ATF guy of yours. He seems like a real straight shooter. I wish you both all the best."

Best of what? Allie thought. Why was it everyone seemed to know what was going on with Jake except her?

"We've got a little news of our own," Barb said. Dan reached over and caught her hand. "Dan and I are unofficially engaged. We plan to take our time, really get to know each other, but he's asked, and I've said yes. We wanted you to be the first to know."

"Oh, Barb, I'm so happy for you. For both of you. And I'm proud of you for taking a chance."

"I wouldn't have done it if it hadn't been for you."

Dan grinned and slid an arm around Barb's waist. "I appreciate the help, Allie. To tell you the truth, I wasn't doing all that well on my own."

"He's really good with the boys," Barb said. "They think he walks on water."

"I'm teaching them to sail," Dan explained with a glance at Barb. "Barb's a natural-born sailor."

"Last weekend we all went camping," Barb put in. "It was really a lot of fun. I never knew what it was like to be a family. I never thought it could ever be this good."

Dan squeezed her hand. "It's only going to get better, sweetheart."

Abruptly, the door swung open and a stout, gray-haired nurse in a starched white uniform stuck her head into the room. "Sorry, folks, visiting hours are over. Time to go."

Barb walked over and took hold of Allie's hand. "The roses are from Dawson?"

Allie nodded.

"I hope things work out for you, too, honey."

Allie gave her an uncertain smile. "So do I." But the truth was she had no idea what Jake planned to do.

The day Allie was released from the hospital, Jake was there to pick her up. Except for a couple of days at the beginning of the week, he had come by to see her every day. He had told her he was madly in love with her, and she had said the same thing to him, but he had never mentioned the future, or any plans he might have made that included her.

That morning, with the help of a nurse, Allie washed and dried her hair, dressed in jeans and an oversize blue plaid shirt that buttoned up the front and left room for the bandages around her chest and shoulder, then sat down in a wheelchair for her exit from the building. Hospital policy, they told her when she complained that she could make it on her own.

Jake was waiting out in the hall with yet another bouquet of roses, and for the first time since the shooting, the haunted look was gone from his face.

"Good morning, gorgeous," he said with a grin. "You look terrific."

Allie glanced up at him, wondering at his mood

and the devilish glint in his eyes. "You're certainly in a good mood today."

As for herself, Allie was feeling a little churlish. Jake might love her, but he might also be grinning because he had just received a new assignment. The lure of adventure would always be there for him. It appealed to her, too, she'd discovered. But she wanted more out of life than just a career. Like a husband and family of her own.

Jake was whistling as he wheeled her down the hall. She didn't even know he knew how. His steps were nearly buoyant and her irritation grew. Something was going on. Dammit, he owed her at least an explanation, not a quick I-love-you and goodbye.

Jake pushed the wheelchair through the revolving door of the hospital onto a big stretch of cement out in front. Holding the bouquet in her arms, she started to get out of the wheelchair.

"Before you do that, I think you might want to stay sitting down for just a little while longer."

"What are you talking about?"

"I've got a surprise for you."

"I'm not really crazy about surprises, Jake."

"Yeah, I know what you mean. But you're gonna like this one—I promise."

He wheeled her around, and for a moment, she couldn't believe her eyes. A small brown Mexican boy with a rosebud stuck over one ear rushed toward her, his arms thrown open wide.

"Señorita Allie! Señorita Allie!"

The bouquet fell from her lap as she shot to her feet. "Miguel!" Jake caught the boy an instant before he threw himself into her arms.

"Take it easy, sport. Remember, Allie just got out of the hospital. How about a real soft hug?"

Allie went down on her knees and the little boy very gently wrapped his arms around her neck. "I missed you—*mucho*," he said. Allie hugged him, ignoring the pain in her shoulder, tears rolling down her cheeks.

"I missed you, too. So much."

When she let him go, he reached into the pocket of a brand-new pair of jeans and pulled out the driver's license with her photo on it she had given him the day she'd left Belize. It was completely dog-eared, as if he had gazed at her photo dozens of times.

"I never forget you. I prayed to the Blessed Virgin that you would come for me." He stared up at Jake as if he had hung the moon. "Major Jake—he send me on a big silver airplane. He say you are waiting for me here. He say you are going to be my mother."

Allie swallowed past the thick lump in her throat. She turned to Jake and simply walked into his arms. "Thank you. Thank you so much."

"Will you marry me, honey? If you say yes, you'll have the family you've been wanting—ready-made."

Allie looked up at him, brushed at the tears on her cheeks. "What . . . what about your job?"

"I quit my job the day after we got Baranoff. At the time, I wasn't exactly sure what I was going to do, but I knew whatever it was, it had to include you. No matter what I did, I knew I could never be happy without you."

"I love you so much," Allie said.

"Is that a yes?"

She nodded. "It's a yes."

Miguel tugged on her jeans. "Are you going to marry Major Jake?"

"Yes, sweetheart. We're going to be a family."

"Will we all live here together?"

Allie looked up at Jake. He was grinning again.

"If it's all right with you," he said, "I've grown kind of fond of San Diego. I thought maybe we'd get a house on Coronado Island, open that private investigation firm I've been thinking about for the last few years."

"I don't know, Jake." She bit down on her lip, hating to be a spoilsport when Jake looked so optimistic. "That's a really nice idea, but it costs a lot of money for something like that. I don't think there's any way we could afford it."

Jake's grin only widened. "I think maybe we can."

"What did you do? Steal the money in Baranoff's briefcase?"

"Not quite. You remember that dry-cleaning business my father owned?"

She nodded. "I remember."

"I might have neglected to mention he owned a whole chain of them—Twinkle Dry Cleaning and Laundry—more than a hundred across the country."

"There's some here in San Diego."

"Yeah, well, they're worth over thirty million dollars. And guess what, honey? My dad left the business to me."

Allie slowly sank back down in the wheelchair, and little Miguel took hold of her hand.

"Are you sick, Señorita Allie?"

"No, sweetheart. I'm fine." She looked over at Jake. "I think."

Jake was no longer grinning. He glanced off toward the ocean barely visible in the distance. "I spoke to my cousin, Rachael, the morning of the funeral. I explained about you being shot and told her I wouldn't be able to make it. She said I should at least be there for the reading of the will. She didn't sound too happy about it. On Monday, Dad's lawyer called and insisted I come. When I got to there, I found out why."

"You didn't think you'd be named?"

"My father cut me out of his will the day I joined the Army. The night we fought about Michael, he told me in no uncertain terms I'd never see a dime of his money. I told him I wasn't interested in his money. I never had been. But Rachael and her husband were damned interested. They'd been sucking up to my dad for years. I figured he'd leave his estate to them."

"And instead he left it to you."

He nodded. "They played a videotape my father made a couple of months before he died. Dad said he was sorry for the way he had treated me. He said I had a right to my own life and he should have been proud of me for having the courage to go after what I wanted. He said he wished he had helped me find my son. He wanted me to take the money from the sale of the business and use part of it for that." Jake turned to face her. "And that's exactly what I'm going to do."

"Oh, Jake." Allie came out of the wheelchair. She framed his face between her hands and very gently kissed him. "We'll find him, Jake. We won't give up until we do."

"*Sí*, Señorita Allie. We find Major Jake's son and then you have two Miguels."

Allie smiled and wiped away more tears. She was tiring rapidly, her knees beginning to shake from all the excitement. But this was the happiest day of her life and she had Jake to thank for it.

"I love you both so very much."

Jake scooped her up in his arms. "Let's go home, baby. As soon as you're up to it, we're going house hunting."

And they did. Jake bought Allie a two-story white wood-frame house with a charming little picket fence and a view of the ocean. It looked like something out of *Leave It to Beaver,* exactly the sort of home she had always dreamed of. She hadn't yet mentioned that as soon as Jake was ready to open his security firm, she planned to go to work for him—at least part time.

The shooting hadn't changed her mind about police work. If anything, the night they had captured Felix Baranoff had only made her more certain she had finally found out what she wanted to do with her life.

But that particular discussion—and Jake's very predictable protests—could come later.

At present, she was enjoying the man who had swept like a storm into her life. As far as Allie was concerned, it was as close to happily-ever-after as any woman could get.

Epilogue

One Year Later

Dawson Security occupied half the bottom floor of a two-story white stucco building off Harbor Drive near the Embarcadero. Jake had bought the newly remodeled structure a month after the shooting, hung a sign above the door—DAWSON SECURITY SERVICES—and immediately begun what turned out to be a highly successful campaign to attract clientele.

Though he had never been interested in running a chain of dry-cleaning stores, he had learned a few things from his father along the way.

He was doing so well that just last week, he had opened a second business in the same location, Dawson and Dawson, Private Investigations.

He grinned to think of the look on Allie's face

when she had seen the sign. In the year since the shooting, she had been taking courses at San Diego State during kindergarten school hours, working to get a second degree, this one in law enforcement. In the meantime, she had nagged him daily to teach her everything he knew about being a cop.

He had moaned and groaned about it, but secretly enjoyed every lesson he gave her. And he had to admit she had a knack for it.

The only thing she did better was be the mother of their sons.

Jake glanced down at his wristwatch then walked over to the window. A couple of minutes later, Allie's brand-new maroon and silver Subaru Outback pulled up to the curb. She still drove her little green Volkswagen when she was tooling around town by herself, but with two little boys, the Dawson family needed something bigger. The Subaru got great mileage and he liked the safety features.

He watched his wife get out of the car and open the back door of the Outback. *My wife,* he thought, loving the sound. In fact, he loved everything about her. From her sexy little body to her shiny gold hair and especially her smile. He never got tired of seeing it.

The boys scrambled out of the car onto the sidewalk. Jake could hear them laughing, and emotion swelled in his chest. Even after making a settlement with his cousins for part of the money he had inherited, the sale of Twinkle Dry Cleaning and Laundry had left him a multimillionaire. With those kinds of resources, he was able to hire the very best investigators in the country, a small army of them.

Six months ago, Phil Goldstein at Goldstein and Richards Investigations had located Marla. She

was using the alias "Marla Jennings," her grand-
mother's maiden name, and living in a low-rent
district in Miami. She was working as a waitress,
drinking and carousing until all hours of the night,
and badly in need of money. Jake offered her a
sum she couldn't refuse in exchange for custody
of Michael.

Marla had agreed.

Outside the office, Jake watched the boys tugging
Allie toward the glass door at the front of the building, each child clinging to one of her hands. It was
Saturday. They were going to the zoo this afternoon. He'd had a few things to do at the office
before they left, but his work was done, and Allie
had stopped by to pick him up.

She didn't bother to knock since she worked
part time in the office next to his. She turned
the brass knob on the door leading in from the
reception area, closed for the weekend, and the
moment she saw him, a smile brightened her face.

"Hi," she said softly.

"Hi." Every time she looked at him that way, his
heart clutched and it was suddenly hard to breathe.

The boys raced toward him, and Jake knelt and
hugged both of them at once. "Hi, guys!" He was
the father of two sons now, both of them named
Michael, though Miguel kept the Spanish pronun-
ciation of his name. The boys had bonded almost
as soon as they were introduced, Miguel the more
outgoing of the two and desperately wanting a
brother, Michael shy at first, but unable to resist
Miguel's innocent charm.

Both boys had black hair, though Miguel's skin
was a little browner, his hair straight instead of
wavy. Though they were the same age within a
couple of months, it was obvious Michael was going

to be a much larger boy. Maybe that was the reason he was so protective of his brother.

Or perhaps, having known what it was like to lose one of his parents, he could imagine only too well what it must have been like for Miguel to lose them both.

Whatever the reason, Jake was proud of his sons. He loved them with every ounce of his soul, and every day he thanked God that they were his.

"Come on, Dad," Michael said. "Let's get going. I want to see the tigers."

"Yeah, Dad, me, too," said Miguel.

"The kids are right." Allie grinned up at him. "We're burnin' daylight here."

Jake laughed. He couldn't help it. Every day he spent with Allie was just plain fun. You never knew exactly what was going to happen and that suited Jake just fine. "All right, let's hit the road."

The boys raced out the door and off to the car parked at the curb. Allie started after them, but Jake caught her hand, turned her around, and pulled her into his arms.

"Have I told you lately how much I love you?" he said.

She smiled. "Not since the great sex we had this morning."

"That was my little head talking. This is my big head talking now."

Allie laughed. "Have I told you how happy you make me?"

"Not since the great sex we had this morning."

"That was my very satisfied body talking. This is my heart talking now." Her expression turned serious. "I love you, Jake. I love our family. Sometimes I think I owe Felix Baranoff a debt of gratitude for stealing those missiles."

"And damned near getting you killed?"

"It was worth it."

Jake gave her another lusty kiss. "We'd better get going. The boys'll never forgive us if they miss the tigers."

Allie grinned. "When we get home, I think I'll try taming a tiger of my own."

A surge of heat went straight to his groin. "Try to tame this tiger, lady, and you just might get eaten."

Allie laughed all the way to the car.

Don't miss *The Secret*,
Kat Martin's spine-tingling blend of suspense and
eerie precognition, available to order now!

THE SECRET

His name is Chance McLain. Wildly good looking,
superbly confident, he's everything Kate Collins doesn't
want when she lands in Lost Peak, Montana.

She's come to change her life, to heal her child,
to find herself—not another man with a sexy smile
and an empty heart. She has a son to raise,
a business to run—and a murder to solve.

Kate may be determined to resist him, but Chance
can't ignore the desire he feels for her—or the suspicion
that somebody wants her to leave Lost Peak.
With the promise of a future together tangled up in
the ghosts of her past, Kate and Chance must believe in
each other before they can believe in love . . .

"Multitalented author Kat Martin continues to make a
name for herself by producing irresistible novels that
blend the eerie and unexplainable with her own
uniquely sensual and exciting style."
—*RT Book Reviews*